THE AGE OF PROPHECY · BOOK ONE

The Lamp of Darkness

The Go Further Addition

DAVE MASON
with MIKE FEUER

LIONSTAIL PRESS

For more details, visit TheAgeofProphecy.com.
Truthfully, you won't find any more copyright information there,
but it's a really cool site and I think you'll enjoy it.

For further permission requests, to place huge book orders, or just to say hi,
contact me at Dave@TheAgeofProphecy.com.

ISBN: 978-1-62393-020-2

Cover Design by the amazing Juan Hernaz.
Check out his other beautiful works at JuanHernaz.com.

Map by the fabulous Erika Givens.
Check out her site at Gleaux-Art-Design.com

Dedication for the Go Further Edition

To our parents, Moshe and Libby Werthan, on
the occasion of their 60th wedding anniversary:
this teacher's edition embodies your
commitment to facilitating Jewish
learning in creative and compelling ways.

August 16, 2019

For Chana, whose patience was tried many a time by my six years of writing, but who stuck by me anyway with undying support.
It wouldn't have happened without you.

Acknowledgements

As a reader, I always marveled at how many people were mentioned in the acknowledgements of books. After all, writing a book seems like such a lone undertaking. As a writer, I'm struck by the huge number of people who played a role in making this book come about. First of all, both Mike and I want to thank our wives Chana and Karen for supporting us throughout. My son Aryeh Lev, with his love of stories and desire to deepen his understanding, was a constant source of motivation. And of course our parents, without whom, none of this would have happened.

The origins of this book go back to when I was learning the books of the early prophets with Rabbi Aaron Liebowitz and studying the inner workings of prophecy with Rabbi Yaakov Moshe Pupko, both at Sulam Yaakov in Jerusalem. Most of this book was written within the walls of Sulam Yaakov, and I'd like to acknowledge the entire crew there, specifically Rabbi Daniel Kohn, whose teachings have been crucial to the development of our understanding of many key points in the book, and David Swidler, whose encyclopedic mind filled in many a random fact.

I'd like to thank Barnea Levi Selavan of Foundation Stone for helping us understand the historical context, Yigal Levin of Bar Ilan University for helping us identify the ancient city of Levonah, and Shoshana Harrari of Harrari Harps for teaching us about Biblical instruments.

Thank you to our editors, Shifrah Devorah Witt, who edited an early draft of the book, and Rebbetzin Yehudis Golshevsky who edited the final two drafts.

I'm incredibly indebted to the dozens of readers who offered comments, corrections, and direction over the years. I can't come close to mentioning them all. But I have to give special mention to: Rabbi Joshua Weisberg, Chaya Lester, Eliezer Israel, Michelle Cahn, Leia Weil, Beth Shapiro, Hadas and Gidon Melmed, Moshe Newman, David Shaffer, Jen Bell Hillel, Rachel Winner, Rabbi David Sperling, Rabbi David Fink, Eitan Press, Josh Fleet, Diana Maryon, and my uncle Sam Firestone.

Thank you all.

Two quick notes before you start reading:

1) We've created an introductory video for anyone who would like more background regarding the world you're about to enter, available at TheAgeofProphecy.com/video.

This video can be viewed at any time. It's not necessary to watch it before beginning. You'll also find both written and video notes on the website providing sources for ideas discussed in the book and deeper insights into key concepts.

2) We are constantly striving to improve the quality of our work as well as the readers' experience. The current publishing revolution not only provides authors previously unknown flexibility, but also allows readers to play a prominent role in the writing process. Accordingly, we've put a feedback form on our site at TheAgeofProphecy.com/feedback.

If there is a specific element for which you'd like us to provide an explanatory video, or if there's a passage that you find confusing, or if you find (heaven forbid) a typo, please let us know.

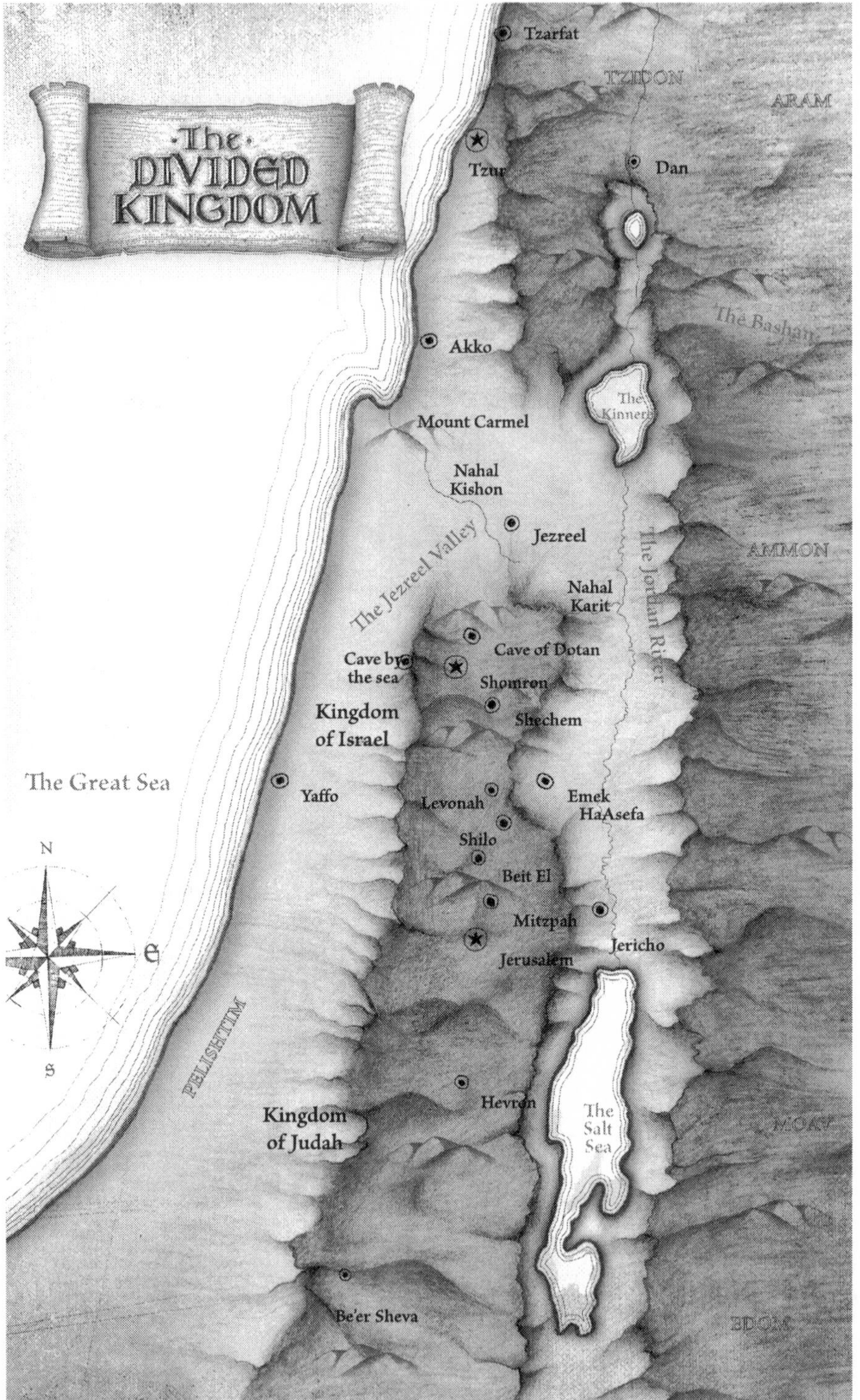

The Divided Kingdom
Tzarfat
Tzidon
Aram
Tzur
Dan
The Bashan
Akko
The Kinneret
Mount Carmel
Nahal Kishon
Jezreel
The Jezreel Valley
The Jordan River
Ammon
Nahal Karit
Cave of Dotan
Cave by the sea
Shomron
Shechem
Kingdom of Israel
The Great Sea
Yaffo
Levonah
Emek HaAsefa
Shilo
Beit El
Mitzpah
Jericho
Jerusalem
N
E
S
Pelishtim
Hevron
Kingdom of Judah
The Salt Sea
Moav
Be'er Sheva
Edom

Hillel said: If I am not for myself, who will be for me? And when I am for myself, what am I? And if not now, when?

Pirkei Avot 1:14

1

A Shepherd's Inheritance

*578 Years After the Exodus**

The day before I was taken from my home, I grazed my uncle's flock on a hillside overlooking the gates of Levonah. Sheltered from the early summer heat beneath a gnarled fig tree, I strummed my kinnor, the small harp that was my only valuable possession, while keeping one eye on the sheep and the other on the travelers approaching the town gates for market day.

This was before the breakout of war, when anyone could safely walk the King's Road, regardless of their loyalties. Few travelers spared a glance for the young shepherd boy, and none stopped to talk until Seguv stepped off the shimmering road in early afternoon, leading his donkey up to my perch on the hillside. Seguv was only a few years older than me and spent half his time traveling the Kingdom with his brothers, selling their father's dates from their estate along the Jordan River. They came to Levonah three or four times a year, but that day was the first time I ever saw Seguv alone. He approached me with a bounce in his step that told of news.

The sheep bleated—strangers spooked them. Seguv barely noticed. He untied one of his saddlebags and rummaged through a thick cushion of flax

until he produced a tiny clay bottle. Its dust-colored exterior disguised the treasure within. His eyes sparkled.

"Is that it?" I asked, my eyes reaching toward the vial.

Seguv nodded.

I leapt to my feet. "Put just a drop my hands. I want to feel it."

With a sly grin, he pulled the flask away. "A drop of this is worth more than one of your reeking sheep, and it would be worth my head if the King found out. I'll let you smell it only."

I reached out to take the bottle, but Seguv tightened his grip. Only when I dropped my hands, did he uncork it and hold it under my nose. The essence flooded my senses, overwhelming the smell of dry grass and stone with the sweetness of wildflowers. I closed my eyes and inhaled. Deeper notes of the scent—mineral, earth, spice—unfolded just as Seguv pulled the flask away. A hot breeze carried the sheep odor back under the tree, and I opened my eyes, confused. "If it's so precious, why are you carrying it?"

Seguv's eyes widened, "My father wants the first batch to go directly to the King."

"But why are *you* taking it?" The roads were safe, and had been ever since the last civil war ended, years ago. Even so, who would send a kingly tribute with a boy selling dates, even if he was of age?

I could tell from the way he smiled, with his tongue flitting between his teeth, that he was waiting for me to ask. "It's early." He raised his thick, dark eyebrows. "This is the first batch of afarsimon oil ever produced in the Kingdom.* The King isn't even expecting a crop this year. My father says there's no better time for my first appearance in Court."

Only the most important men in Levonah ever went to the King's Court—I'd never heard of a fourteen-year-old going to Court on his own. But of course, no family in Levonah was as prominent as Seguv's was. "So that's why you're making the trip alone?"

"Hmm?" Seguv was hardly listening; his attention was focused on packing his precious cargo deep into its flax nest in his saddlebag.

"Is that why you're making the trip without your brothers? To win the favor of the Court?"

"Oh." Seguv closed the saddlebag, his hands fumbling with the straps. "I forgot you didn't know." His breath seeped out of him. "We lost Aviram a few months ago, and now Onan is too sick to travel."

Aviram's laughing face rose in my mind. Gone? I couldn't help but ask, "What happened?"

Seguv's teary eyes rose to meet mine. "It's the waters in Jericho."* His chest swelled and collapsed in short bursts. "Many have died from them, but father says it won't stop the rebuilding."

Seguv tied off the last strap of the saddlebag as a fiery gust blew off the hillside, rustling the broad, handlike leaves of the fig tree. I wanted to comfort him but feared saying the wrong thing. Who knew better than me how easily a misplaced word could hurt? I reached instead for my kinnor—music had soothed my own heart so many times. I lowered my eyelids and quieted my mind. A slow breath filled my chest, and my fingertips found a *nigun*. I plucked the notes gently, passing through the simple melody a few times, and then opened my eyes—it was all I could offer.

The music filled the emptiness between us, its notes softening the silence under the tree. Seguv's head dropped forward as one, two droplets darkened the dry soil at his feet. With a hitch in his breath, he mumbled, "Thank you," and picked his way down the slope, drawing his donkey toward the town's gate.

"Go in peace," I called after him, then added, too quietly for him to hear, "and may the Holy One protect you* from the waters of Jericho."

I closed my eyes back into the melody, playing it louder now. Although it was impossible, I hoped that Seguv could feel the song even in Levonah and that it would bring him comfort there. Like a river, the notes flowed from my kinnor as my fingers swirled across the strings. The repetitive melody and the heat of the day settled down on me, on the road, on the sheep—like a dream.

I was still playing, when a feeling came upon me, a tingling across my back. I had felt this same pricking of warning two moons earlier when a lion stalked the flock in the early morning. Had I responded right away with sling and stones, I might have fought her off. But I had dismissed the feeling—the sheep were quiet. When the lion pounced, I was too late to keep her from making off with one of the lambs.

My back tensed up with the certain knowledge that something was behind me, but I didn't open my eyes or stop playing. The first moment of facing danger was the most important. If only I could identify the threat, I'd gain some advantage. It couldn't be a lion this time—lions almost never hunt at midday. And one wouldn't come this close to the road, certainly not on market day.

I opened my eyes and spun quickly around, hoping to at least catch whatever it was by surprise. There was something there…some*one* there. I almost laughed when I saw that it was just an old man standing on the other side of the fig tree, swaying gently with his eyes closed. The heavy gray eyebrows, broad forehead, and deep wrinkles mapping his weathered face signaled nothing but calm. He held his staff as if it were an extension of his hand, a sure sign that he had walked many a path. Even at some distance, he appeared so very tall.

I couldn't shake the feeling that something was wrong. I hadn't seen the old man step off the road, nor heard any bleating from the flock. Where had he come from, and why was he standing there? Travelers walked quickly, their eyes on the road, rarely returning greetings with more than a glance and a nod. Even the ones I could persuade to share stories of their travels departed before the final words of their tales left their lips. But this white-haired stranger just stood there, swaying. The pricking in my back intensified. Had he stopped to listen to the music? I silenced the strings with the palm of my hand.

The old man stopped swaying and locked his gray-blue eyes onto mine. My chest tightened, shortening my breath. I saw no danger, but the ominous feeling built, like an old memory trying to force itself to the surface. My gaze escaped his hold and found a nearby ewe gnawing a clump of thistle from its wool. I knelt beside the creature and worked at the thistle until the old man stepped back toward the road.

He had left easily enough, but the tight fist in my stomach remained. I just knew that he would return—and return he did. By the time the old man emerged from the town gates, the sun was edging down in the west. He was followed close at heels by a young couple from town. His gaze found the flock first, then narrowed in on me. Our eyes met, and even from a distance I knew: he was coming for me.

The couple remained behind as he scaled the rise up to me. I knew neither of them well, but I would never forget their wedding a month before. The bride's father hired me to perform, the first payment I ever received for playing my kinnor. They stood beneath their wedding canopy, nervous, joyous energy on their faces. Now they stood like stone markers at the edge of the road, huddled and still, waiting.

The sleeve of the old man's linen cloak whispered as he gestured at the trunk of the fig tree, silently indicating his intention to join me. My stomach clenched in dread, but this was common land—I could hardly protest. My fingers kept on with their melody as if moving of their own volition. A cold unease filled me.

He sat down slowly but smoothly—not like the old men of Levonah, whose knees creaked and faces groaned when they lowered themselves to the ground. Once settled, he took a long and penetrating look at me—as if judging my merit. He then nodded in my direction, silently commanding me to go on with the music. Were it not for the couple watching from below and my strange disquiet, I might have thought he sought out the shade for a late afternoon nap. His head sank between his bent knees.* He was perfectly still.

A butterfly came to rest on his motionless elbow, extending and retracting its black and orange wings. I played on in the still air, waiting for a sign from him, not knowing how long I played or even why. The butterfly took flight in a flash of fiery orange as the old man shuddered and a charge filled the air. The hairs on the back of my neck bristled. He trembled for what seemed an age. Was he in some small fit? Should I stop playing? My fingers kept plucking the strings of their own accord while my thoughts spiraled, like dust blown in an eddy. My fingernail caught on a string of my kinnor, slicing it in two.

Just as abruptly as the shuddering began, the old man stilled again. The back that seemed bent over in an impossible curve slowly straightened. Without a word, the stranger unfolded from his position to an impressive height. He raised his aged hand and crooked a finger toward the couple. "Come."

The young man and woman rushed up the slope to meet him. "It rolled behind the wine barrel at the back of the house,"* he said to them. "There it still lies—dirty, but perfectly safe."

The woman put a hand to her chest; a giddy smile brushed her lips. Her husband said, "Now I know you are truly a Seer."* The old man responded with a silent nod. "Shall we escort you back to the city?"

"I remain here with the boy. Go in peace with the blessings of the Holy One."

"Peace and blessings upon you, Master Uriel." The young man took his wife's hand and scampered back toward Levonah

The old man turned his blue-gray eyes on mine, then shifted his gaze to my hands on my kinnor. "It's time to water the sheep and pen them in for the evening. I will come home with you, Lev. I need to speak with your uncle."

How did he know my name?

The King's tower, empty of soldiers during these times of peace, was already casting its shadow across our small farm by the time we returned home in silence. I trudged through my evening chores, my eyes straying like a lost lamb's to watch my uncle in quiet parley with the imposing stranger. It wasn't until the branches of the carob tree blackened against the flaming horizon that I pushed myself to work faster. I filled the watering trough and secured the pen as a curtain of darkness was drawn from east to west.

The rocky spring behind our farm was normally dry by early summer, but this year, a trickle of the heavy winter storms remained. Farmers had cursed the late *malkosh* rains that soaked the barley crop,* spoiling most of it before it could be stored, but I felt only gratitude now as the stream of cool water ran over my curly brown hair and down my sweat-salted, lean frame.

It was nearly full dark when I came inside, the evening meal mostly over. Only Uncle Menachem and my younger cousins Dahlia and Eliav remained at the table; Aunt Leah had already taken the three littlest ones up the ladder for bed. My bread steamed; Dahlia must have reheated it on the hearth when she heard me come. I dipped it in salted cheese, chewing quickly because it was so late. The old man was gone, but his presence was felt in the heavy silence of the table. None of us children would ask about him unless Uncle Menachem mentioned him first, and he said nothing. When I finished, Dahlia rose to clean up while Eliav and I remained at the table for our nightly studies.

"And you shall sanctify the fiftieth year,"* Uncle Menachem chanted the verse that he too had memorized as a child, "and proclaim freedom in the land for all who dwell in it." Eliav and I echoed not only the words but also the melody that strung them together like beads on a strand. "It will be a *Yovel* for you," my uncle continued, "you shall return each man to his ancestral land, and return each man to his family."

"It will be a *Yovel* for you," we repeated, "...you shall return each man to his ancestral land..." Dahlia, setting the crockery in the alcove, pushed a stubborn, russet curl away from her eyes and coughed, "...and return each man to his family." The cough was our signal—she had a question.

"Uncle?"

"Yes, Lev?"

The problem was, I never knew exactly what was bothering Dahlia. "When's the next *Yovel*?" Silence from the alcove—I guessed right.

Uncle Menachem ran his fingers through his wiry beard, newly streaked with gray. "I asked my father the same question when he taught me this verse."

"And what did he tell you?"

"That he had never seen a *Yovel*."

"Have you seen one?"

"No, Lev."

I gripped the edge of the table to contain my excitement. "Then the next one must be coming soon!"

Uncle Menachem shifted on his stool, but the coals in the hearth didn't shed enough light to read his face. "No, Lev. My father had seen more than fifty years when he died. Do not put your hope in the *Yovel*; it's not coming. The land will not return." He rose to his feet though we'd recited just one verse. "That's enough for tonight; it's already late." I sunk my head, avoiding Dahlia's eyes. "Lev, see that the flock is secure and then get to sleep."

I bit my lip hard enough to taste blood. I ought to know better than to get excited over the *Yovel*—another stupid daydream. I grabbed my kinnor from its peg by the door on my way out; its broken string dangled dead at my side. The new moon's tiny sliver had already set, but the summer sky was always clear, and I could pick out shadowy forms by the light of the stars. I tugged first at the gate of the pen, testing that it was well fastened, then skirted the edge of the wall, feeling for fallen stones. There was one faint bleat at the noise, but the flock was settled in for the night.

I lifted a flat rock at the edge of the pen and withdrew a skin pouch from the hole beneath. After a month nestled in cool earth, my new strings were fully cured. I sat on the ground with my back against the pen's low wall and ran my hand across the top of the kinnor until I found the empty spot, a missing tooth in its eight-stringed grin. I threaded one end of the sheep gut through the hole in the olive wood frame, wound the bottom end around its groove at the base of the kinnor, then tied off the other end around its bone key. I stretched and tuned, stretched and tuned, searching for the right sound to match the other strings. When the eight notes were in harmony, I ran my fingers lightly across all eight strings. The voice of the kinnor rippled out into the night.

This was my favorite time of day, when I could be alone with my music. In these moments, there were no responsibilities and no thoughts. I could follow the flow of the rhythm…and forget about my fate. But the music had barely taken hold when a voice broke my focus.

"You must have questions about today," Uncle Menachem said, hovering above me in the starlight.

I silenced the strings and stood. "Yes, Uncle."

"Did you know that old man?"

I thought back to the dread I felt when he first appeared—it seemed rooted in a memory deep within my heart. I reached down for it, but nothing came. "No, Uncle, but he knew my name."

"His name is Master Uriel."

I said nothing, certain he came to tell me more than the old man's name. But why the hesitation?

"He's a *navi.*" Uncle Menachem broke up a clump of dried dirt with the toe of his sandal.

I recalled Uriel's trembling beneath the fig tree, and the couple with their missing item. Was that the spirit of prophecy? Is that how he knew my name?

"Do you know why he's come?" my uncle asked.

Since I first laid eyes on the old man earlier that day, he'd filled my thoughts. An idea struck me. The thought made no sense, but I couldn't drive it away: Uriel came to take me from my family. But, my uncle taught me that silence is a fence for wisdom,* so I kept my mouth shut and shook my head.

"The *nevi'im* have called a gathering in Emek HaAsefa, and they need musicians. Master Uriel seeks to hire you."

"Hire me?" So he did want to take me away. I pictured a hundred men like him, tall and foreboding, trembling in a circle. *Why do they need musicians? Do they dance?* "How long is the gathering?"

"Two months."

"Two months?" I hadn't slept a single night away from home since coming to live with my uncle. "I can't leave for that long—what about the flock?"

"Eliav can look after them. You were also ten when you first took them out alone."

My breath came short. "What did you tell him?"

"I won't refuse a *navi*, Lev. Not without reason."

I said nothing. If having me at home wasn't reason enough, what could I say?

"This will be good for you," Uncle Menachem said, speaking fast. "It won't be long until you're of age, and…" He reached beneath his cloak and pulled out a small pouch, tipping the contents into his hand. "Look here."

I heard the unmistakable sound as my uncle emptied the pouch: the clink of copper. I reached out, and my fingers found the heap of cold metal—there must have been thirty pieces at least. "Whose are these?"

"They're mine, but I weighed them out according to Master Uriel's word. You'll receive the same amount at the end of the gathering." He dropped the pieces back into the pouch, each one ringing in the dark as it fell.

"So many…"

"Enough for a ram and three ewes, with some left over." He tightened the leather strap at the top of the pouch, tying it shut. "It's a shepherd's inheritance."*

I flinched as the word fell like a stone between us: inheritance. "Uncle, tell me again what happened to my father's land."

Uncle Menachem crossed his arms and sighed. "It's as I've told you, Lev. Your inheritance was lost to the King in the civil war. Do not dwell on what is gone. The *Yovel* is not coming." He put his hand on my shoulder. "The Land is wide enough for us all if we each find our place."

I nodded, but knew I had no place. My uncle cared for me like his own, but his land would pass to his sons, not his nephew. I didn't even know where my father's fields lay. It had been foolish to get excited about the *Yovel*—just another futile dream.

"When you return from the gathering, we can start building you a flock of your own." He held the sealed pouch of copper in the palm of his hand as if weighing it. "If that's still what you'll want."

I strained my eyes to read his expression, but it was too dark. Shepherding was the best path for one without land—my uncle taught me this from earliest memory. "Why wouldn't I want that?"

"I'm…I'm sure you will," he said, avoiding my eyes. "You should take that jar of spare strings with you and get to bed. It's late, and you have a long journey tomorrow." He squeezed my shoulder—as much affection as my uncle ever showed—and turned back toward the house.

I lifted the flat rock and retrieved the jar again. When I stood straight, I found Dahlia sitting on the wall of the pen, a dark shadow in the moonless night. "So what does the old man want?"

I sat down next to her. "Weren't you listening?"

"Just tell me."

"He needs a musician for a gathering."

"For how long?"

"Two months."

Dahlia let out a low whistle. "Are you going?"

"Yes."

"Now you won't have to stop travelers to tell me stories of the Kingdom. You can see it for yourself."

I slid along the wall away from Dahlia. "Those are other people's stories."

"They don't have to be." She touched me gently on the cheek, bringing my eyes to hers. Dahlia was the opposite of her father—almost too affectionate. It was fine when we were kids—we were raised like brother and sister—but we were both nearly of age now. Soon we'd be separated, and all her affection would only make it harder. "What's bothering you?"

Dahlia would keep pushing me; she always did. "Your father didn't give me a choice."

"What did he say?"

I examined my hands so I wouldn't have to meet her eyes. "He said it would be good for me, but I know what he meant."

"What?"

I tapped my thumb against the frame of my kinnor, distracting myself enough to keep my voice calm. "That I have to find my place elsewhere because I have no land and can't inherit from him."

Dahlia pulled her hair away from her eyes and tucked an obstinate curl behind her ear. "Neither can I."

"It's different for you. Your father will marry you to Shelah or someone else with land."

Dahlia said nothing, just stared out into the darkness, toward the property of our unmarried neighbor, and shuddered. She was younger than me but would

come of age first, reaching her twelfth birthday in less than six months. There was no telling how long her father would wait before seeking a match for her.

"I'll be thirteen in less than a year. Without land, I'll have no choice but to become a shepherd, following the grasses from pasture to pasture."

"You won't have to leave here when you come of age."

"Not right away, but your father's already sending me away so I can earn enough copper to start a flock. It won't be more than three years until it's too big to keep here."

"Where will you go then?"

I stared at the hills to the east, black against the stars. "To the edge of the wilderness, away from the villages."

"That's so far. When would we see you?"

I shrugged. "A shepherd doesn't just leave his flock." That was true, but there were other truths that Dahlia, who clung to her dreams as if they were the morning sun, refused to accept. Even when I did visit, I might not see her, and we'd certainly never be allowed to speak alone like this.

Dahlia tugged her knees to her chest. "You don't know what will be in three years' time."

Fire blazed in my chest. "You think I'll inherit my father's land? Your father already told me it won't be returned—I don't even know where it is. What will be different in three years?"

"I…" Dahlia's eyes glistened in the starlight. "I don't know, but when you come home—"

"What's going to change when I come home?"

"Well, if the *Yovel* isn't coming—"

"If the *Yovel* isn't coming, my land will never be returned."

Dahlia shook her head. "If the *Yovel* isn't coming, then any land you buy will be yours forever."

I gave a bitter laugh. "Do you know how many years I'd have to herd a flock just to buy a small piece of rocky hillside? It's better not to dream at all."

"Is it?" Dahlia also had a fire in her—we were of the same stock, after all. "This morning you thought you were stuck in Levonah, and tomorrow you're leaving with the old man. You never know what can happen."

"His name is Master Uriel." I pictured his piercing eyes. Blood rushed to my face at the mention of the prophet, and I was glad for the cover of darkness. "There's something strange about him."

"He's a *navi*. My mother told me."

The memory of him saying my name on the hillside brought a fresh dread down my spine. My voice faded. "There's something more."

"I knew it!" Dahlia lowered her voice and leaned in. "Your eyes were so dark when you came home." That was the annoying part about Dahlia: she could always tell my moods so easily. She said my amber eyes darkened to match my thoughts. How could I explain my unease when I first saw the *navi*?

I kept my voice low. "Your father knows more than he says."

Dahlia sighed and lay down on the broad, stone wall of the pen. "The stars are bright tonight."

"What do you think he's hiding?"

"Look at the stars, Lev. Aren't they beautiful?"

"Why don't you answer me?"

"I'm trying to." Dahlia pushed me lightly with her bare foot. "Look at the stars. Whatever's going to happen is already written there. It doesn't matter what Father's hiding; he didn't give you a choice."

I pushed her foot away but turned my eyes upwards. "No, he didn't."

"Try to remember everything you see at the gathering. I want to hear all about it when you get back—it'll give me something to look forward to."

I woke to the drumming of my heart and shot upright. My forehead was clammy with sweat, my breath came fast, and I choked back a scream. Waking from the dream was like a sudden burst to the surface after being submerged in dark waters. It was the old dream, I could feel it, even as it evaporated from my mind before I could grab hold of it. How long had it been since the last time? A month? There was a time when it had been with me night after night, when I was a little boy, alone in the dark, learning not to cry out and wake the others.

I pulled my tunic over my head in the faint dawn light—today wasn't a day to dwell on dreams. I arranged my few belongings on my sheepskin sleeping mat: the extra strings, my pouch. Together with my kinnor, sandals, and tunic, this was all I owned. I started rolling them in a bundle when something heavy dropped on the mat.

"This was your father's knife," Uncle Menachem whispered, trying not to wake the younger children. "I intended to give it to you when you came of age, but it may serve you well on your journey."

My fingers trembled as I picked up the knife. The stone of the handle felt smooth in my hand. I brought the knife up to the high, square window that offered the only light in the loft. A worn ox-hide sheath pulled off with a tug, revealing a blade that was flint rather than iron, a full two handbreadths long. I'd never seen one like it. A copper inlay decorated the hilt; the worn design resembled two claws with three toes each, the inner toe of each claw gently touching.

A lump blocked my throat. My father had held this knife.

"Lev…" My uncle sounded far away, but there was a quiver to his voice that got my attention. "The *nevi'im* are the chief servants of the Holy One. They mean only good; I believe that." I was confused by the mixture of emotions I saw on his face: love, loss, reluctance, even a touch of fear. Twice he looked as if he was about to say more, then he turned to go so quickly that I had no chance to respond.

I sheathed the knife, added it to the pile on the mat, rolled it up, and tied it together. I descended the ladder to find Aunt Leah standing at the hearth. "Sit down and eat before you go," she said. There was a plate on the table with cheese and my special bread. Ever since I could remember, she had set aside the first piece of bread baked each day for me.

"Thank you, Aunt Leah." I washed my hands and sat down without meeting her gaze. I ate quickly, mostly as an excuse to keep my attention on my food. She sat opposite me, and other than rubbing her eyes with the back of her hands, my aunt didn't budge, just sat watching me, expectant. There was no use putting it off; she wasn't going to let me leave without talking. Without looking up, I said, "You don't want me going, do you, Aunt Leah?"

Tears ran down her cheeks, and she forced a half smile. "Yes, I do."

My eyes rose up to meet hers. "You do?"

"I do." She wiped the tears with her palm. "Menachem said you were too young, but I told him you were ready."

So, my uncle hadn't wanted me going—that explained the reluctance. "If you want me to go, then why are you crying?"

She smiled as two more tears spilled over her cheeks. "Hasn't your uncle taught you that more than the lamb wants to suck, the ewe wants to give milk?"*

Why was she suddenly talking about the flock?

Aunt Leah laughed, releasing more tears. "You don't understand now, but when you're blessed with children, you will. You're my sister's son, but you know you're the same to me as one of my own, don't you Lev?"

A wet stinging filled my eyes—I hoped my aunt didn't notice. "Yes, Aunt Leah."

"And no matter what happens, you'll always have a home here."

I nodded—no words would come.

There was a soft knock.

My aunt rose and opened the door. Uriel stood with his back to us, leaving us the space to say goodbye. Aunt Leah held me in a tight embrace, her quiet crying so loud in my ear, her tears wetting my face. I took a final glance at my home over her shoulder as I hugged her back, my eyes open and dry. Though I was destined to return, I always remembered this as the moment I left home for good.

Shimon ben Azai said: Do not despise any person, and do not dismiss any thing, for there is no one who does not have his hour, and no thing that does not have its place.

Pirkei Avot 4:3

2

The Three Keys

Looking off into the brightening east, Uriel stood at the edge of Uncle Menachem's land, hands folded over the top of his staff. "Why have you come, Lev?"

I stared up into the prophet's ancient face, but couldn't read his eyes; his shaggy brows cast their own shadow. "My uncle told me I was hired…" I held up my kinnor, "…for my music."

The *navi* pushed himself to his full height, towering a full head and a half above me. I craned my neck to hold his eyes. "So you are here because you were sent?" His face was unreadable as a stone.

I hitched my sack higher on my shoulder, wishing I could put it on the donkey that waited at his side. I hadn't asked this old man to tear me from my family—what did he want from me?

"Know, if it is only by your Uncle's will that you come to join us, then it is my will that you remain here."

I glanced over my shoulder at the olivewood door of the house. My family's reactions to my early return flashed through my mind: my aunt's disappointment, Eliav's sly grin. Would Dahlia be happy I was back, or think I'd failed?

"You fear being shamed for turning back." Uriel gave voice to my thoughts. "Do not. Your uncle will be relieved. There is much you can do here to help your family."

"Are you offering me the choice?" The last word caught in my throat. My family's rhythms were ruled by routine, and my own life had been shaped by the decisions of others. I had never chosen to come live with my uncle, nor had I sought the life of a shepherd. I may have complained to Dahlia about not having a choice, but I never really expected to be given one.

Uriel's eyes kindled. "The *nevi'im* inhabit a world of devotion. Our Way is a path of choice;* its servants are not for hire. So tell me now—do you choose to come with me, or are you being sent?"

A breath of eastern wind pushed the dry scent of the olive grove between us, carrying with it a vision of an unknown future. Was it true? Could I choose to let the prophet leave without me? But the breeze died and the illusion faded. My uncle had spoken, and I would not upset my aunt.

I glanced toward the King's Road in the distance. We wouldn't move until I told the prophet what he wanted to hear. I drew in a deep breath, drinking in the smell of dew on the leaves of my uncle's grapevines. This narrow valley held the only life I knew. Straightening my posture to mirror Uriel's, I peered into the prophet's eyes and lied. "I choose to come with you."

Uriel held my gaze, as if he had heard all my thoughts, weighed my words, and knew them to be empty. "So be it," he said at last. "Put your belongings on Balaam." The sharp lines of his face relaxed as he stroked the lone, ragged ear of his ancient donkey, whose head sank with a murmur of enjoyment.

When I finished tying down my things, Uriel clicked his tongue and started down the path; his donkey followed without being drawn. The footpath from my uncle's farm skirted the city walls. When it joined the cart track that zig-zagged down from the town gate, Uriel increased his pace and extended his strides, moving nothing like an old man. The donkey trotted, and I pushed myself to keep up.

I knew every rock and tree along this stretch, the spots where the first shoots showed after the early *yoreh* rains, and where small pockets of grass could be found even in late summer. We passed my favorite fig tree, the heavy bottoms of its tear-shaped fruits already ripening to a reddish brown. In two months' time, the fruits would all be gone, the low-hanging ones eaten by other mouths, the higher ones fallen to the ground to rot. My eyes lingered on the shade beneath the leaves, the place where I'd seen Uriel shaken by prophecy the day before.

I felt the prophet's eyes upon me. "You have a question?"

How did he know? "Yes…" I caught myself before using his name. The couple yesterday called him Master Uriel, so did my uncle—was it disrespectful for me to do so? I could just call him Master, but I was hired to play music, not serve. Grandfather? It worked for the village elders but didn't seem right for a prophet. Better not to address him at all. "Yesterday, when the couple came to you," I glanced back at the fig tree, "You used prophecy to find something of theirs?"

"They lost a valuable ring."

"You find *rings*?"

Uriel chuckled, slowed his pace, and turned toward me. "You thought *navua* was only for more important things?"

"Well...yes."

"I assure you," Uriel's eyes no longer laughed, "that ring was immensely important to them." He turned back toward the road, resuming his driving pace.

The silence felt heavy as I followed behind. I hadn't meant to say that what he did was unimportant—I was just surprised. I ought to keep silent.

But there was another question I wanted to ask, one that had been on my mind since I woke that morning, and hadn't my uncle always said that the bashful never learn?* I increased my pace until I was back at the old man's side. "And then you received *navua* about me?"

The old prophet slowed his pace again and fixed me with a hard gaze. "About you?"

"Yes, about hiring me?"

Uriel's arrow-straight posture relaxed just slightly, and he again turned his eyes up the road. "No, Lev, I did not receive a *navua* about hiring you."

"Then why?"

Uriel watched me out of the corner of his eyes. "Why what?"

The tips of my ears grew hot as a faint smile pulled at the edge of his mouth. Was he playing with me? "Why me?"

"What do you mean?"

I took a few more steps in silence, sharpening my question. "I mean, why *me*? There must be better musicians. I'm just..." My voice trailed off. What was I?

The donkey's grunts were the only sound as Uriel contemplated the question. "So you want to know what, other than *navua,* would have driven me to hire a shepherd boy to play for the prophets?"

I nodded.

"That is a wise question, and thus deserves a response." Uriel stopped and faced me. "My heart told me."

His heart? Those blue-gray eyes scanned mine as I thought about his answer. I started walking again so I could drop my eyes. "You didn't want to..." I scratched the back of my sweaty neck, "...check?"

"I have learned never to use prophecy to question my heart."

"But prophecy—"

"An open heart knows more than you realize. At times its intuition is more valuable than prophecy. There is no faster way to dull its voice than to doubt it."

Even if he was right, what did it matter? How many times had I watched the distant hills, dreaming of a mother who would never return? How many times had I questioned my uncle about land that would never be mine? I learned long ago that an open heart could also betray. "Isn't prophecy more powerful than intuition? Your heart couldn't have found that lost ring, could it?"

Uriel combed his long fingers through his thick gray hair. "True, it could not. Yet, my heart is mine to know, while prophecy is not at my command.* Yesterday I was unable to receive *navua* until I heard your kinnor."

"My kinnor?"

"Your music is pure and beautiful.* It cleared away many barriers."

The road from Levonah dropped into a broad valley where it met the King's Road. An expanse of vineyards flowed into the distance all around the crossroads, on land owned by one of the noble families of Shomron, the Kingdom's capital, and worked by farmers from the village. As we turned south, I recalled the stories my uncle told me about the prophets. Beauty was rarely involved.

"You are confused," Uriel said. "Your uncle told me you learn the stories of our Fathers. Tell me, after Joseph's brothers sold him into slavery, how did they deceive their father Jacob?"*

"They dipped Joseph's coat in the blood of a goat. Jacob thought Joseph was killed by a wild beast."

"Good, I see you know the story."

Every boy in Israel probably knew that story, but I still stepped lighter with the praise. I plucked a fennel blossom from its tall stalk off the side of the road and squeezed its seeds into my hand.

"Now, do you understand it?"

My hand paused on the way to my mouth.

"Jacob was a *navi* and a wealthy man. Shouldn't he have known his sons were lying to him? Couldn't the Holy One tell him where Joseph was held in Egypt? Why didn't he go down and redeem him from slavery?"

I stopped walking. I'd known this story most of my life—at least I thought I did. "I don't know."

Uriel continued in silence. I followed but didn't push myself to keep up, drifting further behind as I chewed on his question. I popped the fennel seeds into my mouth, savoring their pungent flavor. How could I know why Jacob didn't ask the Holy One—and what did that have to do with my music? I focused on Uriel's back as if the answer lay somewhere between his shoulder blades.

My uncle told me that Jacob mourned his son every day he was gone as if he'd died that very morning. That's why the story stuck in my mind. I knew the darkness of grieving, like a black hole in my chest. What was left to me of my parents? A memory of lavender wafting from Mother's hair, the weight of Father's broad and heavy hands on my forehead—every shard of memory was shrouded with longing. Had Jacob felt that way for twenty-two years? I tore ahead, slowing only when I drew even with the elderly prophet. "Was it his grief?"

Uriel slowed his pace without turning his head. "Are you asking me a question or giving me an answer?" *The prophet has no interest in making things easy for me.*

A hot breeze drove a parched thornbush across the road. *Where had the vineyards gone?* We'd already crossed into wilder country, without my noticing. I inhaled deeply and replied in a clear voice. "Jacob couldn't receive prophecy because he was mourning the loss of Joseph."

Uriel smiled, the first show of warmth I felt from him that day. "Indeed. Sadness seals the heart. Only in joy can it receive."

The road sank between low, terraced hills that blocked any breeze, and sweat ran down my neck as a white sun burned directly overhead. Ahead, a man sliced the last of his wheat, grabbing handfuls of stalks with his left hand and hacking at their bases with a curved iron blade. A young woman collected the cut wheat, laying it flat to dry. As soon as she caught sight of us, the woman dropped her stalks to the ground and smoothed her skirt. Her swollen belly nearly overwhelmed her narrow frame as she carefully picked her way down the uneven ground to the road. She bowed her head low. "Master Uriel, won't you turn aside and eat a meal from your maidservant?"

I felt a rush of affection for her. The handful of almonds we ate at mid-morning were long gone, the hour for the midday meal had passed, and even my aching legs were protesting their hunger. Yet the prophet had shown no signs of slowing. He nodded to her request, and I sighed as we stepped into the slim shade of a carob tree by the side of the road. The woman weaved her way back to her husband, whispering and gesturing off into the distance. He dropped his sheaves to the ground and ran through the fields.

She returned and led us across the furrowed field to a poor dwelling tucked into the shadow of the hills. Its mud brick walls marked them as among the humblest of Israel, but the roof was freshly thatched, and a jasmine bush near the door gave off a welcoming scent. We entered a tight, dark room, the entirety of their home. She seated us at a low table, poured a small bowl of wine into a pitcher, filled the rest with water, and placed it before us with two clay cups.

"Thank you, Milcah." Uriel poured for the two of us. She brought out freshly salted cheese, then quickly patted dough into two cakes and placed them directly on the coals in the hearth.

Soon after the bread was done, the husband returned leading a donkey carrying a second woman, who looked like Milcah but with a slight body and pinched face. Milcah's husband helped her off the donkey, and she stepped into the house, walking directly to the prophet.

"Peace unto you, Master Uriel." Her eyes were resolute. "I have come for another blessing."

Uriel laid down his bread and swallowed the bit in his mouth. "Another, Rumah? Has the first brought what you sought?"

"Of course not!" Blood drained from her face and her eyes burned.

"Why then do you ask for another?"

Her shrill cry pierced the small room. "Any fool can look at the two of us and see why." She turned to Milcah, the fire in her eyes departing as they fell on her, and soon they brimmed with tears. "My sister and I received the same blessing from you nine months ago. Now here she is with her belly between her teeth,* and I'm just as I was, but for being older."

Uriel's only response was a slight nod, and her anger flared again.

"Why? Why her and not me? She'd been married for two years when we came to you, I for almost ten. People say you can work miracles. Why didn't your blessing work for me?"

"It is not truly my blessing, but that of the Holy One."

"What does that mean?" Rumah's voice cracked. "I told my pain to *you*. It was *you* who promised me a child. Of course the Holy One is the source of life, but *you* are a *navi*."

"I never promised you a child." Uriel rose from his stool, his thick, gray hair brushing the smoke-blackened rafters of the low roof. He peered down at Rumah, small and frail but unshrinking in his shadow. "There are three keys that the Holy One does not surrender to any servant,* even the *nevi'im*: the key to the womb, the key to the grave, and the key to the heavens. Without them, there can be no birth, no resurrection, no rain. Even our father Jacob turned away our mother Rachel when she wept before him, demanding a child. And despite what you may have heard, my power is as nothing compared to Jacob's." His fist clenched around the handle of his staff. "I say his words to you now, 'Am I in the place of the Holy One who has withheld the fruit of your womb?'"*

Even in the dim light, I recoiled at the hard glint in Uriel's eyes. His words shattered Rumah's anger into tears, and she wept into her empty hands.

"So then you can do nothing?" She cried out. "I am lost?"

"No blessing is in vain," he replied, his voice softer now, "but the blessing alone may not be enough."

"But the Holy One heard my sister's cry." Rumah glanced in Milcah's direction and wheeled back, stung by what she saw. "Why does she merit and not me?"

"It is not always a question of merit. Many things can block the channels of blessing. Perhaps your desires lead you astray, and you have not come into this world for the children you wish to bear. And perhaps you yourself are closed to the blessing which is ready to be born into your life. When I left here last, what did you do?"

"You know exactly what I did. I went to my husband—what else would I do to conceive?"

Uriel turned to Milcah, "And what did you do?"

"I also went to my husband." Milcah took the pitcher and added more wine to Uriel's almost full cup, her neck flushing as she spoke. "I'm not sure what else you mean?"

"I mean, when did you start preparing for the baby?"

"Well, it's silly." Pink blotches rose from her neck to her cheeks as she reached for a loosely woven fabric of heavy wool. "The next day I started weaving this blanket. At first, my husband laughed at me, but then he started building that cradle."

"Yes, that is right." Uriel smiled as he contemplated the woven basket next to their reed sleeping mats.

The older sister pursed her lips and glared at the blanket. "You're not suggesting that if I wove a blanket, I would have conceived too, are you?"

"Of course not. The blanket itself was insignificant, as was the cradle. Your sister's conviction made her a fitting vessel." Rumah's mouth was a thin line, and her eyes darted back and forth between the blanket and Uriel. "Milcah acted as if the blessing was already fulfilled. She created a space in her heart for the blessing to rest, allowing it to bear fruit." Rumah's hands unclenched as her eyes settled on his face. "Do you remember what you thought when you left me last?"

"I do." She bent her head with a short laugh. "I even remember talking to my husband when I got home. He asked me, 'Do you think it will work?'

I told him, 'Who can tell? Milcah thinks it will. What harm could there be in going along?'" Her eyes rose back to Uriel's, filled with a new light. "So if I believe, it will work?"

"I cannot promise you that. As I said, the key of birth is beyond my grasp." Uriel's words extinguished the light in her eyes, but his face remained radiant.

"And if it fails? If there is no child?"

I knew the look in her eyes well; I imagine such a look also brightened my eyes whenever my hopes rose. Despite the misery I'd suffered from dashed hopes, despite all the dangers, I wanted Uriel to keep her hope alive. Milcah turned away from her sister, as I held my breath.

"Then you have a choice. You can embrace your present state, receiving it as the will of the Holy One, and seeing it as an opportunity for growth in this world. Or you can struggle against it. But know now that your struggle will not succeed.* I cannot say that joy in this decree will provide what you desire, but bitterness certainly dries up the wellsprings of blessing."

One Year Later

In the Cave of Dotan

"Master, is it true that our futures can be read in the stars?"

Hesitation lingered in the black air. Was it wrong of me to mention the stars, which my master surely knew he would never see again? I twisted a loose string on my worn tunic.

"It is true," he eventually responded, "…most of the time."

"Do the nevi'im read the future there?"

"No, Lev. We keep far from that path."

"Why, Master?"

"The stars are a bridge between this world and the one beyond. One skilled at reading their movements can see what is coming into this world before it arrives."*

"Then why avoid them, Master?"

"Our father Abraham was a master stargazer and read in the heavens that he and his wife were never to have children together. But the Holy One raised Abraham above the stars, promising him that they would no longer bind him and his descendants."*

"So the fortunes of Israel don't lie in the stars?"

"Most of the time our destiny can be seen there as well. But when we choose a higher path, our destiny is ruled directly by the Holy One, bypassing the stars. That is why the prophets avoid their guidance: they do not wish to limit the future to the confines of the present."*

Rabbi Eliezer said: Warm yourself by the fire of the Sages, but beware of their glowing coals lest you get burnt—for their bite is the bite of a fox, their sting is the sting of a scorpion, their hiss is the hiss of a serpent, and all their words are like fiery coals.

Pirkei Avot 2:15

ג

Honoring the Calf

"When you find Yosef ben Avner," Uriel's voice was soft, but no less commanding, in the dawn light, "tell him we shall meet tomorrow at the junction."

I peered across the mist rising from the valley, westward toward the ancient walls of Beit El. "How will I find him?"

"Quite easily, I imagine. There is no other like him in the city."

"But where does he live?"

"He once lived in the weavers' quarter, but I do not know if he has remained there. I have not entered Beit El in upward of sixty years."

My head swung back to stare at the prophet. *Sixty years?* The men in Levonah who reached sixty years ground their food to mash before eating it, yet Uriel still had a full set of teeth. Just how old was he?

The prophet waved at my untouched bread. "Eat. There is no knowing how long you'll be gone."

I took a bite of the dry loaf, forcing myself to chew—I shouldn't fail in my task because of hunger. Uriel walked out to a precipice that cast a shadow over the junction below and sat down on its rocky edge.

"Are you going to sit here alone all day?"

"Probably, though sometimes visitors come to me even in this place."

I swallowed another bite. "Why haven't you entered Beit El in sixty years?"

The prophet shifted his eyes to a cloud of dust rising above the road in the distance, and my question evaporated in the morning light. "That looks like a royal messenger riding toward Beit El. If you hurry, you can catch him. There might be news."

I shoved the last chunk of bread into my mouth, slung my water skin over my shoulder, and raced toward the path. My legs ached from the long march the day before, their stiffness resisting every step. Hoofbeats echoed in the distance, and I pushed myself into a run down the steep, rock-strewn path. This was a mistake. I didn't notice a cluster of loose pebbles until my foot was upon it. My arms shot out for balance, a weak compensation for fumbled footing. My backside hit the ground first, and I slid down the hard-packed trail until my left knee banged into a boulder.

I glared up at the old man. I was a musician, not a messenger. Why should I have to run after some horse and search out a stranger in a city I didn't know while he just sat and waited? But the prophet's eyes were closed, impervious to my anger or the pain in my knee. I got up, rubbed my leg, and limped carefully down the path.

By the time I reached the crossroads, my legs were loose, despite the throbbing in my knee. I was only halfway up the steep incline to the city when the horseman reached the junction below. I pushed myself back into a run, but it was no use. The rider's tunic, emblazoned with the royal ox, whipped in the air as he thundered past, leaving me coughing in a cloud of dust.

The messenger rounded one of the massive stone towers flanking the entrance to the city and disappeared through its gates. Three ram's horn blasts echoed over the surrounding hills—a public announcement.

My lungs raging, I pushed onward. This was no longer just about Uriel's command. A public announcement directly from a royal messenger was something we heard in Levonah only three or four times a year. I rounded the tower and raced through the narrow gateway, past a guard who barely glanced my way. A crowd already surrounded the horseman in the city square, but some of the dignitaries were still making their way from the chambers in the city gate—the announcement wouldn't start without them. My lungs heaved as I hobbled to a stop and doubled over to get my breath. I had made it in time.

A thin beard shaded the messenger's cheeks; he couldn't have seen more than twenty summers. He was covered in dust and sweat traced thin lines down his face. He sat stiffly, chin held high, gazing over the heads of the crowd. When the last of the officials reached the square, he brought a silver tipped ram's horn to his lips and blew a single blast. "By authority of the great King Ahav!" A hush fell across the square. "It gives His Majesty great pleasure to announce the royal betrothal!"

The rider didn't flinch, but his horse sidestepped nervously at the crowd's roar. Still gasping for breath, I added a feeble cheer. Aunt Leah always said, "It's not good for a man to be alone."* To her, even a king was lacking without a wife. The last time she'd said this, her words came with a sad glance at me.

The messenger cleared his throat and waited for silence. "King Ahav will marry Princess Izevel of Tzidon on the ninth day of the fifth month* in the royal capital of Shomron. Let all of Israel come and rejoice!"

I was ready this time and let loose a loud "*Hedad*!" but my voice was nearly alone. I cut my cry short, feeling the stares of the crowd.

The messenger lowered his gaze and sneered at the stunned looks on the faces in the crowd. He kicked his mount, swung it around, and was not yet clear of the crowd when he pushed it into a gallop. I still stood bent over, catching my breath, when someone grabbed the back of my tunic and yanked me out of the horse's way. I tried to thank him, but he was already talking to the man beside him. The thud of hooves was soon drowned out by the babble of voices discussing the news.

I searched the faces of the crowd, seeking a friendly one I could ask for help. I wasn't sure why news of the King's engagement would incense the people, but the confused fury written on their faces extinguished my desire to approach any of them. With the messenger gone, now was the time to find out about Yosef ben Avner before the crowd dispersed. I bit my lower lip. I never liked asking for help, especially from strangers. But there was no other choice—I'd just have to pick someone.

"Are you Lev?"

I spun around to meet the smiling eyes of a squat young man, appearing some five years older than me, with a bushy black beard and bent nose. "Yes, I am."

"Excellent. I am Raphael ben Eshek. Master Yosef sent me to find you. Come, he is waiting."

A warm glow spread through my chest; finding Yosef had gone far easier than I feared. Without another word, Raphael turned to go, and I hastened to follow, hobbling on my bruised knee. I felt comfortable with Raphael from the first, but as we entered the streets of Beit El, my ease faded. If Yosef knew who I was and where I would be, what else might he know about me? Feeling suddenly exposed, I wrapped my arms across my chest.

Raphael interrupted my thoughts. "How long have you been with Master Uriel?"

At least Raphael didn't know everything about me. My first instinct was to tell him that I wasn't really with the prophet, just a musician he'd hired for the gathering, but I swallowed the objection. "Two days."

"Ahhhhh," he chuckled. "My first week with my master, half the time I had no idea what was happening."

I laughed louder than I intended. "That's how I feel right now."

Raphael glanced down at my swelling knee and the trail of dried blood that marred my shin. "Is this fresh?"

I nodded.

"We'll put something on that when we arrive. For now, let me help you." Raphael thrust his stout arm under mine and supported my limp toward a narrow, stone-paved street that radiated out from the city square.

As my body sank onto his shoulder, I caught a side glance at my new friend. He smelled clean, like a fresh rosemary bush. Could he tell that I had not properly bathed since the last new moon? I inspected his tunic; it was not the rough wool of a servant's. Who was he exactly? "Are you Yosef's assistant?"

"No," Raphael grunted at the burden of my weight, "his disciple."

"You're *training* to become a prophet?" My uncle's tales of the prophets were among my favorite stories, but I couldn't recall any that involved training.

"Yes." Raphael beamed, revealing a set of large, crooked teeth that filled his wide grin. I couldn't help but smile back; his eyes gleamed like those of my young cousins whenever Aunt Leah treated them to roasted nuts.

"How long have you been with Yosef?"

"Five years."

"*Five years*?" I spent only six months going out with my uncle before I was ready to take the flock by myself.

"Oh yes. Prophecy comes only after many years of training—if at all."

"Have you received prophecy yet?"

"No, I'm still counted among the *bnei nevi'im*,* not the *nevi'im*."

We stopped in front of a flat-roofed house made from chiseled stone, its street side broken only by a plain wooden door. The door swung outward, and an old man stepped into the street, his coal black eyes fixed unblinking on my face. I turned away from the intensity of his gaze and inspected him out of the corner of my eye. His gray hair and beard were darker and better groomed than Uriel's. The bright white of his linen robes contrasted with the raven black *totafot* boxes bound to his arm and forehead. Uriel had also worn *totafot* in the early morning but removed them before eating.

"Welcome Lev ben Yochanan, I am Yosef ben Avner. I am aware of Uriel's instructions to you; nonetheless, speak your message and fulfill your master's command."

It was one thing for Raphael to assume that I was Uriel's servant, but it was another for Yosef, a prophet, to call him my master. I wanted to protest, but thought better of it—I could already see that Yosef wasn't someone to argue with. "The time has come for the gathering." My voice sounded hollow. "Master Uriel has informed the others. He will await you at the junction in the morning."

"Very good. We will be there." Yosef continued to bore into my eyes, even as I turned away. I tried to catch a glimpse of what was happening inside the prophet's house, in vain.

"Raphael, I see that Lev's knee needs care. In my quarters, you will find clean fabric and ointment in the remedy box next to my mat."

Raphael entered the house, and Yosef turned back to me. "You would like to observe my disciples." He had the same unnerving practice as Uriel of telling me what I was thinking. "They are engaged in training now, and it is not desirable to disturb them." His eyes flickered over me from head to toe. "Yet, there is a way you can help my disciples. Then you may enter and enhance, rather than disturb."

Curious though I was to see what was going on inside, Yosef's piercing eyes made me glad I had a ready excuse. "My kinnor is with Master Uriel."

"No matter, you will not need it."

Raphael returned with a cloth and a bowl of water and bent down to clean the wound. He opened a small clay jar filled with some evil-smelling substance. I clenched my teeth when the herbs touched my knee, but the sting lasted only a moment. A layer of yellowish ointment coated the wound, which I could suddenly barely feel. I eyed the wooden doorway narrowly and asked Yosef, "What else would I do?"

"You will see a stool in the middle of the room." Yosef nodded to Raphael, who entered the house, closing the door behind him. "All you must do is walk in and sit down."

"That's it?"

"That is all."

I had no more excuses to give Yosef, and it did seem a small price to satisfy my curiosity, yet my tongue turned pasty as I stepped toward the door. How could sitting on a stool help the disciples in their training unless they were to do something to me while I sat defenseless?

My moist palm took hold of the iron door handle. A floor of beaten earth met my footfalls inside, where the room was heavy with quiet. Eight disciples were ranged along the walls, each seated on a reed mat, legs folded, eyes closed. An alcove high in the wall contained over a hundred scrolls, far more than I'd ever seen, many brown and cracking with age. In the middle of the room sat the sole piece of furniture, an empty stool.

I limped quietly to my place, and sat down, my knee protesting. No one reacted to my entrance. Other than one disciple who scratched his nose, no sound or movement disturbed their rhythmic breathing. Yosef leaned against the doorframe and watched.

I rubbed the back of my neck, suddenly hot and itchy. I couldn't see that they were acting upon me in any way, but these were not ordinary men; they were *bnei nevi'im,* disciples of the prophets. Uriel and Yosef both knew things about me without being told, sensing my thoughts as if they were spoken aloud. Is that what the disciples were doing now, reading my thoughts? Would I even know it if they were? I fought the desire to press my hands over my ears as if to block the way to my mind, knowing how useless such a move would be.

I had agreed to help, but my thoughts were my own. My forehead creased as I tried to empty my mind. It didn't work. Memories came pouring in on me, the very ones I least wanted to share: Dahlia surprising me while I bathed at the spring; almost losing the flock in a thunderstorm; the feel of Mother's hair on my cheek. Sweat beaded on my forehead, but my failed efforts only proved I couldn't clear my mind by force. My kinnor provided my only refuge from thought, but it was far away. Silence pressed down on me. *My kinnor.* The kinnor channeled my music, but it wasn't the source of it. Closing my eyes, I reached for a *nigun* to play in my mind. A melody whispered in my ears, and my shoulders relaxed. Thought and memory faded as my fingers worked strings they couldn't feel, plucking the notes sharper in my mind than I ever did with my hands.

Yosef finally broke the silence. "What can you tell me about our guest?"

The disciples turned toward their teacher, eyes still closed. I blushed, hoping no one would mention the incident with Dahlia at the spring. One replied, "He is a boy, Master."

"Why do you say so?"

"His footsteps. It took him eight steps to get from the door to the chair. It takes me five or six. Also, his steps were soft, lighter than a man's, but not hesitant like a woman's would be on entering."

"But slightly uneven," the disciple next to him added, "as if he's walking with a limp." I touched my left knee, still aching from the fall that morning.

Yosef was not yet satisfied. "What else?"

"He's a musician, Master."

"Interesting. Why do you say so Nadav?"

"He's tapping his feet." I peered down; I hadn't realized my feet were tapping out the melody in my head.

"Do only musicians tap their feet?"

"No, I even do it myself sometimes." The disciple cocked his head to the side. "But there's something different about the way he taps, the rhythm is more…complex…than when I do it."

"I see." Yosef's voice gave nothing away, but he was smiling. "What else?"

The *navi*'s eyes swept back and forth across the disciples, but no one responded. Finally, the one who scratched his nose earlier said, "He's uncomfortable with us speaking about him."

"What tells you this, Elad?"

"When Nadav described him tapping his feet, he stopped, and he's breathing faster than he was before." Instantly my cheeks grew hot.

"Very perceptive."

This was my first experience with using the ears to see, and I was amazed at how much the disciples were able to learn just by listening. Yet, within half a year, the skills of these disciples would seem basic to me. When one enters a place that light cannot penetrate, his ears become his eyes. I would learn to hear the difference between a wall and a doorway and to distinguish the footstep of friend from enemy.

"The time has come to take mercy on our guest who has provided an opportunity for so much insight. Open your eyes and greet Lev, a musician that Master Uriel has hired to play for us during the gathering." Yosef smiled at Nadav, the one who had guessed I was a musician, and from the look of gratitude on his face, I gathered that a smile from Yosef was a rare reward.

"I must ask you to excuse us now, Lev. We will meet again tomorrow at the junction."

The sun was approaching its midpoint in the sky when I left Yosef's house. I walked back, barely thinking about where I was going, mulling over everything I'd seen and heard. In all the stories my uncle had taught me, the Holy One simply chose the prophet—there was never any mention of disciples or training. Yet, Raphael said that all prophets, every single one of them, had trained. Some could have learned from other prophets, as Raphael was learning from Yosef, but what about the others? Abraham and Moses had been alone, cut off from any other prophets—where could they have trained?

Unbidden, an image rose in my mind of sitting on the ground in our *sukkah*, listening to Uncle Menachem tell the stories of the prophets. This was my favorite time of year, after the grape harvest, when we moved outside for the seven-day festival, sheltered only by a roof of fallen branches. During *Sukkot*, we worked as little as possible, spending our time inside the *sukkah*, singing, feasting on a roasted ram, and telling stories. I couldn't remember having my nightmare even once while sleeping inside the fragile walls of the *sukkah*.

These days, most men considered shepherds little better than illiterate thieves, respecting no man's boundaries, and ignorant of the ways of Israel. But on each night of *Sukkot*, Uncle Menachem told the story of one of the seven shepherds of Israel:* Abraham, Isaac, Jacob, Moses, Aharon, Joseph and David. It always seemed strange that our greatest leaders came from a trade so widely despised, but I never thought to question how they became prophets. In the stories the Holy One simply addressed them—that was all.

I turned the stories over in my mind as I wound through the streets of Beit El. It couldn't just be coincidence that they were all shepherds—could they have trained for prophecy while in the wilderness with their flocks?

As my mind wandered, my feet led me back to the gate of Beit El. I stopped just inside the heavy wooden doors, realizing that Uriel would not look for me much before sundown. I had time for myself, a rarity in Levonah. I turned my head up and sniffed—the scent of roasting meat hung in the air. I immediately knew where I wanted to go; I just needed to get there.

I hurried back to the main square and spotted a farmer drawing a lamb up a wide thoroughfare. I crossed the square to follow, and the enticing aroma of sizzling fat and meat thickened as I left the open plaza. I was on the right trail.

The road climbed gently, the stone pavers underfoot polished by the steps of countless feet. Flights of two or three stairs occasionally broke its smooth incline. Before long, we had walked enough to cross all of Levonah twice, yet we weren't even at the center of the city. Of course, Levonah was little more than a farming village compared to the Holy City of Beit El, where Jacob—one of the seven shepherds himself—had built an altar a thousand years before.* The street broadened into a marketplace. Open storefronts lined the sides, and freestanding stalls ran down the middle. The man leading the lamb disappeared into the crowd, but it no longer mattered—I had arrived.

The familiar animal odor of earth, blood and manure filled the air, and sheep bleated from a storefront on my right. I stepped in, seeing that the store opened out to a pen in the back, where lambs lapped water from a trough. "How much for one of those?" I asked, though I knew I didn't have enough copper to buy one.

The burly shopkeeper eyed my dirty tunic. "The lambs start at three shekel silver, the rams go up to eight."

"Eight shekel silver? We get only half of that for a ram that size."

"A shepherd on your first trip to Beit El, eh? The sheep you sell are for eating; it doesn't matter if they have a bad eye or walk with a limp. Mine have no flaws. If you get any big ones in your flock like that, bring them to me. I'll give you a lot more than you'll get from the slaughterers."

A rhythmic cooing rose from dozens of holes carved into the wall. "How much for a dove?"

"I can give you a good one for half a shekel." He pulled a small iron weight from a pocket of his smock and put it on one end of a scale. On the second pan, I dropped a few copper pieces, my earnings from the wedding earlier in the summer. Just as my fourth copper piece landed on the pan, it sank, bobbing up and down until it came level with the iron. It was most of what I owned, but I couldn't miss this chance—plus a hefty sum awaited me at the end of the gathering. An image of Dahlia floated into my mind, her nose crinkling with envy when she heard I'd gone to Beit El a year early.

The shopkeeper stepped onto a short ladder, untied the reed cover over one of the holes, slipped both hands in, and deftly pulled out a dove. It struggled, then relaxed in his grip. "Hold it like this, with both hands over its wings." He passed me the brown bird streaked with its purple feather-tips. "You don't want it to fly away." I gripped it the way I was shown. The small body squirmed in my hands, its heart beat wildly. Its feathers barely contained the bird's fine bones; I felt as though they'd crack if I squeezed too tightly.

"Hold it firm," he chided me. "If you let it struggle, it might get hurt. A pity to waste your copper on an unfit offering."

I tightened my grip and the bird relaxed. "What do I do now?"

"Take it to the altar. Follow the crowd uphill toward the smoke." Unable to contain my excitement, I snorted out a laugh. The shopkeeper's eyes narrowed, and his beefy hand clapped onto my shoulder. "Wait, I forgot to ask. You're of age, are you not?"

I shook my head. "Not for another year."

He wrapped his big hands around mine, taking control of the passive dove and shaking his head with a half-smile. "I should've asked first. You can't make an offering until you're of age. I'll not have you sin on my account." He stepped up the ladder and returned the bird carefully to its hole, then placed my coppers back in my empty hand.

A stone rose in my throat. "Is there nothing I can do?"

"Go and bow before the Holy One. Anyone can do that."

I stepped out of the shop and continued up the center of the marketplace, picturing Eliav laughing at me if he ever heard about the dove—I'd have to tell Dahlia when we were alone. As the street rose, the scent of incense overpowered the musky reek of sheep. Once I cleared the last of the stalls, the clamor of the caged animals faded and a new sound caught my ear. Floating above the hum of the crowd was a song unlike any I'd ever heard. The precision and delicacy of notes weaving into one another bespoke exceptional skill and countless hours of practice. I closed my eyes and filtered out the noise of the marketplace to better focus on the music. An elbow in my back broke my concentration as a thickset farmer stumbled against me and cursed. I'd chosen a poor spot to stop and gawk.

Slipping through the crowd, I sought the source of the music. The street leveled, opening out into a large square. Across the plaza, I found what I was looking for: seven musicians standing on a wooden platform, brilliant red robes falling to their feet. In the open air of the plaza, the incense was no longer just fragrant; it was intoxicating. Music floated on a cloud of cinnamon, clove, and myrrh, filling the open square.

The cry of a frightened sheep tore my attention from the melody. With the instincts of a shepherd, I sought out the distressed animal, but the thick cloud of smoke billowing up from the incense altar obscured my sight.

There was another sharp bleat, cut short by a grunt, and I spotted the lamb. Its blood flowed out in jets into a stone bowl held ready to receive it. The creature's body sagged, lifeless, as a barefoot priest robed in white hoisted it on his shoulders and carried it up a ramp to the altar. A second priest lifted the bowl of blood and splashed it in a stiff-armed arc across the base of the altar.

Just beyond the bloodstain, a tall banner fell from the horns of the altar to its base, displaying the royal ox of the House of King Omri.* As I stared, the cloth billowed out in the breeze, revealing a crack in the stone hidden beneath. The fissure ran almost the entire height of the altar, with a thin trail of ash surfacing from its depths.

Uriel's words from the morning before came back to me: *The prophets live in a world of devotion; the places they go are reached only by choice*. I hadn't really chosen to follow the old prophet; I only told him what he wanted to hear. But it was my choice to come to the altar and bow down before the Holy One.

I crossed the square and ascended to a platform of massive stone blocks towering over the plaza. A second platform stood above the first. Four limestone pillars supported a roof of woven reeds shading the sacred object: The Golden Calf.*

The Calf wasn't as immense as I'd imagined. Its eyes would barely have reached my knees, but the burnished gold reflected the sun as brightly as a mirror. Its expression was exactly that of a real calf wishing to nurse, and even from where I stood I could see the texture of its hide.

I always expected my first trip to Beit El would be with my uncle, during the annual pilgrimage, and now my pride at coming on my own was tempered by not knowing what to do. My face grew hot as I avoided the gaze of the priests guarding the Golden Calf. A gray-haired man ascended next to me. From the corner of my eye, I watched him stand for a moment, gazing up into the Calf's eyes. He lowered his knees onto the chiseled stone. I copied him, wincing as my wound hit the ground.

I felt the Calf's eyes watching over me, over all the faithful of Israel, as it had for generations. How many prayers had it heard?

This was my chance to speak directly to the Holy One. I recalled my earliest memories of prayer, of how I would cry out for my mother to come back. I wasn't sure how long that went on, probably for years, until one day Uncle Menachem took me aside and explained that wasn't the way prayer worked. "We don't pray for the impossible," he said, "and we don't pray to change what already is. But we can pray for things that haven't happened yet, like strong rains, a good harvest, or that the flock should be safe."

So for years, I did just that; I prayed that the flock would be safe from lions and wolves, and in the two years I led the flock, I had lost only three lambs. But now, standing before the Holy One, with the flock so far away, the words sounded hollow to my heart. This was my chance to pray for what I really wanted. Not the return of my parents or the inheritance of my land—it was still forbidden to pray for the impossible.

Yet, how quickly our visions of what is possible can change. At the last new moon, I would have said that I was destined to become nothing more than a lowly shepherd. Perhaps Dahlia was right, perhaps circumstances could change, even for me. After all, here I was, just a few days later, bowing down in Beit El. If the altar of the Holy One, the holiest place in the Kingdom, could have a crack, then could I, with all of my flaws, also attain holiness?

Raphael said that his master had put him on the path to prophecy five years ago. When I asked Uriel yesterday why he had taken me for the gathering, he said it was for my music. But there was something he was holding back—I was sure of it. Could this be it? Had he brought me to the gathering so that I could catch a glimpse of a different future? Had he put me on the path to prophecy without my even knowing it?

This was finally something meaningful to pray for, a path of devotion to something greater than just my sheep or my stomach. If it was my fate to become a shepherd in the wilderness, then I wanted to be like the seven shepherds of Israel, a shepherd-prophet.

My fellow worshiper was already stretched out on the flagstones, arms extended before his head, legs trailing out behind him. I copied his position, placing my palms flat before me. Lowering my forehead to the cold stone, my hands trembled at my first act of devotion.

Joshua ben Perachyah said: Choose a master for yourself, acquire a friend, and judge every person favorably.

Pirkei Avot 1:6

4

The Knife

"Darkness is rising upon the land."

These were the only words the prophet uttered when I told him of the King's engagement. For the rest of the night, he sat on the precipice, deep in thought. I didn't even get to tell him about bowing before the Holy One.

We met Yosef and his disciples soon after dawn. The two masters embraced, then led us eastward on the broad road toward Jericho. The disciples and I waited until the masters were far enough ahead to speak without being overheard, then we started off behind. Our route led down the dry wilderness slope that bridged the fertile mountain plateau, where I had spent my entire life, and the Jordan valley below. A herd of gazelles leapt along the ridge, leaving gray tracks on the barren terrain. One stopped to nibble at the dark green leaves of a lone hyssop bush that had fought its way through the rocky soil. Halfway down the slope, we turned north onto a smaller footpath that followed the ridge-line along the edge of the wilderness. A hot wind swirled with dust, and I tasted grit between my teeth. Only the toughest creatures could call this steep, arid land home. Two rough, migrant shepherds clicked their tongues to guide a flock of coarse-haired goats toward a patch of brown grasses growing in a catch-basin between the hills.

This is me in a few years' time.

At what point had my family made clear this was my future? Was it all at once or only little by little? This was my first time in the true wild, and I saw how the sparse grass and the distant springs made shepherding here strenuous work. At the same time, a quiet serenity rested between the hillsides. Though life here would be hard, my decision to train for prophecy bolstered me. It was the perfect place for learning to hear the words of the Holy One.

My enthusiasm only lasted until mid-day, when we passed a shepherd's tent. Outside its goatskin walls, the shepherd's wife sat baking their bread directly on the coals of her fire. She responded to Uriel's greeting with a ghastly smile, baring toothless gums and stretching the weathered skin of her face. There were no children around the tent—she hardly looked healthy enough to have any. Was her blighted condition a result of the harshness of their lives, or were the prospects of a wilderness shepherd so poor that her husband could marry no better? Either alternative was enough to make me cringe.

Even as the springs came closer together, returning a haze of green to the landscape, I still couldn't clear that image of the shepherd's wife from my thoughts. Perhaps I should bring Dahlia here to see the worn woman herself? Then she would abandon her silly dream of following me on my path, and leave me to walk it alone.

I was torn from my thoughts of Dahlia only when Raphael announced, "Welcome to Emek HaAsefa, Lev." He swept his hands toward a valley nestled between the hills below us, its gently sloping clearing already in shadow.

I spotted black openings along the steep rock face. "Are those caves?"

"Yes. They will be our homes during the gathering." Raphael stepped off the road onto a trail down to the valley. "And those are just the ones you can see."

Raphael descended directly to the clearing where white-robed servants were laying out food. I stopped first at the animal pens to find Balaam already in the enclosure, snuffing loudly while eating alongside twenty or more donkeys and three horses. As I retrieved my belongings from the saddlebags, my eyes appraised the horses—had nobles come to the gathering?

In the eating area, I found a table laid out with hot bread, chickpea mash, and beet tops lightly cooked to a bright green. An Israelite indentured servant spooned out food for the disciples,* while another baked bread over a clay dome. The servant took one glance at me, and his eyes narrowed. "Are you Lev?" I nodded. "Master Uriel had us set this aside for you." From behind the cooking area, he retrieved a piece of bread dotted with small amounts of the chickpea and beet tops. After a full day's march, I had hoped for more food than this. The servant must have caught my expression. "You can take more. I don't care." He put down his spoon, with the handle facing toward me, then went to help with the cooking, leaving me to serve myself. I added only a modest amount, remembering my uncle's resentment at how much the hired workers had eaten during last year's olive harvest.

Food in hand, I gazed around until I found Raphael, who sat with two other disciples on the gently sloping hillside. The disciples ate in silence, chewing each morsel dozens of times before taking another. When he saw me approach, Raphael swallowed the bite in his mouth to greet me. "Hi Lev, looking for the musicians? They're sitting over there." I caught myself before sitting down—did the musicians not eat with the disciples?

I followed Raphael's gesture and saw three people sitting together in a corner of the field. Their garments immediately caught my eye; they were all dressed in heavy woolen tunics like my own. The whole time we walked together, I hadn't thought how much my clothes, so hot and itchy in the summer sun, must have made me stand out from my companions, who undoubtedly wore wool only in the wintertime. As I weaved through the disciples, I became intensely aware of my tunic, its dank odor, and how it had been crudely stitched together by Aunt Leah and Dahlia. The linen garments of the *bnei nevi'im* were doubtless made by master weavers. I kept my gaze ahead on the musicians so I wouldn't have to meet the eyes of the disciples.

Two of the musicians were youths, one a thickset boy about my age who sat hunched over his food. The other, a few years older, leaned back on one of his elbows and ran a hand through his wavy hair as he watched me approach. The third musician was a man, younger than my uncle, who sat erect, his narrow beard almost reaching his waist. "Are you Lev?" the man asked. I nodded and sat down next to him. "Excellent, then we're all gathered. I'm Daniel ben Eliezer, the master musician here. This is Yonaton ben Baruch," he pointed to the younger boy, "and Zimri ben—"

"Just Zim," the wavy-haired one interjected, his mouth half full. Juice and vegetables dripped from the bottom of his rolled-up bread, and he ate at a pace that made me wonder how long it had been since his last meal.

Yonaton offered a hesitant smile. Like me, he'd just taken small amounts of each dish, and sat with his flatbread spread out on his lap, the different foods on it not touching. I sat down next to him and bit into my bread, glad for the distraction of food that excused us from conversation.

The first stars appeared in the sky, and the chatter among the disciples died down. All turned their attention toward the serving table where Uriel,

Yosef, and a third white-haired sage stood between three torches in a circle of flickering light. "May all who have come be blessed," Uriel said.

"Many are the paths we have walked to reach this point, and many are the places from which we have come. Together, we seek a true bond* with the Holy One, one in which Divine Light will flow to the Nation of Israel, and through us to all of creation. The hour is late, and for many of you the journey has been long; nevertheless, our time is short,* our task is great, and our Master is pressing." He gazed over the crowd of disciples, torchlight glittering in his eyes. "Know too that the reward is great if you pursue the Way with discipline and commitment. We expect nothing less from each of you."

Uriel stepped back into shadow as Yosef replaced him in the torchlight. "When you are dismissed, you will go directly to sleep. You will be woken in the second watch of the night to begin your training. Remember your dreams; even ordinary dreams are one-sixtieth prophecy.* Each night you will discuss your dreams with a master to decipher their—"

"This isn't for us," Daniel whispered. "Come, we can speak in the musicians' cave."

I stood and reluctantly followed Daniel. I knew that prophecy could come through dreams—Jacob's vision of the ladder came in a dream—but I had never known that my own dreams might contain prophecy. I longed to hear about unlocking their secrets, but as I followed Daniel away from the eating area, I realized that it didn't matter much. Yosef said that to decipher your dreams, you needed to remember them. There was only one dream I really wanted to understand, but I could never remember the slightest detail of my old nightmare. Besides, if I ever could remember what the dream contained, I was pretty sure I wouldn't need a master to help me interpret it—it felt more like an evil memory than a prophecy.

Pale blue light still filled the western horizon, but with the moon only a sliver, the trail was little more than a gray smudge on dark ground. Daniel led us, walking with the comfort of one who knew his way.

"Will they also wake us in the middle of the night?" Zim asked.

"No, they don't need us until an hour or two after sunrise."

"Good, because the second watch is when I normally go to sleep."

Thistles snagged the hem of my tunic as the path narrowed at the foot of the cliff. It wound upwards, in some spots little more than a ledge bound by a sheer drop, widening out as we passed cave openings. We stayed close to Daniel, the darkness forcing us to rely on his position to avoid a deadly misstep.

"Why do you go to sleep so late?" Yonaton asked Zim.

"It's when I play my best music—there's a special energy to the night."

"I wouldn't know," Yonaton replied. "In my house, we go to sleep as soon as we can after sunset and wake before dawn. My father says sleep is the body's reward. I couldn't get up if I stayed awake playing."

"That's why I never rise before the third hour of the day if I can help it."

My jaw dropped. "Are you royalty?"

Zim laughed, "Why would you say that?"

"Whenever I'm slow out of bed, my uncle tells me that only princes sleep until the third hour of the day."*

"No, I have no noble blood. My father's a farmer, and so was his. But farming's not for me. I left home for good a year ago."

The path flattened out, and we stepped onto a rock ledge at the mouth of the highest cave. The cliff face rose above us into the darkness. Even in the dim light, I saw a circle of boulders out front, surrounding a fire pit dark with charcoal.

"Then how do you eat?" Yonaton asked.

"My music." Zim retrieved a drum from inside the cave, sat down on one of the boulders, and gently tapped the taut hide with his fingertips. Though hardly focused on his drumming, his sense of rhythm was excellent. "I've found enough work between weddings and festivals."

"What kind of festivals?"

"All kinds. The best is coming up at the full moon in Shiloh—I never miss it."

I swung my kinnor off my shoulder and straddled one of the boulders. "But you'll still be here then, won't you?"

"When Master Yosef hired me I told him I'd come only if I could still play Shiloh."

"How about you, Daniel? Is that what you do too?" Yonaton asked.

"Me?" Daniel chuckled as he sat down, clutching his nevel, a standup harp twice the size of my kinnor. "No, I have a wife and three daughters; I can't be running around to festivals all the time. It's only while my wheat is drying that I can devote myself to music."

"Isn't it hard being away from your family?" Yonaton asked.

"Sure it's hard, but my nevel is easier to work than my land, and copper doesn't spoil." Daniel began to pick out notes and tighten strings.

Zim cocked his head toward Yonaton, "First time away from home?"

Yonaton nodded, "I've never even slept away before."

"How far did you come?" I asked.

"Not far. We live just on the other side of that hill."

"So why not go home at night?"

"My father told me I can't expect the prophets to send someone round to the farm every time they need me. Still, it's nice to know I can run home if

I need to, and my sisters said they'd visit." Yonaton pulled a halil, a wooden fife two handbreadths long, from his belt. "How about you, Lev? Do you play festivals or do you also work your father's land?"

I plucked the strings of my kinnor, feeling their eyes but not looking up. "My father's dead. My mother too. I shepherd my uncle's flock."

My words killed the conversation. I knew this moment, having experienced it so many times in the past—the awkward quiet, the eyes turning away. Zim filled the silence with his drumming, increasing his pace and power. Daniel joined in, picking up Zim's beat, with crisp plucks against the long strings of his nevel, the notes reverberating into the cool evening air. Only Yonaton remained silent. My eyes were dry—I learned long ago that tears would neither bring back my parents nor water the flock—but I was surprised to see that Yonaton's reflected more of the night sky than my dry eyes ever could. I smiled and raised my kinnor, indicating that there was no more to say. Yonaton wiped his eyes across his sleeve, smiled back, and raised his halil to his lips.

The stars were already bright in the sky when I saw twinkling lights ascend the trail toward the caves. "What are those lights?"

"Lamps," Daniel said. "The disciples are going to sleep."

"And they carry their own lamps?" At my uncle's house, lamps were reserved for holy times—olive oil was too precious to burn during the week.

The disciples reached their caves, and the lights went out. "I'm glad I'm not one of them," Zim said.

My hand dropped from the strings of my kinnor, and I stared across at Zim. "Is it really so hard to go to sleep early?"

Zim laughed and leaned into his drum. His right hand tapped out higher-pitched notes on the drum's edge as his left palm pounded the center with a booming bass.

And then it suddenly occurred to me: there could be only one explanation for his lack of interest. "You've never seen them taken by prophecy, have you?"

Zim met my eyes without breaking his rhythm. "No. Have you?"

"Yes." That one word was enough to silence Zim and draw the stares of Daniel and Yonaton, but I wasn't done. "When you see it, you'll understand—"

"Don't envy the prophets, Lev." Daniel let his hands rest on his nevel and our song unraveled—only Zim kept up the beat.

I turned on Daniel, "What's not to envy?"

Daniel sighed, "Theirs is a path that will lead you nowhere."

"Why nowhere?" Yonaton asked. "Look at the masters—"

"Yes, Yonaton, look at the masters. Take Master Uriel. Where do you think he'll be come harvest time when *our* backs are bent with labor? Out in the fields with *us*?" Zim snorted, and Daniel turned to me. "Can you imagine him chasing your sheep over the hillsides?"

He leaned over his nevel to press his point. "I've been playing here for twelve years. The first day, there's always a musician or two who dreams of becoming a prophet; but soon enough they learn that's all they are—dreams. And you'll learn too."

I recalled my last conversation with Dahlia, how she said that there was no telling where my future would lead. "But even dreams can come true—can't they?"

"Not this one. It's as King Solomon said: Wisdom is good with an inheritance."*

I winced at the word inheritance. "What does that mean?"

"It means that it doesn't matter how wise or holy you are, Lev, you'll never become a *navi*. Look at the *bnei nevi'im*: servants prepare their food, they light lamps to walk back to their caves—some even arrived on their own horses. They don't dress like you. They don't smell like you." Zim chortled. Yonaton quietly sniffed his tunic. "Most of the disciples study for years before receiving *navua*, if they receive it at all. Who do you think watches their farms or their flocks while they're searching for the Holy One?"

I shrugged.

"You have to be rich to become a prophet; there's never been one that wasn't. As far as I can tell, it's part of their Way."

I opened my mouth to respond but shut it again. What could I say? Uncle Menachem always told me that the smart man learns from his mistakes, but I never seemed to. When would I stop falling into the trap of clinging to dreams that could never come true? I was like the fool in Eliav's favorite story, the one who sat by a pool of still water, the moon reflected in its surface. Such a beautiful stone, he thought, if he could only get it for himself, he'd be a rich man. But when he grabbed for it, his hands plunged into the cold water and the moon disappeared. He cursed himself for his stupidity, but when the water calmed, the moon reappeared, and he thought that perhaps this time he'd be lucky.

Daniel watched me closely. "Don't look like that. You have a surer path open to you."

"What's that?" I asked, daring him to tout the joys of shepherding.

"The *nevi'im* use your music to lift themselves beyond this world. You may not reach prophecy, but it can uplift you as well. You just need to learn to play properly—start with this." Daniel leaned his nevel against the boulder, came around behind me, and laid his hands over mine. He pulled my left hand further down the front of my kinnor and placed it in an unfamiliar hold. He twisted the angle of my plucking hand, my right. I didn't like the feel of his hands on mine—after what he just told me I would have preferred to be left alone—but I didn't fight him. "Grip it like this, firm up your left hand, but loosen your right. Now listen." Daniel plucked the highest string, and the kinnor let out a crisp, clear note.

"It feels awkward."

"You're used to doing it wrong. Give it time—you'll bring out the full voice of your kinnor. It's a fine, fine instrument."

Yonaton pulled his halil away from his lips. "They don't smell like us?"

Daniel laughed, "Sniff one tomorrow. They're obsessed with purity. Most bathe at least once a day." He returned to his nevel and picked up the melody again. "The way I see it, how much do they really have to tie them to this world? That must be why they can rise above it so easily."

"It's not so easy," Zim said, drumming now with his fingertips so as not to drown out his voice. "They need us."

"Just the disciples—the masters don't need musicians."

"But Master Uriel did." I sat straighter now that I knew something that Daniel didn't. "The day we met, he came to me for my music. That's how I was hired."

Daniel inclined his head to the side and stared at me again, then turned his eyes away and shrugged. "I've never seen a master use a musician before."

Zim waved off our words with the back of his hand. "Enough of this. We may not be prophets, but we know what we need." He stepped up his playing, and the rest of us followed his lead, bringing the conversation to an end.

The music indeed was unlike any I'd ever played. Few in Levonah had the time or patience to play instruments outside of festivals and celebrations. For the first time in years, I found myself in the presence of clearly superior musicians in Daniel and Zim, and even Yonaton harmonized beautifully, if quietly, on his halil. I closed my eyes into the rhythm and felt a tingling in my fingertips as they plucked out the melody. I soon left my concerns about the *nevi'im* behind.

A servant shook each of us roughly by the shoulder the next morning. "Master Uriel requires you." He stepped out of the cave before I'd even sat up.

I squinted in the sunlight. I'd never slept so far into the morning—nor had I ever stayed up so late. By the time Daniel finally made us go to sleep, the eastern sky had already brightened to a dark gray. All through the night, I was telling myself I'd regret not getting to bed, but the music fixed me there.

Guided by Daniel's nimble nevel and driven by Zim's rhythms, I discovered sounds in my kinnor that I never knew existed.

Several buckets of water awaited us outside the cave, and we quickly washed our hands and faces. The cold water chased sleep from my eyes. Daylight offered me a chance to see my new home properly. The niche in the wall where I slept seemed carved out for that very purpose. None of the cave walls were smooth like the ones near Levonah; they were all grooved, as if hewn out with iron tools. They couldn't have been made for the annual gatherings—caves were hardly necessary in the summer, and the grooves had rounded edges, not the sharp lines of freshly cut stone—they looked old. *Hundreds of years old, maybe? But who would have gone to so much trouble to carve out caves in the wilderness?*

As the others started down the trail, my eyes fell on the outline of my father's knife beneath my sleeping mat. I wasn't afraid of anyone taking it—but it didn't seem right leaving it behind. I took out one of my spare strings and used it to secure the sheath around my waist, under my tunic. Then I ran down toward the valley floor to catch up with the others.

Twelve disciples sat in the shade of a large carob tree, its branches heavy with green pods browning in the early summer heat. Daniel directed us toward a smaller pomegranate tree nearby, where we immediately warmed up. Uriel acknowledged us with a nod, then addressed the disciples.

"Envision your soul like a pool of water. When perfectly still, it reflects what is above. The slightest ripple on the surface, however, distorts the image and destroys any hope for vision. Music helps us quiet the mind and calm the pool."* I grinned at this description, thinking again of the fool who tried to grab the moon, but erased the smile as the prophet faced us. "Daniel, just a simple melody, this is the first trial for many."

Daniel plucked a slow tune, and the rest of us joined in once we caught the rhythm. I took advantage of the easy pace to practice the holds that Daniel had taught me the night before—my wrists ached from the strange position. The melody barely held my attention. Was it the simplicity of the music, our lack of sleep, or was Zim correct that there was just something special about the night?

If Uriel noticed anything absent, he didn't show it. He walked among the disciples, correcting their posture and whispering advice. One disciple appeared older than the rest; milky scars mapped his face. He sat upright with legs crossed and eyes closed, swaying gently with the *nigun*. He listened to Uriel's whispering, nodded once, then returned to his swaying.

My heavy eyelids kept fighting to close. All the things I normally did to keep myself awake—pacing, talking, even playing faster or harder—would have disturbed the disciples. Only one of the *bnei nevi'im* appeared to be struggling with sleep himself, even though the disciples had woken at the second watch of the night and were now doing nothing more than listening to our dull music. I recognized him as Elad, the disciple of Yosef's who'd scratched his nose two days earlier during their training, the one who surmised that I was uncomfortable with the disciples discussing me. Elad's head drooped forward and jerked back up as he fought off sleep. The rest of the *bnei nevi'im* indicated through their straight posture and gentle rocking that they somehow remained engaged.

It was a relief when the session finally ended, and we were given a break before the midday meal.

"Do you mind holding my pipe?" Yonaton asked me. "I want to run home; I'm sure my mother's worried."

"I don't mind." I suspected Yonaton was running home less for his mother's need than his own.

He handed me his halil. The delicately whittled piece of olive wood seemed out of place in his thick farmer hands. "I'll be back in time for the meal."

I watched him go until he passed over the hill, out of sight and wondered how my family was doing in Levonah. Eliav would be out with the sheep; Dahlia would already be baking the midday bread. Did they miss me?

I lay down on my back, enjoying the sun on my face, thinking about what I would tell Dahlia at the end of the gathering. The look of awe in her eyes was the last thing I saw as I drifted off to sleep.

I awoke to Yonaton's figure standing over me, a melon in his hands. "We're going to miss the meal."

"What? Oh, right." I sat up, stretched my arms above my head, and followed Yonaton down to the eating area.

Bread, cheese and bright green leeks were still laid out on the serving table. Again, one of the servants handed me a prepared dish, but only me, and he offered no explanation as to why he had not done the same for Yonaton. My portion was a bit bigger than the night before but lacked cheese. Did Uriel really feel that I deserved so little, especially when Yonaton was allowed to take as much as he wanted? Well if he objected to my taking more, he'd have to tell me himself. As Yonaton helped himself to everything from the serving table, I took more leeks and laid a big spoonful of cheese over the top. Food in hand, we sat down next to Zim, who was already finishing his meal.

"So that was prophecy?" Yonaton asked, dipping his bread in the runny cheese.

I shook my head and fought back a smile. "No one there received *navua.* It looks more like this—" I put down my bread, leaned over, and trembled the way Uriel had done. Two passing disciples flashed me cold stares.

"Whoa," Yonaton's eyes grew wide. "So what do we do when it happens?"

"We keep playing, right?" Zim said through a mouthful of bread. "If they need us for prophecy, we have to keep going."

"I don't think it matters. When Uriel had *navua,* it didn't seem as if he'd notice anything, really."

"So he was completely vulnerable?" Zim asked. "Anyone could just come over and slit his throat?"

I recoiled at the brutish question. "I guess so."

"But he's a prophet," Yonaton said. "He can see things no one else can. He would know if he's in danger."

"You think?" Zim asked. "From what I've heard, prophets see only really important things."

"But if someone wanted to hurt him, that would be really important to him—don't you think, Lev?"

"It would be." I tried to sound confident but felt shaken. Zim might actually be right: Uriel had seemed completely removed from this world while receiving prophecy. But if Uriel was vulnerable, it seemed best not to share that information. "Besides, prophets see things all the time that aren't so important; they just don't tell stories about them. I saw Uriel find a lost ring."

Zim stood up to leave, his remaining bread still piled high with more leeks than Yonaton and I had taken together. "You're not finishing your meal?" Yonaton asked.

"These are almost raw." Zim pointed to the leeks. "They've got all these servants, why don't they cook their food?" He walked off toward our cave, shaking his head.

The two of us were the last to finish eating. When we were done, Yonaton hefted his melon. "You want to split this with me?"

"Sure."

Yonaton took the fruit over to a large rock and lifted it over his head.

"Wait, no need to smash it, I've got a knife." I reached under my tunic and pulled out my father's knife. I cut off two pieces, then thrust the knife back into the melon.

Yonaton bit into his slice, and his eyes caught the inlaid handle sticking out from the fruit. "Where did you get that knife? I've never seen one like it."

I turned away, wishing I hadn't brought it out. "This is a great melon. Did you grow it?"

"It's from my own plot." Yonaton grinned as wide as the melon slice. "I just saw it was ripe when I went home."

"Where did you get that?" We both jumped at the rumble of the deep voice behind us. We turned to see the disciple with the scars pointing at the melon. The three of us were now alone in the clearing.

"From my family's farm on the other side of the hill. Cut yourself off a slice if you like."

"Not the melon, boy. The knife." He plucked it out of the fruit and held it up before his eyes. The flint blade absorbed the sun's light instead of reflecting it.

My mouth went dry as I held out my hand to take it back. "It was my father's. Now it's mine. Give it here."

The man ignored my outstretched hand. "Your father's you say?" His eyes moved from the knife to me, his scars knotting as he spoke. "And what's your name?" The exposed blade in his hand made the simple question a threat.

"Lev."

"Lev ben?"

There was something about him I didn't trust. "Lev ben Menachem," I lied. "And yours?"

His scars stretched as he let out a harsh laugh. "Shimon ben Naftali. Very wise to use your uncle's name, Lev ben Yochanan." He took a step toward me, holding my blade in his left hand, and pulling a dagger from his belt with his right. I was defenseless.

Yonaton jumped to his feet, snatched a rock from the ground, and cocked his arm back, ready to throw at the first sign of attack.

I stood paralyzed, hand still extended, gaping at this stranger who knew my father's name.

Shimon ignored both our reactions, his eyes returning to my knife as he turned his small dagger around and offered me the hilt. "Take this."

I reached out and took the weapon—though if we were going to fight, I'd rather have my knife back. But Shimon simply wiped my knife clean on the hem of his tunic and laid it down next to the melon. He bent down, facing me eye to eye. "Never let anyone see this knife. The danger it brings is very real." His words mystified me, but I saw truth in his eyes. "Besides, this is not a tool for cutting fruit. It has only one purpose and should be used for nothing else. If you want to cut melon, use that one." He pointed to the dagger in my hand. "You can keep it. I've got another."

Without another word, Shimon turned and headed down the hill, in the opposite direction from where the disciples were gathering. I examined the bronze weapon in my hand. Its value was equal to two sheep at least, probably three. Even if the disciples were rich, surely they didn't just give away such valuable gifts for nothing? My eyes moved to my father's knife, still moist from the melon. It didn't look dangerous—what was he afraid of? But I had a more pressing question. "Wait!" I shouted at Shimon's back. "How did you know my name?"

Shimon didn't break his stride down the trail, only turned his head to reply over his shoulder. "I brought you to your uncle."

Rabbi Elazar HaKapar said: Envy, desire, and the pursuit of honor remove a person from the world.

Pirkei Avot 4:28

5

The Song of the World

"What just happened?" Yonaton's arm dropped to his side, but his fist still gripped the rock he'd picked up to defend me.

My eyes remained fixed on Shimon's dagger. "My parents were killed when I was two."

"Killed? By who?"

"I don't know. It was during the civil war." I didn't look up—I couldn't bear seeing the pity in his eyes. "All I know is that a stranger left me at my uncle's house…after. I guess now I know who that was." I pushed my thumb into the edge of the dagger, not hard enough to draw blood, just enough to distract myself from the dark hole in my chest. "Are we playing again today?"

Yonaton's shoulders relaxed at the change of subject. "No, the masters gave us the rest of the day to prepare for Shabbat. I know a spring not far from here where we can bathe."

It was the best answer I could have hoped for. I was in no mood for the slow music we played that morning—it left my mind too free to wander. I tucked Shimon's blade into my belt, picked up my father's knife, and followed Yonaton toward the hills at the edge of the valley.

"I've never seen a knife like that—what's it for?"

For Yonaton, who could run home to his mother between sittings, it must have seemed obvious that I knew the purpose of my father's knife. But there was so much I didn't know. "I've never seen one like it either. My uncle gave it to me the day I left, but he didn't tell me anything about it. Just that it belonged to my father."

"Can I hold it?"

It was a natural question, but I still recoiled, weighing the knife in my hand as we walked. It was my father's—my only inheritance. Yonaton threw the rock in his hand at a distant boulder and was rewarded with the resounding clap of stone on stone. He had good aim and a strong arm; I couldn't have hit that boulder even if I could have thrown that far. Yonaton hadn't picked up that rock to throw it at some boulder; he picked it up to defend me from Shimon. I turned the knife around and held it out, handle first.

Yonaton received it with open palms. He ran a finger over the dark, gray edge. "I never knew stone could be so sharp. It looks ancient." He turned his attention to the insignia on the hilt. "Are these claws?"

"I think so, but I don't know what they mean."

"It looks like a small sword." He swung the broad blade in short, chopping arcs.

I thought back to Shimon's warning. "But who would get so upset about using a sword to cut a melon?"

Yonaton shrugged and handed back the knife. My chest relaxed as I slipped it back under my tunic, nestling it safely against my thigh.

We reached the foot of the hills and eased down a well-worn path leading into a shaded ravine. The gorge was lined by stunted oak trees, a sure sign of water. A disciple stood by the side of the path, hands extended toward the sky, eyes squeezed shut, tears flowing down his cheeks, mumbling something I couldn't understand. I forced myself to look away as we passed, fighting the desire to stare at his indecency. Daniel was right; whatever these *bnei nevi'im* were involved in wasn't for the likes of me.

Our trail wound through high brush as the ravine walls narrowed around us, ending at a crumbling, white cliff. Clear water bubbled out of a crack at its base and flowed into a pool formed by a cut in the bedrock.

Yonaton stripped quickly and winced as he slipped into the frigid spring. I hung the knife over a branch of an olive tree, laid my tunic over it, and sat down at the edge of the pool. Despite the bright sun and appeal of cold water, I didn't enter. My mind was fixed on Shimon. *He brought me to my uncle. Does he know how my parents died?*

"Come in!" A splash of water hit me in the face. Yonaton smacked the surface again, and I raised my hands in a useless attempt to block the spray. I peered down at my attacker, submerged up to his chest, his head still dry. My legs kicked a waterfall down on Yonaton. I soaked myself in the process but no longer cared. Yonaton fought back with the full force of both arms, drenching me. I pushed off the edge of the pool, dove under the water, and pulled my new friend's legs out from under him.

We were still laughing when we returned to our cave late in the afternoon. Zim stood at the entrance with a polished bronze mirror in one hand, shaping his long hair into a wave with the other. He had changed his tunic of plain wool for one of reddish brown that left watery red marks on his neck—he must have stained it himself with berries. Anything dyed with madder or henna would have been expensive beyond even his wildest dreams. Zim nodded as we walked in, without glancing up from his mirror.

"Have you ever seen a boy with his own mirror before?" Yonaton whispered in my ear.

I shook my head. "My aunt has one, but she doesn't look in it this long."

"If I was your aunt, I wouldn't either," Zim said, entering the cave. "You should be more careful if you're going to talk about me. I may drum loudly, but my hearing is excellent." My ears grew hot, and Yonaton turned away, but Zim wore the same carefree expression as always. "Laugh if you like, but if you ever want to feed yourself with your music, you should think about getting one yourself."

"A mirror won't help our playing," Yonaton said.

"True, but it will get you more work. All eyes are on the musicians—you get hired for more festivals if you look right." Though answering Yonaton, Zim held out his mirror to me.

I took the sheet of flat, shiny metal. It had been a long time since I'd seen my reflection, and the mirror was clearer than any pool I'd peeked in. My brown hair was curled from the water, and the hairs on my lip were thicker, like a long shadow under my nose, but I was mostly struck by my eyes. They were light today, the color of bee honey, and seemed older than I felt.

From the valley rose the blast of a ram's horn, the signal of the coming Shabbat. The three of us headed down to the clearing where we joined Daniel. Like Zim, he had a second tunic for Shabbat, made from finer wool than the one he wore during the week. The food was a measure better than the night before;

the vegetables were still barely cooked, but the smell of roasted lamb also filled the clearing. My mouth watered. Aunt Leah prepared meat only for festivals.

Again, a servant handed me a piece of bread and a portion of beet greens that had been set aside for me behind the cooking area, where they had already turned cold. I received no meat, and the amount, though larger for Shabbat, didn't come close to meeting my appetite. Daniel, Zim, and Yonaton all eyed my food curiously; none of them had rations set aside. I took the bread and piled meat onto it, making sure the servant saw I wouldn't quietly accept such meager portions. But my greed still seemed small next to Zim's, who crowded as much lamb on his bread as it would hold, not wasting any space on the vegetables. Daniel pointed out a spot for us closer to the *bnei nevi'im* than we had sat the night before. As soon as his bottom hit the ground, Zim raised a chunk of lamb to his mouth, but Daniel grabbed his wrist. "On Shabbat, we wait."

Uriel stood in the middle of the clearing holding a goblet of wine.* His voice rose in a chant that spoke of the six days of creation and the day of rest. I was familiar with the words from my uncle's house, but not with the drawn-out pace of the prophet's melody. It was hard to concentrate on the words with such savory smells wafting up from the food.

When the blessing was complete, Uriel drained the goblet in a single motion and handed it to a waiting servant. "Now can I eat?" Zim asked Daniel.

"Patience."

The prophet now held up two loaves of bread, one on top of the other. "The Holy One tested our fathers with manna in the wilderness,* giving them each morning enough food for that day, but no more. On the sixth day, they received a second portion for Shabbat. The blessing of Shabbat is that we do not receive; it is the blessing of knowing that we already possess what we require. I bless us all on our quest for holiness to know that the Divine light we seek is already within us."

Uriel had barely broken the bottom loaf when Zim's hand starting moving toward his mouth. "Now?"

"Yes."

My hand hadn't been poised like Zim's, but my stomach was just as ready to pounce. The meat was pink and tender, and the vegetables were so well flavored that I almost didn't mind that they were undercooked. Though I had taken a large portion, I soon went back for more of everything.

I was just finishing my second helping when conversation among the disciples died. Tzadok, the ancient, third master, stood by the fire in the center of the eating area. Zim still ate, but Yonaton and I stood, knowing that when the masters spoke it was time for us to go. Daniel put a hand on each of our shoulders. "On Shabbat we stay."

Tzadok closed his eyes, filled his chest, and opened his mouth in song. I would never have guessed that such a resonant voice could emerge from so frail a body. The melody was simple and repetitive. Daniel and a number of the disciples joined him immediately, and more of us merged with them as we picked up the *nigun*, until we all sang together. I closed my eyes, and my body swayed, swept up in the current of the song.

Our voices echoed in the open air of the valley. The melody folded over on itself and amplified the collective energy with each turn. For the first time since coming to the gathering, I felt united with the *bnei nevi'im*. When Tzadok reached the end, he lifted his voice higher, holding the final note until his breath ran out. His silence brought the song to a close, and quiet settled over the clearing.

I opened my eyes to see Uriel standing alone, his face illuminated unevenly by the red light of the dwindling fire.

"There was once a man who lived in a kingdom in the middle of the desert." The prophet spoke softly, but in the stillness of the night, his voice carried across the open ground. "Every morning as he went out to his field and again in the evening when he walked home, this man walked past the King's palace. Each time he wondered, 'Why is it that the King has so much while I have so little?' His envy of the King grew and grew until he was unable to pass the palace without anger.

"The man formed a plan: he would dig a tunnel under the palace, come up inside the treasury, and take a tiny amount for himself. He worked for years on his tunnel, and as his labors grew, so did his desire, until he no longer felt the need to leave the King anything at all. Finally, the tunnel was complete, and he broke through the floor of the palace in the middle of the night. He expected to see piles of gold and gems, but found himself in an empty hallway, just outside the treasury. If he kept on digging, there was a chance he could still access the treasury and escape before dawn. But now that he had broken through the floor, fear struck his heart—he could be discovered at any time, and discovery would cost him his head. So he stepped back into his tunnel and fled the palace with nothing.

"It happened that a second thief, who knew nothing of the first, had formed an identical plan to rob the King and tunneled into the palace on the very same night. Unlike the first, he emerged inside the treasury itself. He saw mountains of gold and streams of jewels, and filled his bags and pockets with treasure. As he was about to leave, he spotted a large ruby in the corner of the treasury, so beautiful that he could not imagine leaving it behind. Lacking any room for it in his bags or pockets, he placed the gem in his mouth.

"The thief lowered his bags into the tunnel and was about to jump in, when he stopped. He spit the gem back into his hand and restored it gently to its place. Then, he emptied his bags and pockets, returned the treasure, and climbed into his tunnel—leaving the palace with nothing.

"The next morning, the two tunnels were discovered. The head of the guards came running to the King. *My King, two thieves tunneled into the palace last night.*

"The King was shocked. No one had ever broken into his palace before. *How much did they take?* he asked.

"The guard said, *It is unfathomable my King—they didn't take anything. One thief missed the treasury and left with nothing. The second thief entered the treasury, but we've counted the reserves, and nothing is missing.*

"The King said, *I want to meet these two men. Let it be known that they will not be punished if they come forward.*

"Such was the power of the King that both thieves presented themselves at the palace by day's end. The guards brought the first thief before the King. *Explain how it was that you broke into my palace and left with nothing?*

"The thief stood shaking before the King and said, *I planned to tunnel into the royal treasury, but when I came out I found that I had not dug far enough. I feared that if I ventured further, I would be caught, so I went back into my tunnel and fled.*

"The King said, *Very well. Had you remained, you might have caused me great loss, but as it transpired, you turned away from the evil. As promised, you will not be punished. I reward your honesty today with your life. You may go.*

"Guards then escorted in the second thief. The King turned to him and asked, *Explain how it was that you broke into my treasury and left empty-handed.*

"The second thief dropped his head. *I did intend to rob you, sire. When I emerged inside your treasury, I filled all my bags, my pockets, and even my mouth with your treasure. Then, when I was about to climb into the tunnel and escape, an image of your face came to my mind. You have been a just and generous king to your people. I should be proud to serve such a king. How could I rob you? So I returned all the treasure to its rightful place and left.*

"A tear came to the King's eye. *Guard,* he called, *I want you to take this man into the treasury and let him take anything he wants.*"

Uriel paused, staring into the glowing coals. "There are two ways to turn from evil in this world. If we right our way from fear of punishment then, like the first thief, we are forgiven. But there is a higher way—to rectify our deeds out of great love for our King. Then our very sins bring us merit, for the Holy One knows how far along the path of evil we have gone and how great an effort it took to reverse our course. If we return in love,* our rectification will be great indeed."

The prophet rose taller in the dark, his voice loud in the silence. "Some of you are here because you desire the prophets' power. You want to cry out, to correct the errors of the people, and when your cries are not heard, you will be tempted to coerce. You must remember that the Holy One seeks true service of the heart. To threaten the people, to give them a glimpse of the awesome power of the Holy One, may sway them, but only through fear.

"As *nevi'im,* we must inspire Israel to rectify their deeds out of love. I wish you all a peaceful Shabbat."

"Blessed is the One who divides between the sacred and the mundane,"* Uriel chanted the following evening at the close of Shabbat, "between light and darkness, between Israel and the nations, between the seventh day and the six days of creating—"

"And between the *nevi'im* and the musicians," Zim chortled, just loud enough for the three of us to hear.

I ignored him, gazing up at the stars first breaking through the dark sky. The sun had set some time ago, leaving an inky stain on the western horizon. Uriel lifted the goblet of wine in his hand, sanctifying the end of Shabbat as he had its beginning. When he marked the division between light and darkness, a disciple touched together the wicks of two lamps, merging their flames into one.

"Can we play now?" Zim asked.

"Yes." Daniel's voice was strained. "Let's go back to the cave."

When he and Zim played music together, they worked off each other beautifully. But instruments were forbidden in Emek HaAsefa on Shabbat and had sat idle the past night and all that day. Throughout the Shabbat day, while I enjoyed the quiet, walking through the valley and playing stones with Yonaton, Zim lay in the cave, his eyes straying again and again to his untouched drum in the corner.

At midday on Shabbat, Daniel had sat with eyes closed, listening. "I love coming to this valley," he said. "It's so peaceful. When our music is stilled, you can really hear the song of the world."

"The world has a song?" I asked.

"Each thing in the world has its own melody. Together their notes rise to form the song of the world."

Zim, who had said little since the morning meal, rolled over at this. "Call it the noise of the world if you must—what you're hearing is too much silence. You're right that there's beautiful music in the world, and you'll hear it as soon as I can get my drum."

Now that Shabbat was finally over, Zim sped up the dark trail and was already seated outside and tapping at his drum when the rest of us reached the cave. I retrieved my kinnor, took my place on one of the boulders, and fell into rhythm with Zim. Yonaton piped in with his halil, but Daniel didn't come out to join us. Would the tension left over between Daniel and Zim from Shabbat keep them from playing together? The thought had hardly been formed in my mind when Daniel stepped out, nevel in hand.

Zim gave a last roll, and removed his hands from his drum, bringing our brief song to an end. He waved toward Daniel in a gesture that said, "You lead." Daniel tightened his strings, then struck up the *nigun* that Tzadok had led us in the night before. He began the song slowly, increasing his pace with each pass through the melody. We played on into the night, not speaking, letting the music reunite us in a way that words could not. On our first night together we'd jumped from melody to melody, but tonight Daniel never strayed from Tzadok's *nigun*, increasing the speed and intensity with each round.

It was rare in Levonah that I found the time to play my kinnor without having to keep one eye on my sheep. All I had were those few precious moments after the evening meal each night when I could let myself dive fully into my music. But even those moments were short-lived, as it was never long before my uncle, or exhaustion, called me in for bed. That night in Emek HaAsefa, Daniel drew me deeper into music than I had ever ventured before. We must have passed through the melody a hundred times or more, but it never grew old. Before long, the notes came of their own off the strings, without thought. I felt the notes flow through me, vibrating up through my chest, and saw them behind closed eyes in tones of blue and orange. For the first time, I sensed what the prophets were seeking in our music and why Daniel had said that it could transport me as well.

Well after the moon set, after the ram's horn sounded to wake the disciples, Daniel finally broke off the *nigun*. My eyes scanned Zim's expression, expecting a protest; his energy had only increased as the night went on. No disappointment registered on his face, though. It was only after I lay down, when I heard neither snoring nor tossing from the bedroll next to me, that I realized Zim hadn't rejoined us in the cave.

Sometime later, a hand shook me awake. "Don't make a sound. Get dressed and follow me," Zim whispered in my ear.

I knew how much time had passed only when I stepped out and saw how far the stars had wheeled across the sky—I guessed we were late into the second watch of the night. The hair on my arms stood on end without the comfort of my warm bed. "Why did you wake me?"

"I want to show you what I found. Come." He turned without further explanation, and I was too clouded by sleep to protest. Zim all but ran down the path, and I hurried to keep up, careful not to stumble into the darkness below. It was only when I paused to catch my breath, and the sound of my footfalls ceased, that I heard it: a low, bass hum. "Zim, what's that sound?"

"You've finally heard it? I was beginning to wonder whether you three were deaf or I was crazy. I've heard it every night since we've arrived, but tonight I finally found the source. Come."

We reached the valley floor, continued along the base of the cliff and onto a faint trail that rose to the black mouth of a cave. The sound grew deeper, its rhythm vibrating along stone walls. When we stepped inside, the sound reverberated in my bones. The cavern floor sloped steadily down into darkness. Sightless, I kept one hand on the wall and followed Zim's breathing.

There would come a time when I would grow used to the underground world, but at this moment I was still a child of the sun. As we descended deeper toward the source of the sound, I felt the weight of the rock pressing above me. Had I been alone, I certainly would have fled back to the comfort of the starlight. But I continued after Zim, preferring to tremble in darkness rather than face his scorn.

Salvation came in the form of a dim, yellow light in the distance. It grew brighter as we approached and finally took the shape of a lamp burning in a niche carved into the tunnel wall. Below it was a short drop of less than a body's length; the lamp was surely there to prevent anyone from falling. Zim climbed down first, then silently showed me where to place my hands and feet. As we moved on, the security of the light tugged at me from behind, but in a few steps, the tunnel turned and once again we were dependent on our hands and feet to see.

I lost count of my footsteps as we descended into the earth, the deep notes expanding as they echoed up to us. As we approached the source, it assumed a layered quality. The complexity was beyond anything but a stringed instrument, no number of voices woven together could accomplish that. *Could they?* A second light gleamed in the distance, and the tunnel widened out to meet it.

Torches high on the wall lit the floor of the cavern, but its roof remained shrouded in darkness. Flickering light danced over three circles of men swaying in rhythm, mouths pouring out their song. The power of the *nigun* we sang over Shabbat was in its repetition, in its slowly building pace. This *nigun*, sung underground, had a fullness that the other one lacked. Somehow, I knew the chant was ancient, each voice a thread in a fabric that stretched back ages. Tones stitched endlessly on themselves, notes braided into sacred layers, building ever more elaborate structures of sound. The song vibrated in harmony with the echoes thrown back by the cave walls, and the torchlight seemed to grow brighter as the intensity built.

I edged toward the swaying men, eager to join them in their song, but Zim grabbed my arm and pulled me back into the shadows, shaking his head. In my desire for the music, I'd forgotten that the prophets wouldn't welcome intruders. I nodded, and Zim released me. Holding our breath, we crept along the cool and damp wall of the cave, outside the circle of light, and tucked ourselves into a crevice where we could see, but not be seen.

Tzadok again led the *nigun*, his hands on his knees, his body loose as he rocked forward and back. Even Yosef swayed with the melody, his dark eyes hooded by closed lids, the sharp lines of his face softened by the warm light.

What had saved me from drowning in my grief? Music. What had freed me when my pain was too much to bear? Music. But here I felt a new power: I saw the prophets and their disciples attaining a true unity on the strength of the *nigun*. I saw that music that flows from the heart can convey a depth of emotion that words cannot.

The song had been steadily building since we entered the cave, and now the momentum came to a head. Their voices rose to a peak in a unity that almost brought me to my knees—then ceased all at once. The silence deep in the earth held me like a newborn child.

The disciples' clothing rustled as they stood. Once they left the circle of light, we would no longer be hidden. Zim's voice trembled in my ear, "We have to get out of here."

We crept back along the wall, moving as quickly as possible without making a sound, and reached the tunnel without mishap, though I couldn't be sure we'd escaped unnoticed. We scurried faster now, still careful to muffle our footsteps, but taking comfort in being out of view.

The breeze from the cavern's mouth flowed toward us in a cool stream. I raised my hand to my face, surprised to find a touch of moisture on my cheek, and quickly wiped my eyes. I didn't risk my first words until we were beneath the stars again. "Warming to the prophets now, are you?"

"I'd no idea they had music like this." Zim shook his head. "Imagine having such power and keeping it hidden underground!"

We increased our pace now that we were out of the total blackness of the cave. "What else should they do with it?"

"What else? You heard Uriel on Shabbat: the prophets must uplift the people. So, what do they do? They travel the land teaching the Law. If they want to inspire, they should bring their music out into the daylight!"

"It looks as if they don't agree with you."

"Of course they don't, and the more fools they are. They don't know how to use what they have—but we can." Zim's face glowed in the starlight.

"We work for them."

"Just for the gathering. In two months, we'll be free."

"Free? Once the gathering ends, I have to go home."

Zim led the way up the narrow trail crossing the cliff face. "You mean to your uncle's? And how long will that last? I heard you talking to Yonaton yesterday."

I scratched the back of my neck. "I thought you were asleep."

"I told you, you have to be careful what you say around me." Zim grabbed my arm and yanked me away from the edge of a precipice. "You have three years left at most in your uncle's house. Then what will you do? Wander alone through the wilderness, dreaming only of green grasses and fresh water for your flock?"

The words stung, and I hung my head. "What choice do I have?"

"Fool, you have your kinnor! If we spent our nights in this cave, learning the ancient *nigunim* of the prophets, think what it would do for us. We could go anywhere—even to Shomron to play for the King."

"The King?" Zim was clearly repeating some fantasy of his.

He stopped in his tracks and faced me. "Yes, the King! Why not? Come with me."

Suddenly, I understood why Zim had handed *me* his mirror the other day, even while speaking to Yonaton. It was the same reason that he woke me alone to hear the prophets' chant. I was the one with no future. I could go anywhere and hardly be missed. And two wandering musicians would be better than one; we could keep each other company, perhaps even find more work. As we reached our quarters, I was glad for an excuse to break off the conversation. "I don't know, Zim."

Zim appeared ready to say more, but Daniel rolled over in his sleep, and he held back.

I dropped exhausted onto my sleeping skin, eager for sleep. But neither of us got what we wanted. Zim never did make it back to the chanting cave, nor did I get a good night's rest.

The stars were fading when I next opened my eyes, my mind still cloudy from lack of sleep. I didn't know what woke me a second time before the sun, but there was a simple solution to such a problem. I wrapped myself more tightly and turned away from the dim light at the cave's opening.

As I drifted back toward sleep, my mind floated on the tide of birdsong rising from the valley below. The first trills and whistles were rhythmic enough to be a *nigun*, the blending together of so many voices strangely reminiscent of the song in the chanting cave. The world began to fade back into a sweet swirl of sound and light when I felt a hand on my back. I rolled over and saw Daniel's lanky body silhouetted by a pre-dawn glow. I stared up with blinking eyes and cocked my head to the side in an unspoken question. He put a finger to his lips and beckoned me to follow. I slipped my tunic over my head, wondering for the second time that night why I was leaving my warm nest behind.

Out now in the open air, the birdsong grew expansive. I hugged my arms to my chest, stepped out into the lightening morning, and inhaled the fresh scent of dew. Daniel hurried along one of the trails and turned to wave me on without a word. I kept my eyes on my feet and tried hard not to stumble as I sped down after Daniel. What could be so pressing at this hour?

At first, I thought Daniel was bringing me back to the chanting cave, but then he left the path and slowed his pace, stepping through the tall yellow grass, heavy with dew. "What are we doing here?"

He put a finger back to his lips. A few paces on, he stopped, dropped to his knees, and crawled on the ground, his eyes fixed on a single point. I followed behind, my tired eyes registering only a blur of brown and yellow. Gradually I gained focus; there, on a stalk of wild barley, sat a grasshopper, its green body muted to dark gray in the morning light. I turned to Daniel and mouthed, "What are we doing here?"

Daniel put a hand to his ear and pointed to the grasshopper. I closed my eyes to listen. The birdsong of the morning was so strong that it overwhelmed the high-pitched chirps of the tiny creature. I leaned in closer, focusing on its piping, steadily blocking out all other sounds. As the rest of the world receded, I sensed deeper rhythms and more tones in the grasshopper's calls. I felt a gentle touch on my back and brought my eyes up to Daniel's. "Why are we here so early?"

"The birdsong is loudest before sunrise."

"But doesn't that make it harder to hear the grasshopper?"

"You think I woke you to listen to a grasshopper? To hear the song of the world you need to hear everything*—the grasshopper *and* the birds."

I closed my eyes and leaned back in, listening without filtering out the birdsong. But I couldn't hold the two sounds at once—the song of the birds was so powerful, the chirps of the grasshopper insignificant. I gave up and got back to my feet. "Why'd you bring me here?"

"I told you, to hear the song of the world."

"Why didn't you wake the others?"

"Not everyone can hear it. Look at Zim, he has no interest in listening to birdsong or the sound of the wind blowing through the trees."

"And why not Yonaton?"

Daniel placed a hand on my shoulder. "Yonaton will be a farmer. His time is better spent learning to sow than learning to listen."

"You think I'm different because I can play music while watching my sheep?"

Daniel shook his head. "Yonaton's an only son, just like I was. He has no choice but to inherit his father's farm and care for his parents when they grow old. You have a choice."

I snorted, "The choice to be a landless orphan?"

"The choice to pursue your music."

Daniel must have overheard the end of my conversation with Zim earlier. "So you also think I should leave my sheep to play festivals and weddings with Zim?"

Again, Daniel shook his head. "That's a desolate life. Besides, to play festivals and weddings you don't need to hear the song of the world."

"Then what?"

"I saw your face the other night when we were speaking about the prophets. It's not only in the summer that they need musicians. One who can hear the song of the world could play for them all year round."

"I couldn't hear the cricket and the birds together. I'm not even sure what I'm listening for." I once again thought how similar the birdsong was to the *nigun* from the chanting cave. Was that the secret? Were the *nigunim* of the prophets somehow connected to the song of the world?

"It takes practice, but you can learn. I already hear the song of the sheep in your music—it's subtle, but it's there."

"Sheep sing?" The bird-calls sounded like a song, but the bleating of my sheep—that was music?

Daniel started back across the meadow toward the path. "I heard a story many years ago from my master,* who played before the prophets for forty years, and who first taught me to hear the song of the world. When King David finished writing the Psalms, he said to the Holy One, 'Is there any creature in this world that sings more songs and praises than I?' A frog came and said, 'Do not become proud David. I sing more songs and praises than you do.'"

"The frog could talk?"

"It's a story. But after hearing the frog, David set out to discover the songs and praises of other creatures. How he understood them I don't know, but he wrote their meanings down in a scroll." Daniel studied my face. "You find this hard to accept?"

"I've never heard any praises from my sheep."

"Neither have I. But we can hear the rhythms of the animals, and we can help the *bnei nevi'im* hear them too. Listening to the world is one of their tools, it helps them find their Way."

"I thought we play to bring them joy?"

"True, but joy is only one thing we can do for them." Daniel stretched his arms up over his head in a yawn.

"So are the songs we play part of the song of the world?"

Daniel paused at the cave mouth. "I don't know if we sing in the song of the world. You'd have to ask one of the masters that."

I lay down and spread my tunic over me. As I settled in, the bulge of my father's knife beneath my mat dug into my spine. It seemed that everyone had an opinion on my future. I hadn't always liked what my uncle taught me, but I always believed it: that without land I had one choice—to become a shepherd. Since arriving at the gathering, new paths had opened before me, but did they hold any greater promise?

Zim wanted me as a companion; we'd wander from place to place, looking for enough work to feed ourselves. A desolate life Daniel called it. Daniel thought I should learn to hear the song of the world and play before the prophets. Perhaps that was a little better: I wouldn't have to move so much and it would be easier to build a family. But even if I could hear the song, wouldn't I be just like the grasshopper, whose chirps were drowned out before the powerful birdsong? Was that my destiny—to become the servant of prophecy, playing a part no one would notice?

As a shepherd, at least I could be my own master, have my own flock, and my own successes. One last thought floated through my mind as I drifted back to sleep: my uncle had chosen wisely.

Rabbi Akiva said: All that will be is already known, yet one still has the power to choose.

Pirkei Avot 3:19

6

The Rogue Vision

It began as a halting vibration in Raphael's hand, like the twitch of a heavy sleeper. I exhaled to relax my chest muscles, a technique Daniel had shown me the night before. I sucked my breath in quickly as Raphael's back arched and his forehead extended upward, drawn by an invisible cord. Zim increased his pace, reaching for the power of our nighttime sessions. I pushed myself to keep up with the raw blasts of rhythm pouring off his drum.

The invisible cord snapped, and Raphael slumped forward, motionless. A tremor crept up his arms, meeting at the base of his neck. His head snapped up, and convulsions overran his slack body like a powerful tide. This was more than I'd seen when Uriel received *navua* outside of Levonah.

Yonaton stopped playing and stood mouth agape. He caught my eye with an expression that said, "Now I see what you mean." He quickly returned his halil to his lips, blushing at having stopped playing. But the music was hardly necessary; Raphael could no longer hear it. The other disciples broke out of their meditations, some as dumbstruck as the musicians, and watched the first storm of prophecy since the gathering began.

Raphael's arms gave a final jolt. The tension slowly returned to his body, and he pushed himself into a sitting position, his eyes wide and unfocused. Only when his gaze fell on Uriel did he really seem to return to us. "I saw the King's servant."*

"Ovadia?" Uriel asked, eyebrows raised.

"Yes."

"What was he doing?"

Raphael's forehead creased and his eyes narrowed. "He is coming." Raphael closed his eyes and rocked gently. "And there was a voice."

"A voice? What did it say?"

"Heed his request."

Uriel's forehead tightened. "Who should heed his request?"

"You should, Master."

"*Me*?" Uriel pulled the collar of his tunic away from his throat. "Was there anything more?"

"That's all I heard."

In the heavy silence that followed Raphael's announcement, hoofbeats thudded faintly in the distance. The tremor grew to a rumble, indicating steeds driven hard. Four chestnut horses, with one rider apiece, turned off the road at the head of the valley and descended toward the clearing. Yosef and Tzadok emerged from their caves to join Uriel, and they stood like a wall, awaiting the arrival of the riders.

Three soldiers reined in their horses at a distance, their flanks heaving from the sprint into the valley. The fourth rider approached the masters, his eyes scanning the area rapidly as he dismounted, pausing briefly when his gaze fell on the musicians. He had thick red hair, ruddy skin, and was dressed like no servant I'd ever seen. He wore an embroidered blue tunic adorned with silver, a leather belt studded with copper, and a short sword at his hip. A beam of sunlight glinted off a seal hanging from his neck. I knew from watching Yoel ben Beerah in Levonah that the King's men wore seals around their necks—but I'd never seen one that reflected the sun.

He embraced each of the masters, holding Uriel longer than the other two. "Is there a place we can speak?"

"Let us go to my cave," Uriel said. "You are hungry after your journey, Ovadia?"

"I'll eat when you eat; I never have much appetite after a hard ride." There was a nasal tone to his speech—was the servant of the King not of Israel?

Uriel's eyes fell on me, and I felt the same sense of foreboding as when we first met. "Lev, please bring us wine."

I laid down my kinnor and ran to the cooking area where fires burned in three large, earthen hearths. I approached a harried servant sweating over the midday meal. "I need a wine skin."

The cook's lip rose in a sneer. "If the musicians desire wine, they'll just have to wait." He turned back abruptly.

Observing his profile, I wondered what he had done to become an indentured servant. Normally, such men were debt slaves, thieves sold by the court into servitude for up to six years to pay back double what they'd stolen. Why would the prophets surround themselves with such people? "It's not for us, it's for the masters and an emissary from the King."

"Ah, you should have said so." The sneer disappeared, and the servant retrieved a skin and four clay cups.

I ran to Uriel's cave and found the prophets and their guest seated around a low table. "So Ovadia," Uriel said, "To what do we owe your visit?"

"Let us wait until we're alone." Yosef nodded in my direction.

"No, no, it is fine that he hears," Ovadia said lightly. "It concerns him as well. You see, I've come for the musicians." I was filling the cups and nearly splashed a stream of wine on the table.

"Why would you want the musicians?" Yosef asked.

"For the wedding, of course. The King heard that the prophets assemble excellent musicians for their gathering, and he wants the very best in the land for his wedding."

"Interesting." Uriel leaned forward to take one of the cups. "Thank you for the wine, Lev." The wrinkled skin between his eyes creased in thought. "It's a little dark in here, would you mind lighting the lamps as well?"

Sunlight shone into the mouth of the cave, making it quite easy to see. Yet, in my eagerness to hear more, I neither argued nor hesitated to fetch fire from the cooking area.

"I won't consent to send them," Yosef said as I reentered the cave. I stepped quietly toward a lamp in the back and took my time lighting it, extending my opportunity to overhear as long as possible.

Ovadia's eyes widened as his hand clenched. "How can you refuse your king? He has the right to anything in the land that he desires."*

"He may be the King, but the full allegiance of the *nevi'im* is not to any king of flesh and blood. I've heard about Ahav's bride, and I can only imagine what this wedding will be like. Are we, the *nevi'im,* meant to contribute to such a travesty? And we also have a duty to the musicians in our service. They come here to play before disciples striving for holiness." Yosef turned now to Uriel. "How can we expose them to such practices?"

Uriel broke eye contact with Yosef and focused on Ovadia. "There are two things I don't understand. I'm surprised to hear the King is even aware of our gathering, and all the more that we hire talented musicians to play for us. And even if he is aware and wants our musicians, why not send a simple messenger to retrieve them? Why send the steward of the palace on such a journey?"

"Two excellent questions." Ovadia grinned as Eliav would when caught taking extra wine. "The King knows about the gathering and the caliber of your musicians because I told him. He sent me here because I advised him to handle the *nevi'im* tactfully before the wedding, something we could not depend on an ordinary messenger to do. I convinced him of this so that King Ahav would suggest that I go personally."

"Why would you do such a thing?"

"Because there are serious matters that I need to discuss with you, and I needed a reason to come."

The cave fell silent as the prophets pondered Ovadia's words. Yosef cocked his head toward his guest. "Ovadia, you have come to us many times in the past. Why should you suddenly need an excuse?"

The King's steward raised his cup to his mouth but returned it to the table without tasting it. "Everything's changed since the King's engagement. He knows that many oppose the marriage and fears that his servants will turn against him as well."

"And this is why the wedding has been so rushed…?" Yosef posed more of a statement than a question.

Ovadia nodded. "He wants it over before opposition can be raised. He is constantly on the watch now for who is loyal and who is not. For me to meet with you there needed to be a reason, otherwise, it would arouse the King's suspicions. He assumes that you are opposed to the match."

"That still doesn't justify taking our musicians to play before such a ceremony," Yosef responded. "Uriel, you must agree with me?"

Uriel held Yosef's gaze for a long moment, then dropped his eyes to his cup. "I'm inclined to let them go. Whether the request is fitting or not, King Ahav has the right to anything in the land. And now is not the time to make an enemy of him."

Yosef scowled but didn't respond. He turned to Tzadok. "We have given our opinions; it is up to you to decide."

There was a pause as Tzadok shut his eyes to consider the issue. Opening them, he glanced at each of the masters, and then, without a word, nodded in Uriel's direction.

"Very well," Yosef said, "I won't oppose both of you. The musicians may go. Now tell us, Ovadia, what is so important that you had to invent such an excuse?"

Uriel cut across Ovadia before he could speak. "Thank you, Lev, that is enough light for now. Please make sure the soldiers are fed and their horses looked after."

Yosef surveyed me with his dark, unblinking eyes. Had he forgotten my presence, or was he simply annoyed that Uriel had allowed me to stay and listen? I turned away but felt Yosef's eyes following me. I kept my expression blank as I walked toward the mouth of the cave. Once outside, though, I broke into a run. I had to find Yonaton. There was much to tell him—and we had to pack.

"What do you think they're talking about?" Yonaton asked me for the third time as we gathered our things.

"I wish I knew, but I don't think that we're going to find out. Master Uriel seemed to want me to hear the first part, but not the rest."

"My father always said my time would be better spent working the land than playing my halil. I wonder if this will change his mind?"

"What are you packing for?" Zim asked as he and Daniel walked into the cave. "Does this have anything to do with the King's servant and the mysterious request Raphael was talking about? Lev, did you overhear anything when you brought them their wine?"

"Yes." Yonaton's voice cracked with excitement. "Ovadia came to get us to play at the wedding."

"We're going to play for the King?" Zim snatched up his drum with one hand and pounded it with the other. "I knew it! I knew my moment would come!"

Daniel sat down, his forehead furrowed in thought. "If that's all he came for, we should be leaving already."

"Well—" Yonaton began, but I cut him off.

"Yosef didn't want us to go. They were still discussing it when I left." Yonaton shot me a glance that the other two missed, but I'd overheard a private conversation; it wasn't my place to tell Zim and Daniel everything that I'd heard. Somehow telling Yonaton felt different.

Zim turned to Daniel. "You don't sound so excited."

"I've played for the King before. As soon as he came out of mourning for his father, he celebrated his coronation and gathered musicians from around the land. But don't think we're going to play before the King as we play before the prophets. There will be many musicians there. We may not even see the King."

"I've never even been to Shomron." Zim tapped the edge of his drum with his fingertips. "The King keeps a small group of musicians to play in the palace." He winked in my direction. "You never know what could happen…"

Ovadia spoke with the masters until the sun burned a fiery gold in the western sky. When they emerged from the cave, Uriel sent word that we would leave in the morning.

"I'm going to tell my parents," Yonaton told me. "Do you want to come? They want to meet you anyway."

I nodded and laid my kinnor on my sleeping mat, but when we stepped out, we saw one of the servants climbing the path toward us. "Master Uriel wishes to speak with you, Lev." His tone was soft, with none of the brutishness of the cook I spoke to earlier in the day.

"Me?"

"Yes, he awaits you in his cave."

I waved goodbye to Yonaton and followed the white-robed servant down the trail. As we turned on one of the switchbacks on the path, I noticed a puncture in his right ear; not a piercing of the lobe, but a hole in the ear itself large enough to see through. Only one thing could have mangled him in that way. I shuddered at the thought, a motion that was not lost upon the servant.

"You are staring at my ear?"

I turned red, but the man's smile didn't waver. "Does that mean—?"

"That when my first service was complete, I chose not to go free. Yes, I am a slave until the *Yovel**...if it ever comes. Forever, probably."

"And your master...?"

"Master Yosef stood me up against a door and drove an awl through my ear, yes."

I couldn't tear my eyes away from the mark of bondage. "But you could have been free."

"Free to do what? Go back to being a thief?" His smile grew broader, showing no signs of shame. "We all serve, Lev. Before I served my appetites. Now I serve a worthy master."

When we reached Uriel's cave, the servant gestured to me to enter alone. Uriel sat in the same spot I had seen him earlier that day. He waved me toward the stool opposite him. I sat, my chest suddenly tight. "You heard quite a bit today."

I nodded, my eyes on the table. Was he upset that I lit the lamps so slowly?

"There is something on your mind, Lev. You may speak."

"I was surprised you let me hear as much as I did," I said quietly.

"As was I."

So, Uriel had wanted me there. Then why did I still feel the pressure in my chest? "Why did you let me stay?"

"My heart told me I should." I raised my eyes as far as Uriel's beard. "I can see the question on your face; you want to know the real reason why."

I nodded in response.

"It began with Raphael—such an unusual way to receive a prophecy."

"It didn't seem very different from when I saw you, just more intense."

"True, it is not at all unusual for a *navi* to receive a message for others. But *nevi'im* are rarely given messages to deliver to other *nevi'im*. If the Holy One wished to send me a message, why not send it to me directly? This is the first time I've ever received a prophecy through another prophet." Uriel bent his head forward, and his eyes met mine. "Questions are the gateway to wisdom. You may ask."

What did he want from me? I dropped my eyes to the table again and asked the next logical question. "Why do you think you received the prophecy this way?"

"I wondered the same. It could be that the end of my life is drawing near. *Nevi'im* often lose their *navua* near the end of their lives.* Or it could be that the Holy One has decreed that I no longer deserve *navua*." His right hand raked through his beard and held it. "But my heart tells me that neither was the cause of today's events."

"What then?"

"I believe that the prophecy was not directed to me alone."

"Then why didn't you tell Master Yosef about it? Wouldn't that have been easier than arguing?"

"Yes, it would. And since Raphael spoke publicly, I could have shared his words if I desired. But the fact that the message was not addressed to Yosef gave me pause. I was told to heed Ovadia's request, but he was not. He was right to rely on his own understanding."

"But you said the message wasn't intended only for you. If not for Master Yosef, then who else?"

Uriel paused until I glanced up. "I believe that it was for you."

A shiver passed through my body. "Me?"

Uriel hesitated, as if weighing his words. "I noticed Ovadia looking intently at the musicians when he arrived. He clearly had an interest in the four of you."

Even if that were the case, the prophecy could just as easily have been for one of the others. "There's more, isn't there?"

"Yes," Uriel replied, but said no more.

I felt blood rising to my cheeks and reached under my tunic for my father's knife, which I now kept with me at all times. The weapon hit the table with a dull thud. "It has something to do with this, doesn't it?"

Uriel picked up the sheathed knife with a faraway look in his eye. At that moment, I was certain he'd seen the knife before. "Yes." He gazed directly at me but offering no more information.

"What are you hiding from me?"

Uriel sighed. "I understand how difficult this must be, but it is not yet safe to tell you all that I know."

"If it's my safety, shouldn't I be able to decide—"

"No!"

My head jerked back at his sharp word.

Uriel's eyes glinted as he leaned across the table. "When I took you with me, I promised your uncle I would look after you. I question his judgment in giving you this knife. I can only conclude that he is unaware of its significance. You heard what Ovadia said—we are entering dangerous times!"

Uriel lowered his forehead into his hands, as though needing their help to carry its weight. When he lifted it, there was a softer expression in his eyes. "Much as I would like to protect you, Raphael's prophecy shows that there is a greater will than my own involved. I must…I will allow events to take their course."

The prophet met my eyes again. "Do the others know your father's name?"

I sat up at the question. "Only Yonaton and Shimon, the one with the scars."

"Good. From now on, call yourself Lev ben Menachem. Tell Yonaton so he won't be surprised, but instruct him not to tell the others. I'm not concerned about Shimon."

Uriel rose. "Be careful in Shomron. Darkness is rising in the Kingdom—I have felt it building for some time. Trust your heart. If something feels wrong to you, it probably is. And keep your eyes open. I won't be in Shomron to see for myself, so I'm counting on you to be my eyes and tell me everything when you return." Uriel walked me to the mouth of the cave, placing his hands on my shoulders. "Perhaps it is best if you leave the knife here with me?"

I shook my head—it was my only inheritance.

"Very well, take it with you, but show it to no one."

"Put your gear on the donkeys," Ovadia told the four of us the next morning. "We'll be riding the horses."

The prophets lent us two donkeys for the journey, and I hitched my sleeping roll and kinnor to the smaller one. "You can ride with me," Ovadia said. I stepped onto a large boulder and mounted behind him.

Uriel walked toward us from one of the caves, and Ovadia kicked his horse forward, out of earshot of the soldiers.

"I have given more thought to your question," Uriel said.

"You haven't changed your mind?"

"No, but there is something more I want to tell you."

"Should we speak privately?"

"There is no need, it is just a story."

This didn't seem to me like the time for stories, but Ovadia didn't appear surprised.

"A fox once walked along the banks of a river.* Looking down, he saw fish swimming frantically back and forth. *Why do you rush about from place to place?* he asked them.

"*We are fleeing the nets of the men,* they replied.

"*Come up onto the land with me,* said the fox. *Here you will be safe from the nets of the men, and we can live together as my ancestors lived with your ancestors.*

"*You are supposed to be the cleverest of animals,* replied the fish, *but you talk like a fool. If we are afraid in the water where we know how to live, how much more is there to fear on dry land where we will surely die?*"

Uriel paused. Ovadia said, "I'm not sure I understand."

"Both paths before you are perilous. When forced to choose, remember that the fish may die even in the water, but leaving it brings total destruction."

Shamaya said: Love work, be loath to assume leadership, and do not become intimate with the government.

Pirkei Avot 1:10

Taming the Bear

Exhausted, I slumped forward and gripped the horse's flanks with my knees in a vain effort to save my sore backside. More hills of Israel rose before me that day than I had seen in my entire life as the horses raced past Beit El, then north on the King's Road. We continued past Levonah, then finally headed west until we reached Shomron on the very edge of the mountain plateau. I always imagined Shomron as the largest city in the Kingdom* and was surprised to see that it was less than half the area of Beit El. Despite its smaller size, Shomron did not lack fortifications. Walls twice the height of Levonah's rose above three gateways, one inside the next. We slowed our pace to pass through the triple gate, where four soldiers, each with the royal ox emblazoned on his tunic, stood at attention. Ovadia reined in our horse close to the one carrying Yonaton and spoke in a low voice. "While you're in Shomron, the two of you will stay with me."

"What about Daniel and Zim?" I asked.

"They'll be in the musicians' quarters."

"We don't mind being with the musicians too," Yonaton said.

Ovadia shook his head. "Master Uriel made me promise to look after the two of you while you are here. He wouldn't agree to send you without my giving my word."

The day before, Uriel had insisted that he would let events take their course without interfering. Yet, as the horses carrying Daniel and Zim turned off the main road immediately inside the city gates while Yonaton and I were carried farther up the hillside, it seemed to me that the old *navi* was not done interfering after all. And I was sure of it when we reached Ovadia's house, the largest and most beautiful I'd ever seen. There was an arched entranceway to the courtyard, and the walls were built of hewn stone, containing windows a full arm's length in width. While two maidservants prepared a stew and kneaded dough in the wide kitchen, a manservant carried our meager belongings up the ladder to a room reserved just for us. Ovadia and his wife Batya saw to it that we wanted for nothing, yet they hardly spoke in our presence, even to each other. As I soaked up the last of my stew with my bread, Batya said, "You two look exhausted; you ought to get to sleep."

Though the sun had not yet set, Yonaton nudged my shoulder as if to say, "Don't argue." It was clear the family wanted its privacy. We said goodnight and climbed the ladder to our room where the amber light of late afternoon streamed in through an open window. It shed a soft and inviting glow over two fresh straw beds. I'd never slept on straw before—in my house, only my aunt and uncle enjoyed such luxury. I leaned out the window and took in the view of the palace, which stood upon a raised rock platform cut out of the hilltop. Its high walls glowed, reflecting the setting sun. Soldiers stood guard, stone-faced, at the corners of the parapet. I watched until darkness fell and the palace disappeared from view. Only a week ago, my sheep were my sole audience; now I was in Shomron, about to play my kinnor before the King. Perhaps Dahlia was right: our lives could change in an instant.

In the morning, the manservant directed us to the visiting musicians' quarters, a single room that could comfortably sleep six, but with more than twice that number crammed inside. Except for a wine barrel standing upright in the corner, the floor was completely covered with bodies. We stepped gingerly over a dozen sleeping musicians to reach Daniel and Zim against the far wall. Daniel sat right up when Yonaton jostled his shoulder, but when I shook Zim, he opened his eyes, moaned, and rolled back over.

"Have a late night?" Yonaton asked.

"More like an early morning." Daniel stretched his arms over his head and yawned.

"Well, help us wake the others, we've got to get down to rehearsal." I shook Zim's shoulder again. "Come on, Zim, you've always managed to get up to play for the prophets. This time it's for the King."

"Yes," Daniel mumbled, pulling on his clothes, "But our prophets water down their wine."

After much wrangling, Daniel managed to get all sixteen visiting musicians up, dressed, and out through the city gates. The sodden bunch could barely keep their eyes open as we headed toward an open field where the six court musicians waited with some amusement.

"I'm sure you're all good musicians, otherwise you wouldn't have made it here," said Dov, the chief musician in the King's court. Despite his bearish build, Dov had soft eyes and a warm smile peeking out from behind his graying beard. "We have only two days to learn to play together, so we're going to have to be diligent. The court musicians have been working on the music for the wedding ever since the engagement, so we'll lead. When you feel that you've caught on, join in."

Dov picked up his tall nevel and counted into the first melody—a rousing dance tune that kicked off with strong percussion and two nevelim. The other court musicians set right into their parts without hesitation. The rest of us, one after the other, meandered into the tune as it became more clear. As soon as all of us were well into the melody, Dov laid down his instrument and circulated among us, offering comments and corrections. "You need to slow down," he said to Zim. "Focus on staying in time with the rest of us." Zim, who was still struggling to keep from nodding off, scowled at the criticism, but he did slacken his beat.

Yonaton, whose turn was next, watched the exchange out of the corner of his eye. "I think you've got it," Dov said to him. "Play louder, I want you to come out clearly." Yonaton's shoulders relaxed, and a grin rose from behind his halil. Dov then stopped in front of me and closed his eyes to filter out the other musicians. He opened them, nodded, and walked onto the next player without saying a word.

Once he had finished his rounds, Dov returned to his place, picked up his nevel, played through one full measure with us, then brought the piece to a close. He immediately started a new *nigun*, and the process began again from the beginning.

The King's Road was packed with people pouring in for the wedding when Yonaton and I headed back in through the city gates. Apparently, not all of Israel was as opposed to the match as the people of Beit El. Merchants hawking their wares to the milling crowd lined the main road as it climbed the hill toward the palace. Yonaton stopped before a man selling iron tools and picked up a two-pronged plowshare. "My father could plow twice as fast with one of these."

I grabbed his arm and pulled him away from the cart, "Come on, you can't afford that." Yonaton shrugged and released the plow point, which clanked against the others in the cart. I stopped in front of another cart loaded with milky rocks. I licked my finger, touched it to the rock, and brought it back to my mouth. "Salt!"

"From the Salt Sea itself," the merchant said. "Don't go eating it, and mind your hands now that you've touched it—you could blind yourself if you rub your eyes with this on your fingers. But I promise you, friend, sheep love it. So do shepherds—keeps the flock healthy like nothing else."

I put my hand on the rock again, feeling the sharp points of the crystals pressing into my palm. No shepherd in Levonah had a rock like this. Yonaton tugged on my arm. "You were right, we can't afford this stuff."

"Now, you don't know that." The salt merchant held up both hands to stop us. "A little one costs just this much copper…" He held up a small iron weight and dropped it on one side of a scale.

Yonaton pulled on my arm again, but I couldn't take my eyes away from those rocks. Would it really keep the flock healthy? If we were paid well for the wedding, it might be only two years until my flock grew too large to keep at my uncle's house. Would I have to take final leave of my family at age fourteen?

Unbidden, a new image rose in my mind. It was Dov's face from that morning, smiling at me, the lone musician among our group he hadn't criticized even once during the rehearsal. True, I mainly stood out because I wasn't suffering the effects of wine like the others, but Dov didn't know that. Without even meaning to, I'd impressed the most influential musician in the Kingdom. Perhaps Dov would offer me a place in the King's court if I proved myself? Then being a musician wouldn't mean moving around, hunting for work wherever I could find it. It wouldn't mean living in a cave, playing for prophets who would use my music to enter realms forever closed to me. I could stay in Shomron, play before the King and nobles, and find my place among the elite musicians of the land—even Zim dreamed of that.

Dov's face faded from my mind, replaced by one younger, sweeter, and so much closer to my heart, with stubborn red curls forever falling over a pair of hazel eyes. I was closer to Dahlia than anyone in the world, but she just wouldn't see the fact I could never ignore. There was a stone wall between us. It was something we never talked about, even though I'd gone over what I would have to say endless times in my mind.

The stone wall is like the wall of the pen. I'm on the inside, locked in with the sheep. You're on the outside, feet planted on the soil. The wall is only waist high now—we can gaze at each other, talk together, even touch as we did when we were children—but only because we're young. As soon as we're both of age, this wall is going to rise right over our heads.

We'd been raised like brother and sister, but that was just another part of the illusion. As brother and sister, we could stay close—what husband would be jealous of his wife's brother? But no man would tolerate such closeness with a cousin. Isaac married his cousin, Jacob married his cousin. Cousins could make the ideal marriage partners—they share family and their lands are often side by side.

But Dahlia and I were the exception. Uncle Menachem would never accept the life of the nomadic shepherd for his daughter. A traveling musician or even a player for the prophets would seem no better. But what about a member of the King's court? There was certainly no comparison between a life in the wilderness and a life in Shomron, the seat of nobility.

And then there was the copper. Daniel told me the King paid visiting musicians well—surely he did no worse for members of his own court. It might take me twenty years as a shepherd to save enough to buy a piece of rocky hillside, but all the court musicians that morning were dressed in linen tunics, not the woolen ones farmers and shepherds wore. Perhaps as a court musician, I could buy land in ten, maybe even five, years. And Dahlia was right; if the *Yovel* wasn't coming, then any land I managed to purchase would be mine forever. *Would it be enough, though?*

The salt merchant hadn't taken his eyes off me this entire time. No doubt, he thought I was dreaming of returning to my flock with one of his rocks, but I was no longer interested. Here, finally, was a dream worth leaving my flock over, a path that even a landless orphan could take toward a normal life.

A shrill scream shook me from my thoughts. A woman shrieked in the distance, her voice immediately drowned out by the rough cheers of a crowd of men. The cheers faded and her cries rose again, only to be drowned out a second time by a deep roar.

The salt merchant laughed.

"What's that noise?"

"Go see," he said with a wry grin.

Yonaton and I followed a throng heading off the main road in the direction of the commotion and looped around a pile of boulders jutting out of the hillside. There was another shrill scream, and we scampered up the boulders to peer down on the scene below. I fell behind because of my kinnor slung over my shoulder and called ahead to Yonaton when he reached the top. "Is she all right?"

"The *woman's* fine." Yonaton flinched, and the crowd roared again. "It's her husband that's got the problem."

"What's wrong with him?"

"He might be torn apart by a bear."

"A bear's chasing her husband?"

"No. Her husband's chasing the bear."

Sure enough, an enormous iron cage stood in the clearing below. Inside, a powerfully built man edged closer to a shaggy, brown bear. Over a hundred people cheered him on while his wife pulled at the bars, berating him. He ignored her, his eyes focused on the bear that was crouched on four legs, its head reaching as high as the man's chest. The animal threw open its jaws and roared, and glints of sunlight sparkled off its neck.

"Yonaton, is that bear wearing…?"

"Jewels," he whispered, stupefied.

The man in the cage stepped forward, and the bear reared up on its hind legs. One more step, and the beast swung yellowed claws as long as my fingers, like a set of curved knives, a handsbreadth from the man's face. A spectator reached his hand between the bars of the cage, trying to grab a golden bracelet off the bear's wrist. The beast turned with a snap of its jaws, and the challenger in the cage advanced, arm outstretched.

The bear spun back to him, swatting with its massive, brown paw. The man jumped back, but not far enough, and a sharp claw caught the end of his nose. He brought his hands to his face as the crowd gasped. His wife's cries reached a frenzied pitch at the sight of blood pouring through his fingers. "Get out of that cage!"

The man retreated to the corner, removed his hands from his nose, and wiped the blood on his tunic. He advanced again, circling to the right of the angry bear. The smell of blood only provoked the beast. It launched forward, slashing its paws. The man ducked under its arm and lunged for the back of the bear's neck. His greedy fingers closed around the golden chain of a ruby necklace. The beast whirled around, the back of a paw slammed into the side of its opponent's head. The blow lifted the man completely off his feet. He crashed into the iron bars of the cage and slid down, collapsing at the bear's feet.

Two soldiers with spears leapt into the cage. The bear growled but retreated before the sharp iron points. A third soldier dragged the challenger out and left him in the dirt outside the cage. Awareness slowly returned to his face, now swollen purple. He opened his eyes and sat up, blinking furiously to clear his eyes of the blood flowing from a gash on his forehead. He unclenched his fist and surveyed his palm. It was empty. The bear was pressed against the far side of the cage, the red stone still suspended from its shaggy neck.

Someone from the crowd helped the man to his feet. As he staggered forward, his wife pounced, hitting him in the chest with both fists, less powerfully than the bear, but no less fierce. The crowd's laughter mingled with the wife's screams as she pulled him away. A scrawny man with large, bulging eyes climbed to the top of the cage, and the laughter immediately ceased. "A handsbreadth away from a lifetime of riches! Who will be the next to try?"

Two men stepped forward from different parts of the crowd. "One at a time," the announcer said. "You. You climb in. You can go next. Unless…Ovadia, have you come to try? I'll let you go first!"

The crowd turned to watch Ovadia approach the cage. He stared long and hard at the bear, now back on four legs, circling its enclosure. The crowd was quiet, silenced by the prospect of seeing the King's steward in a death struggle for treasure. "Not today, Aviad." Ovadia's calm gaze met the shaky eyes of the announcer.

But his refusal only excited Aviad. "Come, come…surely one who enters the throne room of the King isn't afraid to step into a bear's den?" The crowd laughed at the bold taunt, but Ovadia shook his head. Aviad raised his voice higher, "Can any man have too many riches?"

"A fool may be blinded by the jewels, Aviad, but a wise man sees the claws."

Ovadia turned away, and his eyes fell upon the two of us. "Ah, boys, I was hoping to find you. Can you come with me?" We followed him away from the crowd. Once out of earshot, Ovadia pulled out a sealed scroll. "Please take this to Uzziah ben Hanan. He is the foreman in charge of readying the gates. Wait for his response, then come report to me at the palace. I'll instruct the guards to allow you entry."

I was anticipating a meal after a long morning of practice, but couldn't bring myself to refuse. We found the city gates thrown open and people streaming through, most on foot, some on donkeys, and quite a few nobles riding horses. Workmen washed the gates and smoothed out rough patches in the road under the supervision of a tall man who walked among them, inspecting their work. Yonaton approached him, "Are you Uzziah ben Hanan?"

He nodded, took the scroll from Yonaton's outstretched hand, and examined the clay seal in the image of a footstool. "So, what does Ovadia want now?" He broke the seal, read the scroll, then turned to one of the workmen washing the gates. "Shama, take your horn and position yourself on that hill. When Tzidon's caravan comes into view, sound three long blasts." He turned back to Yonaton. "You may tell Ovadia that everything has been arranged."

The first part of our task done, we headed back up the hill toward the palace at the top—but something about our errand didn't feel right to me. "Does it seem strange to you…" I asked Yonaton, "…that Ovadia would use us as his messengers?"

"He's far too busy to go himself."

"Of course he is, but he must have other servants."

"Look around, everyone's busy." Indeed they were. All around us pavers were being washed, bushes trimmed, and even a canopy erected below the palace. "He probably needs all the help he can get."

"Maybe." But something still didn't feel right to me. Uriel may have convinced Ovadia to take us into his house, but why would he make us his messengers as well? *If he needs extra help, why not use his personal servants?*

Three guards blocked the palace entrance. One put out his hand to stop us. "We're looking for Ovadia," I said.

The guard caught sight of the kinnor hanging over my shoulder and nodded. "You're the musicians?" He smirked, probably expecting men, not boys. "Go through. You'll find Ovadia in the entryway."

From Ovadia's house, I'd seen only the top of the palace, but as we stepped through the gates, I entered a city within the city. All the houses inside Levonah's town walls combined together would hardly equal the size of the palace. It was at least five times as wide as Ovadia's house and rose to a full three stories. In the courtyard, a double row of thick limestone columns led up to the palace gate. The whole enclosure was buzzing like a beehive: slaves sluiced down the broad flagstones of the courtyard, gardeners pruned grapevines, and servants darted from place to place, each one burdened by his own load.

Under the arched and pillared entryway to the palace, Ovadia inspected a stately oak throne, oiled and buffed to a warm glow in the sunlight. Beside him, a man in linen robes specked with sawdust gestured to an elaborately carved cedar tree on the back of the throne. "Had there been more time—"

"Nonsense," Ovadia said. "No visiting king could expect more. King Ahav will be pleased." He turned at our approach. "Ah boys, everything's been arranged? Excellent. I'm sure you're hungry. You can return to the house and Batya will fix you something to eat. I may join you there soon, once I find servants to carry this into the throne room."

I eyed the throne of dark-tinted wood. It looked heavy, but not too heavy for us to carry. The next time I saw Seguv, he'd surely tell me about his appearance in the King's court. How I'd love to tell him that I'd been there as well.

I might be dreaming of spending the rest of my life playing music at the court, but I know how much my dreams are worth. This might be the only chance I ever get.

Yonaton read my face and nodded—he wanted to do it too. I spoke up, in the deepest tone I could manage. "We can carry it."

Ovadia's lips curled into a bemused smile. "You probably can. But the King is sitting on his throne and will be watching. For all the world, I would not be the one to drop this throne in front of King Ahav."

"We won't drop it." I tried to sound more confident than I felt. The craftsman shifted from foot to foot, clearly displeased with the idea of mere boys carrying his creation. But he wouldn't voice his opposition before Ovadia.

Ovadia ran his eyes slowly over my face, then down to my chest and hands. He gave the same inspection to Yonaton, who was shorter and more solidly built. I expected Ovadia to refuse, but he raised his eyebrows and nodded, appearing pleased with our proposal. "Very well, two stout hearts are worth many strong arms. The throne belongs next to the King, on his left side. It is unacceptable to set it down in the throne room or to show any strain. If you feel it slipping, say 'Where would you like it, sir?' and I will come to your aid."

We picked up the throne and immediately discovered it was heavier than it looked. The effort I saw on Yonaton's face mirrored my own. Ovadia hesitated, but then took a step backward, directing us forward. At his nod, servants opened two tall wooden doors, and Ovadia backed into the throne room. It was long and narrow, with black basalt columns, carved like date palms and just as tall, marching in two lines down the center of the room. Beams of light shined through windows high in the southern wall. The King, a crown of woven gold on his head, sat on a raised platform three steps above the stone floor. The room held noblemen in dyed linen garments, soldiers bearing the emblem of the royal ox, commoners waiting to petition the King, and scribes recording all that occurred—about twenty people in all. We entered, and with great effort wiped the strain from our faces.

Ovadia walked in reverse ahead of us, twisting slightly to avoid showing his back to the King. His approaching presence parted the crowd as he directed us up the long aisle. I could see the tension creeping back into Yonaton's face, and the muscles of my own jaw tightened. Both of us leaned forward, using the back of the throne to hide our faces from the King, but this only made its weight harder to carry. My arms burned, my back was screaming, and I could no longer keep the distress from my face. Hunched and struggling, we carried the throne between the columns to the foot of the dais, but to place it on the platform, we would have to lift it waist high and pass right before the King.

"Where shall we put it, sir?" The strain in Yonaton's voice rang out like a bell.

Ovadia grabbed the back of the throne with two broad hands and lifted it with surprising power. "Right over here." The three of us carried it over the steps with ease, and Yonaton and I were able to relax our expressions before passing the King. We set it down next to him and backed away, bowing as we went.

"Nicely done, Ovadia. It is truly as beautiful as you claimed." A loud cheer came from outside, and everyone but the King turned toward the sound of the commotion. "Has someone just taken a jewel from the bear?"

"I believe so, my King."

"A rather brutal form of entertainment."

"Apparently quite popular in Tzidon. Princess Izevel thought it would amuse our guests."

"They do sound as if they're enjoying themselves. Still, we don't need any more cripples in Shomron—I'm feeding quite enough already."

Three long blasts echoed from outside the city. The King sat up tall and stately, a match for any of the pillars lining his great hall. "Could Tzidon have arrived already?" He sank back into his throne. "Ovadia, go and meet him outside the walls and escort him to me."

"Very good, my King. What of his wife and daughter?"

"Show them to their accommodations first. Women are not fond of holding audience immediately after a long journey." Ovadia bowed and turned to take his leave, motioning to the two of us to follow. "Wait a moment." The King pointed to the kinnor slung across my back. "These boys. Are they the musicians you fetched from the prophets?"

I heard the probing question in the King's voice and recalled the smirk from the guard at the palace gates. Now that the King saw that we were just boys, would he guess that Ovadia's journey had nothing to do with musicians?

If Ovadia was ill at ease, his face belied it. "Yes, my King. These are two of the four I brought."

"You said they are quite talented, correct?"

"Superb, my King."

That was a risky thing for Ovadia to say. What if the King asked us to play and found us wanting? But the King had other ideas. "Bring them with you. It will make a nice impression for them to play upon his arrival."

"An excellent idea, my King." Ovadia bowed again and exited the throne room, with the two of us trailing closely behind.

Once out of the palace, we broke into a run, covering the distance down to the city gates in a quarter of the time it had taken us to climb up to the palace. My stomach growled—I hadn't eaten since before the rehearsal. *No time for food, though.*

We passed through the gates, and Ovadia directed us to a small, grassy hill overlooking the western road. Hearing from Seguv and other travelers about Shomron, I'd always imagined it perched atop the highest mountain in Israel, but that wasn't the case. Shomron was guarded by higher mountains on the north, east, and south, each surmounted by a watchtower. Only from the west, where there was no higher peak, could the chariots of Tzidon approach. I raised my hand to block the glare and strained my eyes to peer past the rich, brown coastal plain. I caught my breath at the sight of a smudge of distant blue along the horizon. *The great sea!* Until that moment, I knew it only through stories. Teeming with life and dangers, it was the gateway to the rest of the world.

"The two of you will play from here," Ovadia said. "When they come into view, I will descend to greet them at the bottom of the hill."

"Who are we waiting for?" Yonaton asked.

"King Ethbaal of Tzidon and his daughter Izevel, who is to marry King Ahav in two days' time."

"Where's Tzidon?"

"It's to the north of Israel, on the sea. The people of Tzidon are great sailors. King Ethbaal has made his capital city into the greatest port in the world."

"Is that why King Ahav wants to marry his daughter?" I asked.

"Yes. An alliance with Tzidon will expand our ability to trade. The King expects this to bring great prosperity to the land."

"Do you think it will?"

"The King's reasoning is sound."

Ovadia hadn't really answered my question. Before I could ask another, a wedge of horsemen came into view, each bearing a pole flying a banner marked by a majestic cedar tree. Behind the horsemen thundered three chariots carrying spearmen and bowmen. They scanned the sides of the road, weapons gripped at the ready.

"I thought this was a wedding," Yonaton said. "They look as if they're going to war."

This vanguard was followed by a single, gilded chariot, much larger than the rest, carrying three passengers seated side by side. In the middle sat an older man draped in purple robes, with a high forehead and neatly groomed beard. He held his chest high as he gazed off into the distance. At his right sat a woman with coronets of steel-gray hair, the sun flashing off her many jewels. On his left sat a woman in a dove-gray dress, her face and hair covered by a white veil. A second line of chariots stretched down the road behind them. At the end of the caravan rode at least a hundred soldiers on horseback, with more coming into view. Each bore the cedar emblem on his chest.

Ovadia signaled to us with a wave. I played the first song that came to mind, one we'd practiced that morning, a fast, dancing melody. It was too cheerful for a march, but Yonaton joined in without objection. King Ethbaal probably couldn't even hear us over the din of the horses. Ovadia walked down the hill, positioned himself by the side of road, and bowed to the royal chariot. He spoke with the King, climbed in beside the driver, and beckoned us to follow. Without stopping our music, we stepped down to the road and returned to the city as part of the royal retinue.

The main road of Shomron was too steep for the chariots, so the party dismounted at the city gates, where a large crowd was assembled to catch a glimpse of the bride. As she descended, four soldiers came forward with a covered litter. She stepped gracefully into a padded seat and drew the curtains around her, displaying nothing more to the disappointed crowd than a thin wrist and long, elegant fingers. The King and Queen walked slowly at the side of her litter as they ascended to the palace, followed by a winding trail of soldiers.

The procession stopped in front of the palace. Another servant ran forward to place steps before the litter, and the veiled bride stepped down, holding the hand of a maidservant for support. Ovadia escorted the royal family into the palace, and a maidservant followed, carrying an intricately embroidered sack made from some rich indigo fabric.

I wasn't sure what we should do, but as no one had told us to stop the music, we continued playing and trailed the royal family toward the palace at a respectful distance. The plaza showed none of its earlier activity, standing empty except for guards. At the inner gates, Ovadia turned to King Ethbaal and asked, "Would the King like to be shown to his room to refresh himself before meeting with King Ahav?"

"No, I'll see Ahav immediately."

"Very well, my master awaits you. Please follow me. I will return immediately to accompany the Queen and the Princess to their chambers."

Once her father had gone, the Princess pointed around the plaza and said something to her mother in a foreign tongue. Her words were meaningless to me, yet the melody of her voice aroused a desire to glimpse beneath her veil. My eyes rested on her hands, the only part of her not hidden from view. Her olive skin shone as if rubbed with oil.

"You Queen of Israel soon," her mother replied in halting Hebrew. "If you wish to enter hearts of people, you must speak their tongue."

"As you say, Mother," the Princess replied, in a Hebrew far more fluid than her mother's. Izevel swept her hand across the plaza again. "It's little more than a fortress."

The Queen examined the carvings around the entrance. "It has some beauty. Remember, palace is Queen's domain. You cannot expect unmarried King to keep it properly."

"I'm so glad you were able to make the journey, Mother. I will miss your wisdom once you are gone. You are right. The dignity of the palace is my responsibility now." The Princess pointed to a painted vase atop a pedestal opposite the palace entrance. "Place it there."

The maidservant put the vase on the floor, replaced it with the indigo sack, and untied its top so that it fell in a heap around the object it held. She then stepped away reverentially. On the pedestal stood a bronze statue* of a man, a jagged lightning sword grasped in his upraised hand. A helmet as long as his torso extended above his head, reaching toward the sky. "Yes." the Princess sighed. "That's better already."

I inhaled sharply and bit my lip. *A statue—an idol—in the palace of the King of Israel?* The shocked silence of the crowd in Beit El returned to me like a cold, ill wind. Even as I stood beneath the summer sky, gooseflesh crept up my arms.

My sleep was broken that night, but not by the old nightmare.

The caged bear, larger and fiercer than before, roared. It reached up its great paws and pounded the iron bars above its head. The sun sparkled off the jewels hanging around its neck, but the ruby pendant was gone—in its place hung the Princess's bronze statue, its upraised arm ready to strike.

The bear curled a paw around a bar above its head and pulled down with all its weight until the bar snapped in its grip. It reached for another bar on the side of the cage and yanked until it broke as well. It grabbed another bar, then another, breaking each one in turn. Once the cage lay in ruins at its feet, the beast stepped free.

No longer confined, the animal grew at a terrifying pace. It climbed uphill, distending with each step until it reached the height of the palace itself. And it kept on growing. Paws the size of chariots whipped along the palace courtyard, hooked yellow claws ripping paving stones from their moorings. The monster grabbed the sides of the palace and tore it from its foundations. It raised the palace and placed it on its head, fitting it as tightly as a crown. In one colossal step, the bear breached the walls of Shomron and lumbered north.

I startled awake, my heart pounding. Unlike my old nightmare, there was no forgetting this time; every detail of this dream remained deeply etched in my waking mind. I slipped out of bed and looked out the window; my shoulders relaxed at the sight of the palace quietly bathed in moonlight. Still trembling, I reached for my kinnor. Nothing calmed me like music.

Growing up in a home where everyone slept in the same loft helped me learn how to quietly slip down the ladder and step out into the cool night air without waking anyone. I didn't want to play near the house lest I disturb others' sleep. It took only a moment to decide where to go.

No one was awake in the streets, though I passed numerous bodies snoring by the side of the road. Ovadia had mentioned that there weren't enough places for everyone to sleep in anticipation of the royal wedding. The city was only ten years old and had never before held so many people.

The bear slept. Its shaggy back rose and fell with each breath. I approached the bars of the cage and assessed the great beast. Its finery was gone, somehow removed for the night, and a deep musk radiated from its hunched form. I crouched nearby and plucked a *nigun* my aunt used to sing to me when I woke from a nightmare, confused and afraid. Despite my delicate picking, the music roused the bear; it sat up and snuffed at the air. I stopped playing, but it was too late. The beast rose to its full height, growled, and thrust its paws between the bars at me. I retreated as it snarled, blinking in the dark.

Standing at a safer distance, I closed my eyes and listened to its voice. Daniel said he heard the song of the sheep in my music. The bear was no different than my sheep, really, only larger and more dangerous, with a slower and more powerful rhythm. I plucked again at my kinnor, searching for the right sound.

After a few fumbling moments, a simple melody began to emerge from the lower register of my instrument. It just felt…right. I opened my eyes to see the bear standing silently, no longer lunging for me through the bars. I stepped forward, closer, but it still didn't move. I began to hum, adding my voice to the notes of the kinnor. The beast tilted its head and released a groaning sigh. I took another step forward—the bear was now within my reach, which meant that I was within its reach too. Still humming, I removed my hand from the strings and extended it between the bars. The bear didn't move. I laid my hand on the back of its mammoth paw, probing the thick fur.

The animal turned its head—I pulled my hand back, fearing a strike that never came. I returned my hand to the strings, quietly strumming the bear's song. The animal closed its eyes with a low grunt. It crouched, lay down, and rested its head on the back of its paws. I reached in through the bars and scratched the bear behind its neck, the same place where the man grabbed for the ruby necklace earlier that day. I continued to stroke the spot until the bear sank again into a deep slumber.

Rabban Gamliel said: Beware of rulers: if they befriend, it is only for their own benefit. They act friendly when it is to their advantage; faithless during times of need.

Pirkei Avot 2:3

The Alliance

The High Priest's presence filled the wedding canopy. His commanding eyes peered from beneath thick, black eyebrows set within a broad forehead. His heavy beard hung over white linen robes hemmed with golden bells, which tinkled as he smoothed a golden sash at his waist. The plaza in front of the canopy was wreathed in living boughs and heaps of summer fruits, blending a threshing floor at harvest with a king's table at feast time. A mass of torch-bearers stepped into the plaza and sliced a path through the crowd of noblemen. Dov struck the first three notes alone, and the rest of us joined in on the fourth, just as we had rehearsed a dozen times the day before. An expectant silence fell over the crowd as all turned their attention up the aisle.

King Ahav appeared in snowy white linen for his wedding day. He walked alone, eyes focused straight ahead, until he took his place next to the High Priest. Only then could I get a good look at his face, which reminded me of Uncle Menachem's when selling a ram for slaughter.

Next appeared a towering man in violet robes that billowed out over husky arms and a muscular chest, his hand cradling the handle of a sword at his side.

Unlike King Ahav, his eyes swept across the aisle, examining the crowd with each step. I knew there were many in Israel opposed to the marriage—is that what he was looking for? Did Princess Izevel need protection at her own wedding? As the man's eyes passed over the musicians, a chill swept through my body, but the cold eyes didn't pause. With a swirl of vivid cloth, he stepped under the canopy and positioned himself next to the High Priest, who took a half step away from the body-guard and peered at him from the corner of his eye.

The royal family of Tzidon now appeared. Princess Izevel stood veiled in the middle, her smooth black hair flowing over her shoulders, dark against the white of her dress. King Ethbaal's proud face tipped upwards, honoring neither crowd nor king with his attention. He led his wife and daughter forward in step with the music. I recalled the harsh gaze that Yosef had fixed upon Ovadia, insisting that he in no way wished to add to this celebration. Yet here I was playing the music that was drawing Izevel, step by step, closer to becoming queen. I swallowed the stone that formed in my throat.

At the end of the aisle, King Ethbaal dropped his gaze to his daughter, lifted her veil and kissed her gently on the forehead. A soft pink flushed in Izevel's light olive cheeks. She appeared only a few years older than me—she couldn't have been more than sixteen. A familiar scent of wildflowers surrounded the Princess, and I suddenly knew what had become of the afarsimon oil Seguv brought to Shomron. The Queen drew her daughter under the canopy and led her in a circle around King Ahav.

The High Priest stepped forward. "May all who have assembled here be blessed. We are the children of Abraham, whose tent opened to all sides *to welcome guests. We placed our canopy under the sky, recalling the Holy One's blessing to Abraham that his children would be as abundant as the stars of the heavens…"

I was barely listening, my attention drawn more to the scene around me, to the royal families and the crowd, than to the words of the High Priest. King Ahav tipped his head upwards, mirroring King Ethbaal. Neither king watched Izevel, still circling King Ahav. But her eyes never left the face of her future husband as she walked the traditional seven circles,* each one tighter than the last.

"…Marriage is the joining of two halves, destined from creation to be one. The first woman was separated from Adam and then returned,* so they could bond together as one flesh. From this union came all men…"

How different my own wedding would be if Uncle Menachem ever allowed me to marry Dahlia. Two of my younger cousins would precede us up the aisle carrying a rooster and a hen; the canopy would be supported by poles cut from the four trees planted when Dahlia was born; we would be surrounded by family and friends, not strangers and dignitaries. I glanced at Dov, leading us with his nevel, who in the final days of rehearsal continued to be impressed by my playing. I hadn't asked him about returning to play in the King's court—I'd have to do that after the wedding.

A murmur ran through the crowd. Princess Izevel, who now stood beside King Ahav, motioned to the High Priest. He broke off his speech and leaned in, allowing the Princess to whisper in his ear. The priest turned to King Ahav, who nodded. The High Priest winced, but restored the calm to his face by the time he stood upright and faced the crowd again. "This marriage is more than a union of two people; it is the joining together of two nations. The High Priest of Tzidon will bless the union as well."

The man in the garish robes, who I'd mistaken for the Princess's bodyguard, stepped forward, his hand still resting on the hilt of his sword. "I am Yambalya. I serve Baal, the mighty storm god, patron god of Tzidon." His voice resonated with the deep tones of a bass drum.

"Long ago, when the heavens were young, the children of El fought for mastery. In his struggle against Ya'am, lord of the seas, Baal turned to Koshar, the craftsman, for weapons that would make him invincible. With these tools in hand, Baal threw down the lord of the seas into the depths, and climbed supreme into the heavens." Yambalya raised his arms skyward, revealing scars running up his forearms.

"As Baal's faithful, we follow his ways. Baal was mighty on his own. But he did not achieve victory until he formed an alliance joining his power with the strengths of another. So too, Tzidon and Israel apart are mighty nations. But their union will be incomparable. With the blessing of Baal, the fertile soil of Israel and the merchants of Tzidon will bring the nations of the world to our feet." A cheer erupted from the crowd, and Yambalya stepped back to the side of the platform.

All eyes again turned to the High Priest of Israel, who stood pale and silent. He didn't resume his speech, but rather nodded to King Ahav, who took a ring from a waiting servant and slid it smoothly onto Princess Izevel's outstretched finger. The High Priest faced the crowd. "I give you King Ahav and Queen Izevel." The crowd cheered as the King and his new Queen clasped hands, stepped out from under the canopy, and headed toward the palace.

Three court musicians escorted the King and Queen while the rest of us followed the guests out through the city gates and into the fields around the city. As long as the King and Queen were in seclusion, the musicians were allowed to eat and enjoy the festivities. The feast area was divided into three sections: one for the soldiers, one for the nobility, and one for the commoners, who were invited to the celebrations but hadn't been allowed into the city for the ceremony.

The aroma of sizzling fat reached my nose, made my stomach rumble, and brought to mind the altar at Beit El. Zim grabbed my arm, "Did you see the size of the cows they're roasting?"

"That's for the nobility," Yonaton said. "Come on, the food on our side looks fine. I'm starving."

"We could get in there if we wanted to." Zim stared beyond the guards at the roasting pit.

"How?" I asked.

"With these." Zim indicated our instruments and the dark red sashes that we'd been issued for the wedding.

"Look at us; we hardly dress like nobility." I'd borrowed Zim's mirror before the wedding, and thought the dyed sash served only to highlight the plain weave of my tunic.

"As long as we look as if we're supposed to be there, the guards will let us through."

"I don't know," Yonaton said. "That one on the left looks pretty mean."

"Stop worrying. Just start playing and follow me—and remember to stare straight ahead." He launched into a weaving rhythm and started off.

Could Zim be right? If we acted as if we belonged, would the guards let us pass? I glanced at Yonaton, who arched his eyebrows as he raised his halil to his lips. I lifted my kinnor, and my heart thumped in my chest from the thrill of the challenge. When we reached the guards, Zim stepped up his beat and closed his eyes. *Just hold the rhythm,* I told myself. *Ignore the guards. Keep moving forward.* Despite his rough tunic and wild hair, Zim passed through, drawing the two of us after him.

"Wait." The guard on the left stepped in front of Yonaton—he had looked. The guard turned to Zim, then back to me, his face knotted in confusion. I stopped playing and took a step back, not waiting for the outburst that was sure to come.

Zim called back to us, "Don't lose the tempo, they're waiting for us." My hands leapt back to the strings—Zim wasn't admitting defeat. His voice carried so much confidence that the guard looked sheepish and stepped out of the way. Once out of earshot, Zim struck a final drum roll, ending in a belly laugh. "Remember: if you believe it, it's true."

The nobility merited a far wider space than the commoners. In the center was a roasting pit, spanned by two whole oxen and numerous lambs, surrounded on three sides by trestles piled high with roasted meats, breads, and salads. My mouth watered at the smell of spices mixed with the smoke of the roasting meat. Zim walked straight to a serving table, wrapped a chunk of roast lamb in bread, and bit into it like a wolf, letting the juices flow down his chin.

My hands were sweating from the ruse we used to get past the guards. Though excited at our success, I couldn't bring myself to touch the fare. If I ate the nobles' meat, I'd be just like the shepherds in Levonah who grazed their flocks across furrowed fields. "I want to go back and eat in our area," I said. Zim laughed, but Yonaton's shoulders relaxed in relief.

"If you two want to go back, I'll come with you. Let me take a little more meat first—it's delicious. Who knows when I'll get another chance at a roast this good."

Yonaton pointed to the far corner of the nobles' area where a small crowd stood gathered around a table. "What's over there?"

"Don't know. Let's see."

From one end of the table to the other lay a carcass covered in scales with sharp teeth and bulging, lifeless eyes. The animal was split open down its middle, and five servants stood shoulder to shoulder dispensing its flesh, steaming and fragrant. "What is it?" Yonaton asked.

"I don't know." I ran my hand over the animal's skin, feeling the smoothness of the scales that crackled between my fingers. "I've never seen anything like it."

A fleck of meat hit me in the ear as someone behind me laughed. "Mountain boys. Go back to your goats." Zim extended his bread to one of the servants who balanced a piece of the creature on top of his already overflowing pile of meats. "Never seen a fish before?" He held his bread in front of us. "Sure you don't want to try?"

Yonaton glanced at me.

"No," I said.

"Just try a bit of mine. I've already taken it, and I'm not taking any more, so no one will lose if you taste it."

I reached out and broke off a small piece of Zim's fish—just a taste.

"See, it's no fun being holy all the time. Isn't it nice to grab what you want just once?"

I put the fish back on Zim's pile of meat and wiped my hand on my tunic. "I don't want it."

Zim laughed. "Please yourself. Just be careful. You don't want to wind up righteous and alone like Uriel." Zim led us back out past the guards, who paid us no heed.

In the commoners' section, Yonaton and I waited in line to get our food. There was no fish, and the meats weren't spiced, but it still smelled wonderful. Food in hand, we rejoined Zim, who handed us each a clay goblet. "I got us wine." His own goblet was already half empty.

Again I hesitated, remembering our first morning in Shomron, when I could barely rouse Zim for all the wine he'd drunk the night before. The only reason I distinguished myself at the rehearsal was because I hadn't stayed up drinking with the musicians. Now Zim was handing me a goblet with far more wine than had ever passed my lips. This was my last opportunity to impress Dov—I couldn't take any chances now. "I'll pass."

"Don't worry. I got it from this side, you don't have to feel bad about drinking it."

"It's not that. I don't want it to hurt my playing."

"A little wine isn't going to hurt your playing—it might even improve it." Zim downed a quarter of his goblet in one gulp, then wiped his mouth with the back of a greasy hand. "You're not with the prophets now. You're at a feast—probably the biggest you'll ever enjoy. Everyone is drinking and having a good time. Stop thinking so much." He held out the goblet again.

Slowly, I reached out and grasped it, then sipped at its pungent sweetness. It was much stronger than I was used to—not watered down at all. All around me people were drinking and laughing. I closed my eyes, took a large swallow, and felt my nervousness melt away.

I was swallowing the dregs of my second goblet when three sharp trumpet blasts sounded from the palace: the signal I was waiting for. The world tilted as I rose to my feet. Not up to running, I did my best to slip quickly through the crowd.

I arrived at the gates before they opened, slung the kinnor off my back, and joined the other musicians in my rotation. We fell into the same upbeat dance tune I'd played when the royal caravan arrived at Shomron. The trumpets sounded a long cry, the palace gates were thrown open, and King Ahav and Queen Izevel came forth to loud cheering. A crowd careened around them as they strode hand in hand down the hill of Shomron, out of the city gates, and over to the mass celebration.

They were led to chairs next to Izevel's parents, upon a dais at the edge of a large clearing. I joined the rest of the musicians in our position just below the stage. Adjacent to us was the section reserved for the sick and crippled, who, according to the King's custom, were given seats at the very front of the commoners' area. Ovadia stood next to the stage and commanded a constant stream of servants, who converged on him and ran off in every direction. He'd been working non-stop since returning to Shomron. Yonaton and I had helped him as much as we could when we weren't in rehearsals, delivering messages and lending our hands to the endless details to which he attended personally. I hadn't even seen him at the ceremony—he must have been too busy preparing the celebration to attend.

A clamor arose as a line of torch-bearers snaked through the crowd. They pushed the crowd back as they advanced, forming the perimeter of an open space before the royal families. Into the opening stepped a man so thin his white robes swayed as if empty. He wore a matching white turban in the same style as the High Priest of Tzidon. Approaching the platform, he bowed deeply to King Ahav. "Your Majesty, I am your humble servant Avidah. My performers and I were brought by the dyers' guild of Tzidon in honor of the royal union. With the King's permission…" King Ahav nodded in assent, "We will begin."

Dov struck the first note, and the musicians jumped into the music we'd prepared for the performance. It was a wild piece in parts, with a foreign rhythm, and despite all our practice, I feared I wouldn't keep up with the driving pace. But the wine loosened my fingertips, my dizziness was gone, and I felt a wonderful sense of freedom in its place.

Avidah withdrew to the side of the circle, just in front of the section set aside for the infirm. One of his performers carried a cedar torch into the clearing; its flame illuminated his blue robes and matching turban, the scent of its burning resin almost overpowering. He raced around the circle, his torch swinging close to the crowd, forcing people to step back to avoid the flame, pushing them farther and farther until he had more than doubled the size of the clearing. With a loud "Hiyah!" he threw his torch high in the air where it broke apart into six, smaller flames. He caught each one in turn, but each barely grazed his hand before it was back in the air again. Once he controlled all six torches, he ran along the edge of the clearing, catching and throwing the torches as he went. The crowd cheered, stomped, and clapped their hands. Back in front of the stage, he caught the torches one by one, catching three in his right hand, two in his left, and the final one in his mouth. He returned all six torches to his right hand and took his place next to Avidah.

A second performer, a sword suspended from the belt of his pink robes, stepped toward the stage holding a woven reed basket. He bowed before Ahav and Izevel, removed several gourds from his basket, and placed them on the ground before him. He drew his sword from its scabbard and held it above his head for everyone to see. The jeweled handle and polished blade glittered in the torchlight. In a flash, he slashed the sword down upon the gourds, splitting each one cleanly in two, and leaving no question: this sword was sharp.

Falling to his knees, the pink-robed performer held the sword straight above him, tipped his head back so far that the tendons on his neck stood out like ropes, and opened his mouth wide. A gasp issued from the crowd as the point of the sword descended toward his wide-stretched mouth. Only hours of steady practice kept my fingers from freezing on the strings of my kinnor. How could a man kill himself just to entertain the King and Queen on their wedding day? Watching the torchlight dance off the polished blade, I swallowed hard—why would he draw out the pain by doing it so slowly?

As the point of the sword entered his mouth, I turned away, not wanting to watch. Women screamed. I plucked furiously at my kinnor, grateful that the complex rhythm demanded so much concentration. Silence fell over the crowd, and I glanced up, expecting to see the man writhing on the ground. My fingers faltered on the strings. The performer was still on his knees, gazing up, with half the length of the sword sticking out of his mouth. How could it be anything but torture? Yet the blade kept descending.

The sword sank until nothing except the jeweled handle remained visible. Head tipped back, he rose to his feet with outstretched arms, spinning in a circle so that all could see. He turned back to the stage, fell to his knees, and grasped the hilt with both hands. In one smooth motion, he drew the sword from his mouth and held it high in the torchlight, showing that it was clean, without a trace of blood.

The swordsman returned his weapon to his belt and called out something in his guttural tongue. The juggler approached and handed him a flaming torch. Again, he threw back his head and lowered it into his mouth. He removed the extinguished torch and handed it back, receiving another one in return. When the final torch was extinguished, both men bowed toward the stage.

King Ahav nodded stiffly, his lips curled in the slightest of smiles. Queen Izevel clenched her hands in her lap, swaying to the music. She beamed at the performers, following them with her eager eyes as they moved to the edge of the clearing and stood next to Avidah. Her eyes fell on those seated behind the performers, on the special section allotted to the sick and crippled, and she stopped rocking. Her eyes narrowed upon the neediest of the land. Her serpentine look was hideous, but it lasted only half a moment. A contortionist walked on his hands into the clearing; his back and neck arched impossibly so that his feet dangled before his face. The crowd bellowed with laughter. The Queen's attention returned to the performance, her expression regaining its graceful composure.

The musicians didn't pause for a moment. Zim was right; despite my initial dizziness, the wine hadn't hurt my playing at all. I felt an unfamiliar looseness, playing faster and with more passion than usual. Dov perceived the change as well—he kept turning to watch me. Every time his eyes fell on me, I felt a jolt of energy and pictured myself dressed in a dyed linen tunic, playing in the King's court during the day, and coming home to Dahlia at night.

But the transformation in me was nothing compared to what came over Zim, who drummed with an abandon I'd never witnessed before. His closed eyes were turned toward the sky, and his hands were a blur. Sweat poured down his head and neck, and he seemed unaware of his surroundings. I wasn't the only one who noticed. Yambalya worked his way over to the musicians, drawn by Zim's ferocious rhythm, and danced to the beat of his drums.

More and more performers came forward to carry out their feats, one after the next. The contortionist was followed by a man who wrestled a bear. He received a terrible blow to the face, but walked away erect and bleeding to the roar of the crowd. The wrestler was followed by a lean man who charmed two poisonous snakes, and a massive green serpent wound itself around his body. When the performers finished, they all came forward and stood in a row opposite the stage. Avidah fell to his knees and pressed his forehead to the ground, followed immediately by his troupe.

The performers stood as one, then exited the clearing in a line. Dov signaled for the musicians to pause. I stretched my fingers and rubbed my palms, never having pushed my hands so hard before.

From beyond the edge of the crowd, a chanting rose in the guttural tongue of Tzidon. It grew louder, and the crowd parted to allow Yambalya to enter the clearing. Ten men dressed in identical violet robes, all wearing swords at their sides, followed behind. Four of them carried a large wooden chest suspended from poles on their shoulders. Yambalya directed them to lower the chest to the ground before the stage.

We hadn't rehearsed any music for this and watched Dov for a signal, but for the first time that evening, he had no plan. With a quick strike of his nevel, he started us back into the piece we'd performed for the juggler, but we didn't get far. Yambalya waved his arms, and the song died on our strings. He patted Zim's shoulder. "Just you. You come play." He drew Zim into the clearing, positioning him next to the wooden chest.

Yambalya faced the stage and raised his arms. "We must now give thanks to Baal for arranging this union, binding it with blood." His voice boomed across the clearing. "We must humble ourselves before Baal. Ask that he bless this union and bring prosperity to this land." A murmur rippled through the crowd. Yambalya signaled Zim, who began a high paced rhythm.

The violet robed priests lifted the heavy cover of their box. From inside, they removed a carved pedestal. Then, with heads bowed, they placed a golden statue upon it. It was a larger version of the bronze statue that Izevel had stationed in the palace, with a jagged sword in its upraised arm and the same helmet rising straight behind its head. Two priests approached Yambalya with a jar and a torch. He raised the jar and chanted in his native tongue, his words rising in a gut-wrenching cry as he splashed blood red wine before the pedestal. Then he knelt, torch in hand, and lit a pile of incense before the statue.

Yambalya touched his forehead to the ground. No longer distracted by the music, my eyes fixed on Yambalya, riveted. When he arose, he tightened his belt and slipped his arms out of his sleeves. The top of his robes fell away, revealing deep scars that snaked across his back and chest. His fellow priests likewise shed the top of their robes, revealing more ropes of scarred flesh.

"We are the servants of Baal!" cried Yambalya in a voice that shook the air. He drew the weapon from his scabbard,* and I gasped as he held it high above his head. It wasn't a sword at all, but a broad, flat knife. Had it been stone rather than iron, it would have been nearly identical to my father's.

"We have no master but Baal!" Yambalya waved the knife in a wide circle above his head. His thick muscles displayed almost enough power to split the statue in two—but no stroke against the idol ever came. Instead, the High Priest of the Baal brought the weapon slowly down and drew its blade across his own chest. Screams arose from the crowd as blood flowed down his torso. He slapped the flat of the blade against his chest, speckling the golden statue with red.

The other priests now drew their own knives, cut themselves, and screamed out, "Baal answer us!" Their knives were identical to Yambalya's, almost indistinguishable from the one I felt bulging against my thigh. Shimon told me my knife had only one purpose and should never be used for anything else. Could this have been the purpose? Was this the reason Uriel didn't want me to know what it was for?

The priests formed a circle around the idol, and the ground grew muddy with their blood. As they slashed and howled, Zim's drumming surged in intensity. The priests circled their god in a gruesome dance, stopping at intervals to tear at their flesh and call out to the star-filled sky. The crowd stood silent now, too stunned to do anything but stare.

Yambalya faced the royal couples. "The offering of blood has been made. We must now bow down. We must humble ourselves before Baal. Then Baal, master of the storm, will hear our pleas. He will bring rain upon this land. And it will flow with his blessing."

Queen Izevel fell quickly to her knees and pressed her face to the ground as her dark hair spread like a stain around her head. She was followed by both her parents, who moved more slowly, but with similar resolution. King Ahav remained seated, his eyes on the crowd, his fingers rubbing the hem of his sleeve. He glanced back and forth between his prostrate bride and the crowd around him. Ovadia stood next to the stage, glaring at Yambalya.

Yambalya turned a slow circle, blood trickling down his chest, scrutinizing the crowd. Few met his gaze. "People of Tzidon," he called out in his booming voice, "Humble yourselves before Baal." There was a rustling of clothes as the foreign guests dropped to the earth.

Yambalya faced King Ahav, whose eyes still jumped between his queen, the priest, and the people. "Great King! You wish prosperity for your land. Humble yourself! Bow down before Baal, most powerful of gods! Only he can fulfill your desire."

Queen Izevel raised her face from the ground. Ahav's eyes stopped straying and sank into his wife's gaze. His hands, held tightly in his lap, loosened. Green eyes wide, Izevel reached toward Ahav with one slender arm rising from the sleeve of her bridal dress. Tapered fingers reached toward him, beckoning. He rose at the coaxing of his young bride, reeling like a man overcome by wine. His eyes still on hers, he knelt to the ground and bowed until his forehead touched the wood of the dais.

"People of Israel. Your King and Queen want rain and prosperity for you. Show Baal that you desire it for yourselves and you will be answered." The crowd remained silent. Zim's drumming filled the clearing, the ecstatic beat echoing off the mountainside. Heads turned, seeking guidance. One by one, noblemen lowered themselves to the ground to bow before the Baal.

Dov hesitated, but once most of the nobles prostrated themselves, he too knelt and pressed his forehead to the ground. At this act of leadership, the rest of the court musicians bowed as well.

My mind focused on the knives wielded by Yambalya and his disciples. *They drew their own blood so easily—would they hesitate to shed the blood of those who defied them?* My hand dropped to my tunic and grasped the bulge of my knife beneath. It would be so easy to join them, to drop to the ground and be spared their wrath. Yonaton's hands trembled on his halil. My knees buckled as if my body had already made up its mind to yield, but my stubborn heart was not ready to give in. Daniel stood resolute, clutching his nevel. Seeing his defiance fortified me. *If he could resist, so could I.* Yonaton moved in closer, and we remained standing together. I gazed toward the stage to see what Ovadia would do, but he was gone.

Most of the nobility were now on the ground, but the majority of the commoners still stood. I glanced at the section next to ours, that special section reserved for the destitute, many of whom depended upon the kindness of King Ahav for their very bread. Yet, among the dozens of broken and poor, not one bowed down. One man, bent with age, who had sat throughout the entire performance, pushed hard upon his walking stick with a trembling hand, and drew himself to his feet. He stared at Yambalya, a fiery challenge in his eye.

The High Priest of the Baal surveyed the crowd. He nodded approvingly at the Israelite nobility, but shook his head as he scanned the rest of the people, almost none of whom met his eyes. He gazed upon the lame, united in their defiance, his eyes meeting those of the bent old man. Their eyes locked. I focused on Yambalya's knife, waiting for him to strike. But he only shook with laughter and turned his back on the old man. He sheathed his knife, lowered himself to his knees, and touched his head to the ground before the golden statue.

When Yambalya stood, everyone on the ground rose with him. He raised his arms again, shaking the dirt and blood from his chest, and danced to Zim's frantic beat. His brother priests joined in, drawing others into the clearing to dance.

On the stage, the two kings and their queens returned to their seats and smiled upon the revelers. Izevel twirled her long, thin wrists in time to the music. Order broke down as people on all sides entered the clearing to dance. Dov signaled that we musicians were on our own. Some picked up their instruments and tried to keep up with Zim; others jumped into the circle to join the revelry.

I picked up my kinnor and started to play, but Yonaton tucked his halil into his belt and said, "Come on, let's dance." My eyes scanned the clearing—the box holding the Baal was gone. What could be the harm in dancing now? I slung my instrument onto my back and followed Yonaton right into the thick of the crowd.

Whoever leads the people on the right path will not come to sin. But one who leads the people astray will not even get a chance to repent.

Pirkei Avot 5:21

The Dispersal

The tight grip on my shoulder woke me, but it was cold rain on my face that forced my eyes open. I lay on my back, squinting dumbly at the clouds hanging just above the mountaintops. Heavy drops pocked the ground, and a fresh wind stirred dust across the clearing.

My head throbbed—I wanted nothing more than to slide back into sleep, rain or no—but Yonaton grabbed my hand and pulled me up. The world tilted as my body came to a sitting position. Bitter bile rose in my throat, bringing with it memories of dancing around the huge bonfire late into the night, whirling until the wine got the better of me. I couldn't recall lying down.

The rain fell heavier, rousing sleepers all around us. Grunts gave way to groans and curses as farmers staggered to their feet. It wasn't just the wet awakening that tried them: it was the season. Still mid-summer, the early *yoreh* rains were not due for another two months.* All across the Kingdom, the abundant wheat harvest—blessed by the same late *malkosh* rains that had destroyed so much of the barley crop—was cut and drying in the fields. If a downpour soaked the grain, it could rot in storage, destroying the year's harvest.

As this knowledge set in, farmers stared wildly at the looming sky above them. Only one man could help them now, and they moved in a pack toward the sound of drumming which still echoed from the clearing. "Come on." Yonaton pulled me to my feet. I stumbled behind him over the uneven ground. The motion made my stomach roll but cleared some of the fog from my head.

The mob swelled on the path, and stifled cries of "The *yoreh*, the *yoreh*!" filled the air. The strands of gray cloud hanging down from the sky evoked no fear in me, though. I'd never seen rains this early before, but had heard other shepherds call them *matnat ro'im*, the shepherd's gift. Even a brief downpour now would bring up grasses in pockets and hollows all around Levonah, perfect grazing to nourish a flock until the winter rains. Farmers might tremble, but to a wise shepherd it was a treasure.

In the clearing, Yambalya and his disciples danced to Zim's thunderous rhythm, which somehow held strong through the night. Their chanting took on new strength as the crowd flowed back like a tide, and they called out in celebration of Baal's speedy answer to their prayers. Yambalya's belly shook with laughter at the panic on the farmers' faces. He stretched his head back so that raindrops fell into his mouth. "Baal is merciful," he called out. "He will not destroy your crops. Not yet. This is but a sign. A sign…" he lowered his gaze to the crowd, "…and a test." The last word came out with a hiss that sent a shudder right through me.

"You will bring in your harvest before Baal unleashes the power of the storm wind." He pointed his finger at the farmers like a father reprimanding his children. "He who fails to heed Baal's power and leaves his grain in the field will surely see his harvest rot."

A circle of cowed Israelites surrounded Yambalya. He raised his muscular arms, and his eyes rolled back into his head. A single drop of blood rolled down one arm from his wrist. As it reached his elbow, he gave a final triumphant shout, and the rain came to an end.

The royal family would continue to celebrate for a full seven days of feasting up at the palace, but the wedding's end signaled the end of the festivities for all but the highest nobility. Most of the revelers had already planned to leave that day, but now, with Yambalya's threat ringing in their ears, they ran to gather their belongings and begin their journeys home straight away.

Yonaton and I walked silently toward Ovadia's house. We were also leaving that day; the court musicians would suffice to play for the week of celebrations, and we were still needed at the gathering. The streets of Shomron were flooded with people, many running past us up the hill and more already heading out.

"You look awful," Batya said as we crossed the threshold. "You boys get ready to go, and I'll fix you something."

When we descended the ladder with our sacks, one of the maidservants poured out two steaming cups of steeped herbs. "Drink that," Batya said. I took a sip and gagged. "I know it tastes awful, but it will help. You boys should also have something to eat. You have a long journey ahead."

We had barely begun our meal when Daniel arrived. "Finish up," he said brusquely. "The donkeys are ready. If we start soon, we might make it back before nightfall."

"We haven't been paid," Yonaton said.

Daniel held up a leather pouch bound with a thong. "Dov came to pay us this morning. I collected for both of you."

Daniel's pouch held more copper than I'd ever owned, almost as much as promised for the entire gathering. I tried to look pleased—if Daniel read the disappointment on my face, he'd ask questions. I remembered all too clearly the first night of the gathering when he'd smashed my dream of studying for prophecy. Even if I was deluding myself with thoughts of playing in the King's court, I wasn't ready for Daniel to crush this dream as well—certainly not with my head already pounding and my stomach barely holding down my morning bread.

No, if this dream was going to collapse, I wanted to hear it from Dov himself. Only he could tell me if there would be a place for my kinnor or not. I hadn't seen him since the dancing began the night before, when he still had a smudge of dirt on his forehead from bowing before the Baal. And it wasn't just him—every one of the court musicians bowed as well. Was that what it would mean to play in the King's court—bowing before the Baal? Would that be the price of getting Dahlia?

The pounding in my head grew more insistent, in a way that had nothing to do with last night's wine. Daniel wouldn't need to smash this dream—it caved in on its own. I hadn't bowed last night, even when I feared that Yambalya's men would run their blades through any who refused. I made my choice, and once my stubborn heart decided on a path, it was set. I wouldn't bow now either, despite the possible rewards.

I took my last bite and rose to follow Daniel, hating myself for falling into another silly dream, but no longer regretting missing Dov. More disappointing was leaving without seeing Ovadia. He was close to both the prophets and the King, the one person I really wanted to ask about the wedding, the Baal, and the rain. But Ovadia was at the palace, and there was no time to find him. We thanked Batya, who handed us a sack of rations for our trip, and hurried out after Daniel.

While we packed the donkeys, Zim strolled over to the house, clutching his drum under one arm. His eyes were glassy, but his smile was wild with joy.

"Hey Zim," Yonaton called. "Where are your things?"

"They're still in the musicians' quarters."

"You better run and get them. We're leaving."

"I'm not coming with you." Zim took his drum out from under his arm and tapped it gently with his fingertips. "I came to say goodbye."

"You're staying for the week of celebrations?" A pang of jealousy cut through me.

"Longer. Yambalya invited me to join him."

"You're not coming back to play for the prophets at all?"

"Playing for Yambalya all through the night, I poured all of my body and soul into my drum." Zim's eyes had a faraway look. "That's what devotion should look like."

I winced at the word *devotion*. Uriel used the same word to describe the Way of the prophets. I pictured Yambalya drawing his knife across his chest. *Is that what devotion looks like to you, Zim?*

"We'll miss you," Yonaton said.

"I'll miss you too. But I have a feeling it won't be for long. You've both got talent, and you're only going to get better. From what I've seen, good musicians rarely stay in one place. Unless they decide to marry like Daniel here." He slapped Daniel on the shoulder.

"So you'll be moving up to Tzur?" I asked.

Zim shook his head with a grin.

"Isn't Tzur the capital of Tzidon?"

"It is, but Yambalya isn't going back. Queen Izevel asked him to stay. She promised to build him a temple right here in Shomron."

Zim put down his drum and threw one arm around me and the other around Yonaton, drawing us both roughly to his body. He released us, picked up his drum, and stood playing while we rode away.

Beyond the mountains ringing Shomron, the road curved south and flattened out. Daniel tied our donkey to his with a lead rope. "Your eyes are barely open," he said in response to my protest. "This way you can sleep and let the donkey do the walking."

The animal's slow plodding drew me wistfully back to our swift ride to the wedding. On horseback, the journey took less than a day, even with the lightly burdened donkeys following along behind. Now I couldn't see how Daniel hoped to get us back to the gathering before nightfall. The donkey rocked and swayed as we ambled over the bumpy road, and before long Yonaton's head slumped forward against my back. I fought to keep my eyes open, but sleep overtook me as well.

I awoke to a shaking, like a tremor at my back. Opening my eyes, I saw steep-sloped mountains surrounding us. Daniel trotted confidently, singing quietly to himself as our donkey followed close behind. What woke me was Yonaton weeping quietly against my back. I lifted my head, but he immediately choked off his soft cry.

"What's wrong?"

"Nothing." Yonaton sat up and wiped his eyes on his sleeve.

"You can tell me." I twisted on the donkey's back so I could catch Yonaton's eyes over my shoulder. *Tears—as if they'll help anything.* The Holy One knows I cried plenty when I was younger. But the tears never did me any good—I was no better off when they stopped flowing than when they started. Aunt Leah cried often, and I always found it hard to look at her when she did. Dahlia mostly stopped a few years ago at the same time I did. She learned quickly that tears were the fastest way to lose my interest.

On that first night of the gathering, Zim and Daniel both turned away at the mention of my parents' deaths. But Yonaton hadn't looked away; his eyes had actually teared, even though mine remained dry. I forced myself to hold Yonaton's eyes. He hadn't looked away then, and I would stay with him now. "What is it?"

Yonaton hesitated, but only for a moment. *He's no orphan; trust comes more easily to him.* "It's my father. I know what he's like. He won't gather in his grain early. He'll say it's betrayal to fear the Baal. What if our harvest is ruined? We don't have enough stored to get us through winter."

"You think Yambalya can make the rains come early?"

Yonaton gazed up at the dark patches of clouds moving across the summer sky. "What if he can?" he said softly.

I didn't know what to say—I was a shepherd, not a farmer. I was about as far from sharing the farmers' worries about the early rains as Yambalya; I looked forward to them. I was no more concerned about the *yoreh* spoiling wheat than I had been a few months earlier when the *malkosh* ruined so much barley. The late rains made grazing easier this summer than in summers past. The early rains would do the same: replenish grasses, keep the flock healthier, and make my life easier.

But Yonaton's pain struck me in an unfamiliar way. A few months ago, it was the farmers who suffered when the barley spoiled. This morning, it was the farmers who would suffer if the rain soaked the wheat. It was easy to bear the pain of farmers I didn't know—especially when they had land and I had none—but it was much harder to gaze into the teary eyes of a friend. *Did his father really fear the Holy One so much that he would let his family starve? Were there many more like him in Israel?* Still not finding any words, I reached back and squeezed Yonaton's hand.

By early afternoon, the clouds burned off, leaving the sky a bright blue. The sun baked the moisture from the ground and Yonaton's melancholy dissipated with the clouds. "You know, I think the wheat will be fine," he said. "The prophets look out for Israel. They wouldn't let Yambalya destroy the harvest of whoever doesn't fear the Baal."

Yonaton's new attitude sounded forced to my ears, perhaps covering up for the shame of having shown his fear. Either way, I breathed more easily, relieved I no longer had to console a weepy friend.

We left the mountains south of Shomron behind and rode through the massive brown hills I knew so well. When we passed the turnoff to Levonah, I searched the road leading toward the gate, hoping to catch sight of my flock on the hills. The land was quiet and empty.

We ate the midday meal under a carob tree just past Levonah. "We're making good time," Daniel said. "With a little luck, we'll arrive before dark."

"But when I came with Master Uriel it took us two days from here," I said. "We were walking, but we weren't moving much slower than we are now."

"You went through Beit El. Our path will be more direct."

Yonaton swallowed the bread in his mouth. "Then why did Ovadia take us on the Beit El road?"

"Our way is too rough for horses. But the donkeys can make it if we lead them."

After the meal, we continued south on the King's Road for a short stretch, then Daniel turned the donkeys onto a narrow path that climbed up a broken hillside before the road to Shiloh. Once over the ridge-line, the path dropped into a gully, and we dismounted to lead the donkeys down the descent. We picked our way down a series of ridges and valleys, dropping ever lower, the hillsides gradually shifting to lighter shades of brown as the vegetation thinned, finally taking on the yellow tone of the hills around Emek HaAsefa. Daniel was right; this way was far shorter than the road through Beit El. I recalled how my legs ached from walking those first days with Uriel. *He couldn't have led us that way just to alert Master Yosef; a simple messenger could have done that.*

When I asked Daniel, he laughed. "How many people have we passed on this path?"

"None."

"There's your answer."

"What do you mean?"

"What do you think Master Uriel does when he's not at the gathering?"

I had never given any thought to the prophet's life before. "Return home to his family?"

Daniel shook his head. "He travels the land. People go to him for prophecy, for advice, for blessings, for judgment of their disputes. It's not his way to seek the shortest path."

I thought back to Zim's comment at the wedding—if I wasn't careful, I'd wind up holy and alone like Uriel. *Did he not have a family?*

The sun dipped below the hills, casting a pink and orange glow across the sky as we descended into Emek HaAsefa. As the caves high on the hillsides came into view, my eye sought out our cave, the highest of them all, with its rock ledge out front where the four of us had first played. I was surprised at a sudden blossoming of warmth in my chest—like coming home.

Daniel approached the servant with the punctured ear who was cleaning up the cooking area after the evening meal. "Is there anything left? We just returned from Shomron."

"Yes, Master Uriel had us put aside dishes for each of you." The servant gestured to a table with three large portions of bread and lentils. A grin curled up my cheeks as I wondered if the prophet had received a vision that Zim wouldn't be returning with us, or if this was another instinct of his heart.

The servant approached me and spoke quietly, so that I alone could hear. "The portion on the right is for you." This pattern of food being set aside for me had recurred at every meal since the gathering began. I always received a small portion of the most basic foods, never any meat or cheese. Why I was the only one restricted in what I could eat, I didn't know, but each time I took my meager portion and rebelliously added anything I wanted. Now the portion set aside for me was no smaller than the other two and even had a helping of cheese. Was Uriel warming to me?

After the evening meal, we walked to our cave in the twilight. "I'll be back later," Yonaton said, just as I rolled out my mat. He laid his belongings beside mine. "I promised my mother I'd tell her when we got back."

"You're going in the dark?"

Yonaton peered out at the indigo sky. "The moon's still up, that'll give me enough light."

I finished laying out my bedroll and retrieved my kinnor. "Then Daniel and I will just have to start playing without you."

Daniel chortled. "You can play on your own." He lay down on his sheepskin mat. "I'm going to sleep."

"Already?" Yonaton asked.

"I need the sleep if I'm going to make it back to my farm tomorrow."

I turned to Daniel. "You're leaving too?"

"I've got to get home and bring in my harvest before it rots in the field. You heard Yambalya, this morning's rain was only a warning. If we fail to heed it, we may not be so blessed in the future. I'm leaving at dawn. Yonaton, if I were you, I'd tell your family to bring in theirs as well."

The thin veil of confidence that masked Yonaton's face all afternoon melted, exposing raw fear. Without another word, he ran out of the cave toward home.

Zim's reaction to Yambalya was one thing—but Daniel? "After all these years playing for the prophets, you're going to heed the Baal?"

Daniel shook his head. "All these years with the prophets have shown me that all kinds of things are possible."

"But you refused to bow at the wedding."

"True, but I also felt the rain on my face this morning." Daniel folded his arms behind his head. "If Yambalya is wrong and I bring in my crops early, what have I lost? But if he's right, and I leave them in the fields…" Daniel sighed, put down his head, and closed his eyes.

I rested my kinnor next to my sleeping mat—I didn't feel like playing alone. I left the cave hoping to catch Yonaton, but he was out of sight—probably halfway home already at the pace he was moving. I made my way down to the valley floor, unsure what I was searching for. All was silent; the servants had finished cleaning up, the disciples were all asleep. I strolled with a heavy step toward the pomegranate tree under which we played, its unripe flower-tipped fruits just visible in the moonlight, and sat down with my back against its smooth and slender trunk. A dark hole opened in my chest, swallowing down the excitement of Shomron and the wedding that had bloomed there. They seemed like a distant memory now. Zim wasn't coming back, and Daniel was leaving. Would Yonaton be next? *Will I have to play on my own for the rest of the gathering?*

I had barely sat down when I stood up again—there was no point in staying awake on my own. I returned slowly along the path, its worn track a pale gray in the light of the two-thirds moon. A lone, tall figure strode ahead of me, reaching the musicians' cave first and stepping inside. I hurried into the cave and almost ran into the man.

"Ah Lev, I was looking for you," Uriel whispered, resting his hand on my shoulder. "I want to hear about the wedding. Let us go to my cave so that we don't wake Daniel."

Uriel led the way back down the path, and I followed behind in silence. Four lamps burned inside his cave, dazzling my eyes as I stepped in from the dark night. I sat opposite Uriel, whose slate-blue eyes fell upon mine, expectant. I wasn't sure what he wanted me to say, so I started at the beginning.

"When we got to Shomron, Ovadia told Yonaton and me that we'd be staying with him, not with Daniel and Zim in the musicians' quarters." I paused, hoping he would direct me, but he only nodded for me to continue.

As words spilled out, I found myself saying more than I intended, talking about things of no importance. Why would the prophet care about us delivering Ovadia's messages, or the commoners wrestling the bear? I kept scrutinizing the *navi* for some sign of what he was after, but was met with a steady gaze that drew the stream of images out of me.

When I finally ran out of words, two of the lamps had burned out—the charcoal smell of their wicks filling the cave. I slumped forward on the stool, exhausted. Uriel stared at me in silence, his face unmoving. The prophet's gaze felt heavier now that I was no longer speaking, and I dropped my eyes to the table.

"So Queen Izevel and her family all bowed before the Baal?"

A knot clenched in my stomach. "Yes."

"Then King Ahav bowed?"

In my mind, I saw the King's hesitation give way before his bride's coaxing. "Yes."

"Then the people bowed as well?"

"Many of them."

"And Ovadia?"

"I looked for him, but he had gone."

"Then in the morning, there was rain?"

"Yes."

"The people were afraid, and in their fear, they turned to the priest of the Baal."

This wasn't a question, but I still answered, "Yes."

Uriel's gaze rose to the ceiling of the cave. "The lamp of darkness is burning brightly once again,"* he said, more to himself than to me. The creases on his face deepened in the unsteady light. "May the Holy One protect Israel."

The prophet suddenly seemed so old and frail. "The lamp of darkness?"

Uriel didn't answer, as though unaware that I'd spoken. He stood quickly, knocking over his stool as he rose. He lowered himself onto a reed mat on the floor, his feet before him, his knees bent to his chest. "I would like you to play for me. We may need to end the gathering early."

"Why?"

"As you said, the rains might be coming. Whoever leaves his crops in the fields risks ruin. Many of our disciples are farmers. We cannot cause them to suffer such losses."

I thought back to what Yonaton said on our journey back to the valley. "But can't the prophets stop the rains?"

"Even if I could, I wouldn't do so."

"Why not?" I couldn't keep the challenge out of my voice. The image of panicked farmers gathering around Yambalya rose in my mind, and the taste of bile returned to my tongue. It was strange—I had cared little for their panic that morning; I was even looking forward to the early rains. But I must have swallowed some of Yonaton's fear on the ride back to the gathering. *Was the prophet also afraid of the Baal?*

"If we stop the rains, it will only bring the people to fear us more than Yambalya," Uriel said with resignation. "It becomes a battle of one fear over another."

"Isn't that what you want, that the people should fear the Holy One more than the Baal?"

"No! A true turning to the Holy One is the end of fear, not a step down its path."

"So none of the prophets will do anything to stop this?"

The old *navi* hesitated. "I don't think so."

I heard Uriel's uncertainty. Did this mean not all the prophets agreed with him? Was there still a chance to stop the rains? Perhaps if Uriel knew, if he really understood how much fear the threat of rain was causing, he'd decide that closing the gathering early wasn't enough—that this was a time to stand up to Yambalya. I had held back only one detail of our journey, one that I left out so as not to embarrass a friend. But even that would be worth it if it could make Uriel comprehend the humiliation of the people…and hold off the rains.

"When we were riding home from the gathering, Yonaton cried. That's how scared he was that his father would refuse to listen to Yambalya and their harvest would be lost." I flushed as I spoke, horrified to think of Yonaton's embarrassment if he ever found out. "Without the wheat harvest, they don't have enough grain to get through the winter. They're not the only ones."

Uriel slipped out of the position he'd assumed in readiness for prophecy, crossing his legs so he could sit up on the reed mat to face me. "And you feel that Yonaton's tears show what?"

"They show suffering. They show fear."

"And weakness?"

I didn't want to call Yonaton weak, but Uriel was right—in that moment riding together, that's exactly what I thought. "Yes."

"You have much to learn about strength, Lev. Would you consider the constipated man strong?" Uriel fixed me with a penetrating glance. *Could he see that I, who cried so much as a child, had blocked my heart, and not cried for over five years?* "Yonaton's tears are not a weakness—they're his greatest strength. Indeed, if all of Israel could cry out as Yonaton has, we would have nothing to fear from Yambalya." Uriel stretched his long legs before him again, rubbing the underside of his thigh. "Now, if you could please play for me."

I swallowed, my body tense. *How would tears hurt Yambalya? The more our tears flowed, the deeper he'd laugh. He'd brush them aside as easily as he had the glare of the old, bent man the night before.* But the time for discussion had passed. I needed to play, which posed a different problem. "I don't have my kinnor."

"I'm sure you will manage."

I surveyed the cave, hoping to find something to make music with. Lacking anything better, I drummed on the table. Tension flowed out through my hands with every beat against the heavy wood, and soon a rhythm took hold. I opened my mouth in song, weaving deep vocal tones into the beat. It wasn't the best music I ever made, but it seemed to work. By the time the third lamp burned out, Uriel trembled with the spirit of prophecy.

I stopped drumming. In the silence, an image of Yambalya rose in my mind, his taut skin covered in scars and sweat, drawing his knife across his chest, showing all of Israel that he didn't fear spilling his own blood. Next, I saw farmers' faces as the rain fell upon the celebrations, and heard Yambalya's deep laughter at their terror. Then I observed Uriel, old and gray, trembling in a heap on the floor. It was easy to guess which of the two the people would follow.

Uriel pushed himself to a sitting position, his face ashen, the creases in his face like knife cuts in the light of the remaining lamp. "The rains are indeed coming." He stretched out a hand for me to help him to his feet. His palm felt rough, like the scales of the fish at the wedding. I overestimated his weight and pulled harder than necessary, causing him to stumble. The prophet regained his balance and smoothed his tunic. "I must speak to the other masters about ending the gathering early."

"You really won't do anything to stop the rains?"

"I will not." Uriel placed both hands on my shoulders this time, holding my eyes in his. "There is no greater blessing than peace,* Lev. Peace is so great that for its sake the Holy One overlooks our failures, even the people bowing to strange gods. But once peace is broken, there is little left but judgment. In a time of judgment, our sins are recalled and accounted for. The devastation may be great indeed. You are too young to remember the wars that ravaged this kingdom not so long ago. Believe me; it is nothing we want to return to."

Uriel took several steps toward the entrance, then turned back to face me. "I know your words come from your courage as much as from your youth. This courage will serve you well. Indeed, it already has. It was no small thing refusing to humble yourself before the Baal."

I stood straighter. "No, I did not bow." Uriel nodded and stepped toward the entrance. I added proudly, "I've bowed only before the Holy One."

The old *navi*'s brow furrowed as he half-turned back to me. "You bowed to the Holy One?"

"Yes," I nodded. "In Beit El. When you sent me to Master Yosef, I also visited the altar. I wanted to make an offering," I added with a sigh, "but I'm still too young."

Uriel turned to face me fully, his eyes narrowed. "But you bowed?"

"Yes."

A tremor passed through me as the prophet's glare pinned me, helpless. My earlier thoughts of Uriel as a weak, old man disappeared. In his suddenly hard eyes, I sensed an untold strength within his aged body. That strength, boiling with anger, now concentrated itself on me. I felt as I had the night before, watching Yambalya, knife in hand, glaring at those who refused to bow—anticipating a strike.

Finally, he turned away and stepped toward the cave entrance, his body sinking back into weariness. "You may sleep now."

The rasp of hide against stone woke me from an uneasy sleep. I opened my eyes to see Daniel rolling up his sheepskin mat in the gleam of an early morning sun. I dressed quietly so as not to wake Yonaton, stepped out of the cave, and sat on one of the boulders where the four of us first played music together. Clouds colored the eastern sky with shades of watered wine as Daniel emerged, his nevel in one hand, a sack slung over his shoulder. "I'll see you next year?" he asked.

I pictured Uriel's expression from the night before. *Would the prophet even want me back?* "I don't know."

"Return if you can." Daniel hitched his sack higher. "But even if you don't make it back, even if you have only your sheep for an audience, never stop playing your kinnor."

I didn't need anyone to tell me to keep playing music; it was the one thing that brought me joy that I could carry with me wherever I would go in the wild.

But Daniel's eyes were suddenly hard, and his beard stiffened on his chest. I had seen him this serious only once before, two nights ago when he refused to bow to the Baal. It was this that made me ask, "Why not?'

Daniel rubbed a hand along the wooden frame of his nevel and stared out over the valley. "Twelve years ago, my master told me the same thing I told you, that I could stay with the prophets, playing for them year-round, just as he did."

"But you didn't want to?"

"I did." His head dropped as he spoke. "I stayed with them for over a year."

"Why did you leave?"

"My father was getting old—he could no longer handle the farm by himself. One day he fell and injured his leg. I had to go back—I had responsibilities. My master was disappointed, but he understood. Before I left, he told me what I've just told you, that I must never stop playing."

"Why not?"

Daniel lifted his head and caught my eye. "The power of music surged inside me. Every power a person has must be expressed, otherwise, it decays, and decay is a small death. The Holy One forbids us to resign ourselves to death."*

"So that's why you return?"

"Yes, every summer, even though I now have a family of my own and my responsibilities have only grown."

Uriel's stern countenance again rose in my mind's eye. I felt even more certain that he wouldn't want me back. "So even if I can't return—"

"Even if you can't return, you must continue to play. Never let this spark inside you die. But I believe you will return. You didn't receive a kinnor like that to play it alone in the wilderness."

My hand slipped to my side where my kinnor normally hung, feeling only empty air. "What do you mean?"

"The workmanship is unmistakable. It's prophet-made."

"Prophet-made? But I got it from my uncle."

Daniel's beard quivered as he shook his head once. "That kinnor was made by no local craftsman. I don't know how it reached your hands, but I doubt whoever gave it to you aspired for you to play before sheep."

"What do you mean 'whoever?' I told you my uncle gave it to me."

Daniel allowed himself a half smile. "I see. And your uncle is quite the musician, is he?"

My head cocked to the side. "No, I've never seen him play."

"A collector then? Your uncle has many fine craftsman-made objects lying about the house that he has no need for?" Daniel didn't bother keeping the scoffing tone from his voice now, and I allowed myself to smirk along with him—we both knew I didn't come from nobility.

"Admit it, Lev," Daniel's tone grew serious again, "even if you did receive that kinnor from your uncle, there's more to the story than you know. When a prophet's treasure winds up in one's hands, it's rarely happenstance. If you ever learn more, let me know; I always appreciate a good story. But now, I must start for home before the sun gets any higher—I have much work ahead of me." Daniel raised a hand in farewell and turned down the trail.

I stepped into the cave and retrieved my kinnor, and examined it in the growing daylight. I ran my fingertips along the olive wood frame, as if seeing for the first time the smoothness of its surface, the precision of the carving, and the flawless joints. Truly, there was nothing in my uncle's house that approached the fineness of it. I'd been so fixated on everything I lacked, I failed to notice all those years I held a treasure.

Yonaton stepped out of the cave into the brightening day, his arms raised in a yawn. "Has Daniel gone?"

"Yes, he's just left for home."

"Too bad, I would have liked to say goodbye."

"How are things with your family?"

"Not good. My father refuses to take in the harvest—he got angry that I even suggested it."

"He might change his mind now. Master Uriel saw last night that the rains are going to come early."

"Oh?" Yonaton's shoulders relaxed, and a smile brightened his face. "If a *navi* says so, that will be enough for my father."

"They're serving the morning meal in the clearing if you want to go."

"Sounds good." Yonaton stretched his arms above his head again. "We've never made it to the morning meal here before."

The sun was rising over the eastern hills, and the disciples were already sitting in the field eating by the time we joined them. One of the cooks handed me a small piece of bread, a single dried fig, and twelve kernels of toasted grain from where it had been set aside in the cooking area. The portion was the smallest I'd ever received. Was this a further sign of Uriel's displeasure? I stepped forward to help myself to more of everything, and again none of the servants protested. Both Yonaton and I took much larger portions than we had on the first night of the gathering. This made me think of Zim, though neither of us could compete with his appetite. I felt suddenly lonely despite Yonaton's presence.

Silence fell over the disciples, and we all shifted our attention to the center of the eating area where the three masters now stood. "We have received word,"

Uriel began. "The rains will indeed come early this year. The gathering will come to a close so that disciples can return home and attend to their harvests." There was a barely audible sigh from the *bnei nevi'im*—had they already heard what had happened at the wedding?

Uriel and Tzadok both appeared calm, their faces serene as they met the searching gazes of the disciples. Yosef scowled at the ground.

Uriel continued, "I will remain here with any wishing to stay and continue training. To those who are leaving, may you be blessed with an early and abundant harvest. You are now free to go."

Most of the disciples hastened to prepare for the trip home. Yonaton and I turned our attention to our meal and were soon among the only ones in the clearing.

A tall disciple named Tuvia approached me. "Master Uriel asked me to escort you back to your uncle's. I need to ride past Levonah on my way back home."

"But I'm not a farmer. I don't need to go back for the harvest."

"Then speak to Master Uriel—but do it quickly, because I need to go. He also asked me to give you these." He handed each of us a pouch of copper.

Yonaton turned his pouch over in his hand and examined the contents. "This is how much we were supposed to receive for the entire gathering, but we haven't even played for a week."

I poured out my pouch and counted as well. Yonaton was right—the entire summer's wages were there.

Tuvia gazed up at a small cloud in the otherwise clear sky. "I'm just the messenger. Speak to Master Uriel if you want, but you'll need to do it quickly."

Uriel was on the far side of the clearing talking to Yosef, his back to us. He wouldn't have arranged a ride home and paid full wages for the entire summer if he wanted me to stay. "I'll get my things."

Tuvia nodded. "I'll wait for you at the top of the hill."

"Master Uriel might not realize that you're not needed for the harvest," Yonaton said. "Maybe you should speak to him."

"He knows." I avoided his eyes. "If he's sending me home, he doesn't want…" I swallowed, "He doesn't need me." I didn't understand why bowing to the Holy One would anger Uriel, but I had no desire to talk about it—not even with Yonaton. "We should go pack."

Neither of us spoke as we gathered our few possessions and descended the trail back to the clearing. Yonaton kicked rocks along the ground. I searched for the right words—saying goodbye to Yonaton felt different than parting from Zim or Daniel. But words were never my strength. I stepped forward and embraced my friend. When I let go, I offered Yonaton a weak smile and turned up the hill.

Tuvia was waiting for me at the top, mounted on a horse. "Tie your things down and climb up."

"How do I get on?" I asked as I strapped my rolled-up sleeping mat on top of his belongings. My only other time on a horse, I used a boulder to climb on behind Ovadia.

"Place your foot in that strap there, and give me your hand. No, your other foot." Tuvia pulled, and I brought my leg over the horse. "Now hold on." I wrapped my arms around Tuvia, and with a kick to the horse's flank we started off toward the road. By the time I thought to glance back, I saw nothing but the hills behind us.

*"Until I arrived at the gathering, I thought prophecy was simply a gift from the Holy One."**

"Indeed, it is a gift."

"I mean, I never realized that nevi'im trained for it."

"We must train, for even gifts can harm one who is ill-equipped to receive them. Under a trained rider, a fast horse is a powerful gift indeed. But it can also throw off and break the back of the untrained."

"So all nevi'im have trained before receiving prophecy, Master?"

"I know of only one exception."

"Who was that?"

*"Balaam, who called himself the man with the open eye."**

The name Balaam made me think of Uriel's old, one-eared donkey. It lived longer than any beast of burden I'd ever known, but was probably gone by now, at a time when so many animals perished from lack of food. Had Uriel really named a donkey after a prophet? "Why did Balaam merit navua if he hadn't trained?"

"Merit? I'm not sure Balaam did merit, but he received it nonetheless."

"I don't understand."

"What training do you recall from the gathering, Lev?"

"Mostly that the bnei nevi'im had to quiet their minds."

"Yes, only a quiet mind is a fit vessel to receive. Music is a particularly good tool for achieving that. What else?"*

"Dreams. I remember Master Yosef saying dreams were one-sixtieth of prophecy, and that all disciples must discuss their dreams with a master."

"Correct, they must also learn to understand the visions of their heart. What else?"

"I cannot think of anything else, Master."

"What remains is the most important step, the path that Balaam could never pursue: the complete refinement of the self."

"I don't understand."

"Many of the new priests of the Baal first began their training with us."

"They were bnei nevi'im?"

"Indeed. Some were drawn to the nevi'im because they wanted power, to control others, to be feared. Others had a desire to serve, but foundered because they failed to master themselves."

Though my master couldn't see me, I nodded, fully aware of how tempting the Baal was to those desiring power or seeking to satisfy their lusts. "Then how did Balaam succeed?"

"Balaam needed to exist. When we left Egypt, the Holy One wanted the nations to see that what made us distinct was not our circumstances, but our choices. We were led by Moses, who spoke to the Holy One face to face. The nations needed a prophet of equal power to dispel any belief that only Moses's navua set us apart. So Balaam was given tremendous powers of navua, so great that the nations could never claim they misunderstood the Holy One's will."

"But why choose him? There must have been one among the nations with a pure heart."

"There were many. But what would happen to one of pure heart who received the prophetic powers of Moses?"

I bit my lower lip as I tried to picture a prophet as great as Moses among the nations. What would he have done when he saw the splitting of the sea? "He would have joined Bnei Israel."

"Indeed. Look at Ovadia, who left his nation to join us even without navua. The Holy One needed to choose a man whose lusts were so strong that even receiving the Divine Will would not make him change his ways."

"But surely prophecy must have refined him somewhat, Master?"

"I do not believe so. We are refined by our choices. For him, navua remained a mere gift."

Rabbi Shimon said: Do not be wicked in your own sight.

Pirkei Avot 2:18

10

Eliav's Choice

Ascending on foot from the King's Road to Levonah, I drank in the smell of young shoots sprouting in the valley. Now that I was forced to return to my flock, the farmers' dread of the rain faded; the prospect of shepherding again was eased by the promise of early pastures. I scanned the hillside for my flock, but it was nowhere to be seen.

I hiked up to the fig tree where I'd met Uriel less than two weeks before, picked a fig that was still green on top, and split its reddish-brown bottom with my fingers. Its flesh wavered before my eyes as thin, white worms fled from the light. I dropped the infested fruit with a shudder and didn't reach for another.

Every rock and tree on the footpath that hugged the city walls whispered of home, yet the familiar landmarks brought constriction to my throat. A different sun shone on everything I knew, casting it in an unfamiliar light. My uncle's house appeared smaller than I remembered. Dahlia saw me first, peeking around the mud dome of the oven. "Lev!"

"Lev?" Aunt Leah stepped outside, two-year-old Ruth grasping the back of her skirts. Tears were already on her cheeks as I hurried forward into her embrace.

"Tell us about the man eating the sword again," six-year-old Shimi asked for the third time.

"As I said, he didn't exactly eat it." I dropped my spoonful of lentil stew—everyone else had finished eating, but my bowl was still half full. "He bent his head back like this and held the sword over his head." I held my spoon over my upturned mouth. "Then he lowered it down his throat." I lowered the handle until I gagged. "But he kept it going all the way down."

"How long was the sword?" Eliav asked.

"About this long." I held my arms out.

"But it must have gone down to his stomach." Dahlia wrinkled her nose. "And it came out without any blood?"

"Not a drop."

"I think you should all let Lev eat," Aunt Leah said. "You can ask him about his adventures tomorrow. He's home now. Come Ruth, Shimi, Naamah. To sleep."

The youngest children followed their mother up the ladder as Dahlia cleared the table. Uncle Menachem didn't recite verses, as was our nightly custom; instead, Eliav went outside to check on the flock, and Uncle Menachem stayed at the table while I finished. He'd passed the meal in silence, hardly taking his eyes off me as he ate.

Eliav returned and climbed the ladder without a word. I wiped the clay bowl with the last of my bread, handed it to Dahlia, then turned toward the door.

"Eliav's already seen to the sheep," Uncle Menachem said.

"I know, Uncle." I walked outside anyway and leaned against the edge of the pen, patting the head of the nearest sheep, which stared up, then pulled away.

"You didn't mention the rest of the wedding." My uncle came up behind me.

"I didn't want to scare them. I wasn't sure if you even knew."

"We felt the rain here too, Lev. It didn't take long to learn the reason why. Everyone's in a panic to gather in their crops." Uncle Menachem tugged at the gate of the locked pen, checking that it was secure. "What does Master Uriel say?"

"The rains will come, just as Yambalya promised. He ended the gathering early."

"That's why he sent you home?"

"No, Uncle. That's not why he sent me away."

"No? What did he say?"

"He didn't say anything. He closed the gathering and told everyone they could go home to bring in the harvest."

"But if the gathering was closed, it was closed."

"No, Uncle." I fought the tremor in my voice. I wanted to understand the

truth, and to do that, I needed to tell my uncle everything. "He stayed behind with any disciples wishing to remain."

"Then it probably wasn't worth paying a musician for just a few disciples."

"No, Uncle. He paid me for the entire summer." One of the sheep crossed the pen to lick my hand. I felt bolstered by the sudden affection. "He sent me away because he's angry."

"Angry?"

"On the way to the gathering, Uriel sent me into Beit El to deliver a message. I finished earlier than I expected. I had time, so I went to the altar to bring an offering, but they wouldn't let me. So I went and bowed to the Holy One. I told him this last night when I returned from the wedding."

Whatever response I may have expected, it wasn't the burst of laughter I received. "You told a *navi* that you bowed to the Golden Calf?"

My face grew hot. "Why not? You taught me that bowing to the calf is bowing to the Holy One. You go every year."

"Yes, yes I do." His smile melted, and even in the fading light, I saw a shadow grow in his eyes. "I'm not proud of it. But I go. And I bow."

"Why wouldn't you be proud? And if you're not proud," I could tell he wanted to look away, but I held his eyes, "then why do you go?"

He sighed, turning aside and resting his arms on the pen. "I didn't use to. Of course, when I came of age, my father took me. But once I married your aunt, your father wouldn't hear of it."

I started at the mention of my father; my uncle almost never spoke of him. "What do you mean?"

"The tale of the calf is a troubled one. Have I ever told you why the Kingdom was split?"*

I sensed a story coming and sat down on the wall of the pen, shaking my head.

"When King Solomon died, the tribes called his son Rechavaum to Shechem to crown him King of all Israel. Now King David was a mighty warrior, and the people followed him with all their hearts. His son Solomon was a great builder who set the people to build the Holy One's Temple and his own palace in Jerusalem. Twenty years of sending people north, thousands at a time, to fell trees and cut stones in the mountains of Tzidon. Twenty years of fathers gone from their families, husbands from their wives, sons from their farms.

"So when Rechavaum came to Shechem, the tribes said to him, 'Your father placed a heavy yoke upon us. Lighten our burden, and we will serve you as we served him.' Now it is no small thing to make demands on the honor of a King. Unwilling to answer right away, Rechavaum took three days to consider.

"The elders who sat at Solomon's feet advised Rechavaum to heed the people. They promised that if the King bent to their will, the people would bow to him all his days. But Rechavaum's friends, the youth of the palace, did not agree. They told him that it was dangerous to meet demands with weakness. They advised him to say, 'My little finger is thicker than Solomon's loins. My father laid a heavy yoke on you, I will add to it. If Solomon beat you with sticks, I will whip you with scorpions.'" Uncle Menachem shook his head with a mirthless laugh.

"Why would they say that?"

"I think they were afraid."

"Afraid? Afraid of what?"

"Of what the tribes would do. Of having to hold together the Kingdom without King Solomon." He stroked his beard and sighed. "And when men are afraid, they feel safer if they can make others afraid as well—afraid of them."

"So he listened to his friends?"

My uncle nodded. "His friends convinced him that the strong hand is the one that holds the whip. But he didn't count on the strength of the tribe of Ephraim. They killed his tax collector and sent Rechavaum fleeing back to Jerusalem. Only his own tribe of Judah and the small tribe of Binyamin stayed loyal to the House of David. The other tribes chose Yeravaum as their king, and he declared the new Kingdom of Israel, independent from the Kingdom of Judah."

"But how could they do that?"

"As I said, Ephraim is a powerful tribe, and the northern tribes resented twenty years of forced labor to build a capital in the south."

"But you told me the Holy One granted an eternal kingdom to the House of David."

Uncle Menachem's eyes narrowed. "Well, this is where your friends, the prophets, enter the story."

"They fought against Yeravaum?"

He shook his head. "King Solomon's weakness for foreign women raised the wrath of the Holy One. Achia of Shiloh, Uriel's master, was sent to anoint Yeravaum as king even during Solomon's lifetime."

"The prophets declared Yeravaum king even before the people rejected Rechavaum?"

My uncle nodded.

"But what does this have to do with my bowing to the calf?"

"Well, Yeravaum had the support of most of the people, especially after it became known he was anointed by a prophet. But there was one thing he didn't have: The Holy Temple. All the men of Israel are obligated to go up to the Temple for the three yearly festivals: Passover, *Shavuot*, and *Sukkot*."

"So?"

"Only a king from the House of David is allowed to sit in the Temple; all others must stand. Yeravaum was afraid that if he allowed the people to go to Jerusalem, they would see Rechavaum sitting in the Temple courts while he stood. Who would look like the greater king then? He feared their loyalty would return to the House of David. So, he closed the roads to Jerusalem and forbade the people from making the pilgrimage."

I pictured the faces of the nobles bowing to the Baal at the wedding. "Yeravaum was afraid, so he frightened the people?"*

Uncle Menachem nodded. "He put soldiers on the road. After he killed the first few who defied his orders, most stopped trying. But Yeravaum understood he couldn't stop the people from serving the Holy One. Their connection was too strong—attack that and the nation would rise against him. And he was not opposed to the Holy One, just to the people going to Jerusalem. So, he crafted two golden calves, placing one in Beit El in the south of the Kingdom and one in Dan in the north, and declared: 'Here are your gods that brought you up from Egypt.' Then he created a new pilgrimage festival one month after *Sukkot*."

"Why did he choose the calf?"

"I think because our ancestors already worshipped the calf in the desert—it was already in our hearts. Your father had some other explanation that I never understood."

"What was that?" I couldn't keep the eagerness out of my voice. I'd never before heard a teaching from my father.

"He said the calf represents the animal half of our souls. That worshiping it was turning toward our animal self, away from our higher destiny."

I rolled the statement over in my mind, wanting badly to understand my father's words. "I don't know what that means," I admitted at last.

"Neither do I."

I ran my hand across the back of one of the sheep, where the wool was just starting to grow in after the spring shearing. "Uncle, if you know all this, why did you start going again?"

Uncle Menachem dropped his eyes. "It's what everyone does, Lev. It's a time for the people to come together and strengthen our connections to each other and the Holy One. I loved going with my father when I was young. Is it better to go to the Temple? Of course. But the road to Jerusalem is closed." He cleared his throat, yet held his gaze low to the ground. "Your father made me ashamed to go, but when he was no longer here, I started again."

I nodded, glad my uncle had answered, but not wanting to push him further. "So you'll be taking out the flock in the morning?"

Now it was my turn to look away. The question had been on my mind the whole journey back. "No," I said, and my uncle's eyes shot up to mine. "I'll go, but only to help Eliav. He leads the flock now."

"Lev, you know you are no less to me than my own children, don't you?"

I swallowed, but didn't reply.

"It's true that you can't inherit the land. But your aunt and I have spoken. We want each of you to inherit part of the flock. You needn't give way to Eliav. You're the elder and the better shepherd. He should help you."

My lower jaw trembled, but I had decided my path—there would be no more silly dreams. "No, I'll help him. Between the prophets and the wedding, I have enough copper to buy seven ewes and two rams in the spring." Uncle Menachem raised his eyebrows. "I'll go out with Eliav through the winter, then start a flock of my own."

Uncle Menachem pulled on his beard. "This is what you want?"

"Yes." My tone didn't ring as clearly as I intended.

"Very well. I'll give you another ram and three ewes from the calves. With that many to start, you should have a strong flock by the time you're ready to marry."

I knew he'd want to help, but hadn't expected such a generous gift. "Thank you, Uncle."

Uncle Menachem stepped back toward the house, then turned to face me. "You're sure this is what you want?"

"Yes," I said with confidence I didn't feel. "Eliav should take the flock."

He peered deeply into my eyes. "I meant, are you sure you want to be a shepherd?"

My gaze rose toward the sky, lit by the last rays of the setting sun. The dream of playing in the King's Court still called to me, but not if it meant bowing to the Baal. "What else would I do?"

Uncle Menachem shrugged. "That morning when you went off with Master Uriel, you didn't see me. I was working in the olive trees and watched you go. I saw your face and wondered if you'd ever return to this life. You have a lot of your father in you."

Three mentions of my father in one conversation. Was Uncle Menachem suddenly willing to talk? "Uncle, what really happened to my parents?"

Uncle Menachem sat down next to me on the stone wall of the pen and stared down at his hands. When he spoke, it was just above a whisper.

"The truth? I don't know most of it. A man came to us in the night with cuts all over his face. Didn't appear as if anyone had treated his wounds at all. He was carrying you. You just kept screaming. You weren't hurt, but it looked as if you'd not been fed all day. Leah was nursing when he came. She handed Dahlia to me and nursed you instead. He told me he saw your parents killed. He wouldn't say any more. I tried to convince him to stay, to eat something and let us care for his wounds. He refused. He just refilled his water skin, took a little food, and left."

I nodded, not trusting my voice—I hadn't known that Aunt Leah had nursed me. Menachem rested his hand on my shoulder, then stepped back toward the house. I sat alone with my thoughts as darkness fell.

"Where's your kinnor?" Eliav asked me the next morning.

"I'm not bringing it." I held a shepherd's staff, which I hadn't carried in over a year. "You're in charge of the flock now. We'll do it your way."

Eliav stared at me with a blank expression, as if unsure whether to be happy about this change or not. With a shrug, he turned his back, unlocked the pen, and let out a sharp "Yah!" that brought the sheep pouring out. I hemmed in the flock with my outstretched staff, and Eliav turned them downhill toward the fields on the back side of the town.

"The rain brought up fresh grasses by the road," I called from behind the flock. "No one's grazed there yet."

Eliav didn't turn. "The rain brought up grasses everywhere. This way's closer."

"But you need to go through Zimmah ben Merari's field this way. They might eat from the cut grain."

Eliav stopped, and the sheep bunched up behind him, bleating and snorting. "All the shepherds pass through his field, and no one grazes there, you know that. But if you'd rather go to the road, we can go to the road."

"It's your flock—I'll follow you."

Eliav spit on the ground, then turned the flock back up toward the road. I took up the rear, keeping the sheep in a tight group with light taps on the hindquarters of the stragglers. Without my kinnor, my mind drifted quickly. How long had it taken Eliav to change my grazing spot? Had he done it the very day I left? And why? Was it because the road was farther or because all the other shepherds went behind the town?

We found good pasture on the slope immediately below the town's gates. Eliav was more confident now with the flock, but he still stood periodically and rushed at any sheep that threatened to stray.

"Don't do that!" I shouted when Eliav popped up for the third time. "You're just as likely to scare them away as bring them back. If you want to tighten up the flock, go past the sheep and just walk back toward the center.

"All right." Eliav avoided my eyes as he spoke. I didn't offer any more advice after that.

By the time the sun passed its midpoint, I missed my kinnor. A staff might keep the sheep in line but was a poor tool for occupying heart and mind. I watched puffy clouds drift by in ones and twos, high over our heads. Clouds like these weren't so unusual this time of year, but they made me think of the coming rains.

I brought my eyes down to earth just in time to notice a rider dressed in violet robes turning up from the King's Road below. Bile rose in my throat. A priest of the Baal in Levonah?

Astride a black mare, the rider made much shorter work of the steep road than I had the day before. Eliav gaped, and I elbowed him so that he wouldn't stare. I needn't have bothered—two shepherd boys were beneath the priest's notice. He approached the gate and addressed the guard loudly in poor Hebrew. "I want Yoel ben Beerah."

Yoel ben Beerah was the King's minister in Levonah—what could a priest of the Baal want with him? Without thinking, I motioned to Eliav to watch the sheep and slipped up to the town wall. I crept along the footpath that hugged the wall, stopping in the shadow of the gate where I could hear without being easily seen. Memories of the wedding celebration flooded my mind, and I fought the urge to spit the bitter taste from my mouth.

The guard slouched in the gate but sat up at attention as the priest approached. "Who seeks the King's officer?"

"A messenger of the Queen." The priest dismounted in a fluid motion, holding out a scroll in one hand.

The guard shot a skeptical frown at the priest, but when he examined the seal on the scroll, the defiance in his eyes died, his face turned pale, and he bowed his head before answering. "He is here in the gatehouse. I will summon him."

The guard retreated into the gate, and I was gripped by an internal battle. A voice in my gut screamed to retreat—I had no business with the Baal or the King's minister—but my curiosity pushed me closer to the gate, yearning to hear what the message contained. Yet, the knife at the priest's side drew my eyes. My heart pumped only fear—if he was willing to cut his own flesh, what would the priest do if he caught a spying shepherd boy?

Yoel ben Beerah stepped into the gate, trailed by two soldiers. He walked with a deliberate step, examining the priest as he approached. "I am Yoel ben Beerah. You may deliver your message."

The priest handed over the scroll and Yoel ben Beerah hastily broke the seal and glanced at the contents of the parchment. He scanned the gate plaza around him, causing me to shrink back against the stone wall. "Come, we must discuss this."

"Lev!" Eliav hissed from below.

I cringed at the sound and scurried down from my perch.

"What were you doing?"

"That's a priest of the Baal bringing a message to Yoel ben Beerah."

Eliav's eyes widened. "How do you know he's a priest of the Baal?"

"I recognized him from the wedding."

A smirk played at the corner of Eliav's mouth, then it turned down into a frown. "You have no business with him, what were you doing? If he had seen you..."

Eliav was right—it was a stupid risk to take. Why did I feel such a strong need to know what they were saying?

"What did he want with Yoel ben Beerah?"

"I don't know." I glared at Eliav. "I had to stop listening."

Eliav gazed up at the clouds. "Do you really think they can bring the rains?"

"Master Uriel says they will come early."

Eliav grinned. "That'll be a blessing."

I leaned away from him. "But what about all the farmers whose crops will be ruined?"

"What about them?" Eliav planted his staff before him and stood. "Let their blood be on their own heads. Yambalya granted them enough time for the harvest, you heard him yourself. It's only those who don't listen whose crops will be ruined. And any rain is good for us, right?"

Again Eliav was right—hadn't I thought like him when I first felt the rains? Yet, now a fury rose within me that I couldn't explain. Not knowing what to say, I stalked off to gather in a stray ram.

The next day was Shabbat. I passed the time feasting with my family and repeating the stories of my travels, mostly at the request of my younger cousins. On the first day of the week, Eliav again directed the flock toward the fields behind the city. This time I didn't bother protesting.

After the evening meal, I retrieved my kinnor for the first time since returning home. It was not to "keep the spark inside me alive," as Daniel had pressed me to do. No, I needed music to smother all those voices rising in my head since my return: my anger at Eliav, my disappointment in Uncle Menachem, my aching desire to be more than a shepherd in the wilderness. I'd made my choice, and my kinnor was my best tool to quiet the tempest within and remain on my path. I leaned against an olive tree opposite the house and gently plucked the strings, trying to replicate the sound of the leaves rustling overhead, imagining myself alone in the wilderness.

"There was no music while you were gone." Dahlia stood over me, a bowl in her hands. "I brought you some toasted wheat."

I grabbed a few wheatberries, still warm from roasting, and popped them into my mouth.

Dahlia sat next to me, pulled her dress down over her feet, and rested the bowl in her lap. "Do you want to sing to me?"

"I don't feel like singing."

"Want to tell me about the wedding again?"

"No," I said, louder than I intended.

She pulled away. "Do you want me to go back in?"

"No, you can stay." We sat silently, listening to the whisper of the leaves and the soft notes of the kinnor. In the distance, there were three heavy thuds, the sound of wood striking wood.

Dahlia broke the silence. "Are you happy to be home?"

I kept on strumming quietly. Had anyone else in the family asked, I would have offered a quick "Yes," but it was different with Dahlia. "I was when I first got back."

"You don't seem happy now." Again, the thudding sound disturbed the twilight peace, this time closer. "I don't think my mother expected you to return."

"Is that why she cried so much when I left?"

"Probably."

"One of the musicians I met was like that. He left home over a year ago, moving from place to place, playing for weddings and festivals."

"He didn't get lonely?"

"I don't think so."

"Would you?"

I closed my eyes, picturing myself moving from festival to festival, carrying a mirror like Zim, never spending more than a couple of weeks in any one place. Maybe if Yonaton was with me, it wouldn't be so bad. "I'd get lonely."

"I don't think she saw you becoming some wandering musician."

"No, she thought I'd stay with Master Uriel." I clamped my hand on the strings of the kinnor. The music died. Whenever I thought of Uriel now, I saw his cold narrowed eyes after he learned that I'd bowed to the calf.

"Yes," Dahlia replied, and we sat in silence once again.

Two men crossed Uncle Menachem's property and approached the house, taking no notice of Dahlia or me in the growing darkness. The man in front raised his staff and banged it three times against the door.

"Who's there?" my uncle called, anger and worry in his voice. We didn't get many visitors at night—certainly not ones who knocked so loudly.

"It is Yoel ben Beerah," the shorter man answered in a voice that carried into the night.

Eliav opened the door, and soft light from the hearth shone from the house, revealing the violet hue of the other man's robes. Uncle Menachem appeared next to Eliav in the doorway. "Good evening, Yoel ben Beerah. Please come in."

"There is no need, we want just a word." His voice was quieter now, but still had the tone of command. "Queen Izevel invites all of Israel to humble ourselves before the Baal prior to the rains so we will be blessed with a bountiful year."

The priest put a box on the ground, opening a flap in the side facing the house.

"I see the Baal. And I see his servant's weapon." My uncle stared at the long knife at the priest's side. "Are we being forced to bow?" Eliav turned to his father, mouth agape.

"Certainly not. Queen Izevel only invites us. Already tonight several men have declined. If they're not concerned for their crops, I cannot help them. We are here for your sake."

The priest fell to his knees in front of the box, stretched out his arms, and pressed his face to the ground. Yoel bowed next to him, supporting himself with his staff until his knees touched the ground, then lay his arms flat.

Dahlia clutched my arm. Would Uncle Menachem bow to the Baal as he did to the Golden Calf?

Uncle Menachem hesitated. Not a sound rose from the priest or the King's servant. I held my breath as Dahlia's grip tightened. This was not like the Calf. Even if Uncle Menachem believed bowing to the Calf was bowing to the Holy One, he could claim no confusion here. It was from my uncle's mouth that I learned the verse, "Do not bow before their gods,* do not serve them, do not follow their practices; rather, tear them apart and destroy their monuments." My uncle's wavering form filled the door—but Eliav moved first. Turning away from his father, Eliav fell to the ground beside Yoel and stretched himself out in the dirt of the doorway.

Uncle Menachem's eyes fell on his son.

Dahlia's nails dug deep into the skin of my arm. I choked back a cry.

My uncle's knees buckled, as if he was trying to hold up a weight greater than himself. Drawn by Eliav, his shaky knees gave way. Once his knees struck earth, his back curved into the same position that I took before the Golden Calf, with his arms reaching out in servitude, his forehead humbled to the ground.

Yoel stood first, brushing dirt and twigs from his cloak. Uncle Menachem followed, grasping at the doorpost for support. Eliav didn't lift himself from the dirt until the priest stood and closed the shrine.

"You are a prudent man, Menachem," Yoel said. "May you receive much blessing for it. Peace to you."

"And peace unto you, Yoel ben Beerah," Uncle Menachem replied, without lifting his face.

The priest handed an object to my uncle. "Gift from Queen." He followed Yoel away into the darkness.

Uncle Menachem stood in the doorway, watching the two men disappear down the path. As he turned back toward the house, his glance paused under the olive tree where Dahlia and I sat. His chin fell to his chest; he stepped inside, and closed the door.

Dahlia's shuddering form shook mine. "I didn't think my father would bow."

"He doesn't like to be different."

The moonlight reflected in two lines down her cheeks. "You're different, but you never seem to mind."

"If I'm different, it's not because I mean to be." I shied away from her tears. "Don't think it's easy."

"If it's not easy, why'd you come back?"

"Where else was I supposed to go? I told you: I don't want to be some wandering musician." I still avoided Dahlia's gaze, wishing she would dry her eyes.

"You said Master Uriel stayed behind with a few disciples. Why don't you return and play for them?"

My eyes shot back up to Dahlia's. "Uriel doesn't want me!"

The bowl of wheatberries toppled to the ground as Dahlia fled toward the house. I yearned to go after her—I hadn't meant to shout. But I didn't move even as she flew in and shut the door fast behind her. Instead, I lifted my eyes to the fluttering leaves of the olive tree and plucked aimlessly at the strings of my kinnor.

"When you received your kinnor, you were still too young to play it."

"Then why was it left with me, Master?"

"Lest your soul need release that your life could not provide."

"So that I would dream of more than my sheep?"

"Precisely."

My daydreams had caused me so much misery over the years. I always thought my kinnor helped me silence my futile aspirations. I never realized it was responsible for creating them.

My Master said softly, "Song is the language of the soul. When music speaks through you, it reveals how the ears that hear and the hands that play are merely its garments."

Rabbi Elazar HaKapar said: Against your will you were created, against your will you were born, against your will you live, against your will you die, and against your will you will come to give an accounting of your deeds.

Pirkei Avot 4:29

11

The Vineyard of Shiloh

A hand gently shook my shoulder, rousing me from sleep. I awoke to total darkness.

"Get dressed," my aunt whispered against my ear. "Pack your things. Wake no one." Her dress swished down the ladder.

Eliav moaned in his sleep as I pulled my tunic over my head. I rolled my sheepskin sleeping mat as quietly as I could so as not to rouse him further. Holding my things under one arm, I slipped down the ladder. The flickering light of the hearth illuminated a clay statue set in a niche in the wall: the gift from the Queen.

Even in the half-light, I could see Aunt Leah's eyes were red.

"Aunt, have you slept?"

"No." Her head sank into her chest.

"What's happening?" I rubbed my eyes to force them awake.

Aunt Leah breathed in a whispered cry as she struggled to maintain eye contact. "It's time for you to leave this house."

"Leave?" The word leapt out of my mouth too loudly. My eyes rose to the loft, but no one stirred.

"Eat. You'll need your strength." Aunt Leah laid a plate of bread and cheese on the table. I sat opposite her and took a small bite, though I had little appetite.

"Do you remember how, before you left with Master Uriel, I told you that you are the same to me as my own children?"

I struggled to swallow the unchewed morsel in my mouth. "Yes."

"Well, I heard everything that happened last night. I know Menachem and Eliav bowed to the Baal. Dahlia told me you saw it too. I couldn't sleep thinking of you. I wish Menachem and Eliav hadn't bowed, but Menachem is my husband and Eliav my son, and I love them. I'd rather not have a Baal in the house, but there it is. I don't want to bow down to it, but if my husband insists, I will.

"I love you too, Lev." Aunt Leah stuffed bread and hard cheese into a sack. "But you're not my son." Tears now rolled freely down her cheeks.

I stared at my food as she sobbed.

"Your parents never would have raised you in a house with that abomination of an idol. My poor sister would never forgive me. For their sake—for yours—you cannot stay." Aunt Leah's head sank into her hands, her body shuddering.

I ate despite my lack of hunger, finding it easier to focus on bread than on its tear-stricken baker. Sleep was still heavy on my eyes, and I wanted nothing so much as to return to my bed.

Aunt Leah sat up, dried her eyes with the back of her hand, and gave me a weak smile that squeezed out two last tears from her eyes.

"Where will I go?" I remembered this time to keep my voice low.

"You could return to Master Uriel—"

"I'm not going back to him."

"Why not?"

"I'm not going back." My words were final. "There must be another choice."

Aunt Leah laid a fragment of parchment on the table before me, brown in color, tattered at its edges. I tilted it to read by the red light of the coals. *Elazar ben Amram, Beit Shemesh* was all it said. "What is this?"

"This is the name of your uncle, your father's brother. He lives in the Kingdom of Judah. You can go to him and still be with your family, just…" She bit her lip. "Just…away from all of this."

"Go to Judah?" It was the first mention I ever heard of family across the border.

"The road is guarded, but there are many paths through the mountains. Take this." She lay a small pile of copper on the table. "Go to Mitzpah. Search there for a guide to lead you through the passes out of the Kingdom."

Ignoring the copper, I lifted the parchment, my heart pounding. "Whose writing is this?"

"It's your father's. He wanted you raised with his family in Judah. Menachem deemed it too dangerous to move you during the war, and then…" Aunt Leah wiped her eyes again on the back of her hand. "But now I see your father was right. It will be better for you there than here."

"Why?" Years of unanswered questions welled up inside. "Am I from the tribe of Judah? Is that why I have no inheritance here?"

"No, you're not from Judah. You have no land there either."

"There's something you're not telling me."

Aunt Leah didn't turn away as she normally did when I asked about my parents. "Master Uriel made us swear never to tell. He said that knowledge would put you at risk. But once you get to Judah, you'll be safe. Your family there can explain everything."

My eyes narrowed. So, Uriel was responsible for the secrets—for no one telling me the truth about my family.

A cough disturbed the quiet of the dark house. "That's your uncle waking. Go now. I won't have the strength to send you away with him here."

Aunt Leah added more bread to the sack and laid it on the table with a full skin of water. "Take the copper. It will get you across."

"I don't need it. I was paid more than that just for the wedding."

"Take it anyway," she said, her eyes pleading. "For me."

I collected the dull pieces of metal and added them to my pouch. It held more wealth than I ever dreamed I'd have at this age. It felt heavy against my thigh but brought me no joy.

Aunt Leah opened the door. Pale gray predawn light illuminated the dirt path before me. Uncle Menachem's heavy foot appeared on the top rung of the ladder, and I hurried through the open doorway.

"I love you, Lev," was the last thing I heard as Aunt Leah closed the door behind me.

An orange glow backlit the eastern mountains as I headed down to the King's Road in the valley below. I fought the desire to turn and look at my house one last time. I was on a path I hadn't chosen, and it seemed best to keep my feet moving; if I hesitated now, I might not start again. As the trail dipped downhill, birdsong echoed around me. Thinking of Daniel, I considered stopping to listen, but it felt invigorating to just walk. I took my first deep breath of the morning, my chest expanding with dew-filled air.

The slip of parchment still tingled in my hand. I hadn't looked at it since learning that it was my father's writing—but I hadn't let go of it either. There was a message in the note, but what was it? I studied it now, and my step faltered. My legs grew heavy at the thought of crossing the mountains into Judah—I'd never heard of anyone trekking that dangerous path. Who would I even ask to help me? Aunt Leah said they would explain everything in Judah. Explain what? Possibilities swirled in my mind, and I stumbled on a rock in my path.

I had to stop.

I dropped down onto a flat boulder by the roadside. I opened the parchment and stared at the scratchy handwriting, in a brown ink I'd never seen before, I willed it to reveal its secret. No guidance came. My face crumpled into my hands. I'd left so many places in the past weeks, but always with a clear destination. But now…now I was all alone.

The impossibility of this journey suddenly descended on me; I squeezed my eyes tight and bent over my trembling knees. Images whirled through my head: jugglers, prophets, musicians. My throat ached. Uriel rejected me; Aunt Leah sent me away. Who was left?

The pressure in my chest swelled, and a groan rose up from deep inside. A shudder passed through my body, and for the first time in five years, I began to cry. It started off slowly, the first drops barely squeezing out with each heave of my chest, as if my eyes had forgotten how. Their salty taste hit my tongue, evoking memories of a past when they'd flowed freely. A wail rose from my chest, and the tears broke free.

My shoulders shook as drops pockmarked the chalky soil at my feet grew pockmarked; my sobs silenced the last birds of the morning.

I don't know how long I cried, but when I gazed up, the wind blew cool against my cheeks. My chest felt loose as I inhaled. My uncle's words echoed in my mind, "Israel is wide enough for us all, if we each find our place."

My head lifted toward the sky, and a plea welled up as I blinked away the last tears. My heart, no longer blocked, called out to the heavens as it never had before, *"Where is my place?"* I squeezed my eyes shut and sent all my will after the call.

The warmth of the newly risen sun caressed my face, and its golden rays penetrated my eyelids. I stood up from my cold stone seat, slipped the parchment with damp with tears into my pouch, slung my sack over my shoulder, and continued down the hill.

The junction with the King's Road appeared ahead, and I paused to gaze back up at Levonah's walls, reflecting the dawn light. I shook myself like a dog emerging from a cold spring. An image of Uriel rose in my mind—not stony with the anger of our last encounter, but suffused with the compassion and wisdom I'd come to know. I could almost hear his advice about trusting my heart.

I reached the junction just ahead of a group of men walking down the King's Road from the north. They were all older than me and wore the worn summer clothes of farmers. *What were seven farmers doing on the King's Road at dawn?* "Peace upon you," I called to the one leading the pack.

"Upon you peace."

"Where are you headed?"

"To the festival at Shiloh," he answered with a smile. "Where goes the young man?"

I opened my mouth to say Mitzpah, but held myself back. The parchment with my father's writing burned in my pouch—it was the key to all my questions. Yet, once I crossed into Judah—if I managed to make it alive—I'd probably never return. That piece of parchment had sat in my uncle's house for ten years; another day or two wouldn't make any difference. And hadn't Zim said that Shiloh wasn't to be missed? Besides, Shiloh was one step closer to Mitzpah. "I'm also going to Shiloh."

"But you're far too young," one of the farmers laughed.

Now the whole group was staring at me—Zim never mentioned anything about age. "I'm a musician," I said, hoping that made a difference.

"Oh, I see. Walk along with us if you like."

"A musician, eh?" a particularly dirty farmer chuckled. "Why don't you play us something?" I wasn't interested in being their entertainment, but it was good to have company. I drew my kinnor forward and played the sheep's watering *nigun* as we walked.

Dozens of men milled around the hill below Shiloh, and all seemed to be between the ages of twenty and forty. A second group gathered at the east side of the hill, but the two groups didn't mix. Nervous laughter ran through the crowd. One of my companions laid a hand on my shoulder and pointed to a cluster of trees at the foot of the hill. "The musicians are over there."

I approached the trees, finding five musicians playing as an older man scrutinized them, dropping comments and critiques. "Excuse me," I said to the man, who took no notice. "Excuse me," I called a little louder.

The old man turned, first looking over my head, then down until he met my eyes. "Yes?"

I'd never asked for work before. "I'm wondering if you…" I started, brandishing my kinnor.

"Ah, you'd like to play with us." He smirked. "I'm sorry, I've got all the musicians I need." The other musicians watched me now, a couple of them grinning. "Keep working on your music. Perhaps in a few years you can come join us."

I nodded, my cheeks burning, and walked away, their music mocking my retreat. The musicians were good, but no better than me. The leader hadn't even listened to me play. As I approached the King's Road, their song faded, all but the drumming, which grew louder with each step.

I pulled the piece of parchment out of my pouch. It was stupid to think I could just show up and play—at least I hadn't lost much time. If I moved quickly, I might still be able to reach Mitzpah by nightfall. All I could hear now was the drum, pounding louder and louder.

"Lev, you came!"

"Zim!" He stopped drumming and wrapped one stout arm around me, squeezing my face into his shoulder. "I thought you were staying in Shomron?"

"I told you, I never miss Shiloh. Yambalya said I could come." Zim released me, and I rubbed my nose, which itched from scraping against his rough tunic. "You're going the wrong way. The musicians set up over there."

"They didn't want me. The leader didn't even listen to me. He thinks I'm too young."

Zim laughed. "I was barely older than you when I started coming. You're not too young—you just look terrified. Come on." Zim walked past, waving for me to follow. "Emanuel!" he called with his habitual confidence.

The old man saw Zim, and a genuine smile stretched across his face. "Zimri. I was hoping you'd come back. We can use your drum." Emanuel caught sight of me. "I told your friend to come back in a couple of years. We don't need any boys playing."

Zim shook with laughter. "You must have some group this year if you think your musicians are better than the King's."

Emanuel started, his eyes lit with curiosity. "The King's?"

"This is Lev ben Menachem. I played with him at the King's wedding. I told him to come to Shiloh—I figured you could use the help."

"But he's just a boy."

"You judge too much by appearances." Zim ran a hand through his wavy, dark hair. "Have you listened to him play?"

"No." Emanuel scratched his beard.

"Lev, let's do that song we played for the juggler. You start, and I'll join in. If the rest of you think you can follow along, feel free to try."

All eyes were on me again, but now it felt completely different. I took my time preparing to play, first stretching out the fingers on my left hand, then on my right. No one spoke as they waited. I closed my eyes and let my fingers go.

Zim picked the right tune. It was fast, and the melody jumped around a complicated rhythm. If I hadn't spent so much time practicing before the wedding, I would never have been able to lead it. As it was, I struggled to play it on my own. Zim let me start solo, then filled in the rhythm underneath. After one round, a nevel added its voice, not quite in rhythm. A halil joined in with a high, warbling note, but struggled to stay in tune and fell away.

Before long, all seven musicians were playing—the quality of the music nothing near the caliber of the wedding. I played the notes as crisply as I could in order to guide the others—suddenly aware of how much my abilities had grown since the gathering began. All of Daniel's lessons had taken hold. I had more power and speed than before, but that wasn't all. I was playing more loosely now, as I did at the wedding after two goblets of the King's wine. This time, though, the freedom couldn't have come from drink. *It must have been from that morning's flood of tears.*

We played through the melody twice, then Zim departed from the rhythm into short rapid beats. I brought the tune to an end, sealing it with a bold final note that continued to reverberate even as I removed my hand from the strings and opened my eyes.

Emanuel's attention was locked on me, eyes wide and mouth slack. Zim held back a laugh. "You can stay," Emanuel said. "Let's try that song again. We can add it tonight if the rest of you get it sharper."

A molten sun faded in the west as a full moon rose over the ridge on the eastern horizon. The crowds on both sides of the hill continued to grow as the day wore on, but still hadn't mingled. The musicians set up on a hillside overlooking an expanse of trellised grapevines, their avenues or arbors forming shadowed lanes over the land that lay between the two gatherings. An old man approached the near group, and chatter ceased as they surrounded him. I could tell that he spoke loudly, but we were too far away to hear what he was saying.

When the old man finished, he left the first group and walked along the edge of the vineyard toward the second, passing directly below the musicians.

I nudged Zim and pointed. "Hey, that's Master Yosef!"

"That's right. He comes here every year. That's how I got hired to play for the prophets this summer—he heard me last year and asked me to come to the gathering."

"I'm surprised to see him at a festival."

"He likes to come and make sure everything happens in '*the right way*.'"*

"What has to happen in the right way?"

Zim cocked his head and examined me slyly out of the corner of his eye. "You really don't know what happens here?"

"No, what?"

Zim threw me a mischievous grin. "You'll see soon enough."

The second group now gathered around Yosef. When he finished speaking, only a smudge of color remained in the western sky, and the moon glowed white and immense above the eastern hills. Yosef waved a flaming torch back and forth above his head.

"That's our signal." Emanuel raised his hand. "Lev, lead us in that song from the wedding." I struck the first notes, and the others joined in, smoother than before, but still struggling.

The signal was not just for us. Both groups moved toward the vineyard, spreading out as they approached. Some men of the near group hesitated before walking under the bowers, but there was no such hesitation from the far-off crowd. Even from a distance, I could see that they were dancing, and moonlight reflected on their brilliant, white garments. Yosef sat beside a bonfire on the hillside below us, next to two of his disciples.

As they reached the edge of the trailing vines, I got a better view of the dancers. "Hey, those are girls!"

"That's right." Zim snickered, his head bobbing to the beat.

"How can Master Yosef agree to this?"

Zim laughed louder. "He says it's one of the holiest days of the year."

The last of the girls danced into the vineyard, and I could no longer make out anyone clearly. Hundreds of shapes moved beneath the vines, limbs twirling, their garments silver against the darkened ground. We performed our fastest songs, one after the other, and my energy surged as I imagined hundreds of girls dancing to my music.

Toward the end of our third song, a couple emerged from the vineyard walking side-by-side up the hill toward Yosef. They stopped before the prophet, faces lit by the fire, staring into each other's eyes. The man appeared neither young nor old, with a severely crooked nose that distorted an otherwise handsome face. She was much younger than he and wore an elaborately embroidered dress, her long braids falling from a white scarf on her head. She was very pretty, and there was something unnervingly familiar about her.

I continued to stare until it came to me—I knew her. Her name was Hadassah, the daughter of one of the poorest families in Levonah. She looked so different tonight, I was surprised I'd recognized her at all. She must have spent hours, if not days, cleaning herself and braiding her hair. I had seen her only in dirty, tattered clothes. *How could her family afford such an ornate dress?*

Yosef addressed them, but his words were lost in the music. The couple glanced at each other and nodded with the expression of children getting away with something forbidden. They bowed their heads, and Yosef placed one hand on the man's head, holding the other just above Hadassah's. When he removed his hands, they gazed at each other again, clasped hands, and withdrew from the fire.

More couples emerged from the vineyard, ascending the hill toward Yosef, and waiting in a line that began to stretch down to its very edge. "What is he saying to them?" I asked Zim.

"Go listen."

"I can't do that."

"Why not?"

Something about the expression in Zim's eyes made my fears seem childish. I peered around for Emanuel, but he was nowhere in sight. With six other musicians playing, I wouldn't be missed if I went quickly. I left my kinnor and crept down the hillside, stooping under a rocky shelf that projected out just behind Yosef. A new couple stood before him now, both rather short and broadly built.

"It's hard to see in the vineyard," Yosef said, "So I want you to take a good look at each other in the firelight." The couple peered at each other and smiled. "You are certain of your choice?"

The man said "Yes," and the woman nodded.

"Very well. Bow your heads. May the Holy One bless your home to be like the tent of Isaac and Rivka. May you be blessed to raise righteous children, and to eat from the bounty of the land." Yosef lowered his hands, indicating the two disciples at his side. "These men are your witnesses that you have been bound today in holiness. You may go." The man stepped away from the fire first, and his bride followed him into the darkness.

I returned to my place among the musicians, my thoughts a whirl. "They're getting married?"

"That's right," Zim said.

"But I've been to plenty of weddings, why—"

"Nobody wants to get married this way.* But some families can't find good matches for their children. They might have no wealth, no connections. And look around, some of these people are just plain ugly. But they all come to Shiloh and find each other in the vineyard."

"I recognized that first girl; she's from my town. Her family is really poor, but she was wearing a fancy dress."

"All the girls borrow dresses—it's part of the rules of Shiloh. No one can tell who is rich or poor in the vineyard."

"So how do they find each other?"

"The girls just go under the vines, dancing and calling out to the men. The pretty ones say 'Come find yourself a beautiful wife.' The ones from good families say 'Find yourself a wife to build a family with.' Inside that vineyard is the only place where the people of Israel don't hold back."

"So what if they aren't beautiful or from good families?"

"They say, 'Choose a wife for the sake of heaven,' though I'm not sure why heaven should prefer an ugly wife!"

A place in Israel where no one holds back—no wonder Zim was drawn to it. "Did you ever think of going into the vineyard and finding a bride for yourself?"

"Me? Get married?" Zim threw back his head with a loud laugh. "I'm living in Shomron now."

"So?"

"So Baal isn't the only god that Izevel brought down with her from Tzidon."

"Who else is there?"

"There's Ashera."

"Who's he?"

"She. She's the mother of Baal, the goddess of the Earth."

"Yeah? Do her priests also cut themselves up?"

"Priestesses. And no, they don't."

"So what's her worship like?"

"A bit like this. Except in the morning, you don't wake up with a wife."

The sun already blazed above the mountains when Zim shook me awake the next morning. My first thought was how strange it was for Zim to be awake before me, and then I realized I was bathed in sweat.

"You were screaming."

"It's nothing," I said, sitting up, "just a nightmare." But it wasn't nothing. For the first time, I remembered a detail from my old dream. There was a horse, driven fast. I wanted to close my eyes, to hold onto the vision, to see more.

"You sure you're alright?" The concern on Zim's face appeared so out of place.

If I was going to talk about my nightmares with anyone, it wasn't Zim. I opened the sack of food my aunt had prepared and pulled out bread and cheese, giving up on any hope of slipping back into the dream to learn more. "Come eat." I watched Zim help himself to a piece of bread and a hunk of cheese. At least it was Zim and not Yonaton who'd heard me screaming. Yonaton's concern wouldn't have been pushed aside so easily, certainly not with a bribe of food.

In the vineyard and the surrounding fields, couples were sitting and walking together. Two groups again formed on opposite sides of the vineyard, each much smaller than the night before. These must be the ones who failed to find a match. *Would they be back next year?*

"So you're heading back to the gathering today?" Zim asked between bites.

It hadn't occurred to me that Zim wouldn't know. "No, the gathering was closed after the wedding."

"Why?"

"So everyone can bring in their harvests before the rains."

Zim's eyes gleamed. "Even the prophets have begun to fear Baal? Yambalya will be pleased."

My first instinct was to defend them, but I held myself back. It did feel as if the prophets were giving way to the Baal.

"You're going home then?"

I stopped eating and stared down. "I can't go home."

"Can't go home? Why not?"

"My aunt sent me away."

"Why? What happened?"

My throat suddenly felt dry, and I swallowed hard. "My uncle brought a Baal into the house. My aunt said that my parents would never accept me living in a house with an idol, so she made me leave. She told me to go to my father's family in Judah."

"Judah? How are you supposed to get across the border?"

"My aunt gave me copper. She said in Mitzpah I'll be able to find someone to guide me over."

"So that's it? You're going? And you'll just hope that whoever takes your payment can get you there alive?"

"What choice do I have?"

Zim shook his head. "Just because your aunt sent you to Judah doesn't mean you have to go. You're almost of age, Lev—it's time to become a man."

I turned away, my heart feeling like a cold stone in my chest.

"She threw you out—it's no longer her choice. Come back to Shomron with me."

"Shomron?"

"Yes, Shomron. Queen Izevel is building two temples, one for Baal, the other for Ashera. The nobility are competing to offer the biggest feasts each day. There aren't enough musicians for all the ceremonies and banquets. Two nights ago, I even played for Uriel's son."

"Uriel's son?'

"The Chief Priest of Israel." Zim laughed at the look on my face. "Didn't you notice their likeness at the wedding? It might have been Uriel forty years ago!"

I pictured the face of the priest. If the thick brows were white and the skin across his broad cheekbones wrinkled, it would have been Uriel. How had I not noticed? "But Uriel hates the Golden Calf. How can his son be its priest?"

Zim shrugged. "You can ask him when we get to Shomron."

"I couldn't do that!"

"Why not? I did."

"You did? What did he say?"

"He said he used to walk in his father's ways. But his father was always traveling, tending to the needs of the people. He wasn't there for his own family. Ten years ago, he decided he'd had enough."

"And you're playing for him?"

"I'm playing for everyone. There aren't enough musicians in Shomron. They need you there."

I dropped the bread in my hand, my hunger forgotten. "You heard what my aunt said—my parents wanted me far away from the Baal."

"Your parents are dead, Lev."

My crying the day before must have unblocked the channel of tears, for fresh drops clouded my vision.

"I know it hurts, but it's true."

My eyes strayed toward the lone men leaving Shiloh with heavy steps.

"You can't live your life for them. Do you even remember what they look like?"

"You don't understand," I said, my voice flat.

"Maybe I don't." Zim placed a hand on my shoulder. "But you need to hear this. Didn't you learn anything last night?"

I shook off Zim's hand. "What do you mean?"

"I mean, look at those couples down there. Every one of them would have preferred to get married in the usual way, but it didn't work out for them. They could have stayed at home and cried about being alone—but they didn't. They decided not to let a rotten past force them into an empty future."

I gazed at the men and women holding hands under the trees.

"They went into that vineyard with all they had, and they left everything they didn't need behind. Now look at them, most of them aren't alone anymore. How do you think they feel?"

"I don't know…Happy?"

Zim shook his head. "Scared. They're starting a new life with someone they hardly know. But they know one thing: It's better to jump into an unknown future than hold onto a dead past."

I cocked my head. "What are you saying?"

"You were one of the best musicians here last night."

I snorted at the flattery.

"No, really. But if I hadn't come along, you would have walked away and never played a note. Emanuel took one look at you and decided you were too young. What did you say back to him?"

"Nothing. I left."

"Exactly! Emanuel tells you to leave, and you go, even though you're better than his musicians. Your aunt tells you to leave, and you go, even though you don't really know why. Did you ever stop to think about what *you* want?"

Zim stood up. "Learn from the girls of Shiloh. Go into that vineyard and leave the past where it belongs. Come out ready to decide your own future, and let nothing stand in your way."

I picked up a piece of cheese. "I hear what you're saying."

"Clearly you don't, because you're still sitting here." Zim grabbed my arm and drew me to my feet. "Go on. Don't come out until you're ready to claim your life."

Zim pushed me downhill. I continued on my own, then turned back to Zim. "Don't eat all my food while I'm gone."

"Don't worry." Zim broke off another hunk of cheese. "There's plenty to eat in Shomron. Go!"

I ducked under the trellised vines, and the smell of warm earth rose up to greet me. Rays of sun peeked between broad, green leaves, painting the thick, twisted vines with swaths of light and shadow. Rows of grapevines stretched out in every direction, leaving the outer world far behind.

What Zim said made sense—I was on my own now. I didn't choose to leave, but now every choice was mine. Hadn't I come to Shiloh rather than going right to Mitzpah as my aunt wanted? I could just as easily go to Shomron—or anywhere else for that matter. Leaves trembled around me as a breeze swept off the hills above. I followed one path into the vineyard, but there were countless ways out. I settled myself at the base of a solid, olivewood post around which two vines were entwined. The young grapes, maroon and growing heavy with juice, hung above my head.

What do I really want? And what path will get me there?

A grasshopper landed at my feet. The wind died, and its rhythmic chirps rang loud on the still air. I closed my eyes and other sounds emerged, the rustling of leaves, a distant dove's cry. I laid my head back against the knotty wood, the notes of the vineyard clear in my mind, and descended into their song.

Though I had walked far into the vineyard, it was easy to find my way back out; I just followed the bass notes of the drum. The sun was high, and my sack of provisions lay empty on the ground by Zim's side. Zim beat out one last flourish and got to his feet. "If we want to get back tonight, we'll need to go now," he said.

I nodded, picked up my belongings, and followed Zim toward the road.

"Put out your hand." Zim dropped three pieces of copper into my palm. "Emanuel paid us while you were gone. It's nothing compared to the wedding, but not bad for a night of music. Are you still going to Judah?"

I inhaled more deeply than I could ever remember. "No. You were right. That's what my aunt wanted—not what I want."

"Excellent. Yambalya lent me a donkey for the trip. If we both ride, we should be able to make it back before they close the gates."

I stopped Zim with a hand on his shoulder. "I'm not going to Shomron either."

Zim cocked his head. "No?"

"No. You go on your own."

"Where will you go?"

"On my own path."

Zim's face glowed. "Good. Then for the second time in a week, we part as friends." Zim embraced me with both arms. "Until our paths cross again."

Rabban Shimon ben Gamliel said: All my days I was raised among the Sages, and I never found anything better for a person than silence.

Pirkei Avot 1:17

12

The Rains

I filled my lungs, soaking in the dry desert air, as the green speckled valley opened out below me. It was late afternoon, and my legs still felt strong. I shook my head at the memory of the exhaustion I'd felt when I first took sight of Emek HaAsefa. I hitched my sack higher and stepped lightly down the trail.

Uriel paced beneath the carob tree. Five disciples sitting before him, heads bowed between their knees. The old man's focus turned uphill, and his sharp eyes fell on me. Neither of us spoke. I went directly to my old spot under the pomegranate tree, swung my kinnor forward, and held my fingers over the strings, awaiting his signal.

The rhythmic whisper of the disciples breathing was the only sound as the old prophet stood motionless, his face a mask. I waited, undeterred by the quivering of my chin. I was so afraid that Uriel would drive me off again. Walking from Shiloh to Emek HaAsefa, I realized that fear had been my constant companion since losing my parents. But knowing this didn't relieve my fear; it only made it stronger. My teeth began to chatter like a *navi* receiving vision as I imagined Uriel rejecting me again. But for the first time I could bear the trembling, even take a strange pleasure in it, having resolved—like the girls of Shiloh—not to let fear stand in my way.

A flock of thrushes circled an oak topping the ridge on the far side of the valley. Their day's end jabbering filled the hollow valley with song just as Uriel relented, dropping his chin in the slightest of nods.

I closed my eyes and softly rippled my fingers across the strings of the kinnor, not wanting to startle the meditating disciples. At each pass through the melody, I increased the pace, the clear tones of the kinnor deepening and the music unfolding. The *nigun* flowed off the strings, through my bones, and settled in my heart as I lost myself in its rhythm.

A firm hand clasped onto my shoulder, and I opened my eyes to find myself alone with the prophet in the clearing. His creased face was expressionless, showing neither kindness nor anger. "You have returned for the rest of the gathering?"

I nodded.

"And after that?"

"If you desire my service, I will go where you go." I bowed my head. "Master."

One eyebrow lifted at the title. All called him Master Uriel, but only a true servant or disciple called him Master. My stomach churned—would the prophet reject me?

"You have chosen to return. I accept you into my service," Uriel said at last. "Is there anything else you wish to say?"

"Yes, Master. If there are times that you do not need me, I would like to help Yonaton's family bring in their harvest before the rains."

"A generous thought. Come and play for us in the mornings. You may spend the rest of the day helping your friend."

"Thank you, Master."

"Put your things away and come eat. You've had quite a journey."

"Lev!" Yonaton dropped the sheaves in his hands and ran out to meet me. I held onto Yonaton's embrace for a long time, my arms wrapped tightly around his back. After being thrown out by my aunt and Uriel's cool reception, being held by an enthusiastic friend felt like coming home.

"Are you back to play for the disciples?" Yonaton asked.

"Yes, and Master Uriel says I can help you with the harvest too."

"We could use it. Come meet my father and sisters." All eyes were on me as we approached their donkey cart. "This is my friend Lev. He came to help us with the harvest."

"You are welcome, Lev. I'm Baruch ben Naftali. Yonaton told us much about you." Baruch had a strong, stocky build and deliberate speech, giving me the impression that he didn't talk much. But he met my eyes with a sincere smile.

"These are my little sisters, Yael and Naomi."

I waved to the girls. Naomi blushed and turned away, but Yael, the younger, continued to stare.

"So what can I do?"

"Right now we need to load the grain onto the cart and bring it to the threshing floor." Yonaton swiped the back of his arm across his sweaty forehead. "What made you come back?"

I glanced toward his father and sisters, who worked near me in a tight group. "I'll tell you later." I collected a bunch of crackling sheaves and tossed them onto the cart. Yonaton's eyes burned with curiosity, but he held his tongue.

I had never harvested grains before. The sheaves of summer wheat were light, and the bending and stretching felt good. As I warmed up, I quietly sang an old shepherding song. Yonaton picked up the tune and joined in, and even Baruch started to hum along. Seeing that the song wasn't a disturbance, I let my voice soar.

I arrived at the farm the next day to find Yonaton absent from the fields. "Morning, Lev." Baruch pointed to the hilltop overlooking the farm. "Yonaton's at the threshing floor. You can join him there."

"I thought we weren't starting threshing until tomorrow?"

Baruch scanned the western sky. "The morning clouds keep getting darker and burning off later in the day. The sooner we start threshing, the more we'll be able to save when…if the rains come." He sighed and returned to gathering the cut wheat.

I climbed up the terraced hillside, past dusty grapevines, and through a grove of olive trees until I reached the broad threshing floor at the very top.

"Good, you're here." Yonaton raised his voice over the wind. "This is a lot easier with two people. You want to lead the team or ride the sled?"

Now that's an easy choice. "I'll ride the sled."

Yonaton hopped off the threshing sled and circled around to the front of the oxen, taking the reins. Until I arrived, he'd been goading and steering the oxen from behind while weighing down the sled himself.

"I thought farm work was going to be hard," I said, lounging on the sled. "I think I might just take a nap."

Yonaton laughed while spreading more grain on the ground before the oxen. "Go ahead. Enjoy your time on the sled. We'll be winnowing soon enough."

"In the meantime, I'll lend you my weight." I closed my eyes, my body vibrating as the flint on the underside of the sled cut into the grain beneath.

Yonaton slowly led the oxen around the threshing floor twice in silence. When he spoke, his voice was tight. "One of Yambalya's priests came by this morning."

"What?" I sat up, my eyes wide. "When?"

"Not long before you came. One of the Queen's soldiers was with him too."

"What soldiers?"

"You remember all those soldiers that came down from Tzidon with King Ethbaal for the wedding? I guess he left some of them behind. I recognized the cedar tree symbol on his tunic."

"What happened?"

"The priest was happy we were bringing in the harvest early. He said we were showing proper fear of the mighty Baal. Then he pulled out a statue and told us we should humble ourselves before Baal so he'd hold off the rains until we finished."

"You didn't, did you?"

"No. My father didn't either. The priest wasn't pleased, but he didn't say anything. The soldier kept fingering his sword, but he never pulled it out. He spat on the ground and followed the priest away. As soon as they left, my father told me to start threshing."

I thought back to my conversation with Baruch—now it made more sense. Yes, the clouds were gathering unusually early, but apparently, that wasn't the only thing pushing him to salvage whatever grain he could.

My mind kept returning to the priest of the Baal and the soldier of Tzidon as I settled down in my spot under the pomegranate tree the next morning. Would they also come to this valley? Surely they would know to steer clear of a prophet of Israel. Wouldn't they?

Though the music was better when I played with Daniel, Zim, and Yonaton, my bond with the disciples strengthened now that I was alone. At a nod from my master, I launched into my opening *nigun*. Although I'd played it countless times before, I immediately sensed something different. The rhythmic breathing of the disciples rippled through the air, and the space around them seemed to contract and expand with each breath. As the *nigun* came back around to its opening note, the sun shone through a break in the clouds, and the disciples collapsed as one, quivering and shaking as if a great wind tossed their bodies like dry leaves in a storm.

My jaw dropped. Uriel stood above the disciples, his face angled upward. "For so many souls to rise together is rare, but it does happen. You felt them go?"

I nodded without a word.

Uriel peered deeply into my eyes. "What is the shadow on your heart, Lev?"

The two of us had hardly spoken since my return three days earlier, but my master was right. Following the tears, my heart was no longer blocked—it ached instead. The aching wasn't just painful; it felt as though my heart wanted to speak to me, but in a language I didn't understand.

"You can put down the kinnor. They can no longer hear you."

I placed the instrument on the ground slowly in order to gather my thoughts. I pictured Yambalya drawing his knife across his chest and the faces of the farmers the following morning at the wedding. Baruch had the same expression yesterday. They all reflected the same thing: fear.

A priest came to my house with the most important man in the community, but assured Uncle Menachem that bowing down was his own free choice. Now another priest visited Yonaton's family with a soldier at his side—they were getting bolder. As their power grew, would they tolerate resistance? Yambalya's booming laughter rang in my ears.

"Master, the power of the Baal is spreading throughout the Kingdom. What will the people do? What will happen to those who refuse to bow? What will happen to you and the rest of the prophets?"

I'd thought he might be afraid, but his eyes betrayed no fear. I thought my question might anger him, but there was no anger there either. I saw only sadness. Uriel sighed. "I do not know what will be, Lev, not for the people nor for the prophets. The visions I have received lately have all been of the present. I see nothing of the future."

"What will you do?"

"As I have always done."

"But won't they try to stop you?" My voice was sharper than I intended. "Queen Izevel has her own soldiers. I saw them in Shomron. They're traveling around with the priests, trying to scare people into bowing down to the Baal. Do you think they'll allow you to travel and speak against them?"

"For now, yes. Their power is only growing, even while the prophets are yet free to travel and denounce them. Open conflict would force the people to choose between us, and they are still seen as foreigners. They will not fight openly until they are certain they hold the hearts of the people. If a struggle is to start sooner, it will be because we begin it."

"And you don't think that will happen?"

"Pitting fear against fear will not bring us the goal we seek."

"What do the other prophets say? Does Master Yosef agree?"

Uriel hesitated. "He is less inclined to this way of thinking than I. But I believe he too would prefer to avoid a conflict. For now."

"So then what will happen?"

"I do not know, Lev."

How could a prophet not know?

My master's wrinkled hand rested on my shoulder. "Lev, you must know there is only one truth. The same hand that fashioned the light also made the darkness."*

We remained in silence while a breeze shook the leaves of the pomegranate tree and the disciples rattled with the strength of their vision. The image of Queen Izevel bowing before the Baal and beckoning with her long hands to King Ahav came to mind. "Why would the Holy One create darkness?"

Uriel sighed. "Without darkness, there is no choice.* Our bodies may grow without darkness, but our souls cannot."

"But if there is just darkness—"

"Then we could not grow either. There must be a balance for our choices to be real. That is why the disciples have progressed so quickly since the wedding. The soul is a spark, but sparks do not shine in the bright light of day. As darkness deepens, the soul reveals its hidden light."

The disciples began to surface from their visions. Their trembling ceased, and the tension of life returned to their bodies. Two of them rose unsteadily to their feet, two remained sitting, and one fell flat on his back, exhausted. "What did you see?" Uriel asked softly.

"The rain will come in three days' time," one of the standing disciples replied.

"Did you all receive the same vision?"

The others nodded in agreement.

"Very well. Lev, you are excused from playing for us for the next few days to help Yonaton's family complete the harvest."

I grabbed my kinnor and raced toward the farm.

By the third day, the winds whipped across the fields. The family's cattle bunched on the leeward side of the stone cottage, their great eyes wild.

Yonaton's father wasn't complaining—we needed wind for winnowing, and better too much than not enough. Normally, they winnowed on the threshing floor, the highest point on the farm. But this time, we hauled the grain down to a more sheltered area so that the gusts wouldn't carry away the harvest.

The effort of winnowing more than made up for the ease of riding the threshing sled. The winnowing fork reached above my head. With it, I hoisted the threshed stalks of grain and threw them as high as I could into the air. The wind did the rest; heavy kernels of grain fell to the ground first, while husks and chaff blew further away, where Yonaton's sisters gathered the debris to use for animal feed and fuel.

Between the back-breaking work and the whistling wind, Yonaton and I gave up trying to talk. When a flash of lightning blazed against the dark skies in the distance, we exchanged a knowing glance and stepped up our pace.

The lightning had barely faded from our vision when Baruch ran over. "Stop winnowing. Gather as much grain as you can. Get it in before it gets wet." Baruch took the fork, tossing the threshed stalks by himself while the rest of us gathered grain and carried it to shelter. I kept gaping as Baruch worked the grain pile, tirelessly throwing it into the air, getting through twice as much by himself as Yonaton and I had together.

When the first drops fell, only a small mound remained of the grain pile, and most of the winnowed grain was gathered. I didn't mind working on in the rain, but as the lightning drew nearer, Baruch ordered us all in the house.

I turned around just before entering to see Baruch lingering beside the pile, the winnowing fork on the ground at his feet. We saved most of the harvest, but whatever remained would now be lost. He glared at the dark sky as drops rolled down his cheeks.

"Master, is it true that one must be wealthy to become a prophet?"

Though I couldn't see my master's face in the darkness of the cave, I felt his amused smile. "It is true that one always finds wealth with the nevi'im, but it is not essential to us. It is simply part of our Way, as are strength, wisdom, and humility." He paused as I absorbed his words. "Take care with what you hear from the uninitiated, my son, for even the truth they speak is lacking."*

"How so?"

"Tell me, who is the wealthiest man in the Kingdom?"

"The King, of course."

"And is the King satisfied with his wealth?"

My first impulse was to say I didn't know—but I stopped myself. I was familiar enough with my master's questions to know I wouldn't be asked anything I couldn't answer. Was the King satisfied with his wealth? How should I know? I thought back to the choices King Ahav had made in the past year, particularly those that drove us into hiding. By his own admission, they were all made to bring greater prosperity to the land. "No, the King isn't satisfied."

"Indeed, whoever can be swayed by wealth does not have enough to become a prophet, yet even a poor man, satisfied with what he has, is wealthy enough."

"And the other traits, are they as they appear? What about strength, master?"

"The strong man's will is more powerful than his desires."

"Wisdom?"

"The wise learn from all."

"And humility, Master?"

"The humble man knows that all is one. Even we the hunted are not distinct from those who pursue us. We are but two rays emanating from the same sun."

Rabbi Yishmael said: Do not judge alone, for only the One may judge alone. Do not say 'accept my view,' for it is for them to decide, not you.

Pirkei Avot 4:10

13

Jericho

The next two months were the quietest of my life. The ceaseless downpour, at times a drizzle, at times a gusty torrent, dampened my desire to speak. But it wasn't just my need for conversation that was subdued, the chatter in my head also diminished. I worried less about the future, finding comfort in the fact that I'd chosen a master, letting the burden of deciding both of our paths fall on him.

Yonaton and I stole away to the old musicians' cave with our instruments whenever he wasn't busy with the grape harvest. Now that it was just the two of us, I grew almost as familiar with his music as with my own. He harmonized wonderfully but struggled to lead. So I became the leader of our duo, developing over time the sense of when to give him free rein and when he needed shepherding. I pushed myself to play crisper notes, and started to rely on small movements of my head, and especially my eyes, to signal changes in the music.

As I grew quiet, other voices emerged around me. I learned to distinguish one birdsong from another, and to discern the direction of the wind by listening to the water dripping off the cave roof. But I wasn't just becoming more sensitive to sound. Silent languages also revealed themselves. Even though I barely spoke with the disciples, my awareness of their moods heightened; I sculpted my music to their needs, playing softer when their eyes were tight, faster when their heads drooped.

Yet, even as I became more peaceful, tension built in my master. The time for the planned ending of the gathering came and went, yet the prophet didn't leave the valley to resume traveling. As the *Sukkot* festival drew near, he became fixated on the rain, standing for hours at a time at the mouth of his cave, observing the windswept clouds churn in the sky. When he wasn't teaching or searching the skies, he spent most of his time in the darkness at the back of his cave, even taking his meals alone.

On the first night of the weeklong festival of *Sukkot*, my master stood with me and the three remaining disciples staring out into the gloom while streams cascaded down the cliffs. A flash of lightning illuminated our rickety *sukkah* getting battered by the wind. A swirling gust rocked its wooden frame to and fro. Rain as hard as hail pelted the few cut palm fronds that remained on top. The *navi* sighed in disgust and returned to the back of the cave where a table of holiday dishes awaited. "Rain on *Sukkot* is a curse;* you feel like a servant who brings his master a drink, and his master throws it back in his face." He broke the pitch seal of a wineskin and filled his goblet for the sanctification. "The rains will not stop in time for us to eat in the *sukkah* tonight. We will celebrate the festival here in the cave instead."

It wasn't a warm invitation to a feast. Despite the succulent aroma of roast lamb, my appetite dwindled as I sat down. Apparently, the disciples felt the same way. The meal was brief and silent, and when it was over, most of the food was left on the table to grow cold.

I woke in the middle of the night, heart pounding, sweat beading on my forehead. I knew the signs well—the old nightmare. It had visited me twice since Shiloh, each time depositing in my memory a little bit more, just small details. Once it was a shawl pulled across my back, another time a sword striking a shield. Now I lay still, trying to remember more, knowing that as soon as I moved, the vision would evaporate.

There was a knife, my father's knife. Also, I felt my master's presence, as if he was there with me, helping me decipher the clues. Lying in the dark, suspended halfway between sleeping and waking, it struck me; until I first met the *navi* in Levonah, the nightmare had always been sealed, like a lockbox of memory. But now details were starting to leak out through cracks in its wood.

I sat up and pulled my sheepskin tightly around my shoulders. The dying coals cast a faint glow, enough for me to just make out the curled-up bodies of the disciples. We'd taken to sleeping in the same cave since the rains, as much for company as for warmth. But my master's bedroll lay empty against the far wall. Where could he have gone? I turned to the mouth of the cave, where he'd sat for weeks watching the rains, but I saw only gray mist creeping up from the valley.

I stepped to the mouth of the cave and shivered in the damp, cold air. The full moon penetrated the clouds enough to emit a dim, silvery light, reflected by the mist that blocked my view of the valley. Unable to see, I closed my eyes and listened—there was a rhythmic splashing coming from somewhere down below. I opened my eyes and peered into the haze, trying to locate the source of the sound. With a sudden gust of wind, the mist parted.

The old *navi* danced barefoot in a puddle of rain, his steps slapping out a wet rhythm. His linen tunic clung to his skin, and even from my distant vantage point, I felt the raw power in his legs. After weaving several wide circles in the downpour, his feet grew silent. Uriel held his hands out wide, tipped his head back toward the heavens, and shook with laughter. He passed both hands over his face, like a child waking from a dream, and started back toward the cave.

I ducked inside and stirred the coals of the fire back to life. Uriel entered, dripping wet and singing quietly, shivering from the cold. His face shone, and he didn't stop his song even as he rubbed his hands together over the blaze. His voice woke the disciples, and all gathered together around the fire. "There is no sorrow on *Sukkot*.* It is a time of joy," Uriel began. "The Presence comes to dwell with us inside the *sukkah*, just as the bride joins her beloved under the wedding canopy. But such a union is possible only in joy. If we cannot rejoice in the *sukkah*, we may not enter." Uriel paused and met the eye of each listener in turn, holding mine the longest. It was a piercing gaze that cut right through to my heart. *Did he know I had watched him dance?* "But joy is a path to union wherever we sit. So, we shall delight in our festival despite the rains. And perhaps we will merit to enter the *sukkah* before the holy days end."

On the fourth day of the festival, a new noise filled the cave. It took me a moment to realize it wasn't actually a sound at all, but rather the lack of one: the rains had stopped. Outside, the wind blew wisps of dark clouds across the skies far above us, but there was no hiss of falling rain. A stillness pervaded the cool, clean air down below. Two disciples rushed out of the cave, waving for me to follow. When we reached the *sukkah*, one dropped to his knee, and I climbed onto his shoulders—as the lightest one, the roof was my responsibility. The other disciple handed up the fallen branches one by one, and I laid them across the top, creating a roof thick enough to provide shade but not shelter. When we'd finished, I examined our rebuilt *sukkah*. The ground was soaked with mud, the walls were battered and barely holding together, and the waterlogged roofing dripped into the interior. Yet, I never felt happier to have a *sukkah*.

The one remaining servant prepared a feast, serving each of us individually, as he had since I returned. Midway through the meal, Uriel's hand paused on the way to his mouth. He stood quickly without explanation, exited the *sukkah*, and strode up the hill that bounded the eastern side of the valley toward the road. The rest of us continued to eat, but our eyes followed the prophet. It wasn't long until we saw what our master had sensed: a donkey trotting along the hillside.

The *navi* reached the road just before the rider passed, and he flagged him down. The man stopped, spoke briefly to Uriel, then continued on his way. There was a shadow on my master's face as he dropped back into the valley, but no trace of it remained by the time he entered the *sukkah*. He stepped inside and, ignoring his meal, burst into song. The rest of us joined in, but though I knew the tune well, I struggled to harmonize. My master sang a bit too fast.

The break in the rain didn't last, and we never returned to our *sukkah*. The eighth day that capped the festival marked the beginning of the rainy season. The ground was already bogged with mud and rain still fell in torrents, but Uriel declared that the prophets had prayed for rain* at the end of *Sukkot* ever since Joshua led our people across the Jordan River, regardless of what the skies held. We gathered at the chilly opening of the cave, wrapped in all our clothing and sheepskin sleeping mats, to hear the prayers of the old prophet as he stood just outside the mouth of the cave, arms wide, calling out in a raw voice.

"Master of the World! For the sake of Abraham our father, who ran to bring water to the tired and thirsty, do not withhold rain from his children."

A gust of wind stuck Uriel's drenched tunic to his body and tossed his hair wildly. "For the sake of Rivka our mother, who ran to bring water to a stranger, and watered even his ten camels, do not withhold rain from her children."

Uriel cried out each petition in turn, rain rolling down his face; at the end of each one, we all shouted, "Amen."

"Holy One! For the sake of Moses our Teacher, father of the prophets, who stood before you forty days without water, do not withhold rain from his disciples!" The *navi* stretched his hands upward toward the heavens, and we drew in closer.

He clenched his hands in the frigid air as the winds rose to a howl. "May the rains come as a blessing and not as a curse!"

"Amen!"

"May they come for life and not for death!"

"Amen!"

"May they come for abundance and not for scarcity!"

"Amen!"

"Master of the World! You and only you cause the wind to blow and the rain to fall!"

"Amen!"

When he turned back from the rain, my master's eyes were aflame. In that moment, I saw the wild dancer in the rain within the old prophet. Uriel pulled two disciples out into the mire and began to dance. The rest of us joined in, finally relishing the drops on our faces. For the first time, they tasted of blessing, not of bitter curse.

No sooner had the sun set that night, marking the close of the festival, than Uriel drew me aside.

"The first day we met, when I was entering Levonah, you were speaking to a boy leading a donkey. Do you recall?"

"Yes, Master."

"There was an emblem on his saddle bag from the city of Jericho."

"That was my friend Seguv. His father Hiel is rebuilding the city."

"Yes, I know that Hiel of Beit El is rebuilding the city; I wanted to know if your friend was his son." Uriel sighed, and his body again appeared as it had before the festival: heavy, as if every movement was an effort. "I'm sorry to tell you that Seguv died six days ago."

Hot tears stung my eyes—they came so easily now. "Is that what the rider told you?"

"Yes, he was on his way to bring tidings to the King."

Seguv told me the King had invested heavily in the rebuilding of the city—of course he would want to know that Hiel had lost another son. But I cared little now about the King or Jericho. My thoughts were on the warm smile, the friendly face that always stopped to greet me whenever he passed through Levonah, bringing the wider world into the small circle of my life. I wiped my cheeks with the back of my hand, "Why did you wait to tell me?"

"*Sukkot* is a time of joy."

Blood rushed to my face. *That's all he had to say? He knew I'd lost a friend and held it back for...joy?* "You should have told me," I nearly spat out the words.

"I know it feels that way."

Uriel's words only made me angrier. "Joy isn't always the right feeling. We need to feel other things, too."

"Not on *Sukkot*.* Don't think joy is so simple—I'm not talking about the empty celebrations of fools. Real joy takes work, inside and out—more than any other emotion."

I avoided his gaze, but the *navi* pressed his point. "On *Sukkot*, we attach ourselves to the Presence, which we can do only in a state of joy. We choose to rejoice even when we don't feel joyous. That's why there is no mourning on *Sukkot*. The mourning period for Seguv will begin now and last for one week. His family will receive anyone wishing to visit."

Uriel paused, but I remained silent. "If you like, you may go."

Now my eyes met his. "You said we would begin traveling immediately after *Sukkot*."

"True. But I will wait for your return. The loss of a friend is a deep wound, and it must be mourned if it's to heal." Uriel let out another long sigh. "There is no time to go and return before Shabbat. If you go, leave early on the first day of the week. You may take Balaam to hasten your journey. You can let me know your decision in the morning."

I walked to the back of the cave and unrolled my sleeping mat. I removed my tunic, laid down, and pulled it over me, not up to my neck as I normally did, but up over my head. Thoughts of death were nothing new to me, but this was different. I knew Seguv; I never knew my parents.

With Seguv there was no lockbox of memories—they all seemed to rise to the surface of my mind at once: Seguv and his brothers laughing as they led their donkey into Levonah; Seguv holding out the afarsimon oil; Seguv standing in the throne room, presenting the oil to King Ahav; Seguv lying on his back, his eyes dark and vacant.

Lying in the darkness, hidden under my tunic, I felt the pain of my open heart. Tears came, and I didn't hold them back. They streaked my face with loss. The disciples could hear me sobbing, but I didn't care. My tunic wasn't over my head to hide me from the disciples, it was to hide them from me. I couldn't bear to see pity in their eyes.

When my eyes finally went dry, I pulled the tunic down and saw that all the others were asleep. The ache in my chest answered my master's offer. I would go to Jericho to mourn my friend.

I reached Jericho on the second day of my journey. In better conditions, I could have made it in one day, but muddy and washed-out roads made for an uneasy ride. I spent the night in a cave so shallow that it was really just a crevice, barely sheltered from the winds and relentless rain, unable to light a fire for lack of dry tinder. As I shivered through the night, I wondered if my decision to go had been rash—I was traveling farther than I'd ever gone, to pay respects to people I'd never met, on the death of a friend I saw only a few times a year. Yet, the emptiness I felt when I pictured Seguv's smiling eyes pushed me forward.

On the morning of the second day, I descended into the great valley of the Jordan River, where the ruins of Jericho lay just north of the Salt Sea. Halfway down the mountains, the air grew lighter, the clouds thinned, and the rain dwindled to a light mist that barely reached the ground. I descended further onto dry roads, and the sunlight glittered off streams of water running down the mountainsides. At the base of the mountains, the road flattened and passed through a grove of tall date palms, where a dozen camels—animals rarely seen in the cooler mountain plateau—grazed in their shade. There were also rows of newly planted trees whose species I didn't recognize. These must be the balm trees Seguv told me about, the source of the afarsimon oil, the justification for rebuilding the destroyed city despite the costs.

The dry air of Jericho drew the wetness from my clothes, and I was grateful to be spared meeting Seguv's parents stinking of soaked wool. No guard sat at the newly erected gates to direct me, but I had no trouble finding Hiel's house. It was the largest one and stood at the highest point in the city—much as the King's palace towered over Shomron. I tied Balaam to an olive tree out front, its trunk thick and gnarled, a remnant of the great city destroyed hundreds of years before. Before passing the threshold, I filled my lungs with clean air before entering a house tainted with death.

I took in the whole room with one glance. A middle-aged couple sat on the floor, barefoot, their clothing torn and their heads dusted with the ashes of mourning. Four men sat opposite them, but no one spoke.* I paused at the threshold, then stepped as softly as I could to an empty stool, not wanting to disturb the stillness.

Sitting down among people I didn't know, I wondered again if I should have come. I wanted to give comfort, but it was not my place to break the silence—and what would I say, anyway? The couple on the floor must be Hiel and his wife, but where was Onan, Seguv's older brother? Could he have died as well?

I realized I was staring and turned my attention to the other guests. Two of the men, wearing dirty work clothes, resembled each other so much, they must have been brothers. A third sat rigidly in his chair. His posture and spotless linen tunic reminded me of the scribes in the throne room of the King. The fourth sat in the corner, eyes on the floor. Whatever he was staring at must have been absorbing, for he didn't stir at all when I entered. His whole appearance bespoke nobility. His hair and beard were trim and neat. He wore a thick belt made of sheep hide— something I'd never seen, even when visiting Shomron. Despite the heat, a vivid crimson mantle was wrapped tightly about his shoulders.

"Were you a friend of Seguv's?" Hiel asked me.

I stole my eyes from the nobleman in the corner. "Yes sir, I was."

A hungry expression entered Hiel's eyes. "How did you know him?"

"I live in Levonah. He came up to sell dates."

"You came all the way from Levonah?"

"No sir, I was in Emek HaAsefa when I heard."

The nobleman with the mantle snapped up his head and examined me. I could feel the heat of his gaze, his black eyes glowing like coals in the heart of a fire.

Hiel also sat up straighter at the mention of Emek HaAsefa. "Are you of the *bnei nevi'im*?"

I gave a weak smile, then thought better of it. "No, sir, I am a musician."

"Oh, you are that shepherd boy that…that Seguv spoke of." My smile almost broke through again when I heard that Seguv spoke about me, but Hiel's voice cracked on his son's name.

"Did he…I mean, were you…" Hiel was foundering.

Without warning, the nobleman with the fiery eyes rose to his feet,* drawing Hiel's attention. "Are you leaving?"

The nobleman motioned with his chin toward the entrance. In the doorway, flanked by two guards, stood King Ahav himself. The other guests and I immediately jumped to our feet. Hiel and his wife attempted to rise from the floor, but Ahav stopped them with a gesture.

"No need to get up, my dear Hiel. The mourner needn't stand before the King. I was broken-hearted when the news reached me." The King pulled my vacated stool toward himself and sat down. "You may wait outside," he said to his two guards. I wasn't sure if I should leave as well, but followed the lead of the other guests and continued to stand respectfully.

The King ignored our presence, his attention fixed on Hiel. "I blame myself, of course."

Hiel's hand rose in protest. "You must not, my King. I knew the risks involved. The dangers of the waters here are well known. I was proud to take on the mission of rebuilding a great city in Israel. Our losses have been tragic, that is true. But we hold you blameless."

King Ahav dropped his eyes and fingered the tassel on his belt, replying quietly, "I'm not talking about the waters. I'm speaking of the curse."

Hiel's eyes grew wide. "My Lord, I thought you did not believe in the curse."

"Well, I didn't. It seemed so ridiculous. Just a story told to children and the ignorant to frighten them away. But now that it has come true, can we continue to deny it?"

"What curse?" I slapped my hand over my mouth, but the question had already leapt out. One didn't just speak in front of the King—certainly not to interrupt such an intimate conversation.

The King turned to me, and for the second time that day I had the impression that I was being examined. But while the nobleman's gaze penetrated to the heart, the King seemed to be weighing my value. "You look familiar," he said at last.

I dropped my hand from my mouth but didn't reply.

King Ahav's eyes held me. "You may speak."

"Thank you, my King." I bowed my head, avoiding looking him in the eye. "I am a musician. I played at the King's wedding."

"Ah yes, I remember." Ahav leaned back with the satisfied smile of one who has made a good purchase. "Yes, the curse. When Joshua conquered Jericho over five hundred years ago, he declared, 'Cursed is the man who will rise up and build this city Jericho. With his oldest son he will lay the foundations, with his youngest son he will erect its gates.'"

Hiel and his wife both started to wail. I shrank back against the wall—I shouldn't have asked.

The King turned back to the couple on the floor. "It's so strange that the curse would come true," he said, a tone of pleading in his voice, but their sobbing only grew louder. "Who would imagine that the curse of the disciple would materialize, when the words of his master failed?"

"And what does that mean?" The air in the room pulsed as the nobleman with the fiery eyes stepped forward, his frame expanding as he stalked out of his corner toward the King. The hard tone of his voice sounded familiar. I'd heard such a tone once before—from Yambalya.

The King snickered. "Come Eliyahu, you know the story better than I. Moses pronounced a curse on the people that if they worship idols, there will be no rain. Go on, recite it for us."

Eliyahu's nostrils flared as Ahav waved a hand for him to speak, but he did not argue with a command from the King. He drew his mantle tightly around him and declared: "Guard yourselves, lest you turn your hearts and serve other gods and bow down to them." Eliyahu's voice shook with rage. "Then the wrath of the Holy One will blaze against you. The heavens will be restrained, there will be no rain, the ground will not give its abundance, and you will be lost from upon the good land the Holy One gave you."

I'd known these verses from the Torah since I was a young boy, but this was the first time they made me tremble.

The King appeared unmoved. "You see," he faced the bereaved couple, "it makes no sense that this curse would come upon you, my dear Hiel. Look around you. The people seek the Baal more every day, yet in my entire life, I never remember the rain being so plentiful. So why should the curse of Joshua cause your family so much misery, when the curse of his teacher Moses has foundered?"

Eliyahu stepped closer to the King. He would have towered over Ahav even if the King hadn't been sitting. Had the guards been in the room, they surely would have removed Eliyahu to a respectful distance—but they were outside. For the first time, the King shrank as he stared up into Eliyahu's fiery gaze.

I could barely breathe—the air grew heavy, like a gathering storm. Eliyahu's voice was barely above a whisper. "As the Holy One, the Lord of Israel, before whom I stand, lives…there will be no dew nor rain during these years except by my word."

A shudder ran down my back. No one moved as Eliyahu locked eyes with the King. The silence pressed down upon us all. Then Eliyahu spun and strode out of the room, his mantle flying behind him like a banner of war.

Both guards rushed in. They couldn't have heard his declaration but must have been alarmed by the fury on Eliyahu's face. "Is everything well, my King?"

"Fine," the King rasped. Clearing his throat loudly, he shook himself and added in a commanding tone, "You may continue to wait for me outside."

The guards bowed and left, and the King turned back to Hiel and his wife. "Always been unyielding, Eliyahu has. He's quite wise, really, but once he gets an idea into his head, there's no reasoning with him."

"Well, he has certainly gone too far this time," Hiel said, no longer crying.

"Nonsense, he's harmless enough. With people like that, it is best to just let them be."

An awkward silence descended on the room.

"And how is the King finding married life?" Hiel asked.

"Ah." Ahav's posture relaxed with the change of subject. "Izevel has been doing wonderful things with the palace. For my father it was a symbol, you know, and for me it's just a home. But she insists that a palace should be a place of devotion. She brought down a beautiful Ashera tree all the way from Tzur to plant at the gates. Are you men leaving?" The two brothers had stepped forward, and the King gestured them ahead, pausing to allow them to take their leave of Hiel and his wife.

I thought this was a good opportunity to slip out as well, and stepped forward once the brothers turned to leave. I leaned down toward Hiel and his wife and repeated the line Uriel made me memorize before I left. "May the Holy One comfort you among the mourners of Israel."*

Hiel and his wife both lowered their heads. I bowed to the King the way the farmers had, and respectfully backed out of the open door.

I peered up the mountain trail once outside the city gates. The return trip would be more strenuous than the downhill journey had been. A roof of black clouds hid the mountain tops, and I hoped the impending rain wouldn't prolong my ride. The distance from my master suddenly felt daunting.

I kicked Balaam into a trot, and we were soon back among the date palms again. The patchwork shade upon the ground made the field a blend of light and darkness. As I watched the trunks flow by, a flash of red caught my eye. Eliyahu's mantle was crumpled at the base of one of the trees. Its owner lay beside it, head between his knees, gripped by the spirit of prophecy.

Rabban Shimon ben Gamliel said: The world rests on three things: on justice, on truth, and on peace.

Pirkei Avot 1:18

14

The Key of Rain

"What happened?" My master sat perched on a boulder at the turnoff to Emek HaAsefa. Whether he'd been waiting for me since daybreak or had arrived just in time to meet me, I couldn't tell. He showed no weariness, only quiet, complete attention. "I want every detail."

The return journey passed faster than I'd expected. The roof of black clouds lifted ahead of me as I ascended the pass above Jericho, and I made it back without encountering any rain. Ragged patches of blue could now be seen through breaks in the gray sky. Uriel led me to his cave where steam rose from a covered pot simmering over glowing coals. I'd eaten my last hard loaf the night before and was eager to break the day's fast, but the urgency on my master's face told me that recounting what I saw would have to come first. Uriel filled a bowl full of fragrant lentil stew and placed it on the table. I sat at the empty spot and prepared to tell my tale while my master ate.

"No, no—sit here." The old *navi* gestured toward the place with the stew. "Eat first, then speak."

The prophet said nothing while I ate, though he supervised every mouthful as if measuring my progress. Why was he so anxious? He'd waited much longer to hear my report after the royal wedding. Though still hungry, I pushed the half-eaten bowl of lentils away. "The road there was all mud and rain, but the plains of Jericho were dry. I could smell the balm trees from the foot of the mountain, though they're not yet in flower." I described the newly built city, its massive walls, and buildings of fresh-cut stone. I told how Hiel had placed his house on a hill, as if he were king of Jericho. "When I entered, I didn't know what to say to Seguv's parents, so I just sat."

"You did well," Uriel said. "Words rarely pass through the fresh pain of loss." He nodded for me to continue.

I described the house, the visitors, Seguv's parents. Uriel nodded as I spoke, saying nothing. I cocked my head at him when he finally interrupted to question me about Eliyahu's mantle. "Why is that important, Master? Who is he?"

"I might ask you the same question. Continue."

I recounted King Ahav's entrance, how I'd been moved by the King's descent all the way to Jericho to comfort his faithful servant.

"And no doubt to strengthen his resolve. The King has much invested in the rebirth of Jericho and its balm." Uriel closed his eyes and waved me on.

I described Seguv's mother wailing as the King conveyed his wonder at the fulfillment of Joshua's curse.

"Yes." The prophet drew out the word. The interruption gave me pause. Pain cut deep folds down his face. The thread of my story frayed and Uriel opened his eyes. "Why do you stop?"

"King Ahav forced Eliyahu to recite Moses's words." These verses were part of a longer passage that my aunt used to recite with me every night before bed, as she still did with my younger cousins, and I recited them with ease. "Guard yourselves,* lest you turn your hearts and serve other gods and bow down to them. Then the wrath of the Holy One will blaze against you, the heavens will be restrained, there will be no rain, the ground will not give its abundance, and you will be lost from upon the good land that the Holy One gave you."

I cleared my throat. "I have said Moses's words many times, but until Eliyahu said them, I never realized they were a curse."

"Not exactly a *curse*." Uriel bit off the last word. "But I do not expect this King to grasp the difference. Go on."

I described Eliyahu's fury. Uriel's hands trembled on the table as I repeated his oath, seared word for word into my memory, "As the Holy One, the Lord of Israel, before whom I stand, lives…there will be no dew nor rain during these years except by my word."

When I shared how I took leave of Hiel and his wife, Uriel's patience finally waned. "And once you left Hiel's home, what happened?"

"I mounted Balaam and rode through the gate. Then, as I was preparing for the ascent up the mountains, I saw...Eliyahu."

Uriel pushed his hands flat on the table and leaned in closer. "And what exactly did you see?"

"He was lying in a date grove at the side of the road, trembling."

"With the spirit of prophecy?"

At my nod, Uriel closed his eyes and leaned back. I eyed my half-eaten meal; the smell of warm lentils teased me as my master mulled over my story.

Then the prophet's eyes snapped open. "But he didn't receive prophecy in the house?"

"No..." I pressed my hand over my eyes, recalling the scene. Eliyahu towered over Ahav, the room shrank around them. The metallic ring of the oath echoed in my ears. That wasn't prophecy. Could Eliyahu have received a prophecy just before speaking out, while I was focused on the King? "I think...I think he received prophecy only after he left the city."

"You *think*, or you know?" Uriel's eyes bored into mine.

"It wasn't prophecy." I sat taller. "I would have noticed if he went into prophecy. And then he was standing there in front of the King..." My voice trailed off, having no words for the experience.

"After you saw Eliyahu in the date grove, what did you do?"

"I continued riding up the mountainside. I feared I wouldn't get back before sundown tonight."

"And the King?"

He and his soldiers passed me soon after. They were all on horses."

"Did anything happen as the King passed?"

"No. I dismounted and stood to the side of the road." I rubbed a rough spot on the table. "The King didn't even look my way as he passed."

Uriel sighed deeply. "You have done well in your tale. It explains much—though one mystery still remains."

"What does it explain, Master?"

"It explains why the heavens are trembling and why the gates of prophecy have swung wide."

I frowned at Uriel. *Prophecy had gates*?

"Eliyahu has taken one of the forbidden keys."*

I shook my head, "Keys?"

"Yes, keys." Uriel nodded as he spoke, as if I understood, then in one quick motion, he stood. "Do you recall the sisters we met on our first day traveling together?"

I nodded, remembering the anguish of the older sister who wanted to conceive.

"I explained then about the three keys that forever remain in the hands of the Holy One: the key to the womb, the key to the grave, and the key to the sky. Eliyahu has taken the last one—the Key of Rain—in many ways the most powerful of the three."

"Taken it?"

"Well, I should say he was given it. Who can take a heavenly key by force? But at the time you stood in Hiel's house, I entered *navua* here in Emek HaAsefa. I saw Eliyahu's soul rise to the highest realms, to the Throne of Glory itself.* There he demanded the Key of Rain. There was an uproar among the angels. It was enough that he reached such an exalted place—how could he demand one of the keys? But the Holy One granted Eliyahu's request."

I'd never heard my master speak like this. "What does that mean?"

"It means that as long as he holds the key, Eliyahu will determine if and when we receive rain."

"And the prayers we're offering—?"

"Will not be answered. The Holy One will not bring rain as long as Eliyahu denies it."

"What about Yambalya and the Baal?"

"They are powerless to bring the rain."

I pictured the faces of the farmers standing in the morning rain at the wedding. "But I saw—"

"There is no Baal." My master spoke calmly, but his eyes burned, reminding me of Eliyahu's. "Remember, the same hand which fashioned the light, made the darkness as well."

Uriel lifted his eyes to the soot-darkened roof of the cave. "That hand has now granted the power to bring rain to Eliyahu, and to him alone. Neither myself nor Yambalya can do anything affecting the rain, other than pleading with Eliyahu."

I grinned at the thought of Yambalya and his priests cutting themselves and calling out to the Baal in vain. "So when Eliyahu swore there'd be no rain other than by his word, he knew he held the key?"

Uriel observed me closely. "A well-placed question, and one that I cannot answer. Did Eliyahu know he would receive the key when he made his oath? Did he already hold it? We may never know."

Encouraged by Uriel's praise, I pressed the point. "But if the key is never given to man, why would he think he could receive it? He wouldn't swear otherwise—he must have known."

"So I believed, that's why I asked you if he received prophecy in Hiel's house." Uriel stroked his beard. "But prophecy is not the only path of power.

What the righteous decree, the Holy One carries out."*

"The righteous can bind the Holy One?"

Uriel nodded, his eyes cast in shadow. "You yourself observed a woeful example of this."

"When?"

"I do not believe the Holy One commanded Joshua to curse the city of Jericho—he was moved by his own spirit to bind the city in ruins forever. But once his lips spoke the curse, the Holy One gave it power."

The weight of Uriel's words slowly penetrated. "That's why Seguv died?"

Uriel nodded. "Hiel's family has been destroyed by a curse uttered five hundred years ago."

I swallowed the lump forming in my throat. "That's what happened with Eliyahu?"

"Perhaps." The cave filled with a whiff of acrid smoke as the morning lamp burned out. Uriel rose and pinched the smoldering wick.

The muscles of my master's shoulders knotted beneath his tunic. "You don't agree with what he did, do you, Master?"

Uriel turned back to me, his eyes cold. Had the question gone too far? "It's not for me to agree or disagree, Lev." His voice was calm, though his body remained tense. "Eliyahu must be an extremely powerful prophet. To wrest a key from the Holy One is something that has never happened; I would have said it was impossible."

Uriel sat down stiffly on his stool. "But it is true that his way is not my way."

"His way?"

"Eliyahu is willing to take a path I will not tread. The people fear power. You saw this in their reaction to Yambalya. Eliyahu wants to show them that the Holy One is the only power to fear. By this, he hopes to win back the heart of the nation."

"Isn't that what you want as well?"

"Indeed."

"But you don't think it'll work?"

"It may work—but will it last?" He rose and stepped toward the mouth of the cave.

I sensed Uriel's impatience with my questions. He preferred to be alone to ponder everything I told him, but I yearned to understand. "Why wouldn't it last?"

Uriel turned back toward me. "Because fear will not bring the devotion that the Holy One seeks. And will the people truly fear the Holy One, or just Eliyahu? Someday Eliyahu will go the way of all flesh, and the darkness will remain. Then what will the people do, if we have trained them to fear?"

"Return to darkness?"

Uriel nodded. "This is why I left the path of fear. It is a tool most fit to the hands of darkness. The powers of darkness always appear to be greater in number, and often in strength as well." Despite the daylight outside the cave, shadow dimmed the prophet's face.

"But Master, why should darkness be more powerful than light?"

"Darkness is not more powerful than light, but in this world, it *seems* to be so. Who would choose night over day? If light and darkness were seen in balance, there would be no real choice between them. The true power of light is masked to enable us to choose."

I thought of Eliav bowing before the Baal. "But why mask it? Doesn't the Holy One want us to choose the path of light?"

"Of course, but it must come of true free will. This world exists so we can perfect ourselves and creation as a whole; we can do this only through making hard choices. If the way is already paved before us, then even the right choice will yield no growth."

Uriel sat down again, but no sooner had he settled on the stool than he was back on his feet. "In the beginning, there was only the light of the Holy One—a light that shone so brightly, nothing else could exist." He took the extinguished lamp from its niche on the wall and set it down before me. "In order to create the world, the Holy One withdrew this light, leaving a space of darkness behind. Only a single ray of light shone into this void. But even this fragment of Divine light filled the emptiness with such radiance that a world of choice could not exist. So, the Holy One made the lamp of darkness as well."*

I fingered the clay lamp on the table. "A lamp of darkness?"

"A lamp that radiates darkness. A lamp that conceals the light as night covers day."

"But why?"

"As I told you, so we can grow. The world is oil and we are the wicks. As we grow, we draw creation through us and reveal the hidden light."

"But you said the Holy One doesn't desire too much light."

"That is true. The more light we shine into the world, the deeper the shadow cast by the lamp of darkness. But that is not our concern—our task is to create more light, no matter the cost."

"Why create light if the lamp of darkness will only cover it up?"

Uriel's lips spread in a sad smile. His shoulders sank, and his pace slowed. "When a child first learns to walk, his father might stand only one or two steps away. But as the child progresses, the father steps farther and farther away, not to punish the child, but to allow him to grow."

In my exhausted state, the image of a father teaching his son was too much for my newly awakened heart. I dropped my eyes to the table, all curiosity about Eliyahu or the lamp of darkness extinguished. I'd never thought of it before, but I must have known how to walk before coming to live with my aunt and uncle. *Had my father taught me? What else had he taught me before he left the world?*

Uriel reached over and touched me gently on the underside of my chin, forcing my moist eyes to meet his. "Your father gave more for you than you can imagine."

I smiled through the tears.

The *navi* stepped to the back of the cave. "The lamp of darkness is now casting a powerful shadow. Since the gathering began, there has been a great rise in idolatry in the land. Traveling among the people has never been more important." He lowered himself onto a reed mat on the floor. "The remaining disciples left while you were in Jericho. The time has come to resume our travels. Play for me, and I will seek our path."

This was my master's voice of command—the time for questioning had passed. As my kinnor was still in the musicians' cave, I drummed on the table, tapping out a complex rhythm I'd learned from Zim at Shiloh. I closed my eyes and chanted softly between the beats.

The sound of chattering teeth alerted me that Uriel had ascended—the prophet could no longer hear my drumming—but I didn't stop. I raised my voice even louder, no longer worried about distracting my master, and the stone walls threw my tones back at me. As I let myself be swept away by the flow of the music, sweat beaded on my forehead, my hands stung, and the tightness in my shoulders released with each slap against the hard wood.

My throat was raw when I felt Uriel's gaze upon me. I broke off my chanting and opened my eyes. My hands faltered on the table. My master's face was clouded; his brow hung low over pensive eyes.

"Where are we going, Master?"

"Nowhere."

"Nowhere?"

"Nowhere. We are to stay here through Shabbat and begin traveling on the first day of the week."

"Why?"

"I do not know. I did not merit a reason in the vision—I thought our work here was finished. All the disciples have gone, and very few people live in the surrounding valleys. But perhaps someone is coming to us. Either way, we will know soon enough."

Hillel saw a skull floating in the water. He said to it: Because you drowned others, you were drowned. And ultimately, those who drowned you will be drowned as well.

Pirkei Avot 2:7

15

The Battle

For days, we practiced patience. Uriel sat in silence while I searched my kinnor for new sounds. My master said perhaps we awaited a visitor, one important enough for the Holy One to delay our travels. Yet, except for Yonaton, who came to visit often, not a soul entered the valley. As first light seeped through the trees at the dawn of the following week, I again asked, "Master, where are we going now?"

The prophet sighed. "I do not know." He lowered himself onto the cave floor. "Please play." No sooner had I reached for my kinnor than a rush swept past me, as if the cave had exhaled its contents. My master's body trembled on the ground; this time, his soul ascended faster than I'd ever seen. Ignoring my instrument, I hitched our things to Balaam.

As I tied the last bag to the donkey, Uriel stepped out of the cave, his face ashen.

"Have you received instruction?"

"Yes. We must go now." The quiver in his voice silenced any further questions.

I led Balaam up the hill toward the road.

"Not that way." Uriel pointed down the hill toward a narrow track that wound north across the valley floor and snaked up the far ridge. "This way," he insisted, already moving as he spoke.

I touched my father's knife, concealed beneath my tunic. Shimon disappeared down that path right after telling me not to use my knife and had not reappeared since. I shook my head to clear the image of Shimon's scarred face, and turned Balaam to follow Uriel.

A voice called out behind me, "Wait! Don't go yet." Yonaton weaved down the rocky hillside, his sister Yael trailing behind. "My parents sent provisions for your journey." Yonaton pulled two large loaves and a cake of pressed figs from the skin slung over his shoulder. Yael struggled under a massive, green-skinned melon.

I untied the top of one of the donkey bags and carefully added Yael's melon. Yonaton placed the bread and figs on top of the swollen fruit. Even though we'd parted only the night before, I was glad to see my friend one more time. We embraced quickly.

"Go in peace. And take care of Master Uriel."

Uriel still descended the trail, heedless of the gift we'd received. I squeezed Yonaton's hand one last time. "I'll see you next year," I said, then led Balaam at a trot after my master.

Early grasses and mud-filled hollows slowed our progress. We traveled all that day along the overgrown trail, encountering no one. When the sun dropped below the horizon, Uriel pointed to a cave on the hillside. As we ascended through the trees, I gathered an armful of firewood. The prophet inspected the shelter while I arranged the wood outside its entrance.

"No, Lev." Uriel emerged from the darkness within. "Tonight, we light the fire inside."

I gazed up at the cloudless sky—it was a shame to spend the night in a smoke-filled cave when we knew there was no chance of rain. Did Uriel think that Eliyahu had relented already? I turned to ask, but my master's gaze was fixed on the breeze whispering through the oak trees below, and I couldn't bring myself to disturb him.

Uriel sat outside, gazing out into the darkness as I cooked dinner. When I finished, Uriel accepted a bowl of wheat porridge without a word, laid it beside him, and turned back to his contemplation.

The two of us had hardly spoken since leaving that morning. I knew he preferred to be left to his own reflections, but questions filled my mind. "Master?" I said quietly.

Uriel turned toward me, firelight flickering in his eyes. "Yes?"

"I've been thinking about Eliyahu. Won't his curse also hurt those who don't bow to the Baal? Like Yonaton's family?"

"Indeed. A curse brings suffering without making distinctions. It falls upon the guilty and the innocent alike." Tears welled in his eyes. "Even the one who called down the curse is not spared its destruction." He turned back to the darkness, his bowl of porridge untouched, congealing in the cool night air.

I thought of Seguv, dead soon after coming of age, never married, never a father. He didn't fall in battle or struggle for his life. He was the victim of a curse uttered five hundred years before he was born.

Yet, it wasn't Seguv's death that brought tears to my master's eyes. Was it Eliyahu's curse? Did he feel the pain of farmers like Yonaton's family, who would suffer without rain despite their loyalty to the Holy One? Was he thinking of Eliyahu himself? I didn't think so. These were not the quick and hot tears of anger or pain; they were the seeping tears of deep sadness. I cried this way when I finally accepted that my mother would never come back for me. These tears sprang from a well deep within.

But it wasn't my place to pry. I turned to serve myself and caught sight of Balaam, grinding his teeth at the side of the cave, our bags still hitched over his back—how had I not noticed he was still burdened? My uncle would have sent me to bed hungry for such callousness. I moved to unload him, but Uriel stopped me with a grunt and a single shake of his head. Apparently, the donkey would have to sleep ready to travel. I left my master to his thoughts and returned to the cave to eat alone.

I dreamed of stars, my shadow floating across the jeweled sky. In the darkness, a mountain rose before me, a palace perched on its crown. Silently, the air shifted, and I flew forward on the breeze. The palace grew until it filled the night sky. A dim light flickered through a window set high in the outer wall. I glided onwards, landing on the sill of the window.

I knew the room below by its tall columns, carved like date palms, marching in two lines down the center, their bases lit by torches, their tops lost in shadow: the throne room of the King. Two thrones presided over the room, just as I remembered; the King's was empty, but Izevel sat arrow-straight on the one crafted for her father. Her hands gripped the heavy wooden arms of the chair, her olive skin glowing in the torchlight. Even though the throne dwarfed her small frame, the fire in her eyes and her air of command made it seem as though it could barely contain her force.

"You summoned me, my Queen?" The deep voice echoed through the cavernous room. In the firelight, Yambalya's violet robes looked nearly bloody, and they swirled

as though carried on a wind as he approached.

"Yes. Have I acted too soon?"

"No, my Queen." Yambalya bowed before her, exposing the laddered scars on the back of his neck. "You were right to act now."

"And the people will not protect them?"

"They are sheep. They will not rise against us without the leadership of their king."

"That they will not have." She moistened her lips with her tongue and curled them in a serpentine smile. Her eyes narrowed as she watched the priest closely. "Baal has not informed you where he is to be found?"

"No, my Queen. The movements of one man, no matter how bold, are not a matter of note to mighty Baal."

Izevel leaned forward, her tapered fingers white on the clawed arms of the throne. "But he stopped the rains."

The cords of Yambalya's neck grew taut. "Yes, he stopped the rains. Their god is still strong in this land. But when their prophets are gone, the people will learn to fear Baal."

"Their prophets, yes. Most of their prophets are weak. But as long as this one remains alive, he gives the people strength. We must find him."

Yambalya's eyes burned in the torchlight. "The servants of Baal seek him even now. They have never failed in the hunt. He has not been seen since casting his curse. We believe he has fled the land."

Izevel laughed. "There is nowhere for him to flee. I watch the roads, and I have sent word to my father. He rules the sea. We will find him."

"Indeed we will, my Queen. I have read his future in the stars."

Izevel bent her head forward, close to Yambalya's. "What have you seen?"

"Eliyahu will not die the natural death of men—to this I will swear."

Izevel settled back in her throne, her face flushed with pleasure. "Excellent. I will hang his body from the walls of Shomron for the crows to devour. Let his death be a message to all who would stand against us."

"Yes, my Queen. It will be done."

Uriel shook me awake before the sun, the image of Izevel still looming in my mind in the half-light. I wanted to ask my master about the dream, but his distant eyes still defied interruption. As I stepped out of the cave, the old prophet stared back up our path in the direction we'd come. He sat down on the earth, placed his head between his knees, and was soon trembling with the spirit of prophecy.

By the time my master returned, our bedrolls were repacked and Balaam ready to travel. Uriel swept past me, stepping out of the cave and down toward the trail. "We have to move quickly. There isn't much time." He didn't elaborate as he dropped into the brush below our camp. Balaam trotted to keep up.

The *navi* kept to a driving pace all day. Daniel once told me that Uriel didn't concern himself with taking the shortest or fastest paths, that his goal was to travel among the people. Yet, we met no one along our path. What had changed?

The late afternoon sun had already reached the western ridge when Uriel finally stopped with a raised hand and gazed back up the trail. I spotted a man in the distance running toward us. Uriel increased his pace, but in that brief pause, a sad smile flit across his face.

The runner drew closer, but Uriel didn't slow or turn again. I kept glancing back over my shoulder, measuring the runner's progress as the trail rolled up and down between the hills, gently climbing toward the west. When our pursuer reached the hilltop directly behind us, he paused and bent forward, hands on knees to catch his wind, then straightened and resumed running down the hill. In that moment, the dying sun illuminated his features, and I realized he wasn't a man at all, just a boy: Yonaton.

Uriel did not pause until Yonaton caught up with us. Gasping for air, he tried to speak, "They're looking—"

Uriel cut him off with his own skin of water. "First drink. You've had a hard journey—it was brave of you to come." The tenderness in Uriel's eyes contrasted with the rigid impatience of his body.

Yonaton gulped down the skin of water and began again to deliver his message. "Yesterday afternoon they came looking for you. They were part of the Queen's personal guard. I recognized them from the wedding. They heard that I played during the gathering. They came to my house and had me lead them to the valley, where they searched all the caves with swords drawn. They asked me where everyone had gone. I told them that you were the last ones to leave that morning. They asked which direction you went, and I pointed them toward Jericho." Exhausted by the flood of words and gasping for breath, Yonaton doubled over.

My mouth went dry. I pictured the long column of soldiers that had escorted Izevel to her wedding. How many had remained behind?

"How many were they?" Uriel asked.

"Four," he forced out. Yonaton held up as many fingers without standing straight.

"You saw them go toward Jericho?"

"Yes. I wanted to come and warn you immediately, but it was already too dark, so I came at first light." I thought of the fire inside the cave and Balaam remaining burdened all night, ready to travel—had Uriel known?

"You brought nothing with you?"

"When I finished my food and water, I dropped the skins so that I could run faster."

My feet ached in sympathy. I had a hard enough time keeping up with Uriel; I couldn't imagine trying to overtake him. Yonaton stood barefoot—had his sandals also slowed him down?

Uriel sighed, turned his eyes to the sky, and shook his head. "Again, that was very brave of you. I doubt you can appreciate how much you risked coming after us. You will need to stay with us now. It is no longer safe to return."

"Why? They don't know I've come."

"They do. You were followed."

Yonaton and I turned as one, but saw nothing other than the wind playing over the low hills in the distance, stirring the brush.

"You won't see them." Uriel shook his head. "They will stay out of sight until they are ready."

I gazed up at my master. "Ready for what?"

"Surely you can reason that out for yourself?" Uriel started again up the trail. "Come, we must go on."

Despite the prophet's words, Yonaton was too drained by his run to do more than trudge along. When the sun set, we were forced to a crawl. Our trail wound through a steep ravine, already deep in shadow. Balaam brayed as he struggled to find footing on the loose rocks. After one particularly loud protest, Uriel laid his hand on the donkey's nose. "Peace, old friend." He gazed up at a rocky outcrop on the hillside above us. "Stay here. I want to examine that cave."

Uriel displayed no sign of fatigue from the day's march as he climbed up the steep slope and disappeared between the shadowed boulders. Moments later he reappeared and yelled down to us, "Come up. This looks like a good place to spend the night. Lev, see to the donkey. Yonaton, gather wood."

It took all of my skill to coax Balaam up to our resting spot. By the time I finished tying up and watering him, Yonaton came back with a double armful of wood. "Build the fire inside the cave," I whispered. "That way it won't be easily seen."

"No, build it outside tonight." Uriel turned away before either of us could question him.

I struggled to prepare the evening meal—a large crack at the back of the cave drew the wind right through the hollow, turning our shelter into a chimney. My eyes stung as smoke swirled in the cross-draft, and the fire licked my fingers from every side. Any feelings of security brought about by finding cover faded with the dying daylight. Our pursuers couldn't be far behind Yonaton. I stared out into the night as I cooked—listening.

Uriel hummed softly to himself in the back of the cave, unpacking and repacking our gear, while Yonaton snored between us. I gazed up at the stars. Was it really less than three months since Dahlia and I lay on the wall watching them, wondering what the future held? Was I now gazing at them for the last time?

Uriel finished packing and came to the mouth of the cave. "Take the food off the fire, it is time to eat."

My eyes watered from the smoke. "It's not done yet, Master."

"We have given it as much time as we can afford. Take it off and wake Yonaton—he must be famished."

Yonaton indeed ate as much as Uriel and myself combined. Once we finished, I picked up the pot to scrape it, but Uriel put up his hand. "There is no time for that. In any case, we cannot take it with us. Yonaton, throw the remaining wood on the fire. As long as it is burning high, it will appear as if it is tended. There will be no attack until they think we're asleep." I could see the whites of Yonaton's eyes as he stared around out into the darkness. "When you're done, we'll leave."

A column of sparks twisted up into the darkness when Yonaton dumped the last armload of wood on the blaze. Uriel led us to the back of the cave and handed us each a pack. "I've gone through and separated out only the most essential things. We'll need all our strength."

"What about Balaam?" I turned back toward the donkey, tied at the entrance.

Uriel sighed. "He stays. Leaving him tethered in front is the best sign that we are still in the cave."

I opened my mouth to protest.

"You think this poor payment for hard service?" Uriel raised his eyebrows. "Fear not. Men do not kill a beast of burden without cause. Balaam is wise. He will make his way with a new master. Or perhaps find his way back to his old one."

I appraised the pile of belongings to be abandoned. My kinnor rested on top. I trusted Uriel that we would need all our strength, but the kinnor wasn't a drain on my strength—it was a source of it. "I won't…" I insisted, "I can't…" I picked up the instrument, cradling it against my chest. "I'll carry it, the extra weight won't slow me down. I promise."

The fire sent shadows jumping and dancing on the cave walls, reflecting crimson on Uriel's tunic. "I'm sorry, Lev." He pulled the instrument from my weakly resisting hands and tucked it on top of a high rock cradled by a furrow in the cave wall. "It is well hidden there. May we merit to retrieve it."

I swallowed the bulge lodged in my throat, avoiding Yonaton's eyes. I laid my index finger to my father's knife beneath my tunic, suddenly grateful that I kept it on me at all times—would Uriel have made me leave that behind as well? Probably not. Shimon's dagger jutted through my belt, and he hadn't mentioned it.

But Yonaton's attention wasn't focused on me anyway. He peered into the crack at the back of the cave that began along the floor and rose into a narrow channel, splitting the cave wall to the ceiling. "You don't expect us to get out this way, do you?"

"There is no other path. They are watching the front."

"But it's too narrow—even Lev won't fit through."

Uriel approached the wall and ran his hand up and down the fissure. Behind him, the new logs burned down and the gathering darkness urged us to hurry. How much longer would our attackers wait? Uriel's eyes rolled back in his head; his voice echoed in the close cave. *"You split the rock for Samson at Lehi,* bringing him water and restoring our spirit. Only You can open our way and bring us out into life."*

The prophet's hand rose above his head like a general's in war, then came down with force, striking the rock with his staff. Nothing happened.

"You opened the mouth of the well for Israel, sustaining us in the wilderness. Open now our way and bring us out into life."* There was a sharp crack as Uriel swung again, with the same result.

Yonaton stared at the dirt floor, his shoulders tense. Balaam brayed in the silence. Was he just restless, or did he sense someone approaching?

Fists now clenched, Uriel leaned in close to the wall and hissed between clenched teeth, *"In the name of the Holy One, I say this is the moment for which you were formed!"**

A low rumble shook the cave. I grabbed Yonaton for support. His bulging eyes met mine as our hands trembled within each other's grasp. When the tremor stopped and the dust settled, the opening at the top of the crack had grown to twice its width.

Uriel led the way. As his feet disappeared, I gripped the rock and pulled myself upwards, taking shallow breaths as I wormed after my master in the darkness. The channel narrowed; sharp rocks scraped my arms and cut into my fingertips. Dirt rained on my hair, and the welcome smell of moist earth reached my nose.

When I emerged into the moonlight, Uriel's arm thrust out like a beam across my chest, holding me back from a deadly misstep. We stood on a slender ledge, overlooking dark tree-tops. Yonaton squeezed out behind me, and I put out a cautionary arm to protect him as well.

We were on the far side of the hill. The half-moon hovered above the horizon in the western sky, casting a silvery light across a different valley than the one we'd hiked that morning. We climbed down the cliff at a slug's pace. At first, I placed my hands and feet wherever my master did, but soon Uriel's long legs carried him over a patch of jagged rocks that I had to scramble through. By the time I bridged the gap, the prophet had disappeared.

The night air blew across my sweaty forehead; I shivered with the chill. I reached out with my right leg, searching for a foothold in the smooth rock. My body tensed, and my knee began an odd jumping motion. Even if I found a foothold, would my leg hold me? I reached farther down and straightened my quivering knee. My moist hands were slick against the rock. My foot slid, and I felt my grip loosen. A call for help died in my throat as I fell.

The ground was rough, but it was only a handsbreadth beneath my foot. The shock of so sudden a landing choked the cry in my throat. Uriel's strong hands kept me from sliding down the slope. Regaining my feet, I saw the prophet in the moonlight beside me, a finger to his lips.

Climbing down in the dark seemed easier for Yonaton. He crouched at the bottom of the cliff, probed with his foot, and dropped lightly to the ground.

We weren't down yet. The ground was a patchwork of brambles and sharp-sided heaps of stone. Awkward as I was descending the rock face, endless days spent chasing sheep over this terrain allowed me to slip smoothly down the hillside. At the bottom, Uriel dropped into a muddy streambed at the base of the hill. I sat down on the edge, swung my feet forward, and landed softly next to my master. A muffled cry came from above. Yonaton slithered down the side of the streambed, hitting the ground with a scrape and a hiss.

Uriel pulled Yonaton into a patch of moonlight to examine his leg—a dark gash marred the white of his hairless shin. Uriel grabbed the end of his own linen cloak, tore off a long strip, wrapped the cut and pulled hard on the ends. Yonaton winced and bit his lip as the prophet tied off the bandage.

We crossed the narrow streambed and picked up a faint trail. Despite his limp, Yonaton scurried uphill, his boyish features set with determination.

Voices drew my attention back toward the opening on the opposite hillside. In the darkness, the remnants of our fire sent a flickering, red glow through the crack that had freed us. It blacked out for an instant as a body slipped through the light's path, moonlight glinting off the sword stretched out before him.

Uriel clamped our shoulders with a grip that urged silence, forcing us to squat on the ground.

The soldier leaned across the ledge and scanned the hillsides. Was the pale moonlight sufficient for him to pick us out among the scrub and boulders? Did his roving head pause when it reached the spot where we crouched? I pictured him sniffing the earth, like the wild dogs in the hills above Levonah. They always found the injured sheep before the shepherds did.

The crack blacked out again as the soldier reentered the cave. Yonaton and I exhaled, but Uriel yanked us to our feet and spun us by our shoulders. "Come, we must move quickly. They'll circle around the hill. It will be faster for them."

"Where are we going?" Yonaton touched the wet wrapping on his leg, where blood already seeped through.

Uriel didn't answer.

The moon dropped beneath the horizon, obscuring the uneven ground, and forcing us to slow our pace even further. But I didn't mind the darkness: it concealed us as well.

I stumbled again and again. Yonaton limped along behind me, grunting whenever his shin brushed against obstacles on the unseen trail. Uriel pushed on ahead, surefooted and silent in the near-total darkness.

Uriel held up a hand and tipped his head back as if sniffing the wind. "Get down," he breathed. We lowered ourselves softly between the boulders at the side of the trail. I turned my head as I lay, my eyes glued to my master. With my ear pressed against the dirt, I felt a pulsing rhythm in the earth. Hoofbeats.

An impossibly tall figure appeared against the stars. As the shadow drew nearer, it revealed itself as a soldier on horseback. The animal stepped slowly between the boulders. Its questing gait indicated the soldier didn't know our location. Loud breathing drew closer, and a soft whinny sounded at our side.

I swallowed my breath, willing my heart to beat more quietly in my chest. The rider, sitting so far above the ground, could not see what lay at his feet. But how much did he trust his horse? How much did he understand it? The soldier could hear nothing above the heavy breathing of his steed, but would he surmise from the horse's agitation what the animal already knew: that three people lay on the ground before him?

Our faces remained pressed to the dirt as the soldier continued past us without breaking stride. Once I could no longer hear the horse's steps, Uriel rose again to his feet and increased his pace. *Where was he going?*

With the moon set, only the slow rotation of the stars marked the progress of the night. The Bear began the night high in the sky, but was almost at the horizon when Uriel rasped for the second time, "Get down." This time, I could barely hear the horse, and it never came close enough to see. Lying on the ground, I wondered what we would do once the sun rose. At least Uriel seemed to have a destination—but would we arrive in time?

We pushed forward, rushing toward the new day, which already made it easier to see pitfalls on the path. Now it was a race. When I saw a faint glow in the darkness ahead, brighter than the dawn quickly emerging behind us, I knew that we'd won. The glow of a welcoming fire grew ever closer. Uriel picked up his pace and we matched him easily, drawn on by the promise of safety. Yet, as we drew nearer to the warm light, it became clear that this blaze would offer us no protection at all.

Had we walked up the trail two days earlier, we would have crossed a clearing to a large house, at least three times the size of Uncle Menachem's. Now, with the roof gone, it seemed even larger. The walls still stood, their stones black with ash. A red glow radiated from burnt remains still smoldering from their destruction.

Uriel staggered forward with a low moan, no longer restraining his voice. He dropped to his knees at the side of a dark figure on the ground, and I flinched as a high-pitched cry broke from my master's lips. The firelight reflected off the silver beard of the corpse, which Uriel stroked lovingly as he wailed. I stepped closer, recognizing familiar wrinkles around the mouth that sang so beautifully it never required words. Tzadok. Other shadows dotted the clearing around the ruin. We'd arrived at the scene of a massacre.

A ram's horn blast split the dawn: a soldier with dark, hawk-eyes had reached the edge of the clearing.

The eerie silence following the blast was marked only by a last mournful wail from Uriel. I expected the soldier to kick his horse into a charge, but he just sat, watching us from a distance.

Uriel rose from Tzadok's side, his eyes now dry, radiating calm and power. "You two run. It's my blood they want. They'll take yours as well, but if you get far enough away, they won't bother giving chase."

Yonaton trembled, but his eyes were resolute. He straightened his shoulders and met my gaze with a short nod. We wouldn't leave the prophet alone to die. "There are three of us," I said. "We'll fight."

Uriel gripped his staff in one hand, the other flexing rhythmically, his muscles growing tense as he eyed his enemy. "If he were going to attack on his own, he would have done so already. He's just watching us until the others arrive. Then it will be one old man and two unarmed boys against four soldiers with swords and horses." He spun us away from the soldier and gave us each a hard push in the back. "Go!"

Uriel barked the command with so much force that my legs reacted before I even considered disobeying. We darted across the clearing, past the destroyed house, and into the cover of thick pine trees on the far side.

Our dark shelter gave me a renewed sense of safety, and I stopped for a last glimpse of my master.

Uriel rose to his full, imposing height; he twirled his staff above his head as the soldier circled, well out of striking range. A second rider charged up the trail. Would they wait for all four, or would the two attack? I staggered back toward Uriel, but Yonaton grabbed my arm. "He told us to get out of here!"

I bit my lip and tasted blood between my teeth. Yonaton was right, there was nothing more we could do for the *navi*. We dodged between the trees, crashed through branches, and stumbled on the uneven ground, no longer caring about keeping quiet, or even where we were going. When the ground dipped onto a trail, we sprinted in earnest, knowing that our lives depended on putting distance between ourselves and Uriel. There was no way he could hope to defeat four armed soldiers with just his staff, yet when I glimpsed back before disappearing into the trees, he was still swinging that staff over his head, keeping the soldiers at bay. I realized that this meager defense, which couldn't preserve his life for more than a few extra moments, wasn't for him at all—it bought the two of us time to escape the certain death he faced.

A boulder blocked the trail ahead, and we swung around it at full speed. Our haste made us careless: We almost ran straight into the third soldier riding hard up the trail. He reined in his horse, and a wide grin split his sharp cheekbones, his eyes falling upon Yonaton. "Thought you'd have a little fun with us chasing shadows down to Jericho, didya? Knew you were lying. Knew you'd bring us right to him. Ought to thank you, I should. But the Queen says no survivors—no prophets, no disciples. Anyone who'd run to warn a prophet sounds like a disciple to me." He kicked the horse's belly and charged.

We dove to opposite sides of the trail, and the soldier pursued Yonaton. "Run!" Yonaton screamed as the soldier raised his sword.

I took one step down the trail, then froze. I may have left my master to face four soldiers, but I wouldn't leave my friend to fight one alone. I snatched a sharp stone from the edge of the path and flung it with all my might at the rider's back. The rock missed its target but came close enough to the soldier's ear to make him flinch. That was enough—Yonaton rolled back onto the trail as the sword plunged into the vacated ground.

The soldier reared his mount and turned, now facing me. I threw a second rock. He ducked it, then raised his sword for the strike. My legs were rooted to the spot. Even if I'd run for the trees, I wouldn't have reached them in time. But the thrust never came—he lurched forward on the horse, hands clutching for balance as bright blood stained his tunic below the shoulder.

A man jumped out of the trees.

My mouth dropped. It was Shimon, his face livid, with dried blood obscuring his scars.

"Give me the other one!" he screamed at me.

I stared, uncomprehending. Shimon ran toward me with hand outstretched, reached into my belt, and pulled out the dagger that he'd given me months before.

The soldier was wounded, but not badly enough. He recovered his balance and kicked his horse forward. Shimon threw the dagger, but the soldier ducked low over his knees to avoid it.

The horse thundered toward us. The rider raised his sword, then screamed out in pain as Yonaton's rock struck his injured shoulder. He checked his mount and swiveled his pale face back and forth between us. He was still better armed, but now it was three against one, and none of us was his intended victim. Pulling up his horse, he turned and thundered back up the trail.

Shimon reached out a quivering hand. "Give it to me."

This time I knew exactly what he meant, as if expecting the request all along. I pulled my father's knife from under my tunic and handed it to the man who told me never to use it.

Shimon gaped at the knife in his hand. He closed his eyes and pressed the flat of the stone blade to his forehead. Tears squeezed out from under his eyelids. When he opened them, his face was transformed. The burning anger was gone, replaced by peaceful clarity. Without a word, he bolted up the hill after his injured enemy. The look in Shimon's eye pushed all thoughts of flight from my mind. I took off after him, waving for Yonaton to follow.

All four soldiers now circled Uriel like wild dogs, jabbing at him with their swords, hemming him in. He swung his staff in broad sweeps, and they cantered just out of reach. He couldn't keep up his defense for long. They would wait for the easy kill.

Shimon bounded from the trees, unnoticed, and leapt onto the closest horse. It reared and kicked as his weight crashed down behind its rider. Shimon threw a powerful arm around the neck and wrenched his enemy into a chokehold. With an upward thrust of his other hand, Shimon drove the knife through the soldier's back. A choking scream escaped the rider's throat as the tip of the blade broke through his chest above his heart. Shimon yanked the knife out and shoved the soldier's limp body off the horse.

The other three turned at their comrade's cry—a mistake. Uriel stepped forward and brought his staff down with a sickening crunch on the knee of a stocky soldier. The rider let out a howl and turned to fight the prophet, while his companions closed in on Shimon.

Two soldiers charged from either side, swords flashing. Shimon turned the first strike aside with the flat of the knife and threw himself backward to dodge the second. He dug his ankles into the horse's belly, and it leapt forward. He rode in a broad circle around the clearing, two riders giving chase while Uriel dueled the stocky one in the middle.

Yonaton and I waited in the shelter of the trees, gripping rocks. As Shimon raced past, we threw. I missed the hawk-eyed soldier's head by a hairsbreadth, but Yonaton's fist-sized chunk of stone hit his companion just above his left eye.

The rider buckled on his horse, lost his balance, and lurched to the side. He struggled to regain control of his mount, and we saw a blood stain below his shoulder—the same soldier we'd faced earlier. He recovered his balance and took off after us, blood streaming into his eye.

Again, he pursued Yonaton, who eluded him by ducking in and out of the trees ringing the clearing. I chased after them throwing rocks, aiming high to avoid hitting Yonaton. I missed twice, but my third throw connected with the back of his skull with a resounding thud.

The soldier screamed out and spun his horse around to face me. Yonaton seized his chance. Jumping out, he grabbed the horse's tail with both hands and pulled down with all his weight. The horse reared its front legs high in the air as its neigh echoed through the trees.

The soldier fell backward, and his sword tumbled from his hand. The combined force of Yonaton's weight and the soldier's desperate attempt to grip its mane caused his steed to lose its balance, and it too fell back on its haunches. The rider hit the ground first. The horse followed, landing on its rider and Yonaton.

The animal kicked its legs and rolled to regain its footing. Yonaton struggled up as well, having absorbed merely the weight of the horse's hind legs in the fall. The soldier took the hardest blow, falling from a height and crushed by the full weight of the horse's heavy body. Blood bubbled from his mouth as he scrambled for his fallen sword.

I dove past Yonaton, arms outstretched, reaching the sword before the soldier could grab hold of it.

I stood over my unarmed enemy, the hilt warm in my hand. The wounded soldier pushed himself upright and let out a raspy cough, his face twisting in pain. I stared down at him, feeling the weight of the iron. My hands trembled.

Yonaton laid a hand on my shoulder. No longer attempting to fight, the soldier opened his mouth to speak, and blood gushed out. I expected him to beg for his life, but the only words that escaped were a whispered plea. "Make it fast."

I pressed the point of the sword to the soldier's chest and squeezed my eyes shut, not wanting to watch. I always turned away when my uncle slaughtered the sheep. I drew the weapon back to gather more power, but my arms froze there.

"Do it!" the soldier cried, the effort forcing out a bloody cough. His chest gurgled—the soldier was dying. The most merciful thing would be to end it quickly. But I couldn't bring myself to deliver the final blow.

A hand closed over mine. I peered into Yonaton's eyes, afraid of finding pity there, but seeing only understanding. Yonaton took the sword and plunged it into the soldier's chest. The man twitched on the end of the blade, then went still.

I gawked at the bloody sword, then crashed to my knees. The little food I'd eaten the night before came up first, followed by heaves of bile.

"Come on!" Yonaton pulled at my tunic. "There are more of them." He yanked the heavy weapon from the corpse and sprinted back toward the heart of the battle.

I pulled myself upright—my master needed me. Wiping the mess from my face, I ran after Yonaton.

We stopped again at the edge of the trees. Even with a sword, we were no match for mounted opponents—we would wait for another opportunity to strike.

In the clearing, the hawk-eyed soldier still chased Shimon. Uriel smashed his staff into the nose of the stocky soldier's horse, and the rider grabbed at the reins to keep his balance as the horse reared. While he fought to get the horse back under control, Uriel slipped in closer, pummeling blows upon them both. Once the soldier regained his seat, he brandished his sword to hold off Uriel's assault.

But the stocky soldier's focus was diverted from the rest of the battle for a moment too long. Shimon saw the opening and veered toward the center of the clearing. The hawk-eyed soldier giving chase called out, but to no avail—all his comrade's attention was fixed on fending off Uriel's attack. He spun at the sound of a horse bearing down on him, but too late. Shimon jammed my knife into the soldier's neck. His eyes bulged and his jaw sank as he looked down upon the hilt of the knife protruding from his throat. He toppled sideways off the horse as the animal broke free.

The hawk-eyed soldier shrieked at the sight of his companion's collapse. He swiped at Uriel as he rode past, but the prophet blocked the blow easily with his staff. He rode on after Shimon, who was now unarmed.

Yonaton called out, "Here!" and thrust the blood-stained sword in the air. Shimon's horse leapt forward, and I launched a rock at the soldier to hold him back. Shimon snatched the weapon from Yonaton's hand and spun in time to block a thrust from the hawk-eyed soldier's sword.

Now Shimon had no need to run. He closed in on his adversary. Shimon's sword descended like a bolt, and the soldier raised his blade to block it. The clang of iron on iron sounded through the clearing as the soldier's sword broke off its hilt from the force of the blow. Shimon swung his sword in a wide circle around his head, then struck true. The soldier tumbled from his horse. His body slammed to the ground with a thud, followed by his head, which rolled to a rest at Uriel's feet, hawk-eyes gaping up at the old prophet.

Hillel said: Be among the disciples of Aharon, loving peace and pursuing peace, loving people and bringing them closer to Torah.

Pirkei Avot 1:12

16

Yochanan's Secret

"I don't understand." Shimon groaned as he and Uriel laid one of the slain prophets beside the ruined house.

"Tell me everything, from the beginning." Uriel approached the next of the fallen.

"I've been here since I left you. You were right; it was better for me here among the masters than it was among the disciples. The Queen's soldiers rode up at sunset, eight of them. Three of us went out to greet them with food—we had no idea. Foolish as it was, that probably saved my life. I don't think that anyone in the house managed to—Lev, no!"

I jumped back at the rebuke. Yonaton and I had approached one of the bodies—why shouldn't we try to help? Did Shimon think we couldn't carry the body? And why did he yell only at me? Yonaton was a bit stronger, but not by much.

Uriel edged over to my side, making himself a barrier between me and the dead. "Yes, why don't the two of you gather wood for the morning meal. We will need all of our strength."

My master's tone was softer than Shimon's, but his command no less clear. I bit back my response, and the two of us retreated from the line of bodies to the first row of trees, where we gathered sticks in silence so as not to miss a word.

Shimon hovered over another of the fallen prophets. "The details of the battle are not important. You see the results before you."

"Did anyone else survive?"

"I think not. We'll know for certain once we have gathered everyone." He studied the blackened corpse at his feet. "I hid in a cave last night."

Uriel placed a hand on Shimon's shoulder. "Flight is also courage when it holds hope for return."

Shimon nodded. "The ram's horn roused me. I wasn't sure if the blast was from friend or foe, so I crept back, keeping to the shelter of the trees. Then I saw one of them go after the boys, so I attacked. I managed to plant my knife in him, and he rode off. Coward. I knew he must be going after you. I couldn't help you barehanded, so I asked Lev for Yochanan's knife."

Shimon limped to the body that still had my father's knife protruding from its neck. He placed a foot on the soldier's back and grasped the hilt. The knife slid out with a jerk. Shimon plunged it into the soft earth a few times to remove the blood, wiped the blade with his palm, and brought the weapon to Uriel.

Uriel examined the knife. "Yes, Lev has shown it to me. For the second time, this blade has saved your life."

"Indeed. But it is a tool of peace, not war. It should never have been used to kill a man."

Uriel rotated the knife, as if examining it for flaws. "It hardly seems you had a choice."

Shimon's forehead sunk toward the ground. "No, there was no choice. Not this time, and not when Yochanan used it to save me." Shimon sighed. "You know, just before it happened, I…I saw him."

Neither of them heard the branches fall from my arms.

Uriel fixed his eyes on Shimon. "You saw Yochanan?"

He nodded once. "I touched the flat of the blade to my forehead and closed my eyes. I recalled that day years ago. My fear, his sacrifice. I was filled with death, the injustice of Yochanan's murder, the horror of yesterday's massacre, and the evil of them trying to kill you now…" Shimon's posture straightened to the height of that morning's battle. "And that's when it happened."

Uriel's eyes bored in on his disciple. Even Yonaton stopped pretending to gather wood. "What did you feel?"

"Power, like nothing I've ever felt. Yesterday I injured my ankle running away, but when I took off after that soldier, I felt no pain—and I ran faster than I ever have." Shimon's hands stretched out in wonder.

"Clarity." Shimon closed his eyes. "I could see every needle on the trees, feel every whisper of the wind. When I charged into battle, I didn't have to decide what to do. My body just…knew. I leapt onto the back of that horse as if it were a pony!" Shimon's eyes popped open, cutting creases across his scars.

"Did you feel anything else?"

"Courage, no fear at all. Last night, I couldn't sleep, despite my exhaustion. I shook all night, petrified that they might hunt me down. But this morning, I wasn't afraid anymore. And so strong. I snapped that soldier's sword in two—I can't do that."

"How did it end?"

"When the last soldier fell, I felt it just…flow out of me. The fear hasn't returned, but my leg is throbbing, and well…" he glanced at his hands, "I won't be shattering any more swords."

Uriel managed a weak smile. "You have sought *navua* for many years, but it always eluded you. Most disciples either succeed or abandon their path—but you persisted. Now you taste the fruits of your commitment."

"This was prophecy?" Shimon's eyebrows furrowed. "This isn't like any *navua* I've ever seen."

"But I have seen far more than you have, Shimon. One can receive the Presence in many ways.* There is a level, close to prophecy, which can come in a time of crisis. One sees injustice and rushes to act without considering oneself. When your heart, mind, and will move you in this way, you can become a fit vessel for the Holy One."

The words made little sense to me, and Shimon didn't seem to understand either. The lines on his forehead only deepened.

"Learn from Samson," Uriel continued. "Drawn after his eyes, he could never receive full *navua*. But when he seized that donkey's jawbone at the battle of Lehi, what filled him in that moment?"

Fear? I asked myself.

My master continued, not waiting for an answer. "The desperate need of Israel. He slew a thousand men that day. Despite his…flaw, Samson was a fit tool in the hand of the Holy One and merited to save our people from the Pelishtim."

"So the Presence brings you strength?"

"Not always. It is a spirit that fills you with the power you need at the moment. Samson, whose way was to fight alone, received the power of an army.

King Shaul, who ran away from kingship, received this spirit in a different way, giving him the power to lead."

Shimon's face shone for a moment, then his eyes brimmed with tears. "But why wasn't I given this power yesterday? Why did so many have to die?"

"Do not take what you received lightly—it is a rare gift. Yesterday you were afraid. Today you were tormented by the massacre, in fear of another slaughter, and then remembered so vividly the sacrifice Yochanan made to save your life. The spirit didn't take you into battle. You were determined to fight, determined to succeed—you just didn't know how. That determination made you a fit vessel for the spirit. You didn't receive the strength of Samson or the leadership of Shaul. But it did bring you enough speed, strength, and knowledge to overcome these four soldiers. For that, I'm grateful."

My head throbbed. Between our journey, the flight from the cave, our march through the night, and the dawn battle, I was exhausted. Uriel's words knocked away my last restraint. I really grasped only one thing from the conversation: Shimon's transformation was connected to my father's knife—to my father's sacrifice for him. My father saved Shimon's life...*at the cost of his own?*

They stood there talking as if I were as deaf as one of the murdered prophets. They thought I couldn't handle carrying the bodies, couldn't be trusted with the truth of my past.

It wasn't my place to interrupt, but they were talking about *my life*. I cut through the clearing in three strides, and faced Uriel and Shimon over the line of the dead. "What's this about my father?"

Shimon gasped—he hadn't heard me approach. He leapt over a corpse and grabbed my shoulder, drawing me back. I shook his arm free, but allowed him to lead me away from the bodies.

"Lev, I'm sorry. But you can't know. Not yet."

I glared at Shimon. He knew. If Shimon owed his life to my father, then he owed me an answer.

Uriel's voice was softer. "Lev, when you returned to me, you said that where I went, you would go. I was moved by the strength of your promise and held it as binding, though you are not yet of age. But even I did not foresee where it would lead. You offered your life this morning, even if it was spared.

"I have served the Holy One faithfully my entire life, but I am an old man. There are more soldiers seeking me, and even if I were not pursued, the time to lie with my fathers is drawing near. It matters not how my soul will leave my body, in sleep or in battle. But your life is ahead of you. I release you from your oath."

Would my master dismiss me rather than tell me the truth?

"The journey to Judah is now too dangerous for you to attempt. Even the smallest passes will be watched. If you wish to return to your aunt, tell her it is with my blessing and she will welcome you home. Your uncle will help you raise a flock of your own. No one will seek your blood. You will marry and build a family. Grow old.

"Or you may continue with me. We will travel fast, eat little, fight if we must. If you go where I go, it may be to the grave before the week is done."

I stared down at the bodies of the massacred prophets on the ground. If I hadn't been there, Uriel could have lain among them. I raised my eyes up to my master's. "Where you go, I will go."

Shimon shuffled next to me. Uriel continued to hold my gaze. "So be it." He bent his knees and brought his eyes in line with mine. "Then it's time to hear the truth about your father. The truth about yourself."

Shimon's mouth dropped open. Uriel held up his hand and it snapped shut. "I have hidden things until now because knowledge can be dangerous. But at this point, you could hardly be in more danger—now ignorance is a liability." The old prophet held out the handle of my knife. "I saw your father's courage in you today. Take the knife."

I asked for the truth, but hadn't expected to get it. My fingers trembled as I grasped the weapon. It felt warm in my palms, having absorbed the heat of Uriel's hands.

"Do you recognize the imprint?"

I traced a finger over the insignia on the hilt. How many times had I wondered about its meaning since leaving home? I saw it in my dreams. My vision grew blurry as I focused on the milky white stone, but no new insight arose. I shrugged. "Claws of some sort?"

Uriel cocked his head to inspect the insignia, then emitted a short, nasal laugh—the first sound of mirth I'd heard in days. "True, it does look like claws now, doesn't it? Much time has passed since I saw it first. Yes, some definition has been lost, but the image is whole. Not three fingers, five. The thumb, two fingers held together, a gap, then two fingers held together. Does that help you?"

"No, Master."

"The *kohanim*, the priests of the Holy One, hold their hands forward just so when they bless the people. This knife was used by the *kohanim* for offerings in the Holy Temple. Your father was a *kohen*." Uriel drew my eyes up from the knife with a gentle touch on my chin. "Which makes you a *kohen* as well. You were born a priest of the Holy One."*

Uriel's words broke through my exhaustion. Fragmented images whirled in my mind. My special bread—my aunt always gave me the first piece of bread. Hadn't Uriel done the same when I came to the gathering, making sure that a portion was always set aside for me? Uncle Menachem taught me that the *kohen* receives the first bread and the first fruits—why had I never made the connection?

Yonaton stood at the edge of the trees, grasping an armful of branches, watching us closely. When the two of us tried to help care for the fallen prophets, only I was rebuked, not him. "Is that why I can't help with the bodies?"

"Yes, you are forbidden contact with the dead."

How many times had I pestered my uncle about my father's land? His response was always the same, that my inheritance had been lost—always using the word inheritance, never once mentioning my father's land or even his tribe. "And this is why I have no land?"

"The *kohanim* are from the tribe of Levi, who received the service of the Holy One as their inheritance. They have no share in the land."

I shook my head, then raised the knife between us. "And this?"

"That knife was used by your ancestors to slaughter offerings in the Holy Temple."

"Shimon said it was for peace, not war."

"Indeed it is. When the hearts of the *kohanim* are pure and the people are devoted to their service, there is peace in the land."

"Why was it dangerous for me to know what I am?"

"Did your uncle teach you about the splitting of the Kingdom?"

"Yes, but only when I went home after the wedding." I wanted it to be clear that I hadn't understood about the Golden Calf when we were in Beit El. "He said that Yeravaum feared that the people would return to the Temple, so he created the calves and commanded the people to worship the Holy One through them."

"Yes, a new form of our old sin in the desert. The annual pilgrimage to the calves will be in one week, at the full moon, exactly one month after Israel should have gone up to the Temple for *Sukkot*. And did Menachem tell you that not all the people accepted this substitution?"

I shook my head.

"The tribe of Levi were the most adamant in their refusal. They rejected the calf in the wilderness and were not going to bow to it here in the Land. The *kohanim* had a double measure of their tribe's indignation."

My chest filled with pride at my tribe's defiance.

"When Yeravaum replaced the Temple, he replaced the *kohanim* as well. New altars meant new priests, an honor bestowed upon one of the most powerful families in the Kingdom, assuring their loyalty to Yeravaum. Most of the *kohanim* in the northern Kingdom of Israel fled south to Judah. Only a few stayed, and their very presence provoked Yeravaum and the kings who came after him."

"Why?"

"Because the Holy One anointed Aharon and his sons as our priests for all time. The only way to serve the Holy One at the altar is to be a descendant of Aharon. As long as his descendants lived in the land, they were a perpetual challenge to Yeravaum and his mock priests."

"So the remaining *kohanim* were hunted down?"

"No. Most went about their lives quietly. They became craftsmen, shepherds, teachers of the young. Yeravaum saw no reason to disturb the peace by dealing harshly with them."

"So why was my father different?"

"Your father refused to flee or conceal his identity. He wouldn't let the people forget. He traveled the Kingdom, taught about the Holy One, and roused the nation to correct its ways."

Pride blazed through me again at this new image of my father, strong and defiant, though I now knew how much his defiance had cost him—and me. "But you also do this. You were never hunted, were you?" I surveyed the soldier's bodies piled next to the ruined house, "…at least until now."

"True. Yeravaum had no desire to break the connection between the people and the Holy One. Just the opposite: he told the people that worshiping his calves was the surest path to cling to the Holy One. Opposing the prophets would have destroyed this illusion, so we remained free to live and teach in the land."

I stared at the severed head of the last soldier to die, and suddenly the battle made more sense. "But Izevel wants to destroy the connection between the people and the Holy One. She wants them to worship the Baal."

"Indeed."

I wiped my eyes with the palms of my hands, feeling suddenly like a little boy again. But I couldn't give myself over to my feelings yet—there was more I needed to understand first. "Was I never to know who I am?" I searched my master's eyes.

Uriel ran his fingers through his grizzled, white beard. "That was to be a question of how you matured. Had you grown into a man who likes to avoid trouble, like the *kohanim* who abandoned their roots, I would never have burdened you with this knowledge."

I squinted at Uriel. "But how could you know which direction I'd take?"

"When we met under the fig tree, I was a stranger to you, but you were well known to me. I have walked the land for over fifty years—almost always alone." Uriel's lips rose in a half smile. "Your father was a rare friend; I would not abandon his son. After he died, I visited your uncle whenever my path brought me close to Levonah. It was I who gave you that kinnor, for music is a channel for the soul. I saw early on that you possessed a rare spirit—a spirit like your father's—but I still needed to know you better. The past can be such a heavy burden. I needed to be sure you could bear it.

"That's why I hired you to accompany me to the gathering. There I was to make my final decision: to leave you in ignorance and allow you to sink into the people of the Kingdom, or to smuggle you to Judah once you came of age. There you could learn the ways of the *kohanim*, and one day serve in the Holy Temple. Your uncle knew this, of course, but he long ago yielded to my desire for secrecy."

"But, Master, I thought you hired me for my music?"

"Your music is beautiful, Lev—it is an expression of the spirit of which I speak. But I didn't need a musician badly enough to take you from your uncle's flock. I sought to know you better. And you needed to taste your father's world before facing the choice: whether to remain here a shepherd or join me on the journey to Judah to learn the way of your tribe."

For years, I grappled with the prospect of a life I hadn't chosen and didn't desire. Yet, all that time, another option lay hidden beneath the surface, waiting for me to take hold of it. Unlike the paths that Zim and Daniel had encouraged me to walk, this path was destined for me from birth; it was the path my father had walked, and his father before him, all the way back to Aharon the first high priest. This realization broke through my last restraint. Tears coursed through the filth on my face, but I didn't wipe them away. The truth ripped open an old wound, but I preferred pain to the numbness I felt during all those years of mystery.

"And what now, Master?"

"Everything has changed. My days of walking the Kingdom are over. We are quarry now—we'd be hunted down within days. The watch on the passes will be doubled as well—the way to Judah is sealed."

Any sense of safety brought on by that morning's victory slipped away. "Where will we go?"

"I don't know. Despite the delay, I must seek vision. Please play for me."

The ancient prophet's knees cracked as he lowered himself to the blood-stained ground. He closed his eyes and dropped his head between his knees, but there was no music. The wind rattled the trees along the edge of the clearing and Uriel gazed back up, deep lines cutting his face. "I forgot we left your kinnor behind. I will attempt it on my own."

My master hunched on the ground, shoulders slumped with exhaustion, neck taut with the tension of a hunted man, while his brother prophets lay silently in a row next to him, awaiting burial. I couldn't imagine harder circumstances to open his heart to prophecy. I might not have my kinnor, but I still had my voice.

I searched for a *nigun*, for some music that could escort Uriel into the state of joy necessary for prophecy. Nothing came. Smoke from the smoldering building burned my throat, my eyes. Where was the joy in this place?

Shimon gently wiped the faces of his masters and set their clothes aright. Had he shown my parents' bodies the same tenderness? The idea of their death was nothing new to me, but now I knew the reason. For the first time, I felt more than just an ache at the thought of my parents' deaths, but a rush of admiration as well. They died because my father was a *kohen*—a *kohen* who wasn't content to flee or hide. I was also a *kohen*. If I ever made it to Judah, I could serve in the Holy Temple. What did the music in the Temple sound like?

I closed my eyes, picturing King Solomon's Temple, with its white walls and crown of gold. I imagined playing my kinnor there before the altar of the Holy One in an act of true devotion. A melody rose in my heart. I sang through the *nigun* once, my parched lips cracking as I opened my mouth wide to the music. As I returned to the beginning, an arm wrapped around my shoulder, and Yonaton's voice joined with mine, picking out deeper tones in the melody.

Shimon stretched an arm around my other shoulder. His voice was raw, and his harmony just awful. Still, there was something stirring about singing with this strange man who'd carried me to safety as a child and had saved my life once again.

The prophet's head remained bowed between his knees for a long time—I couldn't imagine the shadow he was trying to lift from his heart. Uriel sat up, eyes open—was he giving up? He beheld the three of us swaying before him, attempting to sing away his sorrow. He managed a sad smile, and dropped his head again, rocking his body to our music.

A wellspring of emotion bubbled up from the core of my heart. Ten years of emptiness and longing for answers raged like lions. I held them and watched them melt away under the soft glow of the truth. For the first time, I knew who I was. My song broadened, deepened, flowing out like a river. The arms around my shoulders tightened their hold, and the air seemed to crackle with tension. When the tension burst, I didn't need to open my eyes to know my master had ascended.

By the time Uriel stirred, Yonaton and I had built a fire and warmed our stale bread. Curious as I was to question my master, he'd not eaten since the previous night, and my first duty was to him. I handed the prophet a piece of toasted bread and restrained myself from asking about the vision.

"Thank you, Lev." Uriel accepted the food. "But you should not continue to serve me this way."

"Why not, Master?"

"The *kohanim* serve the Holy One, not man."

"But I want to serve you."

Uriel shook his head. "The laws of the *kohanim* are many and complex. Sadly, we have no proper time for your education. I will serve myself, and Shimon is here if I need assistance."

Yonaton popped up at this. "And me."

Uriel again shook his head. "Yesterday you could not go back to your family because of these brutes, but they will tell their tale to no one now. You may safely return home."

The color rose in Yonaton's cheeks. "I want to stay."

"Lev's uncle handed him into my care. Your parents made no such choice. They are expecting you, worrying over you."

Yonaton dug his hands into his hips. "When I told my parents that the soldiers were looking for you, my father told me I had to come. My mother packed me food. They wouldn't want me to leave you." He added quietly, "Not if I can help."

Uriel's tired brow knitted in thought. "There is a way you can help. Very well, you may remain as long as you are needed."

No one spoke as the prophet ate, but all eyes measured his progress. When he swallowed his last bite, Shimon could no longer contain himself. "What did you see?"

"We must contact Ovadia. He is still loyal, and in his position, he'll know how to advise us."

"Ovadia?" Shimon threw his hands up. "How are we supposed to reach *him*? He's in Shomron, the heart of the Kingdom, right under the eye of Queen Izevel. We need to get you to safety. Wouldn't you be better served leaving the Kingdom?"

"No. You forget King Ethbaal has the largest fleet on the seas. There's no kingdom with whom he does not trade, no end to his reach. The people have not yet accepted Queen Izevel's reign here, but once I leave the land, no one has reason to shelter me. I'd be given over immediately."

"And Judah?"

"Indeed, I would be safe there. But that is where Queen Izevel will expect me to go. She'll concentrate her power on the border." Uriel stood up and leaned on his staff. "In any case, I have no intention of fleeing. Do not concern yourself with my safety. My last days will be here in the Kingdom, serving the Holy One in any way I still can."

"Excellent, so we'll resist. But don't throw your life away going to Shomron."

"I didn't say we need to go to Shomron, we just need to contact Ovadia. It will be less dangerous for him to come to us."

"But how can we contact him without going to Shomron?"

Uriel cocked his head and scrutinized Yonaton and me, and his features molded into a grimace. "The boys. The only soldiers we know can connect us with the boys lie right here. You and I are hunted, they are not. Hopefully none of the Queen's other lackeys know the connection between us."

"So what do we do now?"

"We need to find a place to hide until Lev and Yonaton return. We cannot remain here the night; it is too well known as a gathering place. Just because it has been destroyed does not mean that they will not return to pursue others who may flee here."

Hillel said: In a place where there are no men, strive to be a man. Pirkei Avot 2:6

17

The Steward's Wife

I burst to the surface of the frigid water, and the skin on my arms rose in gooseflesh.

"Immerse again," Uriel said. "I saw your hair floating on the water."

I ran a hand through my curly hair, which hadn't been cut since high summer. Each time I dipped under the surface, it rose like a water lily seeking light. I pursed my lips and dunked again, tucking my chin to my knees and curling over in the narrow pool. When I came up, Uriel nodded.

"The impurity of the dead still clings to the rest of us,"* Uriel said. "We will not be fully cleansed until we merit to see the Holy Temple, where the *kohanim* can purify us with the ashes of the red heifer. But for you, Lev, who have not had direct contact with the dead, living waters will suffice."*

Through most of that morning, Uriel and Shimon had cleansed the dead prophets, laying them out in a nearby cave. There they'd rest, like so many sleepers in a row, with their feet pointed toward Jerusalem.* At Uriel's insistence, the bodies of the soldiers were carried into a second cave. Shimon didn't object, but I suspected he would have preferred their flesh be scavenged by the vultures that already circled overhead.

Unable to help with the bodies, I returned to the previous night's cave to retrieve Balaam and the rest of our gear. My heart pounded as I stretched up to grab my kinnor from its hiding place. My grip relaxed as I ran my fingers over the strings and heard its voice, surprisingly still in tune. I was without it just one night, but it felt like greeting an old friend after a long separation.

Yonaton spent the morning working with the soldiers' horses, removing all the Queen's insignia and burning them in the fire, then setting the animals loose in the valley. Though they would have hastened our journey, Uriel felt they'd draw too much attention.

"Where to now, Master?" I shook myself dry.

"West. There's a cave not far from the King's Road where Shimon and I can hide."

Yonaton flushed. Between his run the day before and the horse falling on him that morning, he was struggling to walk. "I don't think I can make it that far."

Uriel shook his head. "Your legs have earned a rest. You may ride Balaam today."

It wasn't yet midday when we started our journey. Before long, our track cut through rolling hills like those around Levonah. I spent most of my life traversing hills just like these, but couldn't see any path that Uriel was following. Nevertheless, by late afternoon we reached our destination—a cave in a hillside just over the ridge from the King's Road, chiseled by hand like those at Emek HaAsefa. A towering carob tree hid the entrance from view.

It hadn't rained since my return from Jericho, but a cold north wind bit into my bones and I craved a hot, hearty meal. Yonaton, who managed to sleep much of the afternoon while riding Balaam, offered, "I'll go look for—"

"No fire tonight," Uriel said.

I surveyed the broad valley that we'd just crossed. Nothing resembling a soldier appeared anywhere on the horizon, but I hadn't seen the first group either. Were there more out there hunting us?

I rose before the sun after tossing and turning throughout the night. Shimon sat in the mouth of the cave, illuminated by flickering firelight. Sniffing at the smell of roasting meat, I untangled myself from my tunic and threw it over my head. I wrapped my sheepskin around my shoulders for extra warmth and joined Shimon next to the small fire. "I was about to wake you to eat," he said. "The Holy One must truly love you. See what leapt right into my hands this morning?" A fat grouse dripped grease onto the smoking coals.

Shimon plucked the bird from the roasting spit and cut off a wing with his dagger. It was the same dagger he'd given me, the one he threw wide of the soldier. Did he use this dagger because the other one, now tucked into his belt, had contact with the dead? Was this another one of the laws of the *kohanim* that Uriel wanted to teach me about? Shimon handed me the steaming wing, almost too hot to handle. "I envy you."

"Why?" The word was muffled by the crisp skin crackling in my mouth.

"You're walking toward danger, but at least your fate is in your hands. I… we…get to sit here and wait, praying we're not discovered and hoping you're successful; knowing little and doing less."

I chewed the savory meat, keeping my mouth full so I wouldn't have to respond. The hot meat warmed my throat, yet hadn't Uriel, who now slept after taking the first watch, warned us against making a fire? I was relieved when Yonaton appeared, rubbing his eyes. Shimon handed him the other wing and repeated the story of the grouse. Yonaton stared at him. "You're just a vessel for blessing, aren't you? First you save our lives, and now you fill our stomachs." The compliment brought a hint of a smile to Shimon's scarred face.

When we finished eating, we tossed the remaining bones into the fire, wiped our greasy hands in the dirt, and descended to where Balaam was tied up for the night.

"You should ride," I told Yonaton. "I'll lead Balaam."

"I can walk."

"You can limp. Balaam can handle your weight, but both of us will be too much for him in the hills. When we reach the road, we'll ride together."

Yonaton sighed and shook his head, but climbed on.

"Be safe." Shimon's hand drifted down toward something inside of his cloak.

"What do you have there?" I asked.

Shimon pulled back his cloak, revealing the hilt of a sword. "It's the one Yonaton handed me during the battle, from the soldier that he killed."

"You kept it?"

"I was blessed to save us with it once. Perhaps I'll be so blessed again." Shimon watched us as we set off and ducked back into the cave only when we reached the ridge.

Yonaton shot a glance behind him. "Shame he's not coming with us."

I said nothing, just led Balaam on the path that Uriel pointed out to us the day before, which climbed gently until it intersected with the road in the distance. The footing was poor, and we trod along the path as the sun rose over the hillsides.

A figure on the far ridge caught my attention—a soldier on horseback. He sat on one of the hillsides overlooking the road, but he wasn't facing the road, he was peering out over the valley where our path crossed. He noticed us at the same time and nudged his horse forward as he rose in the saddle.

My pulse raced. There was no reason to panic—we were just two boys with a donkey. I lifted my hand, hissing out of the corner of my mouth, "Quick, wave."

Yonaton glanced around until he too saw the soldier, and threw a friendly wave. The soldier waved back, then returned to his post on the hilltop.

Yonaton asked, "Was that an Israelite soldier or one of the Queen's?"

"I don't know, but there weren't any Israelite soldiers posted this far away before the wedding."

"You think he's watching the road?"

"He was facing the valley, so he could be watching both or—"

"Or he's keeping an eye out for anyone avoiding the road," Yonaton finished.

"If that's the case, we'll draw less attention on the road. We can cut over this hillside. It'll be quicker, but I think it's too steep for Balaam to carry you."

Yonaton threw his leg over the donkey and lowered himself to the ground. "I can walk."

We saw no more soldiers as we made our way up, over, and onto the road. Both of us climbed onto Balaam for the ride toward Shomron. The donkey brayed in protest when I mounted behind Yonaton—we were quite a load for the old beast—but it nonetheless trotted forward faster than we could walk.

The evening breeze tickled the sweat on the back of my neck as we climbed the approach to Shomron. We passed six more soldiers on the road during our journey, two of them from the Queen's Guard, the other four Israelite. We lay down in the shade of a large carob tree during the hottest part of the afternoon. In order to draw less attention, we planned to enter the city just before sunset, when the gates would be crowded with those returning from the fields. But we underestimated the distance remaining to travel, and the first ram's horn blew before we reached the city. I nudged Balaam with my ankles, urging the donkey to trot faster.

The guard at the gates raised the ram's horn to his lips to blow the final blast before closing the gates. Yonaton called out, "Wait!"

The guard lowered the horn and waved us forward.

I jumped off and ran, drawing Balaam behind me. The guard blew the final blast, waited for us to pass, and pulled the outer gates closed. We couldn't have drawn more attention to our entry if we'd presented the guard with a sealed scroll emblazoned with our names. A second sentry, one of the Queen's men, also watched the gate. Fortunately, his attention was focused on the setting sun, and he was oblivious to two peasant boys.

The courtyards of the houses on Ovadia's street formed a high stone wall, punctuated with gateways and alleys. A deep shadow already filled the paved stone street when we arrived, and before long, Yonaton was glancing back over his shoulder, casting his eyes back and forth between the sides of the street.

"Did we miss it?" I asked.

"No. Well…you know, I'm not so sure." He twisted forward and back now, craning his neck to see the tops of the houses. It had been several months since we were at Ovadia's, but we'd not anticipated any difficulty finding the house. "This is the street, I know it. Let's go back to the crossroad." Even Balaam groaned as we turned around in the fading light.

We passed the length of street two more times before Yonaton let out a loud "Ha!" and called a halt in front of a heavy wooden gate covered in fresh pitch, its stench stinging our noses.

"I don't remember any gate," I said softly.

"There wasn't one," Yonaton replied. "That's what confused me. But this is it, I'm certain. See, there's Ovadia's seal on the lintel."

The footstool carved into the lintel was indeed the same symbol that he used to seal his messages—I'd delivered enough of them before the wedding to remember. I tried the gate, but it was locked.

Yonaton gripped a crude mallet hanging from the door post, and pounded out three solid blows. I flinched at each strike; they rang too loud in the silence of the twilit street. No one answered. We stared at each other. We'd invested all our energy in reaching Shomron and hadn't even thought about what to do if Ovadia was away. I shuddered at the thought of sleeping on the cold stone street.

Yonaton swung the mallet once more, knocking louder. We stepped away from the gate, assessing the dark wall. A door opened, then quickly closed again. The gate swung silently outward on its hinges, and Ovadia stepped into the gloom, fastening the gate behind him. "Hello, boys. A bit late for a visit, isn't it?" He shifted from foot to foot as his eyes darted up and down the dark street.

I opened my mouth to respond, but Ovadia cut me off. "Well then, very good of you to let me know you're back. Come look for me at the palace in the morning, perhaps we can find work for you again. I recently heard Dov say he could use more musicians for all the banquets. Until tomorrow, then." Ovadia turned back to the gate.

I leaned in and breathed at his back, "Master Uriel sent us."

Ovadia whipped around, his eyes shooting up the street again. "Did anyone see you? Were you followed?"

"I don't think so."

Ovadia swept Yonaton, Balaam, and me quickly into the courtyard. He closed and bolted the heavy wooden gate, secured it without a sound, coaxed Balaam over to a corner, tied him to a post near a watering trough, and tossed him a pile of straw. He hustled us through the main entrance—I exhaled only when the door of the house was locked behind us.

Lamps burned in the main room where drawn shutters blocked the moonlight. Batya tucked a loose strand of raven hair under her scarf as her husband dropped us onto stools beside the hearth table. She poured out water in clay bowls while Ovadia paced. I gulped down the cool liquid, wiping my grimy lips only after draining the bowl.

Ovadia dropped onto a stool opposite me. "Uriel is still alive?"

I nodded.

"Is he safe?"

I nodded again.

"Where is he?" I opened my mouth to answer, but Ovadia interjected, "How did you get here?"

"He is safe," I replied. "He sent us to you for help."

Ovadia popped up and redoubled his pacing. "Help? So many need help. She's got eyes everywhere, you know!"

Batya offered us two hot loaves of flat bread. I tore off a hunk, cringing at the dark smudge my filthy hands left on the brown bread. I put the bread down and stepped toward the wash-basin.

Batya would not allow Ovadia to question us while we ate. Soon all four of us were seated at the heavy wooden table—even Ovadia's nerves calmed in the face of warm bread.

I contemplated the changes in Ovadia's house as I ate. Heavy blankets covered shuttered windows, a strange sight on a windless night. In the shadows, a new oven protruded from the wall on the inside of the house, just opposite the oven in the courtyard. I squeezed the warm bread in my hand—had they been baking at night?

Ovadia managed to hold himself back until the bread was gone, but when Batya rose, saying something about pressed figs, he leaned in close to us. "Where is he?"

I swallowed my last bite. "In a cave a day's journey from here."

"Well hidden?"

I nodded. "There's a tree blocking the entrance; I never would have known it was there."

"It must be one of Gidon's caves."*

"Gidon's caves?"

"Built before Gidon's rebellion against the Midianites hundreds of years ago. Some, like those at Emek HaAsefa, were strongholds, others hiding places. Uriel has shown me several; no one knows them as well as he does. I've never heard of the one you speak of."

"That doesn't matter, we can guide you back."

"Me, leave Shomron, to get a prophet?" Ovadia put his forehead into his hands and snorted. "That's just what she's waiting for, an excuse to take off my head."

I stared at Ovadia—he was our only hope. We couldn't return to Uriel alone. What would we do then? Sit in the cave until we starved?

"Of course, you have no idea what's been happening here." He pulled his stool closer to us and lowered his voice. "The Queen has declared war on the prophets."

"We know," I said, an edge to my voice. "We've buried the dead."

The blunt words sank Ovadia into his seat, and he motioned for me to continue. I recounted the events of the last three days, holding nothing back, except Uriel's revelation about my father—I saw no reason to share this new knowledge. Yonaton leaned in close to me the entire time I spoke, but added nothing. As with our music, he seemed happy to let me lead.

When I finished, Ovadia met his wife's eyes with a groan. "It is worse than we feared." He cradled his temples in his palms. "We hoped that her power was limited to Shomron. Further into the hills, the people still love and fear the prophets. I thought they would protect them."

"The people love the prophets," Yonaton said, speaking up for the first time, "but they fear the sword."

Ovadia nodded. "Yet there are worse things than the sword, Yonaton. May you be blessed not to know them." He rose and faced Batya. "It seems that the fate of these boys is bound up with ours, yes?"

Batya gathered the remains of our meal. "You thought these boys were a tool in your hand. Yet, you see now, we are all tools in the hands of the Holy One."

I wondered what she meant, but was distracted by the sight of her collecting breadcrumbs from the table. During the wedding, I never saw her clean. "Where are your servants?"

A soft tear ran down her high-boned cheek. "They're attending to our land."

Attending to their land? Surely enough men attended Ovadia's land that he didn't need the house servants there as well? Perhaps for the harvest, but now? And even so, why should Batya weep over this?

I thought about everything I'd seen since arriving: the gate blocking access to the house; a new oven, built indoors instead of in the courtyard where it belonged; windows sealed on a still evening; hot bread past nightfall; and the servants gone. My eye fell on a waist-high lump in the corner of the room, covered with a woolen blanket.

I rose from my stool. All eyes watched me go, yet neither Ovadia nor Batya hindered me. I lifted the edge of the blanket and peeked beneath, discovering just what I realized must be there: a stack of freshly baked bread.

Ovadia approached and took the edge of the blanket from my hand. "Your eyes are starting to open, Lev. That is good. You will need them in the days ahead. All our servants, as you must have guessed, are gone. Our hired workers were dismissed even before the wedding; that was one reason I relied on you boys so much. Now even our slaves have been sent away to work our land in the Jezreel Valley. No one can know what we're doing."

A lump rose in my throat. "How many are there?"

"Thirty prophets and disciples. Hidden in a cave outside the city."*

Batya gasped and clasped her hand over her mouth.

"As you said, Batya, they were sent by the Holy One. We must trust them."

She nodded without removing her hand.

Yonaton stirred. "But why us?"

Ovadia raised his eyebrows. "Uriel sent you."

"Not now—during the wedding. You said you dismissed your workers and depended on us instead."

"Ah, yes." Ovadia's expression relaxed. "Even then I wondered if you would ask. Did it not seem strange to you that the King's steward, with all the servants at my disposal, was relying on two unknown boys to do my errands?"

"You told us everyone was busy with preparations."

"Indeed they were—like bees in the hive. But I still saw to the most important details myself, and as you know, I often needed help. I commandeered dozens of slaves and servants, but always kept them at a distance."

"But why us?" Yonaton asked again.

Ovadia shifted his focus from Yonaton to me. I felt the challenge in his gaze to figure out this puzzle as I had about the bread. Ovadia dismissed his hired workers and relied instead on two country boys, both plucked from serving the prophets. The answer was suddenly clear, as though inked on clean parchment. "We were safe."

"You were safe." Ovadia nodded. "From the time of the engagement, the King was constantly on the lookout for anyone who could be disloyal."

"But you weren't disloyal then," Yonaton said, "Were you?"

"No, I have always served my King loyally."

"Until now." I grinned.

"Even now." Ovadia jerked out of his seat and strode to the covered window. "This is the Queen's war. *Her* soldiers are after the prophets; the Israelite soldiers haven't been brought into the hunt. The King is doing his best to ignore the Queen's attacks, neither helping nor hindering her."

"But if you're not disloyal," Yonaton asked, "Why dismiss your servants?"

"The very innocence of the question is what made you so valuable."

"Why?"

"I'm known to have relations with the prophets. I'm foreign-born. I'm a natural target."

"For who?"

"For anyone hoping to advance by setting me up for a fall. It makes no difference whether the accusations are true or not. I directed hundreds of servants, but I never let them get too close and never let them deliver my messages."

"Then why us?"

"As Lev said, you were safe. Uriel told me neither of you had ever left home until you came to play for the prophets. You knew nothing of what was happening here in Shomron, and you were hardly looking to make names for yourselves in the court." Dark circles of exhaustion stood out below Ovadia's eyes in the lamplight. "But that was before. Then I had nothing to hide, and feared only lies."

"What changed?" Yonaton asked.

"I don't know. Something happened when the King went to Jericho a week and a half ago. He came back white-faced and silent. He told me nothing, just summoned the Queen to the throne room. Whatever she heard sent her into a rage, and she called in Yambalya. She emerged determined to kill the prophets and their disciples."

"And no one knows why?" Yonaton asked.

Ovadia shook his head. "The King is keeping his hands clean of the blood of the prophets, but there is someone else he commanded me to find. I expect it is connected to him."

"Eliyahu," I said.

"Yes." Ovadia's eyes narrowed on me. "How do you know about Eliyahu? Did Uriel have a vision of what happened in Jericho?"

"He didn't need to. I was there."

"You were in Jericho?"

"Yes."

"Then do you know why we're hunting him? Did he confront the King?"

My face flushed at the memory of Eliyahu's wrath, and of the King cowering under his fiery gaze. "He did."

"Over the Baal?"

"Yes."

"You see Batya, I knew it. The Queen is proud. Eliyahu standing against the King must have prompted her to act before she was ready."

"Ready for what?" Yonaton asked.

"It was clear at the wedding she intended to draw the people after the Baal—Yambalya wouldn't have coerced the guests to bow down except on her orders. Her influence has only grown stronger since then. Much stronger. But not enough to strike against the prophets. In her rage, she acted rashly. If we can reach Uriel, the resistance will have the leader it lacks. Under him, the surviving prophets can rouse the people to throw off Izevel's yoke."

"And the King's?" Yonaton asked.

Ovadia shook his head. "The King is more dedicated to the people than he is to the Queen. Even rebuilding Jericho and marrying Izevel were, in his mind, done for them. If the people rise against the Queen, I believe he won't stand in their way."

Ovadia studied my face with sharp eyes until I began to shift in my seat. "To think that I brought you into my home because you were some innocent boy who knew nothing of the Kingdom or the court! You're finding yourself in the middle of too many events for it to all be chance. There is more to you than you are sharing, Lev, more perhaps than you know yourself."

My hand went to the bulge in my tunic where it covered my father's knife. Ovadia was correct that I was holding something back. *He need not know that I am a kohen, though. It has nothing to do with what we face right now.*

Ovadia broke into a sudden smile. "Uriel would never have led the resistance on his own. He would have put off war as long as possible, allowing Izevel to grow stronger and stronger. But now that Eliyahu has forced his hand, he will have to lead us."

Ovadia stroked his trim beard. "Unless Eliyahu expects to lead—he started this fight. Lev, did it sound to you as though he was planning to lead the people against the Queen? Tell me exactly what he said."

Blood pulsed in my neck, heating my cheeks. I pronounced his words firmly, with only a trace of the fire that had filled Eliyahu's voice at Jericho. "As the Holy One, the Lord of Israel, before whom I stand, lives…there will not be dew nor rain during these years except by my word."

Batya gasped.

Ovadia staggered back against the hearth. "He tried to stop the rains?"

I nodded.

"I've never heard of such a thing. Can he do that?"

"According to Master Uriel, the Holy One indeed gave him the Key of Rain. The heavens are sealed until Eliyahu relents."

"The Holy One gave him the key? That must be why the Queen summoned Yambalya. He would know if Eliyahu spoke the truth—the dark priest is filled with wisdom of their abominations."

Ovadia's eyes closed in, tightening his brow. "What you said didn't sound like prophecy though. It sounded more like an oath. Or…"

"…a curse," I finished.

Silence fell over the room.

I asked Ovadia, "You said Eliyahu wasn't one of the prophets. He is, though. I saw him receiving prophecy after he left Hiel's house. Was he not known as a prophet before?"

"I do not know. In his youth, he was among the last disciples of Achia, Uriel's master. I do not know if he ever achieved prophecy before. I have known him only at the court. He has always been respectful of the monarchy there. Did anything happen in Jericho before he spoke?"

I shifted uncomfortably on my stool. "The King told Hiel that he blamed himself for Seguv's death."

"As he should." Ovadia planted himself opposite me. "To hire a man to rebuild a cursed city…. Of course, Hiel himself is also responsible for agreeing to do it. Did he say anything else?"

"The King thought it strange that the curse of Joshua would work."

"Why did he think that strange? Few prophets were as great as Joshua."

"Because Moses said that if the people worshipped other gods, there would be no rain."

"What does that have to do with Joshua?"

"The King said that the people have turned after the Baal, yet he could never remember having so much rain. He wondered why the curse of Joshua would work when the curse of his master failed."

"What!" Ovadia leapt to his feet again. He drew his hand across his clammy forehead. When he spoke, his voice trembled. "Eliyahu invoked the curse of Moses?"

I remembered Uriel saying that Moses's words were not quite a curse, but they certainly seemed like it to me. "Yes."

All eyes were on Ovadia as he paced the room. "I had it all wrong. This is not a battle—it is a siege."

Yonaton looked confused. "But the battle has already begun."

"By the Queen, yes. But Eliyahu brought a drought. It may take years for its effects to be fully felt." He turned to Batya. "This changes everything—our plan will not work. We need to think of something else."

"But this should make our resistance even stronger!" Batya said.

Ovadia shook his head. "It cannot be done."

"Batya is right." I rose to my feet. "The Holy One gave Eliyahu the Key of Rain! What better weapon could we have? As you said, the Queen acted too soon—the people are still more loyal to the prophets than they are to the Baal. Why change the plan now?"

Ovadia shook his head. "Because the Holy One did not give Eliyahu the Key of Rain to fight Izevel."

"Then what is it for?"

But Ovadia's thoughts were elsewhere. "Nothing, nothing is as we thought."

Batya approached his side. "Tell us what you mean."

"It is the people. The Holy One's wrath will fall on all those who have turned to the Baal—and on all those who have been loyal as well."

Batya took his hand in hers. "But isn't the Queen the cause of their turning away?"

"Maybe. Yes." Ovadia shook his head. "It does not matter. Either way, Izevel will be the last to feel the lack of rain. The poorest will suffer first."

I couldn't understand why Ovadia was suddenly losing resolve. "But won't that rouse them against the Queen and the Baal?"

"Perhaps. But the Queen will tell them this is not just a temporary stop to the rains, it is a drought, brought on by Eliyahu, a prophet. She will claim he's a tyrant and that she has come to rescue the nation from his grip. In their misery, the people could turn against the prophets themselves."

Tears rolled down Batya's cheeks. "Then what do we do? Nothing?"

"We have thirty prophets already hidden. We'll hide as many more as we can."

"But how will we sustain them? We have sufficient barley for the hidden ones only until the new moon. What will you do then, sell land to buy grain?" Terror lit her eyes. "And you're being watched. How long can we keep this up before someone discovers what we're doing?"

"I don't know." Ovadia slammed his fist on the table; our bowls bounced with a clank. "But when it is known that a drought is coming, at least buying a store of grain will not appear suspicious. We must continue hiding the prophets—I see now that any battle will not succeed."

"But why not?" Batya cried.

"Didn't you hear the boy? Eliyahu evoked the curse of Moses. There will never again be a prophet of Moses's strength."

"But shouldn't that make victory even easier?" I asked, but even as the words left my mouth, I recalled Uriel telling me that the forces of light and the forces of darkness had to exist in balance. The more powerful Eliyahu's curse, the more powerful the counteracting forces would be. Perhaps if Eliyahu were leading us into battle, our strength could prevail, but with Eliyahu in hiding, could any force we set into motion be strong enough?

As if answering my thoughts, Ovadia said, "If this war is won, it will not be by ordinary men like me, nor even by the prophets of today. If we send the prophets out of the cave now, we send them to their deaths. We just have to do what we can, help as many as we can, for as long as we have bread. If we fail, we fail."

Ovadia sighed. "We'll need to find a way to get Uriel and Shimon here without being detected."

"Bring them *here*?" The words leapt out of my mouth.

"Yes, here. There's nowhere else I can sustain them."

I shook my head. "Master Uriel doesn't want to hide. He would support your original plan."

"We can save his life!"

"He said he will spend his last days serving the Holy One in any way he can. I don't think he'll go meekly into a cave."

"Shimon won't either," Yonaton added. "He'd rather fight."

Ovadia slapped his palms on the table and bore into my eyes. "Listen to me—it is crucial that Uriel survive."

"He won't want it. He says he doesn't have long to live anyway."

"Uriel must live. In the struggle between Eliyahu and Izevel, he may prove pivotal."

"If Eliyahu fails?"

"No, if Eliyahu succeeds. It may take the wrath of Eliyahu to defeat Izevel. But it will require one like your master to rebuild the nation—and there is none other like him."

"Why?" Yonaton asked.

But I thought I knew. "Master Uriel believes we must turn to the Holy One from love, not fear."

"That's part of it," Ovadia said. "But Uriel is not the only prophet dedicated to the path of love."

"Then why?"

"You're too young to understand what Uriel has been through. Tell him whatever you must, but get him to me."

"And what about Shimon?" Yonaton asked.

"Shimon is loyal to Uriel. If he thinks that his help is needed to save Uriel, I expect he will do what he must. But once Uriel is hidden, Shimon may do as he pleases."

"Even if he agrees to come, how will we get him here? You said you can't travel."

"No, I cannot. The Queen is investing all her efforts into amassing power. Allegiances shift and swirl around her at all times. Those in her favor are advanced, those who are not…" His expression grew sour. "She distrusts me because I will not bow to her abominations. This is not yet required, but refusal is enough to draw her wrath. The King leans on me for many things, so I am safe at present. But I am watched. If I go to Uriel, it will mean the death of us both."

"But what can we do without you?" My heart raced at the thought of traveling the King's Road with the prophet, and I saw my fear reflected in Yonaton's eyes. We were counting on Ovadia's authority to get the *navi* past the soldiers.

"You saw the Queen's soldiers on the road?"

I nodded.

"Perhaps we can risk it anyway. There are many ways into Shomron. It is not the people we have to fear—they are not yet corrupt enough to hunt a prophet—it is only the foreigners. There are many paths they may not know. No one knows these mountains as Uriel does. It was he who first showed me the cave."

I shook my head. "They have lookouts on the hilltops. They're watching the valleys as well as the roads."

Ovadia groaned. "You see, Batya, a craftsman can have the finest tools, but he's an oaf without a plan." He drummed his fingers on the table. "Perhaps at night?"

I recalled our flight from the soldiers two nights before and shuddered. To reach Shomron in the dark, on footpaths, would take three nights at least. That meant finding hiding places during the days on top of the hardship of the night trekking. "Even if we could make it, we'd never get into the city. The Queen's soldiers watch the gates."

"The cave is not in the city. He will not have to pass the gates."

I didn't like the plan, but what choice did we have? "All right. If we can convince Master Uriel, we'll try at night."

"No, you won't." Batya stood, hands on her hips. "You'll go during the day."

This was too much. Hadn't she been listening? "The valleys are watched."

"You won't walk the valleys. You'll take the King's Road."

Ovadia gaped at his wife. "How will they do that?"

A flush rose in Batya's cheeks. "With the crowd returning from the festival."

The edges of her husband's lips curved up in a smile. "Brilliant."

I stared back and forth between them. "What's brilliant?"

"The annual festival of the Calf is in five days." Ovadia slapped one hand into the other. "The King will be there, along with all the nobility of Shomron."

"But if the King is there," Yonaton said, "There are sure to be soldiers as well."

"The King's guard will escort him, but he moves much faster than his subjects. Besides, those are Israelite soldiers—the Queen's guard won't dare attack while they're around. Once the King rides past, Uriel and Shimon can mingle in with the crowd."

"He won't agree."

"I told you, Lev, your master must reach that cave. And I have known him far longer than you have. I do not believe that he wants to die."

I bristled. "If you know my master so well, then you must know his loathing of the Calf. He hasn't even set foot in Beit El for sixty years. Even if he agrees to hide, he won't do it by pretending to be a Calf worshiper."

"It's the only plan we have." Ovadia reached across the table to seize my shoulders. "The Holy One has chosen you to serve your master. Now you must save him. Whatever you need to do, you do." His grip tightened. "Swear to me that you will get Uriel here alive!"

"He's my master, I'm not his."

"I am offering to save his life. Now swear."

Ovadia's eyes locked on mine, sapping my power to resist. "All right, I swear." How would I stand up to a *navi* when I couldn't even stand up to Ovadia?

"But we'll still have to get past the Queen's soldiers on the road," Yonaton protested.

"Yes."

"But how?"

Ovadia released my shoulders and turned to Yonaton. "Once I was traveling the hills of the Bashon alone, on a mission for the King. Just at sunset, I came upon a pack of wild dogs."

I wondered what this had to do with saving my master. Yonaton asked, "What did you do?"

"I sat down in their midst."

Yonaton's eyes grew large. "Weren't you scared?"

"Terrified."

"I don't understand," I said.

"If you run from a dog, it will give chase. But if you act like its master, it will grovel. You are not going to run from the Queen's soldiers, nor will you hide. You will pass them in the middle of the day, in a crowd returning from a festival for the Golden Calf."

My stomach rumbled, and though I knew the navi was tired, I also knew the wise never left their questions unasked. "I have one more, Master."

"One more then."

I could tell from the direction of his voice that my master was lying down. Suddenly my curiosity felt out of place, and I struggled for the right words. "It's about food."

"The righteous eat to satisfy the soul."

"Is that why the prophets don't cook their greens properly?" I almost said "didn't cook their greens properly," but caught myself. Just because it had been months since any prophet I knew had tasted a vegetable didn't mean they'd given up hope.

I rarely heard my master's laugh these days, though its dry rattle didn't convey much humor. "What did you notice about the meals in Emek HaAsefa?"

Despite the total darkness, I closed my eyes to summon up an image of the gathering. "The vegetables were barely cooked; their colors were very bright."

"You saw well. Of all creation, it is only man that cooks his food. The colors tell us when it is ready to be eaten. Leave it on the fire and the color fades, because its vital force is sapped."

"Vegetables tell us when they should be eaten?"

"Indeed. The nevi'im see a generous creation which guides our growth—we need only listen."

Rabbi Yannai said: We cannot grasp the tranquility of the wicked, nor can we understand the suffering of the righteous.

Pirkei Avot 4:19

18

Shimon's Tale

We left the house before first light, before any prying eyes could take notice. Ovadia instructed us not to speak until we reached the main road, yet even there, neither of us broke the silence. When the ram's horn signaled the opening of the gates, we pushed our way through, practically invisible within a group of farmers heading out to their fields.

Ovadia's words turned over in my mind. *Eliyahu's curse evoked the power of Moses. That power was not directed solely against Izevel and the Baal, the battle that Ovadia wanted to fight. The drought would hit all of the people of Israel, those who bowed to the Baal and those who didn't. The power of the curse meant that even a prophet like Uriel couldn't alter its course. Trying to change it would only lead to his destruction.*

Ovadia believed all this, believed Uriel must hide until the devastation passed, and I had sworn to bring my master to him. But would he agree? If Uriel thought that Ovadia was wrong, I was stuck between two oaths; one to Ovadia and one to my master. I shuddered at the thought of what just one oath had done to Seguv and his family.

"Soldiers," Yonaton whispered, his chest pounding against my back.

"I can't see more than their heads." I craned my neck to see into the stone tower that stood above us. The hilltops surrounding Shomron were all topped with such strongholds, the outer ring of the city's defenses. "Are they Israelite or the Queen's Guard?"

"Can't tell."

The soldiers hardly glanced at us, but as we passed under the shadow of the watchtower, a feeling of disquiet rumbled in my stomach. Since swearing to Ovadia, my thoughts had been focused on Uriel, but a bigger problem just occurred to me.

"Yonaton?" His name caught in my throat.

"What is it?"

"Ovadia said that Master Uriel must get to Shomron—at any cost. But what about Shimon?"

"What about him?"

I hesitated. "Well, it's just that…I'm not sure. Do you think he's safe to travel with?"

Yonaton snorted. "Safe? I can't think of a better person to travel with. When was the last time you shattered your enemy's sword?"

I twisted around to face Yonaton. "Yesterday morning he lit a fire."

"He built it to roast us a grouse."

"I know, but Master Uriel told us not to. And Shimon complained about waiting in the cave. It sounds crazy, but I wonder if he wants to be found."

"You think he wants to die?"

"Not to die, to fight."

"The way he fights, I don't blame him."

"But that's not the way he fights—three days ago he ran from battle."

"You heard what Master Uriel said; he received a spirit from the Holy One. Like prophecy."

"Exactly, a spirit like prophecy, which he's pursued for years, and which he lost as soon as the battle ended. You saw the look in his eyes when he told Master Uriel about it. It was hungry."

Yonaton stared at me. "You don't trust him."

I turned back to face the road. "Ovadia made me swear to bring Master Uriel to Dotan. Master Uriel might listen to me, but will Shimon?"

"If Master Uriel agrees, Shimon will come along to make sure he's safe."

"That's what I'm afraid of. The plan is to sneak past the guards, not confront them. If Shimon won't enter the cave, we're better off without him on the road."

"Tell him that. Tell him that if he's not willing to hide, he shouldn't make the journey."

"He thinks he's protecting Master Uriel."

"Tell him *you'll* do that."

"He won't listen to me." I kept my face forward so that Yonaton wouldn't see my shame. "He knows I couldn't kill the soldier. He thinks I'm a coward."

Yonaton shook his head. "He's glad you didn't kill the soldier—the last thing he'd want is for a *kohen* to kill. You heard what Master Uriel said, that *kohanim* are forbidden contact with the dead. Think of the debt he owes your father. He wants to protect you."

"Exactly, which means he's not going to listen to me."

"Listen, I think you're worrying about nothing. You ought to be more concerned about convincing Master Uriel. Will he agree to act like a Calf worshiper and then retreat into a cave?"

"I doubt it, but we have to try. Perhaps we shouldn't tell him about hiding? Whether the plan is to fight or hide, he still needs to get to the cave. Let Ovadia convince him to stay put once we're there."

Yonaton snorted. "He's a prophet, don't be a fool. But if you can convince Master Uriel, I'll work on Shimon. Twice he's told me how I impressed him at the battle. I think he'll listen to me."

Yonaton's willingness to deal with Shimon lightened my breathing. "So you think it's better to bring him along?"

"Shimon's not stupid—he won't fight unless he has to. And if we have to fight, there's no one I'd rather have on my side."

The full heat of the day was just starting to subside when we saw the great carob tree blocking the cave. Ovadia warned us to enter the cave only after dark, so we tethered Balaam by a spring a short distance away and waited.

The first thing I noticed as night fell were flames backlighting the tree. Had Uriel bowed to Shimon's recklessness?

I approached the cave first, lurking in the bushes while I spied out the situation. There was no sign of the prophet or Shimon. The blaze illuminated the cave, casting an eerie glow behind the carob's dancing leaves. A charred cooking pot lay at its edge. From my hiding place, I inspected the cave for any signs of a struggle.

Stones crunched under footsteps, and I snapped my eyes to the path. By the fire's orange glow, I saw Yonaton stepping toward the cave—but he wasn't alone. A shadow broke away from the darkness and rose behind him. I let out a strangled cry at the sound of metal hissing against a leather sheath. A sword rose behind Yonaton.

The arm froze and then dropped. "You have returned." Shimon sheathed his weapon as he eased into the firelight. His scars twisted in a tight smile.

A second figure slipped from the darkness into the cave. "You succeeded." There was no question in Uriel's voice.

I stepped out from my hiding place. "Yes, Master."

"Where are we to go?"

"The cave of Dotan, Master."

Uriel nodded solemnly. "A choice with wisdom. How many are already assembled there?"

"Thirty."

"There will be more."

"Dotan?" Shimon said, digging his heels into the rocky soil. "That's north of Shomron. Did Ovadia say how we're to get there?"

I swallowed. "Yes."

Yonaton stepped toward the entrance. "We shouldn't leave Balaam where he could draw attention. I'll retrieve him."

Uriel waved his hand in answer. "Balaam is fine where he is. It was wise to approach on foot." His eyes grew narrow. "Now the plan."

I'd rehearsed my speech at least ten times in my head on the ride back from Shomron—but the words evaporated in my master's presence.

Uriel fixed me with a piercing stare. "Are we to join the pilgrims returning from Beit El?"

My chest froze, anticipating the prophet's angry protest. "Ovadia says it's the best way. Hopefully, no one will—"

Uriel cut me off. "Very well. So we will do."

My breath seeped out in relief. That part at least was easier than I feared.

Shimon's hand grew white on the hilt of his sword. "We will be considered among those who bowed to the Calf!"

Uriel shook his head. "I will walk hooded and cloaked. You may do the same. No one will know us. If any do, the faithful judge the prophets with favor.* They will understand we are seeking the cover of the crowd. But even if they do believe we bowed, it is worth the risk. As Lev said, it is the best way."

"I agree, Master Uriel, that we must reach Dotan," Shimon said, "but perhaps you should seek vision before you decide how. The Holy One may grant us guidance whether this path is really the—"

"It is not the time for vision."

"But why not? Couldn't—"

"I never use prophecy to question my heart. This is true now more than ever. We are being carried by a powerful stream of events—ascending now could make me deaf to the voice of my own heart."

"Which is what?"

"We were told to seek Ovadia—we must heed his advice. Traveling with those returning from Beit El is the safest way to get to Dotan."

Yonaton sighed in my ear, but Uriel wasn't done. "The only difficulty is the delay. It is essential we get to Dotan quickly. Even now they may be forming plans to resist Izevel. They will need our guidance."

I sucked in my breath again.

The sound drew Uriel's attention. "Is there more, Lev?"

There was no need for Uriel to know the next part until we reached Dotan, but Yonaton was right—he'd know if I was hiding anything. "They are not seeking guidance, Master."

"Then the resistance has already begun? All the more so, they will need leadership."

"No, Master, they seek no leader."

"No leader? What then?"

My throat clenched, so tight I could barely answer. Uriel studied me as I sputtered. "There is to be no resistance."

"No resistance?"

"No, Master."

"Then why assemble in Dotan?"

I swallowed hard. I needed Ovadia here for this.

Uriel held my gaze. "To hide?"

"Yes, Master."

The prophet shook his head. "I am too old to bury myself in a cave. There is no point in dying hidden. Even being struck down by the sword is better than that; then the people might see the brutality of their so-called Queen and rise up against her."

Shimon stepped between the prophet and me. "Then what shall we do, Master?"

"You were right—I must seek vision. Lev, your kinnor." Uriel lowered himself to the stone ground.

I hesitated. Two oaths: one to serve Uriel, one to bring Uriel to Dotan. All that day I pondered what I would do should those two vows conflict. I felt my master's presence, firm on the floor. Was he set on resistance even if his death would only be a symbol? At the very least, Dotan would extend my master's life, whether he wanted that or not. And what if Ovadia was right? What if my master would prove pivotal once the war was over? I saw now why Ovadia made me swear; the oath's power tied me to his purpose. I swallowed again and made my choice. "No, Master."

Uriel raised an eyebrow.

I gripped my tunic in my fists. "You said it yourself, Master, now is not the time for vision. There must be others resisting Izevel, but the Holy One didn't send us to them. We were sent to Ovadia—we should heed his advice."

I felt the heat of Shimon's glare—he would welcome another fight. But I focused on my master, still crouched on the ground.

Fire rose in Uriel's eyes, flashed, and then extinguished. "Perhaps you are correct, Lev, and I should heed Ovadia's word without pursuing further guidance." He stared down at his hands, limp between his knees. "And perhaps you are wrong."

The uncertainty in my master's voice unsettled me. Uriel reached out to Yonaton to help him to his feet. "You boys have traveled far today—I have demanded enough words for now. To sleep. Let us each seek the counsel of our dreams."

The exhaustion of my body overwhelmed the restlessness of my mind, and I quickly fell into a deep slumber. Riding Balaam, it took much of the day to travel from Shomron, but my dreams returned me there in an instant.

The throne room glowed. Oil lamps surrounded the Queen and ringed Yambalya as he knelt before her. It could have been daylight if not for the nearly full moon shining through the eastern windows.

"We killed their prophets and still they resist!" Izevel's voice was shrill.

"It takes time, my Queen, to uproot a people's connection to their god."

"It is Eliyahu. And this drought."

"The people know nothing of Eliyahu, my Queen, nor do they yet realize there's a drought. Once they do, they will have all the more reason to turn against their prophets."

"Or perhaps they will see Eliyahu as stronger than Baal?"

The priest glared at Izevel, eyes smoldering.

"What of the hunt? You claimed your servants have never failed."

"They are Baal's servants, not mine. And they will succeed. I told you, I have seen Eliyahu's future in the stars."

Izevel sat back with a snarl. "Yet, for now, the people still resist."

"Yes, my Queen, but I have a plan."

She leaned forward. "A plan? What will you do?"

"If her Majesty will be guided by me, then before the moon wanes, half the stubborn ones in Shomron will bend their knees before Baal."

Pale light filled the cave when I woke the next morning. Shimon and Yonaton still slept beside me, but Uriel's mat lay empty. My eyes scanned the back of the cave—Balaam's saddlebags were gone. My heart leapt as I pulled my tunic over my head.

Yonaton stirred. "Where are you going?"

"Master Uriel's gone."

Yonaton sat up. "His sleeping mat is still here."

"The saddlebags are missing."

"So?"

Why didn't Yonaton understand? "So Master Uriel would take them only if he intended to travel."

"Without us?" Comprehension filled Yonaton's eyes, and he rose to his feet.

Uriel took the saddlebags and left without waking us, without even taking his cloak, which Yonaton used as a sleeping mat. Had he decided to journey alone so as not to endanger us? And if my master were headed for a place of safety, would he have left so many of his possessions behind? Uriel said last night that it was better to be struck down than hide. Was he riding now toward a final meeting with Izevel's soldiers? Would he even raise his staff to defend himself this time?

We ran down toward the spring where we left Balaam the night before. From a distance, we saw Uriel tying the saddlebags into place. We weren't too late.

"Master," I called, "Don't go!"

Uriel stopped his work. "Lower your voice, Lev. If you are seen with me—"

"Master, Ovadia can protect you."

"I have given much thought to Ovadia's plan, Lev."

"Ovadia made me swear to bring you to Dotan."

Uriel lifted an eyebrow at this. "Ovadia is very devoted." He placed his hand on my shoulder. "As are you."

Resignation filled the prophet's eyes. "It's not just that, Master. The people need you alive."

"I can do little for the people hidden in a cave, Lev."

"But this war won't last forever."

"Not forever, no. But Eliyahu has not attacked with iron chariots. He brought a drought—it may be years until its end."

"You must live. Ovadia says you can save the people."

"Where is the salvation in hiding?"

"When it's over," I urged. "Ovadia said it might take an Eliyahu to defeat Izevel, but we'll need you to heal the people."

Pity curled his eyebrows. "Ovadia is mistaken. He has wisdom, but is still young. He has not seen what I have."

"Which is what, Master?"

"The Holy One always creates the remedy before bringing the malady,* though it remains hidden until its proper time. The nation will not be rebuilt by an old man crawling out of a hole. My time has passed."

Yonaton broke his silence. "My father taught me that the prophets never lose faith. How can you give up your life, Master?"

Uriel started at the title "Master." Only Uriel's servants and disciples called him "Master," rather than Master Uriel. I'd been calling Uriel master since returning to him months earlier, but this was the first time that Yonaton had declared him so. Uriel peered into Yonaton's eyes. "Give up my life? Certainly not. My life may be the only thing I have left to offer the people, but I will not hand it over needlessly."

"But Master," Yonaton said, "You saddled Balaam and left your sleeping mat behind."

"That is because I must travel a road that he cannot follow." Uriel took Balaam's lead rope and placed it in Yonaton's hand. "And neither can you. I cannot be your master, Yonaton, not now. There are two pieces of bread and a skin of water in the saddlebag. It should be enough to get you home."

We both stared dumbly at Uriel. A chill passed through me as the meaning of my master's words struck my heart. *He was sending Yonaton away. Yonaton, who ran an entire day's journey to warn us, who killed the soldier when I could not.*

Yonaton's eyes dropped to the rope in his hand. "But I want to come with you."

"I know." Uriel's expression softened. "You have a strong heart. I promised you could stay with us as long as you could help. You have done much, but you can do no more. You are not yet of age, and your family is waiting. Your path lies with them now."

Yonaton's eyes fell to the ground, and I knew that he would not raise his voice again in protest.

I turned away, not because I still considered his sorrow indecent, but in order to give him the privacy to grieve. I felt grateful for being allowed to continue, though it was Yonaton's path that led to safety.

Uriel scratched his donkey behind his remaining ear. "Take Balaam for me. He has been my faithful companion but can no longer accompany me."

The significance of his words hit me. "Does that mean we're going to Dotan, Master?"

"Yes, to the cave."

"But you said Ovadia was mistaken?"

"Indeed, I believe so. But you were correct last night—I was told to seek Ovadia. There is a power at work beyond my own. I must follow the direction I was given."

Uriel shot a glance toward the sun breaking over the horizon, then back at Yonaton. "Tonight is Shabbat. You must leave now to be home before sunset."

Balaam inched forward and nuzzled Yonaton's hand. Yonaton scratched him behind the ear the way Uriel had a moment earlier, then turned to me, his eyes spilling tears.

I spread my arms and embraced my friend, knowing that it might be for the last time.

"The Cave of Dotan," Yonaton whispered as he tightened his hold around me. "When I'm of age, I'll find you."

"Don't," I replied. "Stay and help your family. There's nothing you can do for us now."

"I...." Yonaton stopped himself short, released me, and pulled the old donkey toward the road. As he had brought no belongings, there was no need for him to return to the cave. I stood watching until he was out of sight. It was only after he disappeared that it occurred to me—I would now have to deal with Shimon on my own.

Before sunset, Shimon and I built the fire high so it would keep on burning into Shabbat. Our gear lacked for any luxuries, except for the last drops from a wineskin which Uriel used to sanctify our meal. Reclining after we ate, Shimon glared at me across the glowing embers. "It seems that we're following you now."

"We're following Ovadia," I responded, "as the Holy One instructed Master Uriel."

"The Holy One sent us to Ovadia, but we're following his guidance because of you."

I didn't want to admit it, but Shimon was right. Uriel had said nothing since Yonaton's parting that morning, as if his remaining energy was sapped by the decision to hide. He stared at the flames, motionless. "You think I'm leading us astray?"

"What I think doesn't matter, the decision has been made. I'll help in any way I can."

Shimon's sword leaned against the wall of the cave, the cedar tree emblem on its hilt reflecting the amber firelight. "Then perhaps you should leave the sword behind," I said.

"Why?"

"It's too easily recognized."

"It will be out of sight. Until needed."

I knew Shimon would refuse, just as I balked at Uriel's suggestion to leave my knife behind during the wedding. Yet, if Uriel had insisted, I would have yielded. But that was the prophet; in Shimon's eyes, I was a child in need of protection. If Yonaton had been with me, perhaps together we could have pressed him. But how could I persuade him on my own that his eagerness to fight was a danger to all our lives?

Shimon answered my unspoken thoughts. "Even if your plan is to sneak past the Queen's soldiers, it's best to be prepared." I leaned in to argue, but he wasn't done. He braced his back against the wall of the cave and shot words sharper than arrows. "Had your father been so prepared, you might be dining with him now in Judah, rather than hiding in this cave."

The old prophet's eyes opened wide for the first time since Yonaton's departure, and shot up to meet Shimon's.

"What do you mean?" My gaze jumped from Shimon to my master. "You said my father was murdered for preaching against the Golden Calf."

"He was," Shimon answered. He had brought up my father to win the argument about the sword, but now he was stuck—we both knew I wouldn't let the matter drop until I heard the whole story. His posture, so defiant a moment earlier, deflated as he leaned in toward the fire. "It was during the Civil War. King Ahav's father, Omri, was locked in a struggle for control of the northern kingdom with Tivni. The armies fought with arms, yes, but mainly the battle was over the hearts of the people. Omri considered the people's reactions to every step he took, and many of them admired your father. Sending soldiers to his house would have driven many into the arms of Tivni."

"But then why kill him at all? Did he support Tivni?"

Shimon turned to Uriel for guidance—did he not know the answer, or was he questioning how much to reveal?

Uriel broke his silence. "Your father supported neither, but both saw him as an opponent."

"Because he was against the Calf?"

Uriel shook his head. "Because he was for real kingship. He dreamed of a reunification of the two kingdoms. To him, only a descendant of David had the right to rule."

I remembered my conversation with Uncle Menachem about the splitting of the Kingdom. Hadn't I also questioned how the Kingdom could split when the House of David was granted an everlasting throne?

Shimon sighed at Uriel's answer. "Omri aimed to catch your father in an act of rebellion."

"My father rebelled?"

"It was only the appearance of rebellion that mattered to Omri. He knew Yochanan traveled to Jerusalem to serve in the Temple for each of the three pilgrimage festivals. The roads were well guarded, but your father would lead anyone he could convince to join him through the mountain passes. Everyone knew the penalty for crossing was death. If Omri caught your father crossing, he could be rid of him without provoking the ire of the people."

"And my mother?" My voice trembled.

Uriel said, "Your father sought my counsel the week before he died. We agreed it was best for you to be raised in the Kingdom of Judah, with his brethren. This is why both you and your mother were with him at the border when the King's soldiers fell upon him."

Shimon fidgeted. "I'm sorry, Lev. I shouldn't have spoken."

"No." I wiped my eyes with my palms. "I want to know. Please, tell me."

Shimon again searched Uriel for direction. The prophet nodded, giving permission to finally lift the cloak that had covered over my past for so many years. Shimon lost his gaze in the fire, staring into the burning coals rather than face me as he spoke. "I was sixteen, making my third journey to Jerusalem with your father. I walked up front near your parents and heard their last conversation."

"What was it about?"

"You."

Something stirred inside me. This was the story that had haunted my dreams since age two. Yet, now that I was about to hear the truth, a strange thing happened. The locked box I'd built to secure the memory all these years could no longer protect me, so it opened on its own. As Shimon spoke in his deliberate way, images unfolded in my mind, matching him phrase for phrase. It was as though I'd returned to a crisp autumn day ten years before.

"Lev's cold." Mother tightened the shawl that bound me to her back, drawing me closer to her body and shifting me a bit higher. Lavender wafted from beneath her headscarf.

"This isn't a place to stop." Father's sharp eyes scanned the mountains on either side of the narrow path. He was older than I imagined, the sides of his beard fully gray, but he stood tall, almost at Uriel's height, with a muscular build.

"How much farther?"

"See that ridge up ahead? Once we pass it, we'll be out of the inheritance of Ephraim and into the territory of Binyamin. Then we'll be in the Kingdom of Judah."

"And then we'll be safe, Yochanan?"

"Omri's soldiers aren't supposed to cross the border. Still, I never feel safe until I get back on the road." Father gazed into her teary eyes, so much like Aunt Leah's. She was much younger than he and had never made the trip before. "I'm sorry, Sarah, I don't mean to scare you."

"It's not that." She collected herself, but her eyes were wet. "I was just thinking I might never return."

He sighed and peeked over his shoulder at the twenty men following him through the mountain pass. "You're going to be all right?"

I grabbed at Mother's ear, and she caressed my small hand in hers, turned her head back toward me, and drew my hand to her mouth to kiss it. "I just need to remember that I'm doing this for him."

Father continued to scan the surrounding hillsides, eventually spotting a lone soldier mounted on horseback. At first he laughed, for there was nothing a single soldier could do against twenty men. The soldier grinned back at my father, raised a ram's horn to his lips, and blew three short, soft blasts.

I stared at Shimon across the fire. "Soft blasts?"

"Yes, soft. It was the softness that alarmed your father. Blasts like that could never be heard all the way in Mitzpah, where the soldiers were garrisoned. As soon as he heard the blasts, he knew it was a trap."

Father turned back to his followers and screamed, "Run!" He grabbed Mother's hand and pulled her along behind him, dragging her toward the safety of the border. The pounding of hoofbeats thundered behind us. I saw no horses, but the panic and rush set me squalling.

One of the men following behind screamed, "No, this way," and ran back into the Kingdom of Israel. The other followers hesitated, then followed their new leader, separating themselves from my family and the border.

Five soldiers broke into the gap between the two groups. Though Mother's shawl must have blocked my vision of the soldiers, somehow I could still see and hear them in my mind. So, my dreams were not just memories. As Master Yosef said, they must contain a drop of prophecy as well.

The officer leading the small pack of soldiers reined in his steed and surveyed the situation. "The two of you, pursue the large group, but don't catch them. It's enough that the dread of King Omri fall upon them." Two soldiers stalked the group fleeing back into Israel, one banging his sword onto his shield, creating a racket that echoed in the mountain pass while keeping his horse at a relaxed trot. The officer addressed the remaining two soldiers. "You follow me." He kicked his horse after us.

Father still ran, moving as fast as he could while pulling us behind him. Turning back, he saw that the three soldiers would overtake him before the border. Pushing Mother ahead of him, he yelled, "You run! It's me they're after. Save yourself and Lev. Get him to my brother's family."

"Yochanan!" She stood frozen as her husband stepped with forced ease back to meet the horses.

"Run, Sarah! If I can follow, I will." He waited until my mother, with me on her back, began running again toward the border, then walked toward the approaching soldiers. Though armed, he didn't reach for his knife. Perhaps if he came to them unarmed, not resisting, they'd have mercy on him.

The soldiers pulled up their horses and surrounded him, with their officer mounted squarely between Father and the border. "Why do you pursue me, Yoav?" Father asked.

"But he must have known why," I insisted.

"Of course he knew," Shimon replied. "But your mother was still running for the border with you on her back. The longer he could keep them talking, the greater chance she would have to reach safety."

"Where were you?"

"Hidden. I couldn't decide which group to follow and found myself stuck in the middle. Just before the horses arrived, I ducked behind a boulder."

A fiery rage rose against him for not standing by my father's side. Then I remembered he was only sixteen, not much older than me. I myself ran away from Uriel when the Queen's soldiers came to take his life. The anger evaporated, and I said nothing, waiting for Shimon to continue.

"You know what this is about, Yochanan," Omri's officer said. "I've warned you myself against defying the King's orders."

"You've already won, Yoav. You've scared away all those following me. Now it's just me, my wife, and my son, and we're leaving Israel, going to join my brethren in Judah." As he spoke, his eyes flitted between Yoav and my mother, who'd reached the ridge and passed safely into the Kingdom of Judah.

"Oh? Never to return?" Yoav sneered.

"I vow, if you let me go, I will never return."

A joyless smile spread across Yoav's face as he drew his sword. "You lie!" The officer drove his weapon forward and Father dove onto the ground to avoid it. He rose to his feet clutching his knife in his hand. Lunging at Yoav, he drove the blade into his leg, just above the knee. Yoav screamed in pain and brought down the hilt of the sword on top of Father's head, knocking him to the ground. "You never know when to quit, Yochanan HaKohen. The rest of your tribe fled to Judah long ago. They knew it was over for them here, but you refused to go, always defying us. Now your time has come to an end."

"I'm leaving, I swear. You don't need to kill me."

"Did my father intend to return?"

"He was moving you and your mother to a safer place, but he had no intention of abandoning the faithful of Israel. Though now that he was caught, I believe he would have given up on his mission in exchange for his life. I never knew him to break a vow."

My head fell forward into my hands and tears streamed through my fingers.

"I'm sorry, Lev. I've said too much."

My palms muffled my voice. "No, please. I want to hear."

My request met only silence.

I raised my face to Shimon's. "I beg of you..."

"Very well. Your father lay pleading for his life. Then Yoav spoke the words that will bring a chill to my heart until I enter the grave. *'I'm not going to kill you,' he said. 'I'm going to let my soldiers kill you. I'm going to make sure the Kingdom of Israel never has to suffer you or your seed ever again.'* And though by this time your mother had already crossed the border, he kicked his mount after her."

"And you did nothing? This whole time?" I couldn't keep accusation out of my voice.

"While Yoav was there, I didn't dare. I would have been throwing away my life."

I nodded, hating my judgment. Who was I to question Shimon's bravery? Yet, when he returned to the tale, I glared at him across the fire, and couldn't go back into the vision.

"When Yoav rode off, your father howled and chased after him. One of the soldiers slashed at his back, carving a deep gash across his shoulder blade. He collapsed, and the soldier drew back his sword for the final blow, his arm trembling like a leaf. Perhaps in his heart he feared the Holy One's judgment. His fear gave me courage. I hurled a rock with all my might, striking him in the ear. His thrust missed its target, hitting the ground instead of your father's neck.

"But now I was exposed. The other rider turned on me—there was nowhere to run. My best cover was the boulder, so I stayed put. Yochanan staggered to his feet, somehow ready to fight. He couldn't beat a mounted soldier, so he attacked the horse, slashing its throat. It fell over sideways and crushed its rider's leg against the rocky ground. Your father left him struggling under his mount, and came to help me.

"I was unarmed, so I kept the boulder between myself and the soldier, forcing him to dismount to get at me. The only thing I had to fend off his attack was my sleeping mat, but reed doesn't hold up for long against iron. That's how I got these." Shimon pointed to his face and pulled back his sleeves to show more scars laddered up his arms. My anger with him disappeared now that he'd joined the fight.

"When I saw Yochanan approaching, I screamed as loud as I could. The soldier thought I was yelling out in pain or fear, but I did it to cover your father's footsteps. I'll never forget the look of surprise on the soldier's face when your father planted that knife in his back."

My hand glided over my leg, feeling the bulge of the knife hidden under my tunic.

"By this time, Yochanan's tunic was soaked with blood, and he wobbled on his feet. He said to me, 'Come…Sarah and Lev.' I seized the soldier's sword and mounted his horse, pulling your father up behind me."

Shimon's bottom lip trembled. He steadied it between his teeth.

"Go on," Uriel whispered. "He should know this part as well."

Shimon swallowed the bitter taste in his mouth. "We had not ridden far when Uriel appeared before us on the trail. He held you screaming in his arms."

I turned to my master. "You were there?"

"I also traveled to Jerusalem for the festivals, but I knew my way and did not need your father's guidance." Uriel's eyes never left the fire. "I was ahead on the path when the ram's horn sounded. I turned back when I heard it. After that, I followed the sound of your cries."

"Will you continue the tale?" Shimon asked.

"No, you should. Now that you've started, he needs to hear it all."

Shimon nodded. "Your father slipped off the horse and took you in his arms—he could barely hold you, he was already so weak. We heard hoofbeats, and Yoav appeared, bearing down on us with his sword drawn. Uriel stepped in front of your father, and Yoav pulled back to avoid trampling him.

So this was it—the reason I recognized Uriel that first day, the reason I'd felt so on edge when I saw him. He must have visited my nightmares for years. The vision tugged at my mind again, drawing me back in.

"Stand aside," Yoav screamed.

"I'm going where he's going," Uriel replied. "Won't you kill me as well?"

"King Omri grants you passage, but I have my duty."

"And I have mine." Uriel planted his staff firmly on the ground before him. "I have two messages, one for you and one for your master."

Yoav's eyes jumped from Uriel to my father to Shimon, who still sat on horseback, sword drawn, then back to Uriel. Outnumbered, Yoav sheathed his sword. "Very well, navi. Give me my master's first."

"In two years' time, Omri will be victorious. Should he turn away from the path of Yeravaum, opening the road and purging idolatry from the land, his will be an everlasting kingdom. Otherwise, his will be as the kingdoms of Yeravaum and Bassa, and dogs will lick the blood of his children."

Yoav's face was set like stone. "And the message for me?"

"Ride home to your wife, for the child comes."

"But it is not yet time!" Yoav's face faltered. He took a deep breath and straightened on his mount. "It is no matter. The child will come with or without me. I cannot leave my post."

"The child you will never know, and your wife is already beyond your help. I am offering you a chance to say goodbye."

Yoav tensed in his saddle. "Goodbye?"

"Goodbye." Uriel drew himself up to his full height, eyes blazing and voice thundering like Eliyahu's in Jericho. "As you judged, so are you found wanting. You struck down Yochanan's wife and son. The lives of your wife and unborn son are forfeit in turn."

"A son?" Yoav beheld me, wailing helplessly in Father's arms. "But Yochanan's son lives!"

"Yes, he lives, but not from your mercy—you left him to die!" Father crumpled to his knees, almost dropping me as he fell. Uriel lifted me from his arms.

Yoav dropped his eyes to the ground. "What if I have mercy on him now?"

"That is not mercy, it is desperation. You think only of yourself, not the child."

"Then she will die? And my son?"

"So it will be."

Yoav studied Father's dying body, his blood raining onto the dry ground. "And what of me? Is my life forfeit for Yochanan's?"

"Your future is in your own hands. You are a man of strength. Turn your strength inward, conquer your anger, and live."

"And if I don't?"

"Then your greatest act of valor will be your last. King Tivni will die by your sword, but you will fall as well."

"Quill," Father said, his voice raspy. All eyes fell upon the kohen, kneeling in a puddle of his own blood. Uriel retrieved a quill and a scrap of parchment from Balaam's saddlebag and steadied Father's hand as well as he could, while Father dipped the quill into the ready pool of red dye at his feet and wrote. "Take," he gasped, handing the scrap of parchment back to Uriel.

Uriel received the scrap and turned back to Yoav. "Yochanan is dying. Let me take his son to his brethren in Judah."

Yoav lifted his eyes to Uriel, then turned at the sound of approaching horses.

The two soldiers he'd sent after Father's followers came to a stop behind him. Yoav straightened himself and faced Uriel, the tone of authority returning to his voice. "I have my duty. King Omri allows you to pass, but no one else."

"Does your duty include killing children, or may he return to his family in Israel?"

Yoav eyed the two soldiers behind him, then turned back to the prophet. "King Omri is just. He does not desire the blood of children. He may return."

"Shimon, take the child." Uriel dropped his voice so that Shimon had to bend down to hear him. "Take him to his uncle in Levonah, Menachem ben Yitzchak." But Uriel didn't hand me to Shimon, he carried me back to Father. "It is time to say goodbye to your child, Yochanan Hakohen."

I reached out. Father reached back, not to take me, but to lay his strong hands upon my head. Our eyes met as he blessed me for the last time. He kissed me on the forehead, leaving a small, crimson mark. At the same time, Uriel, whose body shielded me from the three soldiers, tucked the parchment into my garments.

I threw my arms around Father's neck, not wanting to let go. Even with Uriel still supporting me, my weight was too much for the dying man. The pressure on his chest brought on heaving coughs, each one forcing his eyes closed. "Take him. Don't let him see me die."

Uriel tugged, but I screamed, refusing to release my grip on Father's neck. Uriel pulled my hands apart, drew me away, and cradled me up to Shimon. Shimon placed me straddled on the horse in front of him, but struggled to keep me there as I writhed and screamed, reaching out for Father. "Hold him tighter," Uriel said. Shimon wrapped a quivering arm around me, pulling me closer into his body, and pinned my arms to my side. "Now ride. He will calm down once we're out of sight."

"Wait!" Father called, holding out his knife. "Take this. It is his birthright."

Uriel passed the knife up to Shimon. I pried one of my arms free and grabbed for it, but Shimon held it out of reach and tucked it into his belt. With a last command from Uriel to "Go!" Shimon kicked the horse, handling the reins in his left hand, my protesting body with his right.

Yoav turned to his two soldiers. "I'm going to follow him, make sure he doesn't make another try for the border. Wait here until Yochanan dies."

"And Uriel?" one of the soldiers asked.

"King Omri grants the prophets leave to go where they will." Yoav kicked his horse to pursue Shimon, but as soon as he was out of sight of the others, he turned his horse and galloped toward Mitzpah.

I scowled, feeling no sympathy for my parents' murderer. "He got what he deserved."

Uriel's cheeks were lined with wet tracks. "What he deserved? Perhaps. But could any of us survive in a world where we receive that which we deserve?"

"Wouldn't that be justice?"

"Yes, it would. But when the Holy One created the world in strict justice, it could not stand.* Where only judgment reigns, creation crumbles."

"So Yoav lived because there's no justice?"

"There is justice, but tempered with mercy. We stand on the merit of what could be and are not judged solely by what is."

My fists clenched. "He killed my parents."

"Indeed, and I cursed him for it."

"So where was your mercy then?"

Shimon flinched at the question. This wasn't the way to address my master, but at the moment I didn't care.

Uriel held out his hands to me. "You must understand: we are all vessels for the light of the Holy One. As we expand mercy in ourselves, it expands in the world. So too the opposite. As we judge, judgment increases in the world, and we are often the first to endure its strictures." Uriel dropped his hands and turned back to the fire.

The blaze had collapsed into a pile of glowing embers. In the silence, Uriel's words held me. During Shimon's tale, I'd been focused on myself, hardly noticing the prophet's pain. I assumed Uriel cried for my father, his lost friend. But in the silence that followed, I began to understand.

Ovadia said two nights earlier that it was essential to rescue Uriel. Not because of what he could do, but because of what he'd been through—because of what he'd become. Had this been the transformation? Had Uriel grown from a vessel of strict judgment to one of mercy? Was this the reason that he, alone among the prophets, could heal a nation shattered by Eliyahu's judgment?

I remembered Uriel's words from earlier that week. "A curse brings pain without regard to who receives it. It falls upon the guilty and the innocent alike. Even the one who invokes the curse is not spared its destruction."

Back at Shiloh, sitting with Zim the morning after the festival, I was shocked to learn that Uriel's son served the Golden Calf his father despised. Didn't Zim say he left his father's path ten years ago, exactly when I lost my parents?

"Master?" I trembled. "When you cursed Yoav, were you judged as well?"

The prophet's composure broke as a sob shook his chest. "Indeed." His head dropped between his knees, and he trembled with grief.

Shimon's mouth stood agape—he must not have known this part of the story.

"At the same time that Yoav's wife died, my wife left the world. By then, I had reached Jerusalem and did not know until I returned weeks later. My son was forced to bury his mother alone."

Comprehension dawned on Shimon's face. "That is why he left the Way and turned toward the Calf?"

"So he says. As you know, I spent my life traveling among the people. I was often away, and he resented it. He said that burying his mother alone was the final act that compelled him to leave my path. But even he does not know the full truth, that it was my curse that drove him from me."

"But, Master," I said, "You're not from the family of priests that Yeravaum appointed to replace the *kohanim*, are you?"

Uriel shook his head.

Shimon explained, "This was during the Civil War. Remember what I told you about King Omri. He deliberated on the people's reaction to each of his decisions. Having the son of the great prophet as his priest would increase his stature in the eyes of the nation and help him achieve the throne. When Omri learned that Master Uriel's son Gershon had separated from his father, he moved quickly to offer him the position before King Tivni could win his loyalty."

The prophet's wail echoed from between his knees. "Three families destroyed on a single day!"

Hillel said: Do not believe in yourself until the day you die.

Pirkei Avot 2:5

19

The Final Journey

The full moon blazed like a beacon in the western sky when we set out from the cave. Three days had passed in silence, each of us lost in contemplation in some corner of the small cave. For me, the time was spent digesting Shimon's tale, dwelling on the panic etched on my parents' faces, the eerie sound of their voices, and the image of their brutal deaths—details I'd never before been able to recall. The rebound of Uriel's curse upon his own family struck Shimon harder than I would have imagined. He no longer handled or even examined the captured sword while we remained in the cave. Nevertheless, when it was time to depart for our journey toward Dotan, he retrieved the sword and sheathed it around his waist.

Once on the road, we would just be pilgrims traveling home from the festival, but in the hills, we were potential prey. We trekked under cover of night to limit the risk of detection, but the cloudless sky and the moon's silvery brilliance nevertheless exposed us to prying eyes. There was nothing we could do about that: the festival always fell at the full moon. Uriel scanned the hilltops as we walked. I likewise searched the dark horizon for the outline of a soldier, but saw nothing.

We stopped well before dawn, hiding a stone's throw from the road in a thick clump of bushes. I lay down, my eyes heavy with drowsiness, my fears of discovery insufficient to hold off sleep.

A steady rumbling woke me; it sounded like the echo of a thunderclap off distant hills. I opened my eyes to sunbeams filtering through the thick branches above. "What's that noise?"

"Horses," Uriel replied. "Thirty at least, from the sound of it, being driven hard. The King and his escort."

"Ovadia will be with them?"

"I expect so. You may go back to sleep; we still have a long wait."

I sat up and pulled on my tunic. Anticipation had set in; sleep was no longer an option. The rumbling grew louder until the troop of horses thundered past, their dark shapes barely visible through gaps in the leaves.

Other horsemen followed the King's escort, riding past in ones and twos; then those on donkeys ambled past in small groups. The sun hung mid-sky when a thin stream of hardy farmers, in a hurry to return to their fields, appeared. Before long, the road was thick with travelers, ranging from boys newly of age to old men, who passed by in waves, talking and laughing as they went.

Uriel finally broke our silence. "It is time."

I crept out of the bushes, then circled around and sat beneath a tree on the roadside, resting my back against its trunk. A group of men passed, and when the last of them disappeared, leaving the road in front of me empty, I ran one hand over the strings of my kinnor.

Uriel and Shimon appeared beside me. Small groups of walkers flowed by as we ate our midday meal, appearing like three travelers stopping for a rest. When a large group of men appeared down the road, Uriel said, "We will let them pass, then join in from behind."

The sun beat down as we fell into stride with the group. My hair stuck to my forehead and sweat pooled beneath the rolled-up sheepskin slung over my back. Images of the cool spring near my uncle's house danced in my head, but Levonah was behind us—ahead lay Shomron.

We mingled in at the back of the crowd, moving past the very rear where we might stand out. My eyes flickered to the hilltops above the road, occasionally picking out a soldier stationed on a peak, but my breath remained steady. These were no longer the soldiers we feared—from above they would see nothing strange in this throng returning from Beit El.

The masses moving north on the road thinned throughout the day as men turned off toward home. In the late afternoon, we rounded a bend, and the road dropped into a long decline. We were close to Shomron now, the destination of most of those still walking. We approached a cluster of men stopped ahead, just before the shade of a large carob tree.

"What's going on up there?" Shimon asked.

Uriel stood to his full height. "Soldiers."

"Israelite or foreigners?"

"Foreigners."

I glanced at Shimon, and my heart thumped in my chest. This was the encounter I was dreading. Would he seek conflict with the Queen's soldiers? I was relieved to see no hunger for battle on his face. His expression was calm, almost serene. Learning of Uriel's curse rebounding upon himself seemed to have changed Shimon—as if for ten years he'd hungered to hold the prophet's power to curse, and only now realized its cost. He said, "A roadblock. Should we turn off?"

Uriel nodded toward the sides of the road. "They have soldiers stationed along the hillsides. They will be watching for anyone trying to avoid them. We are better off walking through."

I followed my master's gesture. At first I didn't spot them—they were not like the lookouts sitting mounted on the hilltops. These watchers were further down, in the shadows, where they could see without being seen.

Shimon's body tensed as he studied the soldiers bordering the roadside, and his eyes lost their quiet. His hand slipped under his cloak to the hilt of his sword.

I inched closer to him and whispered, "Remember, Master Uriel must reach Dotan."

Shimon regarded his hand, appearing surprised to find it grasping the sword, as if his battle-hungry instincts had acted of their own accord. He released the hilt and placed his hand on my shoulder instead. "I know the plan."

We drew closer to the roadblock. Uriel said, "There's a priest as well."

"What?" Shimon asked.

"A priest of the Baal. Under the tree."

I craned my neck to see. Sure enough, I caught a glimpse of violet robes in the shade of the carob tree. One soldier stood on each side of the road, while a third blocked the path in front of the waiting men, forcing them to pass through the shade one at a time. A man in a gray cloak was waved through. He stepped under the tree, approached the priest, then dropped to his knees and pressed his forehead to the ground.

"Clever," Uriel said.

"What's clever, Master?"

"Izevel is most powerful in Shomron, but many are opposed to her, even there. So, she waited until all the men of the city left for the festival, then placed a Baal on their path home. Now she can see who will bow and who will resist."

I peered under the tree, trying to glimpse the statue. "We must get through, Master."

"I will not bow before the Baal."

"Even to save your life?" The words rung hollow, Uriel placed too little value on his life. I changed tactics, appealing to his sense of mercy instead. "Even to save my life?" This too failed.

"Some things are more precious than life,* Lev. We are commanded to choose death rather than bow to strange gods. Even you must be willing to die rather than bow."

Shimon's hand sought the hilt of his sword, not absentmindedly as before, but with the same blazing intensity in his eyes as when he first leapt out of the trees to save us the week before. "You see, Lev, I was right to prepare for battle."

"There are three soldiers ahead and at least five more on the hillsides—you can't fight them all!"

"Samson killed a thousand in a single battle. You heard Master Uriel, Lev. The spirit I received was the same as Samson's."

"You don't know if you'll merit that power again."

"No, I don't. But even if I don't, I won't be fighting alone."

"There's not much Uriel or I could do against all these soldiers."

"It's not just the three of us. It's easy to scare the people one at a time, but in their arrogance, they've become reckless. The crowd is moving through too slowly. There are fifty men waiting and more coming up behind us. If we resist, we will draw much support—especially if it's known that we are led by a prophet."

I wanted to believe him, but recalled the fear on the faces of farmers just like these at the wedding. "But these men aren't armed. They'll run at the first sight of blood."

Uriel shook his head. "It matters not if they are armed. Izevel is seeking to strengthen her support, not to spark a rebellion. Her soldiers will not fight so many, even if they could."

My mind raced. The Queen ordered her soldiers to hunt down every prophet in the land. Perhaps Uriel could lead the crowd through the roadblock without bloodshed, but the soldiers were sure to notice that no ordinary man was at their head. They were sure to follow him and call others to their aid.

Any violence would mean abandoning the plan, and I'd sworn to deliver my master safely to Dotan.

We were close enough now to see the statue, a larger version of the one now resting in my uncle's house. Cast in bronze, its long helmet ascending toward the sky, a jagged sword raised, ready to strike, it stood perched on a wooden pedestal beneath the tree. Another farmer stepped forward, and he too bowed before the Baal. A thought occurred to me. "Master, if Izevel is afraid of a rebellion, then her soldiers cannot be killing all those who refuse to bow, can they?"

Uriel shook his head. "No, Lev, you must be correct. There are still too many in Israel, even in Shomron, that would refuse."

"So what happens to them? Are they allowed to pass?"

"Let us watch. There are fifty or more who still stand before us—I would expect at least ten to refuse."

One after another the soldiers waved the men forward. Some bowed quickly, falling to their knees and touching their foreheads to the ground, others hesitated, then bent at the waist, like the men in Jericho bowing before the King. Yet, each and every one of them humbled himself in some way before passing through the shade of the carob tree. The soldiers on the sides of the road barely watched as the travelers passed through.

Hardly ten men now stood between us and the tree, though the newcomers behind us continued to maintain the crowd's size. Shimon's eyes darted back and forth between Uriel and the soldiers. "If we're going to fight, we need to warn the men. Are we agreed?"

Shimon was right. If we were going to act, it must be now. My throat constricted and sweat ran down my forehead. I trusted Uriel's instincts—there was no sign that the soldiers were killing those who refused to bow. If they were, where were the bodies? But no one refused, so I couldn't know for sure. My vow to Ovadia rang in my mind. There was only one chance to prevent the violence that would ruin our plan.

"I'll go."

"What?" Shimon started.

"I'll go to the head of the line. I'll refuse to bow. If they let me through, you follow with Uriel. If they…if not, then fight."

"Wait, Lev, I don't think—"

But I didn't wait to hear what Shimon thought. My small size allowed me to slip easily through the crowd. A few men peered at me in annoyance—probably impatient to get through the roadblock and make it home—but perhaps because of my youth, no one stopped me.

The soldier at the front put out his arm, blocking me from advancing until the man under the tree passed. Like all the others, he too bowed down before the Baal.

The soldier's arm dropped, and I stepped forward.

My eyes were on the priest, but my thoughts were on the soldiers.

The priest approached. "Bow. Then go on."

I stood silent and still, holding my arms tight so they wouldn't tremble.

The priest insisted, "You bow. Do it now, then go."

I held my breath steady, stared back at the priest, but didn't move.

The priest moved closer. "You not bow? Baal angry. Curse the rain."

My mouth filled with a metallic tang. One knee trembled, and I dug my toe into the dirt to still it. One of the soldiers turned to watch me now. But still I didn't move.

The priest leaned in and spoke in a whisper. "Don't bow. Just pick up and go."* He rotated his body, positioning himself between me and the waiting crowd. He dropped a copper piece on the ground before the statue.

A laugh bubbled up from my belly—I swallowed it back with effort. Uriel was right; not all the men ahead of us were willing to bow. That's why they were only allowed through one at a time. Most men, seeing those ahead of them bow, would bow as well. Those who refused just had to pick a piece of copper off the ground. Those behind—who were not watching closely enough to see the precious metal—would think they were bowing from the waist, just enough to humble themselves.

"Pick up. You keep copper."

Questions flashed through my mind as I peered at the shiny metal. Hardly anyone among the men returning from the festival of the Golden Calf would refuse to pick up the copper. But what about those who refused to give even the impression of bowing? Was that the real point of the roadblock? The Queen's soldiers had already attacked the gathering places of the prophets. Now that the faithful were scattered, there was no way to distinguish them from the rest of the people. Was the roadblock intended to weed out the most devout? To find the prophets and disciples hidden among the commoners?

What about Shimon and Uriel? Would they pick up the copper to save their lives?

One of the soldiers stepped in toward me—I had delayed for too long. I could pick up the metal and get past the Baal, but needed to do it in a way that Shimon and Uriel would realize I wasn't bowing. I stepped to the side, then bent down and picked up the copper. Anyone watching closely would see that I wasn't even facing the Baal, but it was enough—the priest waved me through.

Once out of the shade of the carob tree, I turned around to watch. Neither the soldiers nor the priest paid me any mind—to them, I was just a boy waiting for his father to pass through.

The next man scowled at me as he bowed, annoyed at me for jumping ahead of him and then passing so slowly.

Easy as it was to pass through the roadblock, would Shimon still refuse? Shimon objected to even walking among those returning from Beit El—would he be willing to give the impression that he'd bowed to the Baal? If it was just his life, I was certain that he would rather fight than pick up the copper. But would he do it to protect Uriel? I caught Shimon's eye and gave him the slightest of nods, the most communication I could risk with the soldiers so close. But Shimon just glared back, his eyes resolute.

Three more men passed through the roadblock, two dropping quickly to the ground, the third bending to pick up the offered metal. Shimon drifted ahead of Uriel, placing several men between them. When he reached the front of the line, my hands clenched. A farmer under the carob tree pressed his head to the ground, begging loudly for Baal not to withhold the rains. When he rose, Shimon stepped forward.

The soldier on the far side of the road looked up as Shimon approached—his scars distinguished him from the crowd even without the fresh wounds. The Tzidonian's nostrils flared as if smelling him for blood. Four of his comrades had failed to return from duty the week before. Was he on the lookout for their killer?

Shimon stepped up to the priest.

"You bow. Then go on."

Shimon's voice was calm, yet pitched to carry. "The people of Israel do not bow to the Baal."

A murmur rose from the edge of the waiting pack. One of the soldiers left his post at the side of the road and stepped into the circle of shade under the tree. His hand rested on the hilt of his sword, and black dots marched in a tight pattern across his cheeks, becoming jagged lines at his throat before disappearing into his tunic. I'd heard rumors of the coastal people's tattoos, but had never seen them before. The ink gave his face a bestial look.

Shimon met the soldier's gaze.

With a rustle of violet robes, the priest waved the soldier back. He retreated, but kept his eyes on Shimon. The priest leaned close and whispered, dropping a piece of copper to the ground. Shimon peered at the metal, but didn't move.

I wanted to scream at him to take it. I bit my lower lip until I tasted blood. How stupid I'd been. An old man and a boy would have passed through easily.

Shimon had no desire to hide. He'd accompanied us only to help Uriel reach safety. And yet with his scarred face and unyielding nature, he was our greatest danger. Once Uriel had agreed to join the crowd returning from Beit El, the time had come to part ways. I should have confronted him, even without Yonaton. What would happen to my master if Shimon refused?

The soldier stepped forward once more, this time loosening his sword in its sheath. The priest again waved him away, but the soldier retreated just halfway. The priest pulled another piece of metal from his pocket, this time silver. He didn't just drop the silver on the ground, but rolled it to where Shimon could pick it up without even bending in the Baal's direction.

I tried to catch his eye, but Shimon glared at the idol. *Don't look at the statue Shimon. Just pick up the silver and move on.*

Shimon turned from the Baal. For a moment, he locked eyes with the soldier, whose sword was now half drawn. Then he broke eye contact and bent down to pick up the silver.

As Shimon bent over, his cloak parted in front. The hilt of his sword peeked out between the fabric, revealing the cedar tree emblem engraved on the handle. The priest was no longer watching, but the tattooed soldier was.

The soldier leapt forward and drew his sword in a smooth motion. Shimon grabbed for his own weapon, but in his bent position was slower than his enemy. The sword flashed in an executioner's cut. Shimon threw out his empty left hand to block the blow, but bone is no match for metal. His arm shattered, just like the soldier's sword in our last battle. The tattooed soldier aimed another blow and Shimon fell limp to the ground.

My teeth sliced my lip—I must not scream. I swallowed to hold back the tears. Shimon was beyond my help. I must save my master.

The priest ran forward, screaming in his guttural tongue. He slapped the soldier's face and gestured wildly at the men waiting to get through the roadblock. But he was no longer in charge.

The tattooed soldier called to his comrades lining the hillsides flanking the road. They were eight in all, and the tattooed one seemed to be their leader. He pointed to Shimon's body, and another soldier ran forward, grabbed Shimon's arms, and dragged him to the side of the road.

They may have been heavily outnumbered, but the Tzidonians were the only ones armed. They bunched together under the carob tree, backs to the trunk, ready to defend themselves.

Though shock and anger flashed across the faces of the Israelite men, their fear prevailed. No outcry cut through the stillness of the rolling hills at Shimon's murder; no one advanced to attack. The only serene face was Uriel's.

Seeing that they were unchallenged, the soldiers broke their defensive position. The tattooed soldier pushed the priest back toward the Baal. Then he screamed at the man in front of the line, "Come. You bow now!"

The man dropped to the ground, his eyes avoiding the blood-stained earth. The priest reasserted himself and waved the soldiers back to their positions. One soldier returned to the front of the crowd; the others remained clumped under the carob tree.

Another man stepped forward. Uriel stood next in line.

This farmer groveled in the dirt before the Baal. A soldier grew impatient and kicked his hip. The farmer didn't need a second urging to move on; he jumped to his feet and ran toward the open road. Uriel approached.

The prophet stepped up to the priest.

"You bow. Then go on."

Uriel's face had none of Shimon's defiance—it was radiant, his eyes distant, heedless of the priest.

The priest stepped closer to whisper in Uriel's ear, and dropped a copper to the ground.

The smile on Uriel's face stretched as he bent his head forward. My heart leapt—he was bending down to pick up the copper! But Uriel merely brought his chin to his chest and held it there.

At first, I didn't understand what my master was doing. I could barely contain the urge to scream, *"Take it! Take it!"*

Then I understood.

The prophet would neither bow nor pick up the copper. He wouldn't fight or resist. He was offering the back of his neck to the sword. Uriel would give up his life quietly, a martyr before a mass of witnesses. His death would be a symbol of the brutality of the Baal and the Queen. Just as he desired.

I squeezed my eyes shut. Why hadn't I let Shimon fight? He was already armed and surrounded by fifty men. The priest's reaction showed that the soldiers' presence was intended to evoke fear, not to kill. Would they have melted away before an organized resistance?

And Shimon may have received the Divine spirit again—then nothing could have stood before him. But now he lay dead on the side of the road, because he listened to me, while Uriel stood with his neck exposed, awaiting a similar fate.

The tattooed soldier remained by his post at the side of the road, but had still not sheathed his sword. Another group of pilgrims reached the roadblock, swelling the number of Israelites observing the scene to more than sixty men.

I reached under my tunic and gripped the handle of my father's knife. *If I fight, will I receive the same spirit Shimon had? If I'm determined to succeed, will the Holy One give me the strength to battle these foreigners?*

The tattooed soldier advanced toward Uriel. The priest stepped between them, pointing back toward the side of the road. The soldier pushed him out of the way.

I loosened my blade in its sheath, my fingers whitening on the hilt. If I was going to act, the time was now.

A surge of energy tingled through my muscles. As I drew the blade from under my tunic, Zim's voice rose in my heart. "Remember, if you believe it, it's true."

The soldier raised his sword above Uriel.

I sheathed my knife and ran forward screaming, "Grandfather, Grandfather!"

The soldier's arm stopped.

I grabbed Uriel's hand, placing myself between my master and the sword.

"He's not right in the head," I begged the soldier, loud enough for all the Israelite men to hear.

A shadow of doubt dimmed the tattooed soldier's eyes.

"He'd bow to your sandal if you wanted him to, but we'd never get him up off the ground."

"He bow." The soldier swept his arm across the waiting crowd. "They all bow."

"He's just an old man," I insisted.

Murmurs of protest rose from the waiting men. They watched Shimon die, but were now starting to rouse themselves. A tall farmer at the front of the line shoved his chest against the arm of the soldier holding him back. "Let the old man go through!"

I turned to the priest. "Could my grandfather have one of those pieces of copper? It would mean so much to him."

The priest stepped forward, pushing the tattooed soldier back. "Go," he said. "Don't bow, just go." The priest thrust a piece of copper into my hand and pushed the two of us through.

Uriel allowed me to guide him out of the shade of the carob tree, past the remaining soldiers. The radiance departed from his face. He said nothing as we fled, just walked on in silence.

As the roadblock shrank into the distance behind us, the reality of our situation settled in. My success sealed our fate: we were heading into hiding. We'd live in the darkness of the cave until redemption came.

Shimon's scarred face hung above me. He'd saved my life, stood by my father when no one else had, and followed me to his death. Had I been wrong to fight him? Or if I had given in, would Uriel and I now lie beside him?

And how many others suffered a similar fate? Tzadok was gone, Shimon was gone. The enemy had attacked the known gathering places of the prophets. Had they struck Beit El? It was one thing to kill prophets in the remote wilderness, but had they become so bold as to strike in the middle of that city? What about Yosef and Raphael? Were they even still alive?

I thought about Eliyahu—pursued more than any of us. I'd never seen drought myself, but the elders of Levonah spoke of its terrible suffering. How many dry seasons would it take for the people to stand up to the tyranny of Queen Izevel?

Then Dahlia's face rose in my mind, tight russet curls clustered around her smiling hazel eyes. Would she already be married by the time I came out of hiding, those curls forever tucked under a scarf in the way of married women?

As the sky darkened, the number of people on the road continued to thin. The nearly full moon rose above the horizon as we reached the hills ringing Shomron. Still silent, my master pointed toward a small path that turned off the road and wound through a sloping valley. We pressed on through fields and clumps of trees until the moon was directly overhead and we reached an orchard on a steeply terraced hillside. Saplings leaned at odd angles and the scent of freshly dug soil hung in the air. The hillside rose to a cliff above us.

The trail swung to the right at the base of the hill, and Uriel paused before the first terrace. I couldn't see any markings, but my master found what he was searching for. He climbed upward, feet crunching in the dried earth. We wove back and forth across the terraces, climbing steadily higher, until we reached an old olive tree, its roots wrapped around a boulder at the base of a cliff. Uriel stepped behind it, disappearing from view. I followed, slipping sideways through a crack in the cliff wall.

Darkness engulfed us. I crept forward, my fingers brushing the stone walls that squeezed steadily inward. Without warning, I stumbled, nearly falling. The echo of my footsteps reverberated in an open space.

A flame emerged in the distance. It grew from an orange glow to a yellow point, revealing itself as a lamp. A man with a short gray beard smiled when he saw Uriel and placed a finger to his lips. The lamp illuminated a three-way junction. The lamp-bearer turned to the right, and we followed.

We descended a broad passageway, the floor smooth underfoot. Every now and then I felt a draft from the side as we passed openings in the darkness. Once I heard snoring and once the sound of deep and slow chanting. I paused to listen to the complex rhythm until our guide waved me forward.

I quickly lost track of direction. I'd never been in so intricate a cave before, with so many caverns and passageways. Ovadia was fortunate to find such a place to hide the prophets. Was this another one of those caves carved out in the time of Gidon?

Our guide stepped into an empty chamber, and Uriel had to duck to avoid striking his head on the cavern roof. The lamp bearer touched the flame of his lamp to another that sat in a niche cut into the wall, igniting it. Then he bowed to Uriel and stepped back into the darkness.

I surveyed the chamber in the wavering light: my new home. The events of a week had uprooted everything I knew. There would be no sunshine in the cave, no Yonaton, no Dahlia. Yet I was still alive, which was more than could be said for Shimon or Tzadok.

Drained from the journey, I laid out my sleeping mat. Uriel knelt down in front of the lamp and contemplated the flame with unblinking eyes.

Despite my exhaustion, I dared to break the silence we'd maintained since the roadblock. "What do you see, Master?"

"All things above are reflected below. So it is with the Lamp of Darkness, reflected in the flame."

"You see darkness in the flame?"

"Look closely at the center. Darkness surrounds the wick, consuming it, emitting no light."

I moved closer to examine the flame.

"That is the shadow of the lamp of darkness. Beneath the blackness is a thin layer of sapphire, the color of the Throne of Glory,* on which the Holy One sits. The darkness appears greater than the blue, but does not dim its brilliance."

The flame filled my vision. At first, the blue jumped and faded, but as I concentrated, it grew in depth and radiance. "Master, the darkness makes the blue seem even brighter."

"Indeed. So it is with our world. No amount of darkness can destroy the light, no matter how deep the darkness grows."

Uriel sighed. "The order of the world has flipped. Once, light dwelled above and shadows filled the caves. Now darkness will reign over the land and light will retreat underground."

My master turned away from the lamp to face me and fire reflected in his bright eyes. "It appears, Lev ben Yochanan HaKohen, we have the time to begin your education after all."

Dear Reader,

As an avid reader myself, I treasure the feeling of connection with an author that I get from reading a book. But now that I'm an author, I'm struck by the one-sided nature of that relationship: all readers get a glimpse into the mind of the author, but rarely does the author hear back from the readers. With your help, I'd like to rectify this.

The subject matter of this book is a real passion of mine. In fact, it was the vision of one day being able to share this passion with readers such as yourself that drove me through the six years of writing The Lamp of Darkness.

I'd love it if you would take a moment and share a bit of yourself with me as well. I'm so curious to learn who my readers are, where they live, what they do, and what their passions are. I'm also constantly trying to improve my writing, so it would be a great help to me to know what you liked about the book and what you didn't. If you're really willing to engage, please include a picture of yourself holding the book (or your digital device loaded to the book cover). Just note, I intend to post some pictures online, so let me know if you want yours private (and nothing explicit please). My personal email is Dave@TheAgeofProphecy.com, and it's my aim to respond to all who contact me.

Personally, when curious about a new book, the first thing I do is check out reader reviews, normally on Amazon and/or Goodreads. Until recently, I almost never left reviews myself, but then I realized that the more I participate, the more I can help other readers, and the better the entire system works. Before you move on, please take a moment to leave a review online so that others can benefit from your insights as well.

It has been a privilege to share this journey with you.

Dave Mason

P.S. Those of you hungry for more will find an ever-growing library of resources at TheAgeofProphecy.com. Sign up for the newsletter to receive advance notice of new materials, specials, or the next book release. Keep reading for a preview of Book 2, The Key of Rain.

Also, connect with us at:
Facebook.com/TheAgeofProphecy

Glossary

Ahav: Also known as Ahab.

Binyamin: Also known as Benjamin.

Bnei Nevi'im: Literally the children of the prophets, figuratively their students.

Eliyahu: Also known as Elijah.

Emek HaAsefa: Literally, the valley of gathering. A fictional location.

Eved: Slave.

Halil: A straight flute.

Hevron: Also known as Hebron.

Izevel: Also known as Jezebel or Isabel.

Kohanim: Priests (plural).

Kohen: A Priest.

Kinnor: An instrument that most resembles an ancient lyre.

Labneh: A sour, spreadable cheese.

Malkosh: The late rains.

Matnat Ro'im: The shepherd's gift.

Navi: Prophet.

Navi'im: Prophets.

Navua: Prophecy.

Nevel: An instrument that most resembles an ancient harp.

Nigun: A melody, usually without words.

Niggunim: Plural of Nigun.

Shalom: Peace, also used as a greeting.

Shavuot: Also known as Pentecost or the Feast of Weeks.

Shomron: Also known as Samaria.

Sukkah: The temporary huts built during the festival of Sukkot.

Sukkot: The Festival of Booths when we build and live in temporary huts.

Tefillah: Prayer.

Tikun: Fixing.

Totafot: Also known as Tefillin or Phylacteries.

Yoreh: The early rains.

Yovel: The fiftieth year, called Jubilee year in English.

The Go Further Addition

Forward

The Age of Prophecy series is the brainchild of Dave Mason, and since an early stage I have served as its creative midwife. From the outset, our goal in writing these books has been introducing the reader to the world of the prophets, and through them to the depth of passionate and fulfilling life that we have each found in Torah. Originally the narrative was a vehicle for our favourite thoughts in Torah, and thus a complete failure. The transformation into a successful novel happened in two stages. The first came when an editor pointed out that our educational goal would never be served if we failed to write a compelling story. The Torah, which we saw as the ends, was overwhelming the narrative which we had approached only as a means. So we took it all out, stripping the book down to a fun adventure story which I doubt many people would ever have read. The second stage emerged through our creative work together. At some point of grappling with how to make the story real while also allowing to serve our educational goals we realized that when it comes to the Torah, to say that the medium is the message is a vast understatement. We are a people who is a product of the story we have been telling since long before we remember. Suddenly, the characters became our teachers as they struggled through the world which we created together.

It is with tremendous gratitude, excitement and not a little trepidation that I present you with the 'Go further' edition of the Lamp of Darkness. This edition aims to peel back the cover of our narrative and expose the topography of Torah beneath. Whether you are an educator, a student or simply a seeker of meaning it is my hope that it will help you access the depth of our work, and the Divine story which it seeks to tell. For each chapter you will find the texts that are directly referenced, as well as those which serve as the underlying conceptual framework, often quoted in their full format for ease of use. In addition, I have provided questions to deepen your personal and textual reflection.

A few thanks are in order. First to the Werthan family, for their generous support of this project. Also to Jackie Frankel Yaakov and the entire Pardes management team for their belief in and support of my work. To my wife Karen, without whose love, belief and support I would never accomplish anything. To Dave Mason, whose partnership has transformed the meaning of chavruta and taken me to places I never dreamed to go. Finally, to the Holy One who is love, support and belief itself – and much, much more.

Mike Feuer

Prologue

We state that the prologue occurs 579 years after the Exodus. We reached this conclusion from the following collection of sources. Kings I 6:1 says it was 480 years from the Exodus from Egypt until Solomon laid the foundation of the Temple, which occurred in the fourth year of his reign. Solomon ruled for forty years (ibid. 11:42), which brings us to 516 years after the Exodus. Yeravaum ruled for twenty-two years (ibid. 14:20), his son Nadav ruled for two years (ibid. 15:25). Ba'asa reigned for twenty-four years (ibid. 15:33) and his son Elah became king for two years (ibid. 16:8). Zimri ruled for seven days (ibid. 16:15) in the twenty-seventh year of King Asa of Judah. Omri then won a civil war and ruled the kingdom of Israel until his death in the thirty-eighth year of King Asa of Judah (ibid. 16:29), which means there were eleven years from the rule of Zimri to the rule of Ahav son of Omri. Thus, Ahav became King of Israel 577 years after the Exodus from Egypt, and the prologue segment occurs two years into his reign.

For a rabbinic analysis of these biblical dates, see Seder Olam Rabbah ch. 16-17. In order to really grasp the background of the book, it is worth reading the whole first Book of Kings, but the immediate foundational chapters in the Hebrew bible on which the Lamp of Darkness is based are I Kings 16 and 17.

Chapter 1 - A Shepherd's Inheritance

Questions for Learning and Reflection

Reflective

Lev lives life within a very limited horizon, longing for something larger. He watches the road to see travelers, values his friendship with Seguv even though he sees him only passing through, and lives on daydreams of what might be. Nevertheless, when Uriel offers him the opportunity to actually enter a larger world he is frightened and upset. Why? What do you dream about and what can that teach you about yourself? How would you react if life actually offered you your dreams?

Textual

What can the various names of the prophets teach us about the role which they played in their society?

The Torah conceives of three primary vessels for the relationship between God and Israel – the commandments, the land and the historical experience of the people. Looking at the sources offered from this chapter on the rains and inheritance, what is the nature of the relationship which each offers? What other sources and types of relationship can you think of?

Sources

This is the first batch of afarsimon oil ever produced in the kingdom

Anointing with oil has both a legal function and powerful symbolism in Jewish tradition. Moshe was commanded to create the original anointing oil in the wilderness (see Exodus 30:22-33) and once the children of Israel entered the land only the High Priest and the King were anointed. The very word messiah derives from the Hebrew moshiach (משיח) which means anointed. Once the unified kingdom split, the Kings of Israel were anointed with afarsimon oil, while kings of the House of David who ruled over Judah were anointed with the special anointing oil.

Babylonian Talmud Horayot 11b Kings of the house of David are anointed; kings of Israel are not anointed. From where do we derive this? Rava said that the verse states: "Arise, anoint him, for this is he" (I Samuel 16:12): This king, David, requires anointing, but another king does not require anointing. The Master said: Even Jehu, son of Nimshi, king of Israel, was anointed only due to the challenge of Joram. And due to the challenge of Joram, son of Ahav, shall we misuse consecrated anointing oil and anoint a king of Israel, who does not require anointing? It is like that which Rav Pappa said: They anointed him with pure balsam oil, not with anointing oil. So too, with regard to Jehu, they anointed him with pure afarsimon oil, not with anointing oil.

Rambam Mishne Torah Kings and Wars 1:10 The kings of Israel are not anointed with the (special) Anointing Oil, but with afarsimon oil only. They may never be appointed in Jerusalem – only may the descendants of David. Only descendants of David are anointed (with the special Anointing Oil).

It's the waters in Yericho

On the deadly waters of Yericho see II Kings 2:19-22

> The men of the town said to Elisha, "Look, the town is a pleasant place to live in, as my lord can see; but the water is bad and the land causes bereavement." He responded, "Bring me a new dish and put salt in it." They brought it to him; he went to the spring and threw salt into it. And he said, "Thus said the LORD: I heal this water; no longer shall death and bereavement come from it!" The water has remained wholesome to this day, in accordance with the word spoken by Elisha.
>
> The Radak on this verse offers an explanation of the evil of the waters which is reflective of the sins of the people as the actual cause of their deaths.
>
> > "Look, the town is a pleasant place to live..." Up to this point we have no indication that the waters of Jericho were bad, or that they caused bereavement. If it had been so, the people would not have loved it nor would they have transgressed the ban against rebuilding it. Furthermore, if the waters had been bad all along how is it that

> Eliyahu did not heal them? Finally, if they had caused bereavement for the many years they had been settled there the people would have given up and left. Therefore it appears that the evil had come to the waters recently due to the wickedness of the city's residents, and it was the bad waters which caused the ground to be a source of bereavement - killing many who drank from them. From an interpretive perspective, the verse is saying that Jericho was cursed and a source of bereavement because Joshua had cursed it. Then Eliyahu added his own curse in the when Hiel's two sons died and Eliyahu and King Ahav came to comfort him, as described above in I Kings 16:34 and the midrash. The Sages taught "Look, the town is a pleasant place to live in...but the water is bad and the land causes bereavement." What could be good about it?! R' Yochanan said: the inhabitants always see the grace of a place. (Sotah 47a)

As the story progress it will become clear that the rebuilding of Yericho by Hiel, the death of his sons and the interplay between curses and sin serves as a frame for the entire narrative. For more of the background of Hiel's story see the following sources.

> I Kings 16:34 During his reign, Hiel the Bethelite fortified Yericho. He laid its foundations at the cost of Aviram his first-born, and set its gates in place at the cost of Seguv his youngest, in accordance with the words that the LORD had spoken through Joshua son of Nun.

> Babylonian Talmud Sanhedrin 113a "Hiel the Bethelite built Jericho; with Aviram, his firstborn, he laid its foundation, and with his young son Seguv set up its gates" (I Kings 16:34). It is taught in a baraita: From the death of Aviram, his firstborn, the wicked, it was not incumbent upon him to learn not to build Jericho, as Aviram's death could be attributed to chance. But with the death of Seguv his young son, it was incumbent upon him to learn that it was due to Joshua's curse that they died. What did Aviram and Seguv do that they are characterized as wicked, and what is the baraita saying? This is what the baraita is saying: From the death of Aviram, his firstborn, that wicked man Hiel should have learned about the cause of the death of Seguv his young son. By inference from that which is stated: "With Aviram, his firstborn," do I not know that Seguv was his young son? Rather, what is the meaning when the verse states: "His young son Seguv"? It teaches that he

gradually buried all his sons from Aviram through Seguv, and he should have suspected that Joshua's curse caused the deaths.

may the Holy One protect you

There are many names of God used in the Hebrew bible, and a vast traditional and critical literature which attempts to explain why and what these names mean. We choose to use only the term 'Holy One' in the book for a few reasons. One was simply to avoid confusion through any attempt to add another layer of meaning to the dialogue of the prophets. Another was as part of a larger effort to avoid gendered language in reference to God, which though consonant with Israelite culture, can lead to many misunderstandings within our own. Finally, we operate on the belief that the various names of God express different aspects of the relationship between Creator and creation. The Holy One communicates both the sacred and the unified which we felt were critical elements that must be present in our story.

His head sank between his bent knees

The source for the prophetic position of sitting on the ground with the head between the knees is I Kings 18:42 "Elijah meanwhile climbed to the top of Mount Carmel, crouched on the ground, and put his face between his knees."

For a connection between prayer and prophecy via this position see gemara Berachot 34b.

> Rabbi Ḥanina ben Dosa, who went to study Torah before Rabbi Yoḥanan ben Zakkai, and Rabbi Yoḥanan's son fell ill. He said to him: Ḥanina, my son, pray for mercy on behalf of my son so that he will live. Rabbi Ḥanina ben Dosa placed his head between his knees and prayed for mercy upon his behalf, and Rabbi Yoḥanan ben Zakkai's son lived.

For an interesting explanation of why having the head between the knees is significant see Vayikra Rabbah 31:4

> Another interpretation of "Command the Children of Israel" (Leviticus 24:2): Bar Kapparah opened [his discourse]: "It is You who light my

> lamp" (Psalms 18:29) - the Holy One, blessed be He, said to Adam, "Your light is in My hands and My light is in your hands." Your light is in My hands, as it is stated (Proverbs 20:27), "The lamp of the Lord is the soul of man"; and My light is in your hands, as it is stated (Leviticus 24:2), "to light a continual lamp." Rather, the Holy One, blessed be He, said, "If you light My lamp, I will certainly light your lamp." This is [the understanding of] "Command the Children of Israel" (Leviticus 24:2). This is [the understanding of] that which is written (Song of Songs 7:6), "Your head (*roshekha*) upon you is like crimson wool (*karmel*), the locks of your head are like purple" - the Holy One, blessed be He, said to Israel, "The poor (*rashim*) among you are as beloved to Me as Eliyahu, when he went up to [Mount] Carmel." This is [the understanding of] "and Elijah climbed to the top of Mount Carmel, crouched on the ground, and put his face between his knees." And why did he put his face between his knees? He said, "Master of the world, if we do not have any merit, look to the covenant of circumcision."

It rolled behind the wine barrel

We typically think of prophets through the lens of the works of the later prophets like Isaiah and Jeremiah, looking at them as an institute on par with the kingship. The source which shows that the prophets also served the common need as finders of lost objects is I Samuel 9:5-9

> When they reached the district of Zuph, Saul said to the servant who was with him, "Let us turn back, or my father will stop worrying about the asses and begin to worry about us." But he replied, "There is a man of God in that town, and the man is highly esteemed; everything that he says comes true. Let us go there; perhaps he will tell us about the errand on which we set out." "But if we go," Saul said to his servant, "what can we bring the man? For the food in our bags is all gone, and there is nothing we can bring to the man of God as a present. What have we got?" The servant answered Saul again, "I happen to have a quarter-shekel of silver. I can give that to the man of God and he will tell us about our errand."— Formerly in Israel, when a man went to inquire of God, he would say, "Come, let us go to the seer," for the prophet of today was formerly called a seer.—

Now I know you are truly a Seer

Seer is one of the many names by which the prophets are known.

> Avot d'Rabbi Natan 34:8 The prophet is called by ten names. An envoy, as it says "I have received tidings from the LORD, And an envoy is sent out among the nations..." (Jer. 49:14) Trusted, as it says "...he is trusted throughout My household." (Bamidbar 12:7) Servant, as it says "Not so with My servant Moses..." (ibid.) Representative, as it says 'And an envoy is sent out among the nations (?)' (see Jer. 49:14 and Shemot 4:13) Seer, as it says "...the word of the LORD had come to the prophet Gad, David's seer." (Shmuel II 24:11) Watchman, as it says "O mortal, I appoint you watchman for the House of Israel..." (Ezk. 3:17) Seer, as it says "...for the prophet of today was formerly called a seer." (Shmuel I 9:9) Dreamer, as it says "...do not heed the words of that prophet or that dream-diviner." (Dev. 13:4) Prophet, as it says "...since he is a prophet..." (Bereshit 20:7) Man of God, as it says "There is a man of God in that town..." (Shmuel I 9:6)

Farmers had cursed the late malkosh rains that soaked the barley crop

The relationship between the barley harvest and the wheat harvest are embodied in the Torah and rabbinic literature through the relationship between the *Omer* barley offering which marked the beginning of the harvest immediately following Passover and the two loaves of wheat bread offered on the Shavuot festival seven weeks later. See for example Leviticus 23:10-17

> Say to the children of Israel, When you have come to the land which I will give you, and have harvested the grain from its fields, take some of the first-fruits of the grain to the priest; And let the grain be waved before the Lord, so that you may be pleasing to him; on the day after the Sabbath let it be waved by the priest. And on the day of the waving of the grain, you are to give a male lamb of the first year, without any mark, for a burned offering to the Lord. And let the meal offering with it be two tenth parts of an ephah of the best meal mixed with oil, an offering made by fire to the Lord for a sweet smell; and the drink offering with it is to be of wine, the fourth part of a hin. And you may take no bread or dry grain or new grain for food till the very day on which you have given the offering for your God: this is a rule for ever through all your generations wherever

> you are living. And you shall count seven full weeks from the day after the Sabbath, the day when you give the grain for the wave offering; Let fifty days be numbered, to the day after the seventh Sabbath; then you are to give a new meal offering to the Lord. Take from your houses two cakes of bread, made of a fifth part of an ephah of the best meal, cooked with leaven, to be waved for first-fruits to the Lord.

Together they represent an evolution from the animal to the human, as in this comment from R' A.Y. Hakohen Kook Orot, Orot Yisrael 8:1

> Therefore, Pesach is linked to Shavuot through the counting of the Omer in the Temple, that links together the barley sacrifice, animal feed, the instinct, to the wheat offering, human food, the spiritual intellect, "the tree of knowledge was wheat". (Berachot 40a) These two basic forces reveal their full strength and action, in the depths of the soul and in the breadth of life, when each is expressed in its own full and independent way, with no restrictions, and when they fuse together to a higher unified system.

The first rains (*yoreh*) and the last rains (*malkosh*) are essential aspects of the agricultural cycle in the land of Israel. The bible sees their regular function as a sign of God's covenant with Israel, as in Deuteronomy 11:13-17

> If, then, you obey the commandments that I enjoin upon you this day, loving the LORD your God and serving Him with all your heart and soul, I will grant the rain for your land in season, the early rain (*yoreh*) and the late (*malkosh*). You shall gather in your new grain and wine and oil— I will also provide grass in the fields for your cattle—and thus you shall eat your fill. Take care not to be lured away to serve other gods and bow to them. For the LORD's anger will flare up against you, and He will shut up the skies so that there will be no rain and the ground will not yield its produce; and you will soon perish from the good land that the LORD is assigning to you.
>
> For a rabbinic exploration of the terms which combines meaning and meteorology, see Babylonian Talmud Ta'anit 6a
>
> > The Sages taught in a baraita: The first rain [yoreh] is called by this name due to the fact that it instructs [moreh] people to plaster their roofs and to bring in their produce from the fields and to attend to all their needs. Alternatively, that it moistens [marve] the earth and

waters it to the depths, as it is stated: "Watering [ravvei] its ridges abundantly, settling down its furrows, You make it soft with showers, You bless its growth"(Psalms 65:11). Alternatively, yoreh means that it falls gently and it does not fall vehemently. Or perhaps that is not the case; rather, yoreh means that the rain causes the fruit to drop from the trees, washes the seeds away, and washes the trees away in a destructive manner. Therefore the verse states: "Last rain [malkosh]" (Deuteronomy 11:14); just as malkosh refers specifically to rains that are for a blessing, so too, yoreh is for a blessing. Or perhaps that is not the case; rather, malkosh means that the rain falls so hard [kashe] that it knocks down the houses, shatters the trees and brings up the locusts? Therefore, the verse states: "Yoreh," just as yoreh is for a blessing, so too,malkosh is for a blessing. And with regard to yoreh itself, from where do we derive that it is referring to rain that falls for a blessing? As it is written: "You children of Zion, be glad and rejoice in the Lord your God, for He has given you the first rain [moreh] in His kindness, and He caused to come down for you the rain, the first rain [moreh] and the last rain [malkosh], in the first month" (Joel 2:23). The Sages taught: The first rain falls in Marḥeshvan and the last rain in Nisan. Do you say that the first rain is in Marḥeshvan and the last rain in Nisan, or perhaps it is only that the first rain falls in Tishrei and the last rain in Iyyar? Therefore, the verse states: "I shall give the rain of your land in its due time" (Deuteronomy 11:14). The last rain [malkosh]. Rav Nehilai bar Idi said that Shmuel said: It is a matter that circumcises [mal] the stubbornness [kashyuteihen] of the Jewish people, i.e., it penetrates to the hearts of the Jewish people, as when rain does not fall in its time, they turn to God in repentance. The school of Rabbi Yishmael taught: it is a matter that fills out [memalle] produce in its stalks [bekasheha]. It was taught in a baraita: Malkosh is a matter that comes down on the ears [melilot] and on the stalks [kashin].

And you shall sanctify the fiftieth year

The verse they are reciting is Leviticus 25:10. The question of whether Israel successfully kept the *shemitta/yovel* (sabbatical/Jubilee) cycle during the 1st Temple period is not a simple one, and the connection which it draws between moral rectitude, financial security and national safety is a theme which will unfold through the series. The following sources seem to make it clear that the cycle broke down:

> Jeremiah 34:13–17 Thus said the LORD, the God of Israel: I made a covenant with your fathers when I brought them out of the land of Egypt, the house of bondage, saying: "In the seventh year each of you must let go any fellow Hebrew who may be sold to you; when he has served you six years, you must set him free." But your fathers would not obey Me or give ear. Lately you turned about and did what is proper in My sight, and each of you proclaimed a release to his countrymen; and you made a covenant accordingly before Me in the House which bears My name. But now you have turned back and have profaned My name; each of you has brought back the men and women whom you had given their freedom, and forced them to be your slaves again. Assuredly, thus said the LORD: You would not obey Me and proclaim a release, each to his kinsman and countryman. Lo! I proclaim your release—declares the LORD—to the sword, to pestilence, and to famine; and I will make you a horror to all the kingdoms of the earth.
>
> 2 Chronicles 36:19–21 They burned the House of God and tore down the wall of Jerusalem, burned down all its mansions, and consigned all its precious objects to destruction. Those who survived the sword he exiled to Babylon, and they became his and his sons' servants till the rise of the Persian kingdom, in fulfillment of the word of the LORD spoken by Jeremiah, until the land paid back its sabbaths; as long as it lay desolate it kept sabbath, till seventy years were completed.
>
> For the connection between how a failure to keep the sabbatical year was connected to exile already in the Torah (before the people entered the land), see Babylonian Talmud Shabbat 33a
>
>> Due to the sin of prohibited sexual relations, and idol worship, and failure to let the land lie fallow during the Sabbatical and Jubilee Years, exile comes to the world and they exile the Jewish people from their land, and others come and settle in their place.

Silence is a fence for wisdom: Pirkei Avot 3:17

It's a shepherd's inheritance

The concept of inheritance is essential to the way in which the Torah articulates the relationship between the people of Israel and the land of Israel. It appears in countless places, perhaps the most fundamental is found in Numbers 26:52-56

> The LORD spoke to Moses, saying, "Among these shall the land be apportioned as shares, according to the listed names: with larger groups increase the share, with smaller groups reduce the share. Each is to be assigned its share according to its enrollment. The land, moreover, is to be apportioned by lot; and the allotment shall be made according to the listings of their ancestral tribes. Each portion shall be assigned by lot, whether for larger or smaller groups."

The source for the tribal inheritance which has been alienated from its original owner through sale returning in the Jubilee year is Leviticus 25:10 (quoted on page 8)

> "and you shall hallow the fiftieth year. You shall proclaim release throughout the land for all its inhabitants. It shall be a jubilee for you: each of you shall return to his holding and each of you shall return to his family."

The link between the Sabbatical and Jubilee cycles and all of the tribes of Israel being settled on their inheritance, with messianic implications, is made explicit by the Babylonian Talmud Arakhin 32b

> From the time that the tribe of Reuben and the tribe of Gad and half the tribe of Manasseh were exiled, the counting of Jubilee Years was nullified, as it is stated: "And you shall proclaim liberty throughout the land to all its inhabitants; it shall be a Jubilee for you" (Leviticus 25:10), indicating that the laws of the Jubilee Year apply only when all its inhabitants are in the land of Israel, and not when some of them have been exiled. The baraita continues: One might have thought that if all the Jews were living in the land of Israel, but they are intermingled, e.g., the tribe of Benjamin is living in the portion of the tribe of Judah, and the tribe of Judah in the portion of the tribe of Benjamin, that the Jubilee Year should be in effect. Therefore, the verse states: "To all

its inhabitants," which teaches that the Jubilee Year applies only when its inhabitants are living according to their proper arrangement, and not when they are intermingled.

More than the lamb wants to suck, the ewe wants to give milk

The source for this is in Babylonian Talmud Pesachim 112a. There it refers to a teacher's desire to teach being even greater than a student's desire to learn

Chapter 2 - The Three Keys

Questions for Learning and Reflection

Reflective

Uriel says that the prophets inhabit a world of devotion (*avodah*, עבודה) which is defined by the ability to make our own choices. What is the difference between a life of choice and one of obedience? How can Uriel say this if the Torah is filled with commandments? What significant choices have you made and how did they shape your life? What role has obedience played in your choices?

Have you ever been in an emotional state that left you unable to achieve what you wanted? Perhaps because you were too angry to engage or too depressed to motivate yourself? The prophets often used music to change their states. What tools do you use to change yours?

Textual

Why would joy be a necessary precondition for prophecy? How do you define joy?

Despite the fact that fertility plays a central role in the biblical blessings, Sarah (Genesis 16:1), Rivkah (Genesis 25:21), Rachel (Genesis 29:31) and Hannah (I Samuel 1:5) were all barren. Why do you think this might have been? Note the role that prayer and Divine relationship play in these four stories – what is the connection? In this light, how do you understand the words of the Babylonian Talmud Chullin 60b "the Holy One, Blessed be He, desires the prayers of the righteous"?

Sources

Our Way is a path of choice

Most of our actions in life are constrained by necessity - be it situational, societal, biological or otherwise. Many people see the Torah, with its emphasis on commandment, as a further constrain on their freedom. Nevertheless, there is a rich literature on the critical role which choice plays in cultivating the Divine relationship. The Rambam discusses the link between choice and devotion in Mishneh Torah Laws of Repentance 5:1 - 5:4

5:1 Every man was endowed with a free will; if he desires to bend himself toward the good path and to be just it is within the power of his hand to reach out for it, and if he desires to bend himself to a bad path and to be wicked it is within the power of his hand to reach out for it. This is known from what it is written in the Torah, saying: "Behold, the man is become as one of us, to know good and evil" (Gen. 3.22), that is as if saying: "Behold, this species, man, stands alone in the world, and there is no other kind like him, as regards this subject of being able of his own accord, by his reason and thought, to know the good and the evil, and to do whatever his inclination dictates him with none to stay his hand from either doing good or evil; and, being that he is so, 'Lest he put forth his hand, and take also from the tree of life, and eat, and live forever'" (Ibid.)

5:2 Permit not your thought to dwell upon that which ridiculous fools of other peoples and a majority of asinine individuals among the children of Israel say, that the Holy One, blessed is He! decrees at the very embryonic state of every man whether he should be just or wicked. The matter is not so. Every man is capable of being as just as Moses our Master or as wicked as Yeravaum, wise or incony, merciful or human, miser or philanthropist, and so in all other tendencies. There is none to either force things upon him or to decree things against him; either to pull him one way or draw him another way, but he alone, of his own free will, with the consent of his mind, bends to any path he may desire to follow. It is concerning this that Jeremiah said: "Out of the mouth of the Most High proceedeth not the evil and the good" (Lam. 3. 38), which is as if saying, the Creator decrees not that man should be either good or bad. Now, this being so, the consequence hereof is that the sinner alone brought harm upon himself. It is, therefore, meet that he should lament and shed tears because he sinned, and because of what he did to his soul and rewarded it with evil. Even this is the meaning of the succeeding Verse: "Wherefore doth a living man complain, or a strong man? Because of his sins" (Ibid.) Again, he continues, in the succeeding Verse seeing that it all is in our power, and we did all the evil of our own free will and accord, it is, indeed meet for us to turn in repentance and abandon our wickedness, for our free will is in our hands now as well as at the time we committed the sins saying: "Let us search and try our ways, and return to the Lord" (Ibid.–40).

5:3 And, this matter is a great and component part, the very pillar of the Torah and its precepts, even as it is said: "See, I have set before thee this day life and good, and death and evil" (Deut. 30.15), and it is, moreover, written: "Behold, I set before you this day a blessing and curse" (Ibid. 11.26). This is as if saying, the power is in your hand, and whatever human activity man may be inclined to carry on he has a free will to elect either good or evil. And, because of this very subject it is said: "Oh, who would grant that they had such a heart as this, to fear Me, and to keep all my commandments at all times" (Ibid. 5.26). This is as if saying, that the Creator forces not the sons of man, and makes no decrees against them that they should do good or evil, but that it all is in their own keeping.

5:4 Had the decree of God prompted man to be either just or wicked, or had there been a fundamentally inborn something to draw man to either of the paths, or to any one branch of knowledge, or to a given tendency of the tendencies, or to particular act of all actions as the astrologists maintain by their foolish inventions, how did He charge us by the prophets, to do thus and not to do such, improve your ways, and do not follow your wickedness, whereas man from his embryonic state already had a decree of his conduct issued, or his inborn nature draws him toward a given path of conduct from which he can not deviate? Moreover, what need would there be, under such circumstances, for the Torah altogether? And by what law, and under what system of justice could the wicked be punished, or the just rewarded? Shall the judge of the whole earth not exercise justice? Now, do not wonder and ask: "How is it possible for man to do what his heart desires, and have his entire course of action lodged within himself seeing that he can not do aught in the world without the permission of his Master and without His Will, even as the Verse says: "Whatsoever the Lord pleased, that hath He done, in heaven and in earth, in the seas and in all deeps" (Ps. 135.6)? Know all that man does is in accordance with His Will, although our actions are really in our own keeping. For example? Even as it is the Creator's Will that fire and air shall ascend upward, and that water and earth shall descend downward, or that the sphere shall revolve in a circle, and that other creatures of the universe should likewise follow their respective natural laws, as it was His Will for them to be, so was it His Will that man shall have the free choice of conduct in his own hand, and that all his actions should be lodged within him, and that

> he should be neither forced or drawn, but he, of his own free will accord, as God endowed him with, he exercises in all that is poss for man to do. He is, therefore, judged according to actions; if he good, his is rewarded with good; and if he did wrong, he is punisl This is in harmony with what the prophet said: "This hath bee your own doing" (Mal. 1.9); and: "According as they have chosen t own ways" (Is. 66.3); and of this very subject Solomon said: "Rej O young man, in thy youth, and let thy heart cheer thee in the d of thy youth, and walk in the ways of thy heart, and in the sigh thine eyes; but know thou, that for all these things God will br thee into judgment" (Ecc. 11. 9); as if saying: "True, it is within power of thine hand to do so, but thou art to render an account on the day of judgment".

hadn't my uncle always said the bashful never learn

This is a paraphrase of a section from the Mishnah in Pirkei Avot 2:5

> He used to say: A brute is not sin-fearing, nor is an ignorant pers pious; nor can a timid person learn, nor can an impatient person tea nor will someone who engages too much in business become wise. a place where there are no men, strive to be a man.

prophecy is not at my command

The idea that prophecy is not an ability which the prophet can exerci anytime they desire has many implications for the Divine relationship. S Rambam Mishneh Torah Foundations of the Torah 7:4

> All the prophets do not prophesy every time they may desire, but they mu prepare their minds, rest in a state of exultation and hearty contentmer and in undisturbed solitude; for, prophecy does not rest upon any proph either when he is in a state of melancholy or in a state of indolence, but whe he is in a state of delightfulness. Therefore, the disciples of the prophe had before them the harp, the timbrel, the flute and the violin when the were seeking the spirit of prophecy, whereof it is said: "And they strove t prophecy" (I Sam. 10.5), meaning, they followed the path of prophecy unt they did prophesy, as one says: "Yonder is one aspiring to become great.

Your music is pure and beautiful

For more on the idea that the Divine Presence only comes to rest on one who is in a state of joy, particularly that induced by music, see the Rambam cited in the comment on page 21 and Babylonian Talmud Shabbat 30b

> The praise of joy mentioned here is to teach you that the Divine Presence rests upon an individual neither from an atmosphere of sadness, nor from an atmosphere of laziness, nor from an atmosphere of laughter, nor from an atmosphere of frivolity, nor from an atmosphere of idle conversation, nor from an atmosphere of idle chatter, but rather from an atmosphere imbued with the joy of a mitzva. As it was stated with regard to Elisha that after he became angry at the king of Israel, his prophetic spirit left him until he requested: "But now bring me a minstrel; and it came to pass, when the minstrel played, that the hand of the Lord came upon him" (II Kings 3:15).

The story of Yosef's sale into slavery is found in Genesis chapters 37-46

Here she is with her belly between her teeth.

This phrase comes directly from the Mishnah Rosh Hashanah 2:8.

There are three keys that the Holy One does not surrender to any servant

The idea of three keys which are never given into the hand of man comes from the Babylonian Talmud Taanit 2a-b

> Rabbi Yoḥanan said: There are three keys in the hand of the Holy One, Blessed be He, which were not transmitted to an intermediary. And they are: The key of rain, the key of birthing, and the key of the resurrection of the dead. The key of rain, as it is stated: "The Lord will open for you His good treasure, the heavens, to give the rain of your land in its due time"(Deuteronomy 28:12).From where is it derived that the key of birthing is maintained by God? As it is written: "And God remembered Rachel and listened to her, and He opened her womb" (Genesis 30:22). From where is it derived that the key of the resurrection of the dead is maintained by God?As it is written: "And you shall know that I am the Lord when I

have opened your graves" (Ezekiel 37:13). In the West, they say: The key of livelihood is also in God's hand, as it is written: "You open Your hand and satisfy every living thing with favor" (Psalms 145:16). And what is the reason that Rabbi Yoḥanan did not consider this in his list? Rabbi Yoḥanan would have said to you: Rain is the same as livelihood in this regard...

Am I in the place of the Holy One who has withheld the fruit of your womb?

This is a quote from Genesis 30:2. Look at chapter 30 there for the larger story of Rachel's struggle to give birth.

for growth in this world

The intent of the word growth here parallels the Hebrew word *tikkun* (תיקון). Its biblical meaning is to straighten something which has become bent, as in Ecclesiastes 1:15

> "A twisted thing that cannot be made straight, A lack that cannot be made good."

It can also mean to establish something on right foundations and in its intended place, as in this usage from Midrash Genesis Rabbahh 4:6

> "And God made the firmament" (Genesis 1:7) ...Why doesn't it say "it was good" on the second day of creation? R' Yochanan taught in the name of R' Yosi bar Chalafta, because gehennom was created on the second day, as it says "The topheth has been ready for him since yesterday..." (Isaiah 30:33), a day that has a yesterday but not two days ago. Another reason that it does not say "it was good" on the second day, R' Chanina says it is because division was created on the second day, as it says: "and it (the heavens) should separate between the two bodies of water" (Genesis 1:7). R' Tavyomi said: if division whose purpose is to fix and settle the world (לתקונו של עולם ולישובו) does not merit 'it was good,' all the more so division whose purpose is to mix up the world.

The Sages of the Mishnah saw *tikkun olam* (fixing the world) as the responsibility to manage the legal system in order to prevent legal but non-desirable outcomes, as in Mishna Gittin 4:6

> If a man sells his slave to a Gentile or [to someone living] outside the land [of Israel] the slave goes free. Captives should not be redeemed for more than their value, because of tikkun olam. Captives should not be helped to escape, because of tikkun olam. Rabbahn Shimon ben Gamaliel says [that the reason is] to prevent the ill-treatment of fellow captives. Torah scrolls of the law, tefillin and mezuzoth are not bought from Gentiles at more than their value, because of tikkun olam.

In the hands of the early modern kabbalists, particularly the Arizal of Tzefat, the idea of tikkun took on a much more expansive meaning. In their cosmogony the world in which we live is made up of the shattered remnants of the original world which God intended to create. Mixed in with these shards are sparks of the original light of creation and the purpose of human existence is to find and set free these sparks. This is done through acts of tikkun. Every religious act requires contemplative concentration on the various dimensions of divinity and the various combinations of the divine name in order to "raise up the fallen sparks." Once all the sparks are lifted up and the vessels are prepared, the world undergoes a renewal known as tikkun olam – the restoration/repair of the world.

1st Prophecy Conversation

The stars are a bridge between this world and the one beyond

R' Moshe Chaim Luzatto (the Ramchal) says in his work Derech Hashem II ch. 7 sec. 1-2 that the stars are the bridge between the spiritual world of the Divine will and the physical world of manifestation.

> 1. Behold, I have already explained in section one that all physical items have their root in transcendent powers. In truth all these items are rooted there in every necessary fashion, and only afterwards are drawn down and translated into physicality in the manner required of them. The heavenly spheres with all their stars were prepared for this purpose. Through their rotation all that is rooted and prepared above in the spiritual world is drawn down and translated into our physical world here below, set in its proper place. The number of the stars, their various levels and divisions, are set according to the highest wisdom

> in order to achieve this translation. The power of existence flows from the stars to every physical item below, they are the means to transform everything from its transcendent form above to its manifest form below.
>
> 2. There is another matter which the Holy One engraved into the stars. All the events of the physical world are prepared above and only then drawn down by the stars in they way in which they are meant to occur. For example - matters of life, wealth, wisdom, children and the like are all prepared above in the roots and made manifest below through the stars in their proper manner. Each of these happen though well-known divisions, particular groupings and known orbits assigned to them. Among all these are divided everything which occurs in the physical world. All physical matters are under their control, functioning according to the influences of their orders and connections to each and every individual.

The idea that the star gazers see some but not all of the Divine intention is rooted in the Sage's understanding of Isaiah 47:13 as expressed in Bereshit Rabbahh 85:2

> You are helpless, despite all your art. Let them stand up and help you now, The scanners of heaven, the star-gazers, Who announce, month by month, Whatever will come upon you.
>
> What is written above the matter? "And the Midianites sold him to Egypt" [and then it interrupts with the story of Yehuda and Tamar:] "And it was at that time." And the reading (narrative) only required it to [immediately] say "And Yosef was taken down to Egypt" (Genesis 39:1) And because of what was this section made proximate to that? Rabbi Elazar and Rabbi Yochanan [answered this]: Rabbi Elazar said, "In order to make one descent proximate to the other descent." Rabbi Yochanan said, "In order to make [one use of the word,] "recognize," proximate to [another use of the word,] "recognize." Rabbi Shmuel bar Nachman said, "In order to make the story of Tamar proximate to the story of Pothiphar's wife; [to tell you that] just as that one (the incident of Tamar) was for the sake of Heaven, so too this one (the incident of Potiphar's wife) was meant for the sake of Heaven." As Rabbi Yehoshua ben Levi said, "She saw through her astrology that she was destined to raise a child from him (Yosef), but she did not know if [it would be]

from her or from her daughter." This is [the meaning of] what is written (Isaiah 47:13), "let the diviners of months inform you from that which will come to you" - Rabbi Eibo said, "'From that' and not 'all that.'"

See also Rambam Mishneh Torah Foundations of the Torah 10:3

Are not the necromancers and astrologists foretelling what is to come to pass, what, then, is the difference between a prophet and such as they? Forsooth, necromancers, astrologists and their like, some of their words are established and some of their words are not established, as the subject is spoken of: "Let now the astrologers, the stargazers, the monthly prognosticators, stand up, and save thee from some of the things that shall come upon thee" (Is. 47.13); —of some of the things are spoken, but not of all of the things, because they are not capable to foretell all of the things…

But the Holy One raised Avraham above the stars

The story of Avraham being lifted up 'above the stars' is rooted in Genesis 15:5

"He took him outside and said, "Look toward heaven and count the stars, if you are able to count them." And He added, "So shall your offspring be.""

Rashi on this verse quotes the midrash from Bereshit Rabbahh 44:12 saying 'He took him out of the terrestrial sphere and lifted him above the stars.'

But when we choose a higher path

The idea that Israel is not subject to the influence of the stars (אין מזל לישראל) is the subject of argument among the Sages. Here is the simple disagreement, for the extended discussion see Babylonian Talmud Shabbat 156a

It was stated that Rabbi Ḥanina says: A constellation makes one wise and a constellation makes one wealthy, and there is a constellation for the Jewish people that influences them. Rabbi Yoḥanan said: There is no constellation for the Jewish people that influences them.

Chapter 3 Honoring the Calf

Questions for Learning and Reflection

Reflective

When Lev has an unexpected moment of freedom he decides to do an act of devotion. What does this teach you about his character?

What does it take for something to be an act of devotion? Think of something which you have done which you would characterize as an act of devotion. How did it come about?

Textual

The Golden Calf seems to be gone as a source of idolatry after its original appearance at the foot of Mount Sinai, but it reappears hundreds of years later in the hands of the Kings of Israel. What can this "come back" add to our understanding of the assertion in the midrash that Israel carried the idolatry of the calf with them out of Egypt? (see the sources for pages 39-40.)

Sources

It is not good for a man to be alone

This is a paraphrase of Genesis 2:18

on the ninth day of the fifth month

The ninth day of the fifth month is the 9th of Av in the current Hebrew calendar, the day on which both Temples were destroyed and which is marked by many other tragedies throughout Jewish history. There is no known date for the wedding, so we chose this day for its power in communicating the scale of tragedy which occurred when the King of Israel entered into a marriage with the Queen of an idolatrous people.

No, I'm still counted among the b'nei nevi'im

There are sources for groups of prophets from elsewhere in the Tanach, but the sources for the students of the prophets being known as the children of the prophets (bnei nevi'im) center on the personalities of Elisha and Eliyahu - see II Kings 2:3, II Kings 4:1 and 38, II Kings 6:1

The Rambam makes clear that the bnei nevi'im are those who are seeking prophecy in Mishneh Torah Foundations of the Torah 7:5

> They that seek the spirit of prophecy are called disciples of the prophets, and, although they train their minds well, it is uncertain whether the Shekinah will rest upon them or whether it will not.

Uncle Menachem told the story of one of the seven shepherds of Israel

The origin of the idea of the seven shepherds is Micha 5:4

> And that shall afford safety. Should Assyria invade our land And tread upon our fortresses, We will set up over it seven shepherds, Eight princes of men,

The Babylonian Talmud in Sukkah 52b says

> "Who are these seven shepherds? David is in the middle; Adam, Seth, and Methuselah are to his right; Abraham, Jacob, and Moses are to his left."

The Zohar Emor 103b-104a identifies 7 guests (*ushpizin*) who visit the Sukkah, one on each night of the festival – Avraham, Yitzchak, Yaakov, Moshe, Aaron, Yosef and David. Later kabbalistic and Chassidic sources associate these guests with the Seven Shepherds, and this is how they are known today.

built an altar a thousand years before

The connection between Yaakov and Bet El centers on his famous dream vision of a ladder connecting heaven and earth in Genesis 28:11-19

> He came upon a certain place and stopped there for the night, for the sun had set. Taking one of the stones of that place, he put it under his head and lay down in that place. He had a dream; a stairway was set on the ground and its top reached to the sky, and angels of God were going up and down on it. And the LORD was standing beside him and He said, "I am the LORD, the God of your father Abraham and the God of Isaac: the ground on which you are lying I will assign to you and to your offspring. Your descendants shall be as the dust of the earth; you shall spread out to the west and to the east, to the north and to the south. All the families of the earth shall bless themselves by you and your descendants. Remember, I am with you: I will protect you wherever you go and will bring you back to this land. I will not leave you until I have done what I have promised you." Jacob awoke from his sleep and said, "Surely the LORD is present in this place, and I did not know it!" Shaken, he said, "How awesome is this place! This is none other than the abode of God, and that is the gateway to heaven." Early in the morning, Jacob took the stone that he had put under his head and set it up as a pillar and poured oil on the top of it. He named that site Bethel; but previously the name of the city had been Luz.

The royal ox of the House of King Omri

The text of the Hebrew bible gives no indication of Omri's tribal affiliation. The academic and traditional literature also come to diverse conclusions. Our decision to make him part of the House of Menashe is largely based on Omri's decision to move his capital to the new city of Shomron, in the heart of Menashe's tribal lands. We assumed that after years of civil war, the king would choose to place his new capital in the most secure area, where he had the strongest tribal support.

Revealing a crack in the stone hidden beneath

The story of the crack in the altar at Bet El appears in I Kings 13:1-5

> A man of God arrived at Bethel from Judah at the command of the LORD. While Yeravaum was standing on the altar to present the offering, the man of God, at the command of the LORD, cried out against the altar: "O altar, altar! Thus said the LORD: A son shall be born to the House

> of David, Josiah by name; and he shall slaughter upon you the priests of the shrines who bring offerings upon you. And human bones shall be burned upon you." He gave a portent on that day, saying, "Here is the portent that the LORD has decreed: This altar shall break apart, and the ashes on it shall be spilled." When the king heard what the man of God had proclaimed against the altar in Bethel, Yeravaum stretched out his arm above the altar and cried, "Seize him!" But the arm that he stretched out against him became rigid, and he could not draw it back. The altar broke apart and its ashes were spilled—the very portent that the man of God had announced at the LORD's command.

a roof of woven reeds shading the sacred object: the Golden Calf

King Yeravaum built a golden Calf at Bet El and Dan. For the simple event see I Kings 12:26-33

> Yeravaum said to himself, "Now the kingdom may well return to the House of David. If these people still go up to offer sacrifices at the House of the LORD in Jerusalem, the heart of these people will turn back to their master, King Rehoboam of Judah; they will kill me and go back to King Rehoboam of Judah." So the king took counsel and made two golden calves. He said to the people, "You have been going up to Jerusalem long enough. This is your god, O Israel, who brought you up from the land of Egypt!" He set up one in Bethel and placed the other in Dan. That proved to be a cause of guilt, for the people went to worship [the calf at Bethel and] the one at Dan. He also made cult places and appointed priests from the ranks of the people who were not of Levite descent. He stationed at Bethel the priests of the shrines that he had appointed to sacrifice to the calves that he had made. And Yeravaum established a festival on the fifteenth day of the eighth month; in imitation of the festival in Judah, he established one at Bethel, and he ascended the altar [there]. On the fifteenth day of the eighth month—the month in which he had contrived of his own mind to establish a festival for the Israelites—Yeravaum ascended the altar that he had made in Bethel.

The Golden Calf as a primary idolatrous expression originates in the plain text at Sinai (see Exodus 32) and Babylonian Talmud Sanhedrin 101b argues that Yeravaum's decision to create the calves as a focus of worship was directly related to his fear that the people would question his legitimacy as king. His logic was that only kings of the house of David are permitted to sit in the Temple Courts. When the people saw Solomon's son Rehovam sitting and he Yeravaum standing they would know that Rehovam was the true king. Therefore, he made two calves of gold

In the eyes of the Sages the worship of the Calf is associated with the story of someone known as Micah

> According to Babylonian Talmud Sanhedrin 101b, Micah was one of many children whom the Egyptians crushed between the stones of their buildings to use as mortar. Rashi on that gemara describes a dialogue between God and Moshe which occurs when Moshe wants to save the children from their suffering – "Crushed in the building - of the Egyptians, who put him into the building in the place of a brick as is explained in the aggadah. Moshe said to the Holy One 'You have done evil to this people! Now if they don't have bricks they place the children of Israel into the building!' The Holy One replied to him, 'They are wiping out the thorns, because it is revealed before Me that if these children lived they would be completely wicked. If you want, make a test and remove one.' Moshe went and removed Micah."
>
> Right before the Exodus, Moshe went to remove the bones of Joseph from the Nile where they had been hidden (see Exodus 13:19). In order to retrieve them, the midrash says that Moshe wrote the words 'ascend ox, ascend ox' (the ox was Joseph's symbol) on a chip of metal and threw it into the Nile. When he took the bones, Micah retrieved the chip of metal. At Sinai, when Aaron threw the people's gold into the fire (see Exodus 32:24), Micah threw the chip of metal in after and the Golden Calf emerged.
>
> Babylonian Talmud Sanhedrin 103b "And He shall pass through the sea with affliction and shall strike the waves in the sea" (Zechariah 10:11), Rabbi Yoḥanan says: This affliction is a reference to the idol of Micah, as Micah passed through the sea during the exodus from Egypt. It is taught in a baraita that Rabbi Natan says: The distance from Gerav, where Micah resided, to Shiloh, where the Tabernacle was at that time, was three mil, and the smoke from the arrangement of wood on the altar in Shiloh and the smoke from the worship of the idol of Micah would intermingle with each other.

> Micah "reappears" in the story of the idol of Micah found in the Judges ch.17-18. At the end of that story his idol is taken by the children of Dan to the newly founded village of Dan.
>
> As a final piece in the thread, the Babylonian Talmud in Sanhedrin 101b referenced above, when explaining Micah's name, says "It is taught in a baraita: He is called Nebat, he is called Micah, and he is called Sheba, son of Bichri. Nebat, who looked [nibat] but did not see, Micah, who was crushed [nitmakhmekh] in the building of the storage cities of Pithom and Raamses. And what is his actual name? His name is Sheba, son of Bichri." Nevat is the father of Yeravaum, who rebelled against the House of David and replaced the Temple worship with that of the Golden Calf, one of which is placed at the village of Dan.

There is an interpretive tradition which understands the Golden Calf at Sinai not as an idol meant to replace God but rather as symbolic substitute for Moshe's leadership, without which the people felt lost, as it says in Exodus 32:1

> When the people saw that Moses was so long in coming down from the mountain, the people gathered against Aaron and said to him, "Come, make us a god who shall go before us, for that man Moses, who brought us from the land of Egypt—we do not know what has happened to him."

The chief exponent of this perspective is perhaps R' Yehudah haLevi, who combines it with an understanding of human religious consciousness in the ancient world in Kuzari 1:97

> 97. The Rabbi: All nations were given to idolatry at that time. Even had they been philosophers, discoursing on the unity and government of God, they would have been unable to dispense with images, and would have taught the masses that a divine influence hovered over this image. which was distinguished by some miraculous feature…Now when the people had heard the proclamation of the Ten Commandments, and Moses had ascended the mount in order to receive the inscribed tables which he was to bring down to them, and then make an ark which was to be the point towards which they should direct their gaze during their devotions, they waited for his return clad in the same apparel in which they had witnessed the drama on Sinai, without removing their jewels or changing their clothes, remaining just as he left them, expecting every

moment to see him return. He, however, tarried forty days, although he had not provided himself with food, having only left them with the intention of returning the same day. An evil spirit overpowered a portion of the people, and they began to divide into parties and factions. Many views and opinions were expressed, till at last some decided to do like the other nations, and seek an object in which they could have faith, without, however, prejudicing the supremacy of Him who had brought them out of Egypt...Their sin consisted in the manufacture of an image of a forbidden thing, and in attributing divine power to a creation of their own, something chosen by themselves without the guidance of God... They resembled the fool of whom we spoke, who entered the surgery of a physician and dealt out death instead of healing to those who came there. At the same time the people did not intend to give up their allegiance to God. On the contrary, they were, in theory, more zealous in their devotion. They therefore approached Aaron, and he, desiring to make their plan public, assisted them in their undertaking. For this reason he is to be blamed for changing their theoretical disobedience into a reality. The whole affair is repulsive to us, because in this age the majority of nations have abandoned the worship of images. It appeared less objectionable at that time, because all nations were then idolators. Had their sin consisted in constructing a house of worship of their own, and making a place of prayer, offering and veneration, the matter would not have been so grave, because nowadays we also build our houses of worship, hold them in great respect, and seek blessing through their means. We even say that God dwells in them, and that they are surrounded by angels. If this were not essential for the gathering of our community, it would be as unknown as it was at the time of the kings, when the people were forbidden to erect places of worship, called heights. The pious kings destroyed them, lest they be venerated beside the house chosen by God in which He was to be worshipped according to His own ordinances. There was nothing strange in the form of the cherubim made by His command. In spite of these things, those who worshipped the calf were punished on the same day, and three thousand out of six hundred thousand were slain. The Manna, however, did not cease falling for their maintenance, nor the cloud to give them shade, nor the pillar of fire to guide them. Prophecy continued spreading and increasing among them, and nothing that had been granted was taken from them, except the two tables, which Moses broke. But then he pleaded for their restoration; they were restored, and the sin was forgiven.

Chapter 4 The Knife

Questions for Learning and Reflection

Reflective

Throughout the book Lev entertains various dreams of the possibility for a different life. What "alternative futures" have you dreamt about, and what can they teach you about yourself? When you consider any lessons you might learn about yourself from your dreams, how does this help you understand the notion that dreams are one sixtieth of prophecy?

Textual

Consider the sources on dveikut. What might dveikut look like today?

Why do the Sages see so many prerequisites for prophecy? How do they influence the form in which prophecy is expressed in the world? How does this help you understand the role which the prophets play in the Biblical narrative?

Sources

A Israelite indentured servant spooned out food for the disciples

The Israelite indentured servant (*eved ivri*) is a social institution which first appears in Exodus ch.21. Their standard servitude lasts 6 years, and thus are differentiated from foreign slaves who are considered property by the Torah (compare Leviticus 25:44-46). According to the Torah, an Israelite can be sold as a slave in two situations. The first case is that of one who stole something but is now unable to restore the stolen object or its value. The second case is when a person is forced to sell themselves as a slave because of their poverty. At least in regard to Israelite slaves, the Sages put so many restrictions on their servitude one could say that they strove to push the institution out of existence. As it says in Babylonian Talmud Kiddushin 22a "Anyone who acquires a Hebrew slave is considered like one who acquires a master for himself…"

Together, we seek a true bond

The phrase 'true bond' is our translation of the Hebrew term dveikut (דבקות). In the Torah, dveikut begins as the model for intimacy of human relationship as in Genesis 2:24

> Hence a man leaves his father and mother and clings (*v'davak*) to his wife, so that they become one flesh.

and develops into a model for human/Divine relationship, as in Deuteronomy 11:22

> If, then, you faithfully keep all this Instruction that I command you, loving the LORD your God, walking in all His ways, and holding fast to Him,

In the context of the prophets and their disciples it is worth seeing the Rambam's understanding of the Torah commandment for dveikut in Mishne Torah Laws of Human Dispositions 6:2

> It is a mandatory commandment to cleave to the wise and their disciples, in order to learn of their deeds, even as it is said on the subject: "And to Him shalt thou cleave" (Deut. 10.20). Is it possible to cleave to the Shekinah? But even thus the wise men commented upon in interpreting this commandment, saying: "Cleave to the wise men and their disciples" (Ketubot, 111b). Man shall, therefore, find the necessary means to take to wife the daughter of a disciple of the wise, and to give his daughter in marriage to a disciple of the wise; to eat and drink with the disciples of the wise, to do business for and with the disciples of the wise, and to associate with them in every form of companionship, even as it is said, "And to cleave to him" (Deut. 11.22). Even so have the wise men commanded, saying: "Sit amidst the dust of their feet, and drink their words with thirst" (Pirkei Avot 1:4).

The Ramchal, R' Moshe Chaim Luzatto, saw dveikut as characteristic of prophecy, not only because of the Divine intimacy involved but also because it began as a human effort and ended as a Divine gift, as expressed in Mesilat Yesharim 26:2-4

> The exertion is that when a man completely detaches and removes himself from the physical, and clings always, at all periods and times

> to his G-d. In this manner, the prophets were called "angels", as said of Aharon: "For a priest's lips shall guard knowledge, and Torah shall be sought from his mouth; for he is an angel of the L-ord of Hosts" (Malachi 2:7), and it is said: "but they mocked the angels (prophets) of G-d" (Divrei Hayamim II 36:16). Even when he is engaged in physical actions required for his bodily side, his soul will not budge from its clinging on high. This is as written: "my soul clings after You; Your right hand supports me"(Tehilim 63:9). However, it is impossible for a man to place himself in such a state. For it is beyond his ability. He is after all a physical creature, of flesh and blood. Thus I said that the end of Holiness is a gift. For that which is in man's ability to do is the initial exertion, pursuing true knowledge and continual thought on the sanctification of deed. But the end is that the Holy One, blessed be He, will guide him on this path he desires to follow and imbue His holiness upon him, and sanctify him. Then this matter will succeed and he will be able to achieve this clinging with the blessed G-d constantly.
>
> > See also 26:7 where the Ramchal says that a state of dveikut allows one to sanctify even the most mundane of acts, like eating

Dveikut received a novel development in thought and practice by the various schools of Chassidic thought.

> The essential innovation of the founder of Chassidut, the Baal Shem Tov, was that dveikut could be the starting point of Divine service available to all people, rather than the end point achieved by the rare few
>
> The Baal Shem Tov took the idea that 'no place can be void of the Shekhinah' to mean that an awareness of the omnipresence and immanence of God is itself dveikut. He also saw the falling out of the state of dveikut as an idolatrous denial of God's oneness and all-pervading presence.

our time is short

Pirkei Avot 2:15 Rabbi Tarfon said: the day is short, and the work is plentiful, and the laborers are indolent, and the reward is great, and the master of the house is insistent.

dreams are one sixtieth prophecy

Babylonian Talmud Brachot 57B.

There are five matters in our world which are one-sixtieth of their most extreme manifestations. They are: Fire, honey, Shabbat, sleep, and a dream. The Gemara elaborates: Our fire is one-sixtieth of the fire of Gehenna; honey is one-sixtieth of manna; Shabbat is one-sixtieth of the World-to-Come; sleep is one-sixtieth of death; and a dream is one-sixtieth of prophecy.

Only princes sleep until the third hour of the day

This idea comes from Mishnah Berachot 1:2

From what time may one recite the Shema in the morning?From the time that one can distinguish between blue and white. Rabbi Eliezer says: between blue and green. And he must finish it by sunrise. Rabbi Joshua says: until the third hour of the day, for such is the custom of the children of kings, to rise at the third hour. If one recites the Shema later he loses nothing, like one who reads in the Torah.

Wisdom is good with an inheritance

This is a direct quote from Ecclesiastes 7:11 and finds a broader expression in Babylonian Talmud Nedarim 38a

Rabbi Yoḥanan said: The Holy One, Blessed be He, rests His Divine Presence only upon one who is mighty, and wealthy, and wise, and humble.

Music helps us quiet the mind and calm the pool

The connection between music and prophecy is a broad topic which appears in many classical sources and bears on several themes of the book. See for example

I Chronicles 25:1 "David and the officers of the army set apart for service the sons of Asaph, of Heman, and of Jeduthun, who prophesied to the accompaniment of lyres, harps, and cymbals."

Radak I Chronicles 25:1: *who prophesied to the accompaniment of lyres* – The sons of Asaph would play the instruments and the holy spirit would come to rest upon Asaph. Then he would sing along with the voice of the lyres. So too Heman and Jeduthun were all prophets with instruments because the Book of Psalms was said with the holy spirit and there are in it prophecies, predictions, exile and redemption...

II Kings 3:15 "As the musician played, the hand of the LORD came upon him..."

This verse is understood by the Sages as an example of how music can be used to clear away negative emotions which block the prophetic spirit (see also comments on p.21-22.)

Babylonian Talmud Shabbat 30b "...the Divine Presence rests upon an individual neither in sadness, nor in laziness, nor laughter, nor in frivolity, nor idle conversation, nor idle chatter, but rather from the joy of a mitzva. As it was stated: "But now bring me a minstrel; and it came to pass, when the minstrel played, that the hand of the Lord came upon him..."

Radak on II Kings 3:15 – It is said that from the day on which Eliyahu, Elisha's teacher, was removed from the world the spirit of prophecy had not returned to Elisha because of he was in mourning and the holy spirit only comes to rest in joy. And there are those who say that because of his anger toward the king of Israel he was upset...

The connection between prophecy and clarity of mind is rooted in an understanding of the Mishna Berachot 5:1

"The pious ones of old used to wait an hour before praying in order that they might direct their thoughts to God."

The Rambam's commentary on that Mishna explains this 'waiting' (*shohin* in Hebrew: שוהין) in the following manner: The meaning of *shohin* is waiting. That is to say that they would wait for an hour before praying in order to settle their minds and silence their thoughts – then they would begin to pray.

See also Rambam Mishneh Torah Foundations of the Torah 7:4

> All the prophets do not prophesy every time they may desire, but they must prepare their minds, rest in a state of exultation and hearty contentment, and in undisturbed solitude; for, prophecy does not rest upon any prophet either when he is in a state of melancholy or in a state of indolence, but when he is in a state of delightfulness. Therefore, the disciples of the prophets had before them the harp, the timbrel, the flute and the violin when they were seeking the spirit of prophecy, whereof it is said: "And they strove to prophecy" (I Sam. 10.5), meaning, they followed the path of prophecy until they did prophesy, as one says: "Yonder is one aspiring to become great."

Chapter 5 The Song of the World

Questions for Learning and Reflection

Reflective

Many people in this chapter want something for or from Lev, but it is Yonatan who becomes his friend. What is the difference between how Yonatan related to Lev and how Zim or Daniel do? How do you form friendships, are there particular types of experiences that help?

Textual

Shabbat is marked by an act of sanctification at the beginning (*kiddush*) and division at the end (*Havdalah*). How are these two acts the same and how do they differ? How do they combine to make Shabbat a unique day?

How do you relate to the list of distinctions which Uriel states? What benefits and problems does drawing distinctions bring to the world? Why is the distinction between Israel and the nations included in this list? What does it say to you? How is this connected to the Sages' idea that prophecy is the unique inheritance of Israel?

Sources

Uriel stood in the middle of the clearing holding a goblet of wine

The Torah commands us to mark the entrance of Shabbat in Exodus 20:8 "Remember the sabbath day and keep it holy."

The Sages learn that this should be done over a glass of wine in Babylonian Talmud Pesachim 106a

"Our Rabbis taught: Remember the Sabbath day, to keep it holy (Shemot 20:8): remember it over wine"

The Rambam clarifies the Torah level obligation in Mishneh Torah Laws of Shabbat 29:1 and 29:6

> "It is a positive commandment from the Torah to sanctify the Shabbat verbally, as it is written in Exodus 20 'remember the Sabbath day to make it holy…' that is to say remember it with a recollection of praise and sanctity."

The Holy One tested our fathers with manna in the wilderness

The manna is intimately bound up with Shabbat. In fact, the first explicit reference to Shabbat, even before the commandment in Exodus 20:8, is in connection with the absence of the daily manna on the seventh day. The custom to bless two loaves of bread is also connected to the manna. See Exodus 16:22-26

> On the sixth day they gathered double the amount of food, two omers for each; and when all the chieftains of the community came and told Moses, he said to them, "This is what the LORD meant: Tomorrow is a day of rest, a holy sabbath of the LORD. Bake what you would bake and boil what you would boil; and all that is left put aside to be kept until morning." So they put it aside until morning, as Moses had ordered; and it did not turn foul, and there were no maggots in it. Then Moses said, "Eat it today, for today is a sabbath of the LORD; you will not find it today on the plain. Six days you shall gather it; on the seventh day, the sabbath, there will be none."

The idea that the manna was a test is explicit in Deuteronomy 8:16

> "who fed you in the wilderness with manna, which your fathers had never known, in order to test you by hardships only to benefit you in the end—"

According to the Sages the blessing and holiness given by God to Shabbat in Genesis 2:3 found their expression in the manna, as stated in the midrash in Genesis Rabbah 11:2

> "And Elokim blessed the seventh day and sanctified it"- Rabbi Yishmael says: "He blessed it" with manna "and sanctified it" with manna, He blessed it with manna-for all the days of the week one omer [portion] fell [per person], on Friday two omer [portions] fell [per person]. He sanctified it with manna [on Shabbat] it didn't fall at all.

If we return in love

The essential importance of serving God out of love is embodied in the verse Deuteronomy 6:5

> You shall love the LORD your God with all your heart and with all your soul and with all your might.

The difference between the Divine relationship which emerges from serving God out of love and the one which grows out of fear can be found in Rashi's comment on that verse, which itself is based in the Sifrei Deuteronomy 32:1

> (Deuteronomy 6:5) "And you shall love the L-rd your G-d": Act (i.e., serve) out of love. There is a difference between acting out of love and acting out of fear. If one acts out of love, his reward is doubled. It is written (*Ibid.* 6:13) "The L-rd your G-d shall you fear, and Him shall you serve." One may fear his friend, but if he belabors him, he may leave him. But *you*, act out of (absolute) love. And there is no (absolute) love in the place of (i.e., co-existing with [absolute]) fear, and no (absolute) fear in the place of (absolute) love except vis-à-vis the Holy One Blessed be He. (So that if one loves Him absolutely, it follows that he fears him absolutely, and his reward is doubled.)

The idea that repentance which is motivated by love can transform one's transgressions into merits is a complex notion, and Uriel gives a classic explanation of why this might be so. The textual source for the idea is found in Babylonian Talmud Yoma 86b

> Reish Lakish said: Great is repentance, as the penitent's intentional sins are counted for him as unwitting transgressions, as it is stated: "Return, Israel, to the Lord your God, for you have stumbled in your iniquity" (Hosea 14:2). Doesn't "iniquity" mean an intentional sin? Yet the prophet calls it stumbling, implying that one who repents is considered as though he only stumbled accidentally in his transgression. Is that so? Didn't Reish Lakish himself say: Great is repentance, as one's intentional sins are counted for him as merits, as it is stated: "And when the wicked turns from his wickedness, and does that which is lawful and right, he shall live thereby" (Ezekiel 33:19), and all his

deeds, even his transgressions, will become praiseworthy? This is not a difficulty: Here, when one repents out of love, his sins become like merits; there, when one repents out of fear, his sins are counted as unwitting transgressions.

Blessed is the One who divides between the sacred and the mundane

The ceremony marking the end of Shabbat is known as *Havdalah,* which means dividing. We chose to have Uriel recite a version of the text which is used in the present day because it is based on listing the distinctions which the Torah itself presents as foundational to creation.

For the Torah level obligation to verbally mark the leaving of Shabbat just as one does with the entrance, see Rambam Mishneh Torah Laws of Shabbat 29:1 in notes on page 60 above.

The blessing on fire is recited at the end of Shabbat due to the tradition that fire was discovered at the end of the first Shabbat, as noted in Babylonian Talmud Pesachim 54b

> "At the conclusion of Shabbat, the Holy One, Blessed be He, granted Adam knowledge similar to divine knowledge, and he brought two rocks and rubbed them against each other, and the first fire emerged from them."

To hear the song of the world you need to hear everything

The source for the idea of the Song of the World is a book entitled Perek Shirah, the chapter of song. In its current version Perek Shirah is a list of songs and praises sung to God by the various creatures and elements of creation. It consists primarily of Biblical verses, but includes rabbinic sayings as well. Many scholars believe that the unique names given to certain birds in the work indicate that it is Tanaitic in origin (1st century BCE through 2nd century CE) though heavily modified over time. There are hints of references to Perek Shirah in the Talmud, but the first clear reference is found in the geonic era, 10th century CE.

I heard a story many years ago from my master

The story of the frog and King David comes from Yalkut Shimoni on Tanach 889

> They said of King David that when he finished the Book of Psalms he was filled with pride. He said before God: Master of the World! There is nothing in the world which sings songs of praise like me! He happened upon a frog which said to him: don't be so arrogant, because I sing far more praises than you. And for every song of praise I say, I compose upon it three thousand proverbs, as it says "He composed three thousand proverbs, and his songs numbered one thousand and five." (I Kings 5:12)

Here is a beautiful thought from R' Nachman of Breslov (1772-1810) in the spirit of the Song of the World, and Lev's life, from Likutei Moharan part II, Torah 63:1

> For know! each and every shepherd has his own special melody, according to the grasses and specific location where he is grazing. This is because each and every animal has a specific grass which it needs to eat. He also does not always pasture in the same place. Thus, his melody is dictated by the grasses and place he pastures. For each and every grass has a song which it sings. This is the concept of Perek Shirah. And from the grass's song, the shepherd's melody is created.

Chapter 6 The Rogue Vision

Questions for Learning and Reflection

Reflective

Uriel is given a prophetic message which he does not understand, and which actually increases his uncertainty, so that in the end he must trust his heart to guide his actions. What does it mean to trust your heart? How do you deal with uncertainty? What is one time you let events take their course even though you knew there was a risk involved?

Textual

The parable at the end of the chapter is from Babylonian Talmud Berachot 61b. Look at the continuation of the story there and see how it ends for R' Akiva. Does the conclusion change your understanding of the parable? If so, how?

Sources

I saw the king's servant

Ovadiah is named by the Bible as the chief steward of Ahav, king of Israel (I Kings 18:3). He is also labeled as one who greatly feared the Lord (ibid. 4) and his name in Hebrew means servant of God. See I Kings 18:3-16 for the role in which he plays in the war which breaks out between the prophets of Israel and the priests of the ba'al. Due to the role he plays in our story, we were forced to take more liberty in developing Ovadiah's character than in any other personality taken from the Hebrew bible.

Ovadiah was identified by the rabbis in a couple of places both as a convert from the nation of Edom and as the author of the prophetic book of Ovadiah which prophecies the downfall of the kingdom of Edom. See this source from Babylonian Talmud Sanhedrin 39b

> It is written: "And Ahav called Ovadiah, who was over the household; now Ovadiah feared the Lord greatly" (I Kings 18:3). What is the verse saying? Rabbi Yitzḥak says that Ahav said to Ovadiah: It is written with regard to Jacob: "And Laban said to him: If now I have found favor in your eyes, I have observed the signs, and the Lord has blessed me for

your sake" (Genesis 30:27). It is written with regard to Joseph: "The Lord blessed the Egyptian's house for Joseph's sake" (Genesis 39:5). The house of that man, i.e., my house, was not blessed. Perhaps you do not fear God? Immediately, a Divine Voice emerged and said: "Now Ovadiah feared the Lord greatly," but the house of Ahav is not fit for blessing. Rabbi Abba says: The praise that is stated with regard to Ovadiah is greater than that which is stated with regard to Abraham. As with regard to Abraham the verse states: "For now I know that you fear God" (Genesis 22:12), and the term "greatly" is not written, and about Ovadiah the term "greatly" is written. Rabbi Yitzḥak says: For what reason did Ovadiah merit prophecy? It is because he concealed one hundred prophets in a cave, as it is stated: "It was so, when Jezebel cut off the prophets of the Lord, that Ovadiah took one hundred prophets, and hid them, fifty men in a cave, and fed them with bread and water" (I Kings 18:4). What is different to conceal fifty men in each of two caves and not conceal them all together in one cave? Rabbi Elazar says: He learned from the behavior of Jacob to do so, as it is stated: "And he said: If Esau comes to the one camp and smites it, then the camp that is left shall escape" (Genesis 32:9). Rabbi Abbahu says: It is because there is no cave big enough to contain more than fifty people. The verse states: "The vision of Ovadiah. So says the Lord God concerning Edom: We have heard a message from the Lord, and an ambassador is sent among the nations: Arise, and let us rise up against her in battle" (Ovadiah 1:1). What is the reason, that specifically Ovadiah prophesied concerning Edom? Rabbi Yitzḥak says: The Holy One, Blessed be He, said: Let Ovadiah come, who dwells among two wicked ones, Ahav and Jezebel, but did not learn from their actions; and he will prophesy concerning Esau the wicked, the progenitor of Edom, who dwelled among two righteous ones, Isaac and Rebekkah, but did not learn from their actions. Efrayim Miksha'a, a student of Rabbi Meir, said in the name of Rabbi Meir: Ovadiah was an Edomite convert. Consequently, he prophesied with regard to Edom. And this is as people say: From and within the forest comes the ax to it, as the handle for the ax that chops the tree is from the forest itself.

He has the right to anything in the land that he desires

The authority of the kings of Israel was not absolute, as is shown by the Torah's commandment to set up judges, its empowerment of the priests and the institution of the prophets which served as a critique of royal power throughout the Bible. Nevertheless, they have extensive rights when it comes to property. The book of I Samuel (see in particular 8:11-17) details the king's ability to overrule private possession of property. There is an argument from the Tanaitic age down through the Biblical commentators of the late Middle Ages over whether these verses are describing the rights granted to the king or simply the situation of oppression which a king brings in his wake.

This is the opinion of the Rambam in Mishne Torah Kings and Wars 4:3

> "He can enlist artisans, any he so needs, to do his work. But, he must pay them their wages. He can draft all the animals and slaves and maid-servants he needs for his service, but he must pay their wages or pay their worth, as it says, "and to plough his ploughings, and to harvest his harvests, and to make the implements of war and the tools for his chariots…and the best of your slaves and maid-servants and youth and your asses…he shall take; and they shall do his work" (I Samuel 8:12-16).

I am a slave until the Yovel

The process of transformation from Hebrew slave of a temporary (6 year) period into a perpetual servant is found in Deuteronomy 15:16-17

> But should he say to you, "I do not want to leave you"—for he loves you and your household and is happy with you— you shall take an awl and put it through his ear into the door, and he shall become your slave in perpetuity. Do the same with your female slave.

In the eyes of the rabbis, perpetuity here means until the coming of the Yovel year, as in Mekhilta d'Rabbi Yishmael 21:6

> "and he shall serve him forever": until the Jubilee year (Yovel). For it would follow otherwise, viz.: If money, whose "power" is formidable, and which acquires everything, acquires only for six years, then boring, which acquires only bondsmen, how much more so should it acquire (a bondsman) for only six years! It is, therefore, written "and he shall serve him forever" — until the Yovel. But perhaps the meaning is that he acquires him forever — literally! It is, therefore, (to negate this) written (Leviticus 25:10) "And (in the Yovel) you shall return a man

(including a bored bondsman) to his holding." Rebbi says: Come and see that "forever" is fifty years, it being written "and he shall serve him forever" — until the Yovel. How so? With the arrival of the Yovel, he goes free. With the death of the master he goes free.

Nevi'im often lose their nevua toward the end of their lives

The source for the idea that prophets lose prophecy before their death is the Rambam in Guide for the Perplexed 2:45

> "...for ordinary prophets must cease to prophesy a shorter or longer period before their death. Comp. "And the word of the Lord ceased from Jeremiah" (Ezra 1:1); "And these are the last words of David" (2 Sam. 23:1). From these instances it can be inferred that the same is the case with all prophets."

A fox once walked along the banks of a river

The parable of the fox and the fish is found in Babylonian Talmud Berachot 61b

> The Sages taught: One time the evil empire of Rome decreed that Israel may not engage in Torah. Pappos ben Yehuda came and found Rabbi Akiva, who was convening assemblies in public and engaging in Torah study. Pappos said to him: Akiva, are you not afraid of the empire? Rabbi Akiva answered him: I will relate a parable. To what can this be compared? It is like a fox walking along a riverbank when he sees fish gathering and fleeing from place to place. The fox said to them: From what are you fleeing? They said to him: We are fleeing from the nets that people cast upon us. He said to them: Do you wish to come up onto dry land, and we will reside together just as my ancestors resided with your ancestors? The fish said to him: You are the one of whom they say, he is the cleverest of animals? You are not clever; you are a fool. If we are afraid in our natural habitat which gives us life, then in a habitat that causes our death, all the more so. So too, we Jews, now that we sit and engage in Torah, about which it is written: "For that is your life, and the length of your days" (Deuteronomy 30:20), we fear the empire to this extent; if we proceed to sit idle from its study, all the more so.

Chapter 7 Taming the Bear

Questions for Learning and Reflection

Reflective

Lev enters a whole new horizon of life when he arrives in Shomron. Think of sometime in your life when you have 'stepped into a larger world' – what does such an experience offer? What are the challenges it poses? What are the strategies and abilities one needs to succeed in a new environment?

Textual

Ovadia says 'a fool may be blinded by the jewels, but a wise man sees the claws.' Compare this statement to these two classic rabbinic definitions of wisdom. "Who is wise? The one who learns from everyone." (Ethics of our Fathers 4:1) and "Who is wise? The one who sees the consequences of his behavior." (Tamid 32a) What is your definition of wisdom?

Sources

I always imagined Shomron as the largest city in the kingdom

Shomron was a new capital of the northern kingdom, built by King Omri shortly after his ascension to the throne, as recorded in I Kings 16:24

> Then he bought the hill of Shomron from Shemer for two talents of silver; he built [a town] on the hill and named the town which he built Shomron, after Shemer, the owner of the hill.

It is interesting to note that expanding the borders of Israelite sovereignty was so important in the eyes of the Sages that they had the following to say in Babylonian Talmud Sanhedrin 102b

> Rabbi Yoḥanan says: For what virtue was Omri privileged to ascend to the monarchy? Due to the fact that he added one city in the land of Israel, as it is stated: "And he bought the hill of Shomron from Shemer for two talents of silver, and built on the hill, and called the name of the city that he built after Shemer, the owner of the hill, Shomron" (I Kings 16:24).

On the pedestal stood a bronze statue

The bible explicitly associates the marriage between Ahav and Izevel with the introduction of new forms of idol worship into the land. I Kings 16:29-33

> Ahav son of Omri became king over Israel in the thirty-eighth year of King Asa of Judah, and Ahav son of Omri reigned over Israel in Samaria for twenty-two years. Ahav son of Omri did what was displeasing to the LORD, more than all who preceded him. Not content to follow the sins of Yeravaum son of Nebat, he took as wife Jezebel daughter of King Ethbaal of the Phoenicians, and he went and served Baal and worshiped him. He erected an altar to Baal in the temple of Baal which he built in Samaria. Ahav also made a sacred post. Ahav did more to vex the LORD, the God of Israel, than all the kings of Israel who preceded him.

It is interesting to note that the Sages contrast the military strength of Israel under Ahav (something which supported by extra biblical texts as well) with the low spiritual state of the people. While standard Biblical theology sees military security as dependent on spiritual purity, Ahav seems to be the exception. The solution offered by the midrash is the social unity which Israel maintained under his rule. See Vayikra Rabbahh 26:2

> Even though the generation of Ahav were all idolaters, because there were no informers among them then were victorious in war…

Chapter 8 The Alliance

Questions for Learning and Reflection

Reflective

The royal wedding is more than the joining of two people, it is the union of two cultures. This is why two very different stories are told by the High Priest and Yambalya, each of which represents a separate national identity. What stories do you tell which express your personal, familial and national identities?

Textual

Why would the Torah present the model of relationship as a process which begins in separation and ends with union? And why does verse Genesis 2:24 present the end goal of Adam and Eve's relationship as becoming one flesh if that is how they began?

Sources

whose tent opened to all sides

The source for Avraham's tent being open in all directions is Midrash Tehillim 110:1

> "Of David. A psalm. The LORD said to my lord, "Sit at My right hand…" This is what the verse says "Who awakened one from the east whom righteousness met wherever he set his foot?" (Isaiah 41:2) The nations of the world we as if asleep, failing to take shelter beneath the wings of the Divine presence. Who awakened them to come and take shelter? Avraham, as it says: Who awakened one from the east. And not only the nations, but even righteousness itself was sleeping until Avraham awakened it. How did Avraham do this? He made an inn and opened doors in every direction in order to receive all those passing by, as it says "He planted a tamarisk (*eshel*) at Beer-sheba…" (Genesis 21:33) R' Azaria said: what is this *eshel* (אשל)? It is an acronym for eating (אכילה), drinking (שתייה) and escorting one's guests (לוייה). This is "righteousness met wherever he set his foot…"

as she walked the traditional seven circles

The origin of the tradition among Jews (today primarily those of Ashkenazi descent) that the bride circles the groom before the wedding ceremony is obscure. Some trace it to Jeremiah 31:21

> "For the Lord has created something new on the earth, a woman shall circle [after] a man."

Perhaps the bride is also circling her groom seven times in hopes of bringing down any walls between them, just as Joshua and the people circled Jericho seven times before its walls fell (Joshua 6:12-21). In general, the Torah and Jewish tradition use the number seven to represent wholeness.

The first woman was separated from Adam and then returned

The source of woman being separated from man and then rejoined through a different type of union is Genesis 2:21-24.

> "And the Lord God caused a deep sleep to fall upon man, and he slept, and He took one of his sides, and He closed the flesh in its place. And the Lord God built the side that He had taken from man into a woman, and He brought her to man. And man said, "This time, it is bone of my bones and flesh of my flesh. This one shall be called ishah (woman) because this one was taken from ish (man)." Therefore, a man shall leave his father and his mother, and cleave to his wife, and they shall become one flesh."
>
> The idea that this is true for God and Israel, as well as every man and woman in marriage can be found in the Zohar 3:7b
>
> > The following was taught in the section of "Hear oh Israel, the Lord our God, the Lord is One" (Deuteronomy 6:4) What is one? This is Knesset Israel which is unified with the Holy One, blessed be He. As R' Shimon says: the union of male and female is called one. The place where the female dwells, this is called one. What is the reason for this? Because male without female is called half a body, and half is not one. When two halves of the body are connected, they become one body and then they are called one.

He drew the weapon from his scabbard

The source for the priests of the ba'al cutting themselves is I Kings 18:28

> "So they shouted louder, and gashed themselves with knives and spears, according to their practice, until the blood streamed over them.

Chapter 9 The Dispersal

Questions for Learning and Reflection

Reflective

The farmers panic when the rain begins to fall, but at first Lev is ready to see it as beneficial to his life as a shepherd. Have you ever benefited from a situation which brought damage to others? What do you think is the proper response to such a situation in thought, feeling and action?

Textual

Deuteronomy 11:13-21 is the second paragraph in the recitation of the Shema prayer, and it is known as the 'acceptance of the yoke of the commandments.' It presents a Divine promise that if Israel keeps the commandments, God will cause the rain to fall and the crops to grow. In the ancient world, what type of relationship emerges from this promise? How about now in the post-industrial societies of the 21st century?

Sources

Still mid-summer, the early yoreh rains were not due for another two months

For sources on *yoreh* and *malkosh*, the early and late rains, see above the notes on page 8.

For a good example of the threat which rain in harvest time represented in the ancient world see I Samuel 12:16-19

> "Now stand by and see the marvelous thing that the LORD will do before your eyes. It is the season of the wheat harvest. I will pray to the LORD and He will send thunder and rain; then you will take thought and realize what a wicked thing you did in the sight of the LORD when you asked for a king." Samuel prayed to the LORD, and the LORD sent thunder and rain that day, and the people stood in awe of the LORD and of Samuel. The people all said to Samuel, "Intercede for your servants with the LORD your God that we may not die, for we have added to all our sins the wickedness of asking for a king."

The lamp of darkness is burning brightly once again

The concept of a lamp of darkness which emits a shadow that dims the light of the Infinite appears in Zohar 1:15a. The phrase בוצינא דקרדינותא is translated by many as 'a lamp which emits darkness'

> With the beginning of the manifestation of the King's will, that is, when the King desired to emanate and create the world, a דקרדינותא בוצינא (lamp of darkness) made an engraving upon the supernal light. This lamp of darkness, which emanated from the most concealed of all concealed things from the secret of the Endlessness Light took a shapeless form. The lamp was then inserted into the center of a circle that was neither white nor black nor red nor green, nor any color at all. When it began its measurements, it created colors that shone into the empty space and the engraving. From within the lamp - This lamp of darkness - a fountain spouted, from which the shades down below received their colors. From the most concealed of all concealed things, from the secret of the Endlessness Light, emanated two faces: One cleaved and the other did not cleave. Its atmosphere was unknown until forceful blows split Atik, and a concealed supernal point shone. Beyond this point, nothing is knowable and, because of this, it is called by the name Beginning, which means the first of the sayings.

The is no greater blessing than peace

Uriel is quoting Bereshit Rabbah 38:6

> Rebbe said: so great is peace that even if Israel is worshipping idols, so long a there is peace between the it is as if God says 'I cannot rule over them (i.e. punish them), since there is peace between them, as it says "Ephraim is addicted to images— Let him be." (Hoshea 4:17) However, when they are divide what does He say? "Now that his boughs are broken up, He feels his guilt; He himself pulls apart his altars, Smashes his pillars." From this you learn that great is peace and division is hateful.

The Holy One forbids us to resign ourselves to death

While the sources for the value of life are too numerous to list, perhaps the most fundamental is Deuteronomy 30:15-20

> See, I set before you this day life and prosperity, death and adversity. For I command you this day, to love the LORD your God, to walk in His ways, and to keep His commandments, His laws, and His rules, that you may thrive and increase, and that the LORD your God may bless you in the land that you are about to enter and possess. But if your heart turns away and you give no heed, and are lured into the worship and service of other gods, I declare to you this day that you shall certainly perish; you shall not long endure on the soil that you are crossing the Jordan to enter and possess. I call heaven and earth to witness against you this day: I have put before you life and death, blessing and curse. Choose life—if you and your offspring would live— by loving the LORD your God, heeding His commands, and holding fast to Him. For thereby you shall have life and shall long endure upon the soil that the LORD swore to your ancestors, Abraham, Isaac, and Jacob, to give to them.

The Sages also taught that one who was righteous and actualized their full self through Torah is called alive even in death, as in Babylonian Talmud Berachot 18a-b

> "For the living know that they will die, and the dead know nothing and have no more reward, for their memory has been forgotten" (Ecclesiastes 9:5): For the living know that they will die, these are the righteous, who even in their death are called living. As it is stated: "And Benayahu, son of Yehoyada, son of a valiant man of Kabze'el, who had done mighty deeds, he smote the two altar-hearths of Moab; he went down also and slew a lion in the midst of a pit in time of snow" (II Samuel 23:20). He was referred to in the verse as son of a living man. Is that to say, that all others are children of the dead? Rather, The son of a living man who lives forever, who even in death is referred to as living. Man of Kabze'el who had done mighty deeds, as he accumulated and gathered many workers for the sake of the Torah. Who killed the two lion-hearted men [Ariel] of Moab, as after his death he left no one his equal, in either the First Temple or the Second Temple periods, as the Temple is called Ariel (see Isaiah 29:1), and the two Ariel refers to the two Temples.

Prophecy Conversation

I thought prophecy was simply a gift from the Holy One

For sources on how prophecy begins as a training but ends as a Divine gift, see Rambam Guide for the Perplexed, II 32:3

> The third view is that which is taught in Scripture, and which forms one of the principles of our religion. It coincides with the opinion of the philosophers in all points except one. For we believe that, even if one has the capacity for prophecy, and has duly prepared himself, it may yet happen that he does not actually prophesy. It is in that case the will of God [that withholds from him the use of the faculty]. According to my opinion, this fact is as exceptional as any other miracle, and acts in the same way.

It is interesting to note that R' Moshe Chaim Luzatto (the Ramchal) sees holiness in the same light in Mesilat Yesharim ch. 26, section 1

> The matter of holiness is dual. Its beginning is service [of G-d] while its end is reward; its beginning is exertion while its end is a [divine] gift. That is, its beginning is that which a man sanctifies himself, while its end is his being sanctified. This is what our sages, of blessed memory, said: "if a man sanctifies himself a little, he becomes much sanctified. If he sanctifies himself below, he becomes sanctified from above" (Yomah 39a).

Balaam, who called himself the man with the open eye

The story of Balaam can be found in its entirety in Numbers chapters 22-24

The source for Balaam's "necessity" is Midrash Tanchuma Balak 1:1

> Every dignity Israel received, you find that the nations of the world [also] received. In like manner He raised up Moses for Israel, who spoke with him any time that he wanted, [and] he raised up Balaam for the nations of the world, in order that he might speak with Him any time that he wanted. Look at what a difference there is between the prophets of Israel and the prophets of the nations of the world!

> The prophets of Israel warn the nations about transgressions, and so it says (in Jer. 1:5), "I have given you as a prophet to the nations." The prophets who He raised from the nations, however, established a breach to cut off mortals from the world to come. And not only that, but all the prophets had a merciful attitude towards both Israel and the nations of the world; for so did Isaiah say (in Is. 16:11), "Therefore my inner parts throb like a harp for Moab…." And similarly has Ezekiel said (in Ezek. 27:2), "Son of man, 'Raise up a dirge over Tyre.'" But this cruel man rose up to uproot a whole nation without cause, for nothing. Therefore the parashah about Balaam was written to make known why the Holy One, blessed be He, removed the holy spirit from the nations of the world. [It was] because He raised this man out of the nations of the world, and look at what he did!

The source for Balaam's base character is Midrash Tanchuma Balak 6:1

> "Then they came unto Balaam and said to him, 'Thus has Balak ben Zippor said, "[Please do not refrain from coming unto me.] For I will surely honor you greatly."'" [Even] more than what you [wanted] formerly I will give you. Moreover, everything that you desire and whatever you ordain I will do. (Numb. 22:18:) "But Balaam answered and said unto the servants of Balak, '[Even] if Balak should give me his house full of silver and gold, [I could not transgress the command of the Lord my God to do less or more].'" From here you learn that he had three things. And they are an evil eye, a haughty spirit and a greedy soul:23 An evil eye, as it is written (in Numb. 24:2), "Then Balaam raised his eyes and saw Israel." A haughty spirit, as it is written (according to Numb. 22:13), "for the Lord refused to let me go with you." A greedy soul, as it is written (according to Numb. 22:18), "[Even] if Balak should give me [his house full of silver and gold]."

Music is a particularly good tool for achieving that

For sources on the role of music in quieting the mind for prophecy see notes on page 52 above

Chapter 10 Eliav's Choice

Questions for Learning and Reflection

Reflective

Lev says that Uncle Menachem bowed to the ba'al because he doesn't like to be different. When have you done something with which you did not agree in order to avoid looking different? When have you chosen to be different despite the discomfort? What caused you to make different choices in these situations?

Textual

The Babylonian Talmud in Shabbat 56b says that 'anyone who says that Solomon sinned is mistaken,' despite the simple meaning of the verses in I Kings 11:1-9. Try and look at this contradiction from both perspectives – if the verses are correct, then what are the Sages trying to teach? If the Sages are correct, then why would the plain meaning of the verses read as it does?

Sources

Have I ever told you why the Kingdom was split?

In the biblical narrative, the twelve tribes of Israel initially lived as a loose confederation which only united to fight wars, as described in the books of Joshua and Judges. In the face of the rising threat of Philistine invasion in the mid-11th century BCE, the tribes were united under the rule of King Saul. Saul was succeeded by David, who together with his son Solomon ruled over what is known as the United Monarchy. Due to King Solomon's failures (see I Kings 11:4-13) God tore apart Solomon's kingdom, leaving the tribes of Judah and Benjamin under his son's rule as the Kingdom of Judah in the south and creating a new Kingdom of Israel out of the ten remaining tribes in the north. The story of the splitting of the unified kingdom into the northern kingdom of Israel and the southern kingdom of Judah can be found in I Kings 12

Yeravaum son of Nevat had a complex relationship with Solomon, first servant, then rebel and finally rival king appointed by the prophets, see I Kings 11:26-32:

> "Yeravaum son of Nevat, an Ephraimite of Zeredah, the son of a widow whose name was Zeruah, was in Solomon's service; he raised his hand against the king. The circumstances under which he raised his hand against the king were as follows: Solomon built the Millo and repaired the breach of the city of his father, David. This Yeravaum was an able man, and when Solomon saw that the young man was a capable worker, he appointed him over all the forced labor of the House of Joseph. During that time Yeravaum went out of Jerusalem and the prophet Ahijah of Shiloh met him on the way. He had put on a new robe; and when the two were alone in the open country, Ahijah took hold of the new robe he was wearing and tore it into twelve pieces. "Take ten pieces," he said to Yeravaum. "For thus said the LORD, the God of Israel: I am about to tear the kingdom out of Solomon's hands, and I will give you ten tribes. But one tribe shall remain his—for the sake of My servant David and for the sake of Jerusalem, the city that I have chosen out of all the tribes of Israel."

In the beginning, Solomon even tried to kill Yeravaum as a dangerous rival "Solomon sought to put Yeravaum to death, but Yeravaum promptly fled to King Shishak of Egypt; and he remained in Egypt till the death of Solomon." (I Kings 11:40)

See also this source from Babylonian Talmud Sanhedrin 101b

> Rabbi Yoḥanan says: For what virtue was Yeravaum privileged to ascend to monarchy? It is due to the fact that he rebuked Solomon for his sins. And for what misdeed was he punished and lost everything? It is due to the fact that he rebuked Solomon and humiliated him in public, as it is stated: "And this was the cause that he lifted his hand against the king: Solomon built the Millo, and repaired the breaches of the city of David his father"(I Kings 11:27). Yeravaum said to Solomon: David, your father, created breaches in the wall so that the Jewish people could ascend for the pilgrimage Festival, and you sealed them in order to marshal forced labor [angarya] for the daughter of Pharaoh, your wife.

Solomon's weakness for foreign women as the cause for his loss of the kingdom is explicit in I Kings 11:1-9

> "King Solomon loved many foreign women in addition to Pharaoh's daughter—Moabite, Ammonite, Edomite, Phoenician, and Hittite

women, from the nations of which the LORD had said to the Israelites, "None of you shall join them and none of them shall join you, lest they turn your heart away to follow their gods." Such Solomon clung to and loved. He had seven hundred royal wives and three hundred concubines; and his wives turned his heart away. In his old age, his wives turned away Solomon's heart after other gods, and he was not as wholeheartedly devoted to the LORD his God as his father David had been. Solomon followed Ashtoreth the goddess of the Phoenicians, and Milcom the abomination of the Ammonites. Solomon did what was displeasing to the LORD and did not remain loyal to the LORD like his father David. At that time, Solomon built a shrine for Chemosh the abomination of Moab on the hill near Jerusalem, and one for Molech the abomination of the Ammonites. And he did the same for all his foreign wives who offered and sacrificed to their gods. The LORD was angry with Solomon, because his heart turned away from the LORD, the God of Israel, who had appeared to him twice."

The Babylonian Talmud in Shabbat 56b has a prolonged discussion about whether Solomon did or did not go astray after foreign gods. Here is an excerpt -

Rabbi Shmuel bar Naḥmani said that Rabbi Yonatan said: Anyone who says that King Solomon sinned is nothing other than mistaken, as it is stated: "And his heart was not perfect with the Lord his God, as was the heart of David, his father" (I Kings 11:4). By inference: Solomon's heart was not equal to the heart of David, his father; however, he also did not sin. However, how then do I establish the meaning of the verse: "For it came to pass, when Solomon was old, that his wives turned away his heart after other gods" (I Kings 11:4)? That verse is in accordance with the statement of Rabbi Natan; as Rabbi Natan raised a contradiction between the two parts of the verse. On the one hand, it is written: "For it came to pass, when Solomon was old, that his wives turned away his heart after other gods." On the other hand, isn't it written: "And his heart was not perfect with the Lord his God, as was the heart of David his father," indicating that Solomon's heart was not equal to the heart of David his father; however, he also did not sin? Rather, the verse says as follows: For it came to pass, when Solomon was old, that his wives turned away his heart, in an attempt to spur him to go after other gods; however, he did not go after them. ...The Gemara raises another question. Isn't it written: "And Solomon did evil in the sight of the Lord" (I Kings 11:6), clearly indicating that Solomon sinned? Rather, since he should have protested against the conduct of his wives, i.e., their involvement in idolatry, but he did not protest, the verse ascribes to him liability as if he had sinned. Rav Yehuda said that Shmuel said: It would have been preferable for that righteous man, Solomon,to be a servant tasked with drawing water and hewing wood for another matter, i.e., idolatry, and not have the verse write about him: "And he did evil in the sight of the Lord," even though he did not. Rav Yehuda said that Shmuel said: When Solomon married Pharaoh's daughter, she brought to him a thousand musical instruments and said to him: This is the way we do it for this idolatry, and this is the way we do it for that idolatry, and he did not protest that talk. Rav Yehuda said that Shmuel said: When Solomon married Pharaoh's daughter, the angel Gabriel descended from heaven and implanted a reed into the sea, and a sandbar grew around it, growing larger each year, and upon it the great city of Rome was built, which became God's instrument to punish Israel.

Yeravaum was afraid so he frightened the people?

The source for Yeravaum's fear that the people's attachment to the Temple in Jerusalem would lead them back to their allegiance to the kings of the House of David is I Kings 12:26-28

> "Yeravaum said to himself, "Now the kingdom may well return to the House of David. If these people still go up to offer sacrifices at the House of the LORD in Jerusalem, the heart of these people will turn back to their master, King Rehoboam of Judah; they will kill me and go back to King Rehoboam of Judah." So the king took counsel and made two golden calves. He said to the people, "You have been going up to Jerusalem long enough. This is your god, O Israel, who brought you up from the land of Egypt!"

The Babylonian Talmud Sanhedrin 101b fills in Yeravaum's thinking -

> Yeravaum calculated and said: It is learned as a tradition that sitting in the Temple courtyard is permittedonly for kings of the house of Judah alone. Once they see Rehoboam, who is sitting, and they see me standing, they will think: This, Rehoboam, is king, and that, Yeravaum, is the

> servant. And if I sit there, I will beconsidered a traitor against the throne, and they will kill me and follow him. Immediately, the following took place: "And the king took counsel, and made two calves of gold, and said to them: It is too much for you to ascend to Jerusalem; behold your gods, Israel, who brought you up from the land of Egypt. And he placed the one in Bethel and the other he placed in Dan" (I Kings 12:28–29).

Then he created a new pilgrimage festival one month after Sukkot

I Kings 12:33 describes how Yeravaum created a new festival holiday -

> "On the fifteenth day of the eighth month—the month in which he had contrived of his own mind to establish a festival for the Israelites—Yeravaum ascended the altar that he had made in Bethel." (I Kings 12:33)

Do not bow before their gods

The verse quoted is Exodus 23:24

Chapter 11 The Vineyard of Shiloh

Questions for Learning and Reflection

Reflective

After repeated crises, Lev's heart becomes unblocked through his tears and he finally feels free to choose his own path. What are the barriers in your own heart and what might you be able to do if you removed them?

Textual

When the Babylonian Talmud Ta'anit 31a-31b explains why the fifteenth of Av was a day of joy it gives a number of reasons - that this is the day on which the tribe of Benjamin was once again allowed to marry members of other Israelite tribes, that this was the day on which the prohibition against tribal intermarriage was lifted, the day on which the generation which died in the wilderness finally ceased to die, and the day on which the guards whom King Yeravaum had placed on the roads to prevent the people of his kingdom from ascending to Jerusalem were removed. What value or idea do you see uniting these things? Why would this be the source of an annual festival 'to the Lord' at Shiloh?

Sources

He likes to come and make sure everything happens in 'the right way'

For the biblical reference to the festival at Shilo, see Judges 21:19-21

> "They said, "The annual feast of the LORD is now being held at Shiloh." (It lies north of Bethel, east of the highway that runs from Bethel to Shechem, and south of Lebonah.) So they instructed the Benjaminites as follows: "Go and lie in wait in the vineyards. As soon as you see the girls of Shiloh coming out to join in the dances, come out from the vineyards; let each of you seize a wife from among the girls of Shiloh, and be off for the land of Benjamin."

The Mishna Ta'anit 4:8 describes the following scene which would take place at Shiloh -

> Rabbi Shimon ben Gamaliel said: There were no days of joy in Israel greater than the fifteenth of Av and Yom Kippur. On these days the daughters of Jerusalem would go out in borrowed white garments in order not to shame any one who had none. All these garments required immersion. The daughters of Jerusalem come out and dance in the vineyards. What would they say? Young man, lift up your eyes and see what you choose for yourself. Do not set your eyes on beauty but set your eyes on the family. "Grace is deceitful, and beauty is vain, but a woman that fears the Lord, she shall be praised" (Proverbs 31:30).

Nobody wants to get married this way

Zim's description is a paraphrase of the Babylonian Talmud Taanit 31a

> The Sages taught: …all the Jewish people borrow from each other. so as not to embarrass one who did not have her own white garments. All the garments that the women borrowed require immersion, as those who previously wore them before might have been ritually impure. Rabbi Elazar says: Even if the garments were folded and placed in a box [kufsa], The daughters of the Jewish people would go out and dance in the vineyards. A tanna taught: One who did not have a wife would turn to there to find one. Those women of distinguished lineage among them would say: Young man, please lift up your eyes and see what you choose for a wife. The Sages taught: What would the beautiful women among them say? Set your eyes toward beauty, as a wife is only for her beauty. What would those of distinguished lineage among them say? Set your eyes toward family, as a wife is only for children. What would the ugly ones among them say? Acquire your purchase for the sake of Heaven…

Chapter 12 The Rains

Questions for Learning and Reflection

Reflective

In chapter 10 Uncle Menachem told Lev a story about King Yeravaum, who dealt with his fear by making other people afraid. In this chapter Uriel tells Lev that 'pitting fear against fear' will not achieve the goals of the prophets. Do you think this is true? What is an alternative to making people afraid in order to get them to obey? Why do so many people in power choose to use fear?

Textual

Uriel says that the same hand fashioned light and darkness, echoing Isaiah 45:7 "Who forms light and creates darkness, Who makes peace and creates evil; I am the Lord, Who makes all these." If the idea that both good and evil come from God is a theological foundation of Judaism, then why does the liturgy change the verse in Isaiah into the blessing 'Who forms light and creates darkness, Who makes peace and creates everything…'?

Sources

The same hand that fashioned the light also made the darkness

The notion that both light and darkness, good and evil, come from God is a foundational frame for Torah consciousness. It is also too large to give a full treatment here. Nevertheless, consider the following. The essential biblical verse in the discussion is Isaiah 45:7

> Who forms light and creates darkness, Who makes peace and creates evil; I am the Lord, Who makes all these.

Here is a rabbinic perspective on what the origins of evil might be and how it too came from God. Bereshit Rabbahh 9:7

> Rabbi Nahman said in Rabbi Samuel's name: 'Behold, it was good' (Genesis 1:4) refers to the Good Desire; 'And behold, it was very good'

> (Genesis 1:31) refers to the Evil Desire. Can then the Evil Desire be very good? That would be extraordinary! But without the Evil Desire, however, no man would build a house, take a wife and beget children; and thus said Solomon: 'Again, I considered all labour and all excelling in work, that it is a man's rivalry with his neighbour.' (Ecclesiastes 4:4).

This is a philosophical perspective on the question from the Rambam, Guide for the Perplexed 3:10:1-3

> Just as we say of him who puts out the light at night that he has produced darkness, so we say of him who destroyed the sight of any being that he produced blindness, although darkness and blindness are negative properties, and require no agent. In accordance with this view we explain the following passage of Isaiah: "I form the light and create (bore) darkness: I make peace, and create (bore) evil" (Isa. 45:7), for darkness and evil are non-existing things. Consider that the prophet does not say, I make ('oseh) darkness, I make ('oseh) evil, because darkness and evil are not things in positive existence to which the verb "to make" would apply; the verb bara "he created" is used, because in Hebrew this verb is applied to non-existing things e.g., "In the beginning God created" (bara), etc.; here the creation took place from nothing. Only in this sense can non-existence be said to be produced by a certain action of an agent...After these propositions, it must be admitted as a fact that it cannot be said of God that He directly creates evil, or He has the direct intention to produce evil: this is impossible. His works are all perfectly good. He only produces existence, and all existence is good: whilst evils are of a negative character, and cannot be acted upon. Evil can only he attributed to Him in the way we have mentioned. He creates evil only in so far as He produces the corporeal element such as it actually is: it is always connected with negatives, and is on that account the source of all destruction and all evil. Those beings that do not possess this corporeal element are not subject to destruction or evil: consequently the true work of God is all good, since it is existence. The book which enlightened the darkness of the world says therefore, "And God saw everything that He had made, and, behold, it was very good" (Gen. 1:31). Even the existence of this corporeal element, low as it in reality is, because it is the source of death and all evils, is likewise good for the permanence of the Universe and the continuation of the order of things, so that one thing departs and the other succeeds. Rabbi

> Meir therefore explains the words "and behold it was very good" (tob me'od); that even death was good in accordance with what we have observed in this chapter. Remember what I said in this chapter, consider it, and you will understand all that the prophets and our Sages remarked about the perfect goodness of all the direct works of God. In Bereshit Rabbah (chap. i.) the same idea is expressed thus: "No evil comes down from above."

Without darkness there is no choice

The nexus between good, evil and choice is well expressed in the sources from Rambam Mishne Torah Laws of Repentance 5:1-5:4 cited in the notes on p. 19.

R' Moshe Chaim Luzatto (the Ramchal) adds the following perspective on the purpose of this interaction between good, evil and choice in his work Derech Hashem 1:3:1

> As we have discussed, humanity is the creature created for the purpose of drawing close to God. They are placed between perfection and deficiency, and it is in their hands to earn perfection. Humanity must earn this perfection, however, through their own desire and choice because if they were forced to choose perfection then they would not actually be its master, and God's purpose would not be fulfilled. It as therefore necessary to create humanity with free will. One's inclinations are therefore balanced between good and evil and they are not compelled toward either. They have the power of choice, able to choose either side knowingly and willingly, as well as to possess whichever one they wish. Humanity was therefore created with both a good urge and an evil urge. They have the power to incline in whichever direction they choose.

Sparks do not shine in the bright light of day

This is an adaption of a line from Babylonian Talmud Shabbat 63a

The idea that darkness itself gives power and meaning to the light finds powerful expression in Ecclesiastes 2:13 and the comments on this verse in Zohar 3:47b:10

"...As light is superior to darkness." (Ecclesiastes 2:13) The benefit of light only comes from darkness. What is the fixing (tikkun) of white? Black. If it were not for black one would never know white, because blackness causes whiteness to disappear become more precious. R' Yitzchak says, this is like the bitter and the sweet - one does not know what is sweet until they have tasted bitterness. What therefore makes something sweet, wouldn't we say the bitter? This is what is written "...The one no less than the other was God's doing..." (Ecclesiastes 7:14)

Prophecy conversation

It is simply part of our way

The relationship between wealth and prophecy, as well as a number of other attributes, is based in a rabbinic discussion of Moshe's personal character found in Babylonian Talmud Nedarim 38a "Rabbi Yoḥanan said: The Holy One, Blessed be He, rests His Divine Presence only upon one who is mighty, and wealthy, and wise, and humble. And all of these qualities are derived from Moses… Rabbi Yoḥanan said: All the prophets were wealthy."

The rabbinic perspective on some of these attributes is best communicated by Pirkei Avot 4:1

> Ben Zoma said: Who is wise? He who learns from every man, as it is said: "From all who taught me have I gained understanding" (Psalms 119:99). Who is mighty? He who subdues his [evil] inclination, as it is said: "He that is slow to anger is better than the mighty; and he that rules his spirit than he that takes a city" (Proverbs 16:3). Who is rich? He who rejoices in his lot, as it is said: "You shall enjoy the fruit of your labors, you shall be happy and you shall prosper" (Psalms 128:2) "You shall be happy" in this world, "and you shall prosper" in the world to come. Who is he that is honored? He who honors his fellow human beings as it is said: "For I honor those that honor Me, but those who spurn Me shall be dishonored" (I Samuel 2:30).

The humble man knows that all is one

See Maharal of Prague *Netivot Olam, Netiv Hanava* for an advanced understanding of this idea.

It is also important to know that the Torah concept of humility (ענוה) is not the same as lowliness (שפל רוח), each have a separate importance in spiritual character. Humility is knowing exactly who and what one is and never being one ounce more or one ounce less. Thus Moshe could be labelled 'the humblest of men,' (Numbers 12:3) and yet still struggle with Pharaoh, chastise the people and intercede before God.

Chapter 13 Yericho

Questions for Learning and Reflection

Reflective

The suspension of mourning on Shabbat and the Festivals can be one of the hardest aspects of Jewish law to understand. Do you think that it is possible to choose your emotions? Why would the Torah command us to be joyful even when the situation is a sad one? Is it possible to hold both sadness and joy? What does that look like?

Textual

The interaction between Eliyahu and King Ahav is a classic power struggle between king and prophet. It is made more complex by comparing Yehoshua's words to Moshe's. Look back at Yehoshua 6:26, did God command this curse or was it Yehoshua's idea? Look also at Deuteronomy 11:16–17. Is this really a curse from Moshe? If not, what is it? If it is a Divine threat, then why in the midrash (and our story) does it take Eliyahu's oath to make it happen?

Sources

Rain on Sukkot is a curse

According to rabbinic understanding Sukkot is a time of judgment on the rain which will fall in the coming year (see sources on page 183). Nevertheless, we do not add supplication for rain to our prayers until the last day of the festival. Moving out into a temporary, and non-weatherproof, dwelling is both an act of faith and a seeking of Divine intimacy which are precursors to that request. Thus image shared in Mishna Sukkah 2:9

> All seven days of Sukkot, a person renders his sukka his permanent residence and his house his temporary residence. If rain fell, from when is it permitted to vacate the sukka? It is permitted from the point that it is raining so hard that the congealed dish will spoil. The Sages told a parable: To what is this matter comparable? It is comparable to a servant who comes to pour wine for his master, and he pours a jug [kiton] of water in his face to show him that his presence is not desired.

There is no sorrow on Sukkot

The commandment to rejoice in Sukkot (which is ultimately extended to the other festival holidays) is rooted in the verses Deuteronomy 16:14-15

> You shall rejoice in your festival, with your son and daughter, your male and female servant, the Levite, the stranger, the fatherless, and the widow in your communities. You shall hold a festival for the LORD your God seven days, in the place that the LORD will choose; for the LORD your God will bless all your crops and all your undertakings, and you shall have nothing but joy.

One of the classic statements about the power of joy in Divine service is found in the Rambam's Mishne Torah Laws of Shofar, Sukkah and Lulav 8:15

> The joy which a person derives from doing good deeds and from loving God, who has commanded us to practice them, is a supreme form of divine worship. Anyone who refrains from experiencing this joy deserves punishment, as it is written: "Because you have not served the Lord your God with joy and with a glad heart" (Deuteronomy 28:47). Anyone who is arrogant and insists on self-glory on such occasions is both a sinner and a fool. King Solomon had this in mind when he said: "Do not glorify yourself in the presence of the King" (Proverbs 25:6). On the other hand, anyone who humbles himself on such occasions is indeed great and honored, for he serves the Lord out of love. David, King of Israel, expressed this thought when he said: "I will make myself even more contemptible than this, humbling myself in my own eyes" (II Samuel 6:22). True greatness and honor are attained only by rejoicing before the Lord, as it is written: "King David was leaping and dancing before the Lord" (II Samuel 6:16).

For sources on the connection between joy and receiving God' presence, see the sources cited on pages 21-22 above.

There are many traditions that the Divine Presence comes to rest in the Sukkah. One of the earliest is Zohar Emor 103b:8

> "Come and see, when one sits in this place beneath the shade of faith (the Sukkah), the Divine Presence spreads out her wings over them from above…"

Uriel declared that the prophets had prayed for rain at the end of Sukkot ever since

The prayer for rain which is said at the end of Sukkot likely has its origins in the reality of the climate of the land of Israel which exhibits clear wet season/dry season dichotomy. Significant rains rarely begin before the Sukkot festival. In rabbinic tradition Sukkot therefore is a time of judgment on the rain which will fall in the coming year, as it says in Mishna Rosh Hashana 1:2

> At four set times the world is judged: On Pesah in respect to the produce. On Shavuot in respect to the fruit of the tree. On Rosh Hashanah all the people of the world pass before Him like a division of soldier [a numerus], as it says, "He who fashions the hearts of them all, who discerns all their doings" (Psalms 33:15). And on Sukkot they are judged in respect of rain.

The waving of the 'four species' on Sukkot is also connected to the prayer for rain, as it says in the Babylonian Talmud Ta'anit 2b in response to the question of why we begin praying for rain on Sukkot.

> Rabbi Eliezer said: It is since these four species, come only to offer appeasement for water, as they symbolize the rainfall of the coming year. And this symbolism is as follows: Just as these four species cannot exist without water, as they need water to grow, so too, the world cannot exist without water.

The prayer for rain presented here is modeled on the version which is still recited by many Jews around the world at the beginning of the additional service recited on the last day of the Sukkot festival. It was composed by Eleazar Kallir, the 7th century liturgical poet from the land of Israel.

Not on Sukkot

See above the comments on page 181 for the sources on the obligation to be joyful on Sukkot.

Four men sat opposite them, but no one spoke

The tradition of sitting in silence before the mourner until they speak has its textual roots in the book of Job 2:11-13

> When Job's three friends heard about all these calamities that had befallen him, each came from his home...When they saw him from a distance, they could not recognize him, and they broke into loud weeping; each one tore his robe and threw dust into the air onto his head. They sat with him on the ground seven days and seven nights. None spoke a word to him for they saw how very great was his suffering.

Without warning, the nobleman with the fiery eyes rose to his feet

The scene between Ahav and Eliyahu in Hiel's house is taken directly from the Babylonian Talmud Sanhedrin 113a

> Rav Ḥisda says: The reference is to Jericho, as it is written: "And the city shall be devoted, it and all that is in it, to the Lord…And Joshua charged them at that time by oath, saying: Cursed be the man before the Lord, that rises up to build this city Jericho; he shall lay its foundation with his firstborn, and with his youngest son shall he set up the gates of it" (Joshua 6:17, 26). It is taught in a baraita that this includes a prohibition not to build Jericho even after changing its name to the name of another city, and not to build another city after giving it the name of Jericho, as it is written: "Hiel the Bethelite built Jericho; with Aviram, his firstborn, he laid its foundation, and with his young son Seguv set up its gates" (I Kings 16:34). It is taught in a baraita: From the death of Aviram, his firstborn, the wicked, it was not incumbent upon him to learn not to build Jericho, as Aviram's death could be attributed to chance. But with the death of Seguv his young son, it was incumbent upon him to learn that it was due to Joshua's curse that they died. The Gemara asks: What did Aviram and Seguv do that they are characterized as wicked, and what is the baraita saying? The Gemara answers that this is what the baraita is saying: From the death of Aviram, his firstborn, that wicked man Hiel should have learned about the cause of the death of Seguv his young son. By inference from that which is stated: "With Aviram, his firstborn," do I not know that

Seguv was his young son? Rather, what is the meaning when the verse states: "His young son Seguv"? It teaches that he gradually buried all his sons from Aviram through Seguv, and he should have suspected that Joshua's curse caused the deaths. Ahav was Hiel's close friend and groomsman. He and Elijah came to inquire about Hiel's welfare in the house of mourning. Hiel sat and said: Perhaps when Joshua cursed, this is what he cursed: Not to build Jericho even after changing its name to the name of another city, and not to build another city after giving it the name of Jericho. Elijah said to him: Yes, that is the curse. Ahav said to Elijah: Now the curse of Moses is not fulfilled, as it is written: "And you go astray and worship other gods," and it is written: "Then the Lord's anger will flare against you, and He will close the heavens, and there will be no rain" (Deuteronomy 11:16–17). And that man, referring to himself, established an object of idol worship on each and every furrow in the kingdom of Israel, and the rain is so plentiful that it does not allow him to go and worship it; will the curse of his student, Joshua, be fulfilled? The verse relates Elijah's reaction: Immediately: "And Elijah the Tishbite, who was of the inhabitants of Gilead, said to Ahav: As the Lord God of Israel lives, before whom I stand, there shall not be dew or rain these years, but according to my word" (I Kings 17:1). Elijah prayed for mercy and they gave him the key to rainfall enabling him to dictate when it would rain, and he arose and went.

May the Holy One comfort you among the mourners of Israel

There is a powerful exploration to be done around this phrase. The concept of comforting a mourner has many biblical roots on both the individual and national level, see the above quote from Job 2:11-13 for the former and Isaiah 40:1-2 for a classic example of the latter. The word comfort here is a translation of the Hebrew נחם which is also used to convey regret (see for example Genesis 6:6 and I Samuel 15:11.) These seemingly contradictory meanings open up the depth of the concept, because in truth נחם means to change one's perspective after the fact. Combined with the name of God most associated with the comforting of a mourner, the definition of נחם can teach us much about how to do this important task. We had Lev offer this comfort in the name of the Holy One, but the traditional phrase used today is 'May the Makom (lit. the place) comfort you among the mourners of Israel.'

Makom is a unique name of God which appears in early rabbinic literature, like the Mishna Berachot 5:1

> One should not stand up to pray except in a reverent state of mind. The pious men of old used to wait an hour before praying in order that they might direct their thoughts to God (lit. כדי שיכונו לבם למקום align their hearts with the Place.)

Here is an explanation of its importance from R' Daniel Kohn: "The word 'place' in this mishnah has a double meaning, or so it seems at first. On the one hand, it means simply the place where one stands. On the other hand, the Rabbis teach that G-d Himself is 'the Place', because He is the ultimate Place for the world and so it refers to Him (see Bereshit Rabbahh 68:9) … To appreciate how these to 'places' coalesce, and to appreciate the sense in which G-d is the place for the world, you need to contemplate a bit about what 'place' is. Say you're sitting on a chair now. That's your place. But that chair is in a room, so in broader sense you place is the room. But that room is in your house, and that house in your town, and that town in your country, on your continent, in your world, in outer 'space'. But that space too is in a place which holds it, enabling it to be. The irony is, though, that that place, the ultimate space, is no place at all. It is the space in which all things 'are' but it itself is not them. The truth is no 'thing' is truly space: anything which can be defined with dimensions and is distinguishable from some other thing is not the space holding it, but rather occupies a background, an essence, which enables all things to be. This contemplation to a most ironic conclusion: that which is 'no thing' is what holds all things and enables them to be. The truth is that this can only really be known as an experience, and the challenge for most people is that this experience only comes by letting go of 'knowing' anything and simply becoming 'present' to this awareness. This is because in order to 'arrive' at 'place' you need to let go of holding on to things and be alertly aware of... nothing! The truth is, the less you move, think or talk, the more you 'stand still', the more you are 'there' in the 'space of all places'. If you allow this to happen, slowly and calmly following the contemplation above, you might notice that, inside of you, a certain quiet is developing. That quiet comes as thought is let go of and is actually the inner equivalent to 'place', the silence present when no words or thoughts, no mind objects, are there; when there is 'only' inner space. This silent presence of shehiýya is not only the way to align with place, it is the experience of it and its inner manifestation. Here you meet the unchanging, unconditional, essential Place which is 'yours', within you, an ever-present truth of essence. There you experientially meet He Who is, as the Rambam says, the only truth, the place of the world, from which 'all that is manifest' comes." From Prayer Essay Three - Shehiyya: The Stillness Which Is Place, Rav Daniel Kohn

When we "comfort a mourner" in the name of HaMakom, the Place, we are offering them the perspective that there is something outside of their grief. We affirm God as the place of existence in order to remind the mourner that when they are ready to move from the pain of loss into the process of acceptance and integration of that loss into a new phase of life, that perspective is waiting for them. We sit silently in a house of mourning because this is not something which can be given to another person, only held deeply as an inner belief; but we offer the hope for it as our parting words.

Chapter 14: The Key of Rain

Questions for Learning and Reflection

Reflective

When describing the lamp of darkness, Uriel offers one of the classic explanations for *hester panim*, the hiding of God's face which can be experienced as evil, or simply as the absence of God's intervention in one's life or history. In what type of situations do you think that a good (parent, friend, God) should actively intervene to help those they care about and in which do you think they should stand back? What type of relationship results in both cases?

Textual

In light of the sources brought in this and the previous chapter, how do you understand the Sage's assertion that there are three keys never given into the hands of man, together with their teaching that Eliyahu received the key of rain?

Sources

Guard yourselves

The verses quoted by Lev are Deuteronomy 11:16-17. These verses are part of the larger passage (verses 13-21) which make up the second paragraph in the declaration of God's unity, the acceptance of the yoke of Divine kingship and the acceptance of the yoke of Divine commandments which combined are known as קריאת שמע - the recitation of the *shema*.

Eliyahu has taken one of the forbidden keys

See the Babylonian Talmud Sanhedrin 113a brought in the notes on pages 188-190 for the source of Eliyahu taking the key of rain. There is another version of the story found in the midrash Tanna debei Eliyahu Zuta 8

> …And so Israel angered and blasphemed against their Creator, engaging in idolatry for three hundred and ninety years in the age of the First Temple. From where do we learn this? You can know it was so because

Israel was settled in the land for four hundred and ten years while the First Temple stood. Subtract from these the twenty years that the kings of Judah and Israel did not worship idols and you are left with three hundred and ninety in which they did. Every prophet who spoke to Israel would rebuke them, urging that they repent but they did not want the goodness which the prophets offered. The people replied 'we do not want nor do we desire your prophecy.' From where do we know this is true? You can know it was so because King Have asked Elijah the prophet, saying 'is it not written in your Torah "Take care not to be lured away to serve other gods and bow to them. For the LORD's anger will flare up against you, and He will shut up the skies so that there will be no rain and the ground will not yield its produce…" (Deuteronomy 11:16-17)?!' But we worship idols and no drought has come! On the contrary, come and see how much good has come to me, as it says "Ahav son of Omri became king over Israel…Ahav son of Omri did what was displeasing to the LORD, more than all who preceded him…He erected an altar to Baal… During his reign, Hiel the Bethelite fortified Jericho. He laid its foundations at the cost of Aviram his first-born, and set its gates in place at the cost of Seguv his youngest, in accordance with the words that the LORD had spoken through Joshua son of Nun." (I Kings 16:29-34) At once Elijah was filled with great wrath upon Ahav and said to him 'empty one! You have despised the One who created the whole world for his glory, the One who gave the Torah for his glory. Upon your life, I will bring judgement upon you only through your own words, as it says "Elijah the Tishbite, an inhabitant of Gilead, said to Ahav, "As the LORD lives, the God of Israel whom I serve, there will be no dew or rain except at my bidding." (ibid 17:1) At once Elijah took the key of rain and departed. Then a great famine came upon the land…

I saw Eliyahu's soul rise to the highest realms, to the Throne of Glory

The Throne of Glory (כסא הכבוד) is a keystone concept in Torah. Conceptually, a throne is where the Presence of the king comes to rest and holds the king's presence even when the king is not there. The following two points will help you connect this idea to the world of the prophets.

The Throne of Glory is one of the things which preceded the creation of the world.

> Bereshit Rabbahh parshat Bereshit 1 "In the beginning God created…" Six things preceded the creation of the world, some of which were created and some of which 'rose up in thought' to be created. The Torah and the Throne of Glory were created. The Torah, as it is written "The Lord acquired me at the beginning of His way…" (Mishle 8:22) The Throne of Glory, as it is written "Your throne is established of old…" (Tehillim 93:2) The forefathers 'rose up in thought' to be created, as it is written "Your fathers seemed to Me Like the first fig to ripen on a fig tree." (Hoshea 9:10) Israel 'rose up in thought,' as it is written "Remember Your congregation, which You acquired from time immemorial…" (Tehillim 74:2) The Holy Temple 'rose up in thought,' as it is written "As a Throne of Glory, exalted from the beginning, so is the place of our Sanctuary." (Jeremiah 17:12) The name of the Messiah 'rose up in thought,' as it is written "…before the sun, his name will be magnified…" (Tehillim 72:17) R' Ahavah son of R' Zeira said: also teshuvah, this is what is written "Before the mountains were born…" (Tehillim 90:2)

The idea that Yaakov's face is engraved on the Divine throne is a widespread motif in rabbinic writings. Here is one example from the 'Heikhalot literature,' (lit. the Throne room literature) which are some of the earliest Jewish mystical texts preserved. They deal primarily with the means and experience of ascent to God's throne.

> Heikhalot Rabbahti, § 164 Bear witness to them of what testimony you see of me, of what I do to the features of the face of Jacob their father, which is engraved for me on the throne of my glory. For at the time that you say before me "holy," I bend over it, embrace, kiss and fondle to it, and my hands are upon its arms, three times, when you speak before me "holy." As it is said: holy, holy, holy.

Another example is the Targum Yonatan on Genesis 28:12

> "He had a dream; a stairway was set on the ground and its top reached to the sky, and angels of God were going up and down on it." Targum: And he dreamed, and, behold, a ladder was fixed in the earth, and the summit of it reached to the height of heaven. And, behold, the angels who had accompanied him from the house of his father, ascended to make known to the angels on high, saying, Come, see Jacob the pious, whose likeness is in the throne of glory, and whom you have been

desirous to see! And, behold, the holy angels from before the Lord ascended and descended, and looked upon him.

What the righteous decree the Holy One carries out

The origins of this idea in the Biblical text can be traced to Job 22:28

You will decree and it will be fulfilled, And light will shine upon your affairs.

The rabbis address it in Sifrei Bamidbar 135

"Do not speak to Me again about this thing" (Deuteronomy 3:26) He said to him: "Do not ask this thing of Me, but decree a different thing upon me, and I will do it." To what might this be compared? To a king who issues a difficult decree upon his son. When the son asks him to rescind it, the king replies: Do not ask this thing of me, but decree a different thing upon me and I will do it, as it is written (Iyyov 22:28) "You will decree and it will be fulfilled for you." So Moses said: If not, (i.e., If I cannot enter Eretz Yisrael), let me see it. The Lord said: This I will do. "Go up to the summit of Pisgah, etc." (Deuteronomy 3:23)

The Talmud Yerushalmi Ta'anit 16b (3:8) places this doctrine in the mouth of the 1st century BCE Sage Shimon ben Shetach, who says "The Holy One, blessed be he, nullifies his decree when it conflicts with the decree of a righteous person…" See the whole context there, as it also deals with bringing rain to the world.

So the Holy One made the lamp of darkness as well

The concept of a lamp of darkness which emits a shadow that dims the light of the Infinite appears in Zohar 1:15a. The phrase בוצינא דקרדינותא is translated by many as 'a lamp which emits darkness.' See the source on page 126.

This page also contains a simplified description of the concept of *tzimtzum*, the Divine contraction which created the space for creation. A foundational version of this idea is found in the book Etz Chaim 1:2:2

Know that before the emanations were emanated and creations were created, there was a simple, supernal light which filled all of existence; there was no place empty [of the light]. Rather, all was filled with the Light Without End (Ohr Ein Sof). There was no beginning nor end, rather all was a simple, undifferentiated light -- the Light Without End. And when His Will rose to create the worlds and to emanate the emanations, to reveal, in full, His deeds, name, and attributes (this was the reason for the creation of worlds, as explained [elsewhere]) The Infinite Light contracted itself into a central dot, literally in the middle of the Light. And the Light contracted and spread to the sides surrounding the central dot, thus leaving an empty vacuum…

Chapter 15 The Battle

Questions for Learning and Reflection

Reflective

This whole chapter is marked by things that could be seen as miracles or as coincidence. Have you ever had the experience of the world 'going your way' when you most needed it? What brought this about? How did you understand it at the time? How about afterwards?

Textual

Look at the midrash which explains the scene in which Uriel and the boys escape the cave. What types of situation, personal or national, cause nature to return to its conditionality? Looking at the stories to which it refers, does human will have a role in this return, or only Divine will?

Sources

You split the rock for Shimshon at Lehi

The story of Shimshon at Lehi is found in Judges ch. 15, the specific reference is to verses 18-19

> He was very thirsty and he called to the LORD, "You Yourself have granted this great victory through Your servant; and must I now die of thirst and fall into the hands of the uncircumcised?" So God split open the hollow which is at Lehi, and the water gushed out of it; he drank, regained his strength, and revived. That is why it is called to this day "En-hakkore of Lehi."

You opened the mouth of the well for Yisrael

The well which sustained Israel in the wilderness after the Exodus has many appearances in Biblical and rabbinic literature. Uriel is referring to the splitting of the rock in Exodus 17:6-7

> Then the LORD said to Moses, "Pass before the people; take with you some of the elders of Israel, and take along the rod with which you struck the Nile, and set out. I will be standing there before you on the rock at Horeb. Strike the rock and water will issue from it, and the people will drink." And Moses did so in the sight of the elders of Israel.

I say this is the moment for which you were formed

The idea of miracles where God overturns the laws of nature in order to meet some immediate need of the prophet or the people one of the more theologically challenging notions the Bible presents, at least to the philosophical mind. It has troubled philosophers from Philo to Rambam to Spinoza. One of the ways in which the Sages harmonized the idea of there being 'laws of nature' and their belief in the absolute freedom of Divine will to micro-manage when desirable was by asserting that the conditionality of the laws of nature was built-in to creation, as in Genesis Rabbahh 5:5

> The Holy One set preconditions (before creation) with the sea that it split before Israel, as it is written "...at daybreak the sea returned to its normal state (eitano)..." (Exodus 14:27) Meaning that it returned to the conditions (tano) that had been set for it. R' Yermiah ben Elazar said: not with the sea alone did the Holy One set such conditions, but rather with everything created during the six days of creation, as it is written "It was I who made the earth And created man upon it; My own hands stretched out the heavens, And I commanded all their host." (Isaiah 45:12) I commanded the sea that it split before Israel, I commanded the heavens and earth to fall silent before Moshe, as it says "Give ear, O heavens, let me speak; Let the earth hear the words I utter!" (Deuteronomy 32:1) I commanded the sun and moon to stand still before Yehoshua, as it says "Stand still, O sun, at Gibeon, O moon, in the Valley of Ayalon!" (Joshua 10:12) I commanded the ravens to sustain Eliyahu, as it says "The ravens brought him bread and meat every morning and every evening..." (I Kings 17:6) I commanded that the fire not harm Hananya, Mishael and Azarya and I commanded the lions not hurt Daniel. I commanded the heavens to open at the voice of Yechezkiel, as it says "...the heavens opened and I saw visions of God." (Ezekiel 1:1) I commanded the fish to vomit out Jonah, as it says "The LORD spoke to the fish, and it spewed Jonah out upon dry land." (Jonah 2:11)

Chapter 16 Yochanan's secret

Questions for Learning and Reflection

Reflective

What does being a priest mean to you? Is it a duty? A privilege? Something else? Why do you think that God characterizes Israel as "a kingdom of priests and a holy nation," (Exodus 19:6) right before the giving of the Torah at Sinai? What would such a nation look like?

Textual

Look at the at the sources which deal with the priestly gifts and the fact that the kohanim receive no inheritance in the land. What reason do you imagine might lie behind these commandments? How are they connected? What opportunities become available to the kohanim through a lack of inheritance?

Sources

One can receive the Presence in many ways

The story of Shimshon and the battle of Lehi can be found in Judges 15:9-19

The story of King Saul referred to can be found in I Samuel ch. 11

The idea that the gift of power in response to a desire to fight injustice is the first rung on the ladder of prophecy is found in Rambam's The Guide for the Perplex II 45:1

> The first degree of prophecy consists in the divine assistance which is given to a person, and induces and encourages him to do something good and grand, e.g., to deliver a congregation of good men from the hands of evildoers; to save one noble person, or to bring happiness to a large number of people; he finds in himself the cause that moves and urges him to this deed. This degree of divine influence is called "the spirit of the Lord"; and of the person who is under that influence we say that the spirit of the Lord came upon him, clothed him, or rested upon him, or the Lord was with him, and the like. All the judges of Israel possessed

this degree...This faculty was always possessed by Moses from the time he had attained the age of manhood: it moved him to slay the Egyptian, and to prevent evil from the two men that quarreled; it was so strong that, after he had fled from Egypt out of fear, and arrived in Midian, a trembling stranger, he could not restrain himself from interfering when he saw wrong being done; he could not bear it...This faculty did not cause any of the above-named persons to speak on a certain subject, for it only aims at encouraging the person who possesses it to action; it does not encourage him to do everything, but only to help either a distinguished man or a whole congregation when oppressed, or to do something that leads to that end. Just as not all who have a true dream are prophets, so it cannot be said of every one who is assisted in a certain undertaking, as in the acquisition of property, or of some other personal advantage, that the spirit of the Lord came upon him, or that the Lord was with him, or that he performed his actions by the holy spirit. We only apply such phrases to those who have accomplished something very good and grand, or something that leads to that end; e.g., the success of Joseph in the house of the Egyptian, which was the first cause leading evidently to great events that occurred subsequently.

You were born a priest of the Holy One

The revelation that Lev is a kohen not only draws together many aspects of the story, it also lays the groundwork for understanding some of its fundamental themes. In order to reflect on this, we have to clarify the meaning of kohen. It is generally translated as priest, and while this is certainly correct, the English words lacks a specific connotation which is critical to understanding the role of the kohanim within Israel. Rashi on Exodus 28:3 explains:

> "Next you shall instruct all who are skillful, whom I have endowed with the gift of skill, to make Aaron's vestments, for consecrating him to serve Me as priest."
>
> > Rashi: *to sanctify him, to appoint him as priest to me* — to sanctify him, i.e. to install him into the priesthood by means of the garments here specified, so that he may become priest unto Me. The expression of kehuna כהונה denotes service.

The element of service which the word kohen contains makes the translation 'minister' more accurate, as in its usage in II Samuel 20:26 and I Kings 4:5. In essence, a kohen serves the people vis a vis God and God vis a vis the people. This definition has profound implications for the relationship between Israel and the world. Immediately preceding the giving of the Torah at Sinai, God labels Israel "a kingdom of kohanim and a holy nation." (Exodus 19:6) This means that as a people Israel is meant to serve the world vis a vis God and God vis a vis the world.

The idea that the kohanim have no inheritance in the land appears in Numbers 18:20

> And the LORD said to Aaron: You shall, however, have no territorial share among them or own any portion in their midst; I am your portion and your share among the Israelites.

The command to separate the first portion of bread is one of the twenty-four priestly gifts which the Torah grants the kohanim listed in Tosefta Challah 2:8

> Twenty-four priestly gifts were given to Aharon and his sons, in particular, in general and with an everlasting covenant. These are they: ten in the Temple, four in Jerusalem and ten in the surrounding environs. Ten in the Temple: sin offering, guilt offering, communal peace offerings, bird sin offerings, conditional guilt offerings, the oil of the leper's offering, the two loaves of Shavuot, the weekly showbread, the remains of the flour offerings and the Omer offering. Four in Jerusalem: first born animals, first fruits, the elevated portions of the thanksgiving and Nazirite offerings, and the skins of the sacred offerings. Ten in the surrounding environs: the terumah portion of produce, the terumah taken from the Levitical tithe, the first bread (challah), the first fleece, the shoulder, cheek and stomach portion, redemption of the first born male child, redemption of the first born donkey, devoted offerings, a devoted ancestral field which was not redeemed, returned property stolen from a convert who is dead. All of these were given to Aharon and his sons in general, in particular, and with an everlasting covenant in order to create an obligation on the whole and on each particular, to grant a reward on the whole and on each particular. One who transgresses and withholds them is as if they transgressed both on the whole and the particular.

The specific command to separate the first portion of bread (Challah) appears in Numbers 15:17-21

> The LORD spoke to Moses, saying: Speak to the Israelite people and say to them: When you enter the land to which I am taking you and you eat of the bread of the land, you shall set some aside as a gift to the LORD: as the first yield of your baking, you shall set aside a loaf as a gift; you shall set it aside as a gift like the gift from the threshing floor. You shall make a gift to the LORD from the first yield of your baking, throughout the ages.

The connection between the giving of priestly gifts to the kohanim and their landless status is made explicit in Numbers 18:19-20

> All the sacred gifts that the Israelites set aside for the LORD I give to you, to your sons, and to the daughters that are with you, as a due for all time. It shall be an everlasting covenant of salt before the LORD for you and for your offspring as well. And the LORD said to Aaron: You shall, however, have no territorial share among them or own any portion in their midst; I am your portion and your share among the Israelites.

Aside from the practical need to support the kohanim, the priestly gifts, and in particular the bread offering, were seen as a source of blessing for all Israel who gave them. As in Ezekiel 44:30

> All the choice first fruits of every kind, and all the gifts of every kind—of all your contributions—shall go to the priests. You shall further give the first of the yield of your baking to the priest, that a blessing may rest upon your home.

The prohibition against a kohen becoming impure due to the dead is found in Leviticus 19:1-4

> The LORD said to Moses: Speak to the priests, the sons of Aaron, and say to them: None shall defile himself for any [dead] person among his kin, except for the relatives that are closest to him: his mother, his father, his son, his daughter, and his brother; also for a virgin sister, close to him because she has not married, for her he may defile himself. But he shall not defile himself as a kinsman by marriage, and so profane himself.

The Sages understood this prohibition in a very broad fashion which is analyzed in the tractate of the Mishna call Ohalot (tents.) A general rule of thumb is that a kohen cannot make direct contact with or be under any roofed space with a dead body.

The kohanim are a separate family unit within the tribe of Levi. The refusal of the Levites to participate in the sin of the Golden Calf appears in Exodus 32:26

> "Then Moses stood in the gate of the camp, and said: Who is for God, let him come to me; and all the children of Levi gathered to him"

There is one interpretive tradition which even sees the refusal of the Levites to join in the sin of the Golden Calf as the source of their elevation to the position of servants of God, and became an archetype for their steadfast faith in God and Moshe's leadership. See Deuteronomy 10:8

> At that time the LORD set apart the tribe of Levi to carry the Ark of the LORD's Covenant, to stand in attendance upon the LORD, and to bless in His name, as is still the case.
>
> And Rashi Deuteronomy 10:8
>
>> AT THAT TIME accordingly means: In the first year of the Exodus from Egypt, when ye sinned by worshipping the golden calf, but the sons of Levi did not thus sin. — at that time God separated them from you. It places this verse in juxtaposition with the retreat to Bene Jaakon to tell you that in this matter also, the sons of Levi did not sin, but stood steadfast in their faith.

Chapter 17 – The Steward's Wife

Questions for Learning and Reflection

Reflective

On their journey to Shomron, it is their insignificance in the eyes of the soldiers which keeps Lev and Yonatan safe. Has it ever helped you to be unnoticed? How did it feel?

Textual

There is a common expression that 'cleanliness is next to godliness.' How do you understand the Torah's emphasis on immersion in water in order to remove impurity? Is it simply a negative spiritualization of dirt, or something more? And if so, what might it be?

Sources

The impurity of the dead still clings to the rest of us

The Torah has numerous commands to wash with water in order to remove some form of impurity, though the verb used (רחץ) can be understood in many ways. The Sages understood it to mean immersion in flowing water or such waters properly gathered into a bath (*mikve*), as in the midrash halacha Sifra Emor 4:7

> "until he bathes his flesh" (Leviticus 22:6): I might think that he could bathe each limb individually; it is, therefore, written (Leviticus 22:7) "And when the sun sets he shall be clean" — Just as the sun sets as a whole, so the bathing in water must be as a whole (and not limb by limb).

As Uriel notes, the impurity of the dead is only removed through the ritual sprinkling of water mixed with ashes of the red heifer, as described in Numbers chapter 19. We included this scene simply to emphasize Lev's newly discovered status.

Living waters will suffice

The phrase 'living waters' is used in many places to mean water which flows naturally from the ground rather than that which is gathered, as in Genesis 26:19

> But when Isaac's servants, digging in the wadi, found there a well of spring water,

It is connected specifically to rituals of purification in verses like Leviticus 15:13

> When one with a discharge becomes clean of his discharge, he shall count off seven days for his cleansing, wash his clothes, and bathe his body in fresh water; then he shall be clean.

A beautiful explanation of the role that living water plays in purification can be found in the Sefer HaChinuch 173:2

> (2) And about the reason that water purifies everything impure, I would think from the perspective of the simple understanding it is in order that a one see themselves upon immersion as if they are created at that time, [just] like the whole world was water before man was upon it - as it is written (Genesis 1:2), "and the spirit of God floated upon the face of the waters." Through this comparison, the one who immerses can take to heart that just as they are renewed his body, so too they also renew their actions for the good, fixing their actions and becoming exacting in the way of God, blessed be He. Therefore the Sages said that the purification is not fit with water that is in a vessel, but rather only with living water - or collected [water], which is on the ground and, in any case, not in a vessel - in order to place in the heart the idea world in the moment of immersion was entirely water, and [that] one is renewed upon emerging from it, as we said. But if the water was in a vessel - or even if it passed through a vessel - this matter that we said would not be set in the thought of the one immersing as everything within a vessel has limits which are the creation of the hands of man. Therefore, when one immerses in a vessel, they will not think of the whole world as water like at the beginning of Creation, and that they are renewed at that time. 'And the one who accepts, will accept; and the one who refrains will refrain.'

With their feet pointed toward Jerusalem

There is no binding requirement for the direction in which one is buried. However, the belief that upon the resurrection of the dead the newly-living will immediately head to Jerusalem has led many communities over time to develop customs on the matter. Some bury the dead with their feet toward the cemetery exit, some toward the Land of Israel and some toward Jerusalem.

It must be one of Gidon's caves

The source for Gideon's caves is Judges 6:1-2

> Then the Israelites did what was offensive to the LORD, and the LORD delivered them into the hands of the Midianites for seven years. The hand of the Midianites prevailed over Israel; and because of Midian, the Israelites provided themselves with refuges in the caves and strongholds of the mountains.

Hidden in a cave outside the city

The source for Ovadia hiding the prophets from Queen Izevel is I Kings 18:13

> My lord has surely been told what I did when Jezebel was killing the prophets of the LORD, how I hid a hundred of the prophets of the LORD, fifty men to a cave, and provided them with food and drink.

Prophecy Conversation

The righteous eat to satisfy the soul

Mishle 13:25 "The righteous man eats to his heart's content, But the belly of the wicked is empty."

Chapter 18 Shimon's Tale

Questions for Learning and Reflection

Reflective

Most people think of a just world as one in which everyone gets what they deserve. Uriel insists that such a world could not stand and sees the story of his own life as proof. How do you understand the relationship between justice and mercy? How could they work together to build the world? Would the world be better off with strict justice? What would we gain and what would we lose?

Textual

See the source on the obligation to judge another favorably. What do you see as the benefits and risks of such an obligation? How would you define its limits?

Sources

The faithful judge the prophets with favor

There is a general position in rabbinic thought that one has an obligation to judge others with a favorable eye. The Torah verse in which this is rooted is the end of Leviticus 19:15

> You shall not render an unfair decision: do not favor the poor or show deference to the rich; judge your kinsman fairly.

The Babylonian Talmud in Shevuot 30a understands the verse as applying both to legal requirements for fairness and to the personal obligation to judge others favorably. It also narrows the application of the obligation

> "But in righteousness shall you judge your colleague," meaning that you should judge another favorably, and seek to find justification for his actions, even if when interpreted differently his actions could be judged unfavorably. Rav Yosef teaches that from the verse: "But in righteousness shall you judge your colleague [amitekha]," it is derived: With regard

> to one who is with you [im she'itekha] in observance of Torah and in fulfillment of mitzvot, try to judge him favorably…

The Holy One always creates the remedy before bringing the malady

This is a concept which appears in Babylonian Talmud Megillah 13b

> As Reish Lakish said: The Holy One, Blessed be He, does not strike at the Jewish people unless He has already created a remedy for them beforehand, as it is stated: "When I would have healed Israel, then the iniquity of Ephraim was uncovered"(Hosea 7:1). But this is not so with regard to the nations of the world. With them, God first strikes them and only afterward does He create a remedy, as it is stated: "And the Lord shall smite Egypt, smiting and healing" (Isaiah 19:22).

it could not stand

The idea that world cannot stand on strict judgement appears in one of Rashi's comments on Genesis 1:1

> In the beginning of God's creation of the heavens and the earth.
>
> Rashi: *God's creation of the heavens and the earth*: But it does not say "of the Lord's creation of" (i.e., it should say "of the Lord God's creation of" as below 2:4 "on the day that the Lord God made earth and heaven") for in the beginning it was His intention to create it with the Divine Standard of Justice, but he perceived that the world would not endure; so He preceded it with the Divine Standard of Mercy, allying it with the Divine Standard of Justice, and that is the reason it is written: "on the day the Lord God made earth and heaven."

Chapter 19 The final journey

Questions for Learning and Reflection

Reflective

See the sources on the situations in which the Sages determined that observance of the law was more important than life. Are there people, ideas, laws which you see as more important than living?

Textual

The principle of *marit ayin* is based on the idea that people judge the world by what they see, even if they are not judging it correctly. The command to place the blue thread on the corners of one's garment is also based on the connection between one's eyes and the world, that one should see it and recall all the commandments. What do the two have in common and how do they differ?

Sources

Some things are more precious than life

The Torah's injunction to choose life is one of its strongest principles, as expressed in Deuteronomy 30:19

> I call heaven and earth to witness against you this day: I have put before you life and death, blessing and curse. Choose life—if you and your offspring would live—

Nevertheless, the Sages understood there to be three prohibitions which themselves uphold the boundaries that give life its meaning. Therefore, if one is forced to choose between death and violation of these principles, the choice is death. The limitation to three actions is true in normal times, but in a time of persecution when enemies are seeking to uproot the Torah from Israel, every precept becomes a matter of choosing death over violation. See Tosefta Shabbat 16:1

> The precepts were given to Israel for no reason other than for Israel to stay alive, for it is said of the precept, "Which if a man do, he shall

> live by them" (Lev. 18:5) - live by them and not die by them. Therefore, when there is danger to life, no precept is to be insisted on except those prohibiting idolatry, unchastity, and murder. When does the rule apply? Not in a time of religious persecution. But during a time of religious persecution, a man must be willing to give up his life even for the least demanding of precepts, as it is said, "You shall not profane My Holy Name - I am to be hallowed among the children of Israel" (Lev. 22:32).

Don't bow. Just pick up and go.

The situation described here is built upon the rabbinic notion that even if an act is permissible in and of itself, it may be prohibited because it looks like an act forbidden by the Torah (*marit ayin,* lit. within eyesight). The legal source for this scene is in Babylonian Talmud Avodah Zarah 12a

> If a thorn became imbedded in one's foot while he was standing before an object of idol worship, he may not bend down and remove the thorn, because he appears to be bowing down to the object of idol worship; but if he is not seen, it is permitted. If one's coins were scattered while he is before an object of idol worship, he may not bend down and pick them up, because he appears to be bowing down to the object of idol worship; but if he is not seen, it is permitted. Likewise, if there is a spring that runs before an object of idol worship, one may not bend down and drink from it, because he appears to be bowing down to the object of idol worship; but if he is not seen, it is permitted.

It also has a narrative parallel in the Babylonian Talmud Gittin 57b

> "As For Your sake we are killed all the day long; we are reckoned as sheep for the slaughter" (Psalms 44:23). And Rav Yehuda said: This verse applies to the woman and her seven sons who died as martyrs for the sake of the sanctification of God's name. The incident occurred as follows: They brought in the first of the woman's sons before the emperor and said to him: Worship the idol. He said to them: I cannot do so, as it is written in the Torah: "I am the Lord your God" (Exodus 20:2). They immediately took him out and killed him. And they then brought in another son before the emperor, and said to him: Worship the idol. He said to them: I cannot do so, as it

is written in the Torah: "You shall have no other gods beside Me" (Exodus 20:3). And so they took him out and killed him. They then brought in yet another son before the emperor, and said to him: Worship the idol. He said to them: I cannot do so, as it is written in the Torah: "He that sacrifices to any god, save to the Lord only, he shall be utterly destroyed" (Exodus 22:19). And so they took him out and killed him. They then brought in another son, and said to him: Worship the idol. He said to them: I cannot do so, as it is written in the Torah: "You shall not bow down to any other god" (Exodus 34:14). And so they took him out and killed him. They then brought in yet another son, and said to him: Worship the idol. He said to them: I cannot do so, as it is written in the Torah: "Hear, O Israel, the Lord is our God, the Lord is One" (Deuteronomy 6:4). And so they took him out and killed him. They then brought in another son, and said to him: Worship the idol. He said to them: I cannot do so, as it is written in the Torah: "Know therefore this today, and consider it in your heart, that the Lord, He is God in heaven above and upon the earth beneath; there is no other" (Deuteronomy 4:39). And so they took him out and killed him. They then brought in yet another son, and said to him: Worship the idol. He said to them: I cannot do so, as it is written in the Torah: "You have avouched the Lord this day to be your God…and the Lord has avouched you this day to be a people for His own possession" (Deuteronomy 26:17–18). We already took an oath to the Holy One, Blessed be He, that we will not exchange Him for a different god, and He too has taken an oath to us that He will not exchange us for another nation. It was the youngest brother who had said this, and the emperor pitied him. Seeking a way to spare the boy's life, the emperor said to him: I will throw down my seal before you; bend over and pick it up, so that people will say that he has accepted the king's authority [harmana]. The boy said to him: Woe [ḥaval] to you, Caesar, woe to you, Caesar. If you think that for the sake of your honor I should fulfill your command and do this, then for the sake of the honor of the Holy One, Blessed be He, all the more so should I fulfill His command. As they were taking him out to be killed, his mother said to them: Give him to me so that I may give him a small kiss. She said to him: My son, go and say to your father Abraham, You bound one son to the altar, but I bound seven altars. She too in the end went up to the roof, fell, and died. A Divine Voice emerged and said: "A joyful mother of children" (Psalms 113:9)

The color of the Throne of Glory

The color of the Throne of Glory is stated in Ezekiel 1:26

> Above the expanse over their heads was the semblance of a throne, in appearance like sapphire; and on top, upon this semblance of a throne, there was the semblance of a human form

The significance of the color is expressed in the Babylonian Talmud Menachot 43b

> It is taught in a baraita that Rabbi Meir would say: What is different about tekhelet from all other types of colors such that it was chosen for the mitzva of ritual fringes? It is because tekhelet is similar in its color to the sea, and the sea is similar to the sky, and the sky is similar to the Throne of Glory, as it is stated: "And they saw the God of Israel; and there was under His feet the like of a paved work of sapphire stone, and the like of the very heaven for clearness" (Exodus 24:10), indicating that the sky is like a sapphire brickwork. And it is written: "The likeness of a throne, as the appearance of a sapphire stone" (Ezekiel 1:26).

Glossary of authors and works referenced

Mishna

An authoritative collection of the oral tradition of Jewish Law, redacted by R' Yehudah HaNasi in the early 3rd century CE.

Midrash Aggadah

Midrash Haggadah is made up of the interpretation, illustration, or expansion, in a moralizing or edifying manner, of the non-legal portions of the Bible. Many of the works cited above (such as Genesis Rabbah, Tanchuma, Eliyahu Zuta) belong to this category.

Midrash Halacha

Midrash Halacha is the exploration of the traditionally received law through identification of its sources in the Bible and through interpretation of these Scriptural passages as proofs of its authenticity. The term applies also to the derivation of new laws and enactments from the Bible, either by means of interpretation of the meaning of the verses themselves or through the application of certain hermeneutic rules. A few of the works cited above, like the Sifre and the Mekhilta d'Rabbi Yishmael belong to this category.

Seder Olam Rabbah

A 2nd-century CE Hebrew language chronology attributed to the Tanna R' Yose bar Chalifta. It details the dates of biblical events from Creation to Alexander the Great's conquest of Persia.

Babylonian Talmud

A comprehensive work of rabbinic literature comprised of both legal and narrative elements (halacha and Aggadah), built upon the Mishna. The Babylonian Talmud (as opposed to the Jerusalem version) reflects discussions and editing over a period from approximately 250 CE to 600 CE.

Targum Yonatan

A translation of the Torah into the dialect of Aramaic spoken in the land of Israel. Its origins likely are in late antiquity and it includes much narrative material collected from various rabbinic sources.

Heichalot literature

A collection of esoteric and revelatory texts produced some time between late antiquity and the Early Middle Ages, they represent some of the earliest Jewish mystical texts.

Eleazar Kallir

The greatest and most prolific of the early paytanim, the liturgical poets, whose works are still recited today. He apparently lived in the city of Tiberias in the land of Israel in the Byzantine era, though the biographical facts of his life, including his name, are all shrouded in mystery.

Zohar

A commentary on the Torah, written in both Aramaic and Hebrew. It presents a complete mystical theosophy, dealing with the nature of God, the cosmogony and cosmology of the universe, the soul, sin, redemption, good, evil, etc. It first came to light thirteenth century Spain at the hands of R' Moshe ben Shem Tov de Leon. Its authorship is traditionally attributed to the second century Tanna R' Shimon bar Yochai.

Rashi (1040 - 1105 CE)

Shlomo ben Yitzhak, best known by the acronym "Rashi", was an early and influential medieval Torah and Talmud commentator. He was born in Troyes, France, and as a young man he studied in the yeshivot of Worms and Mainz. His commentary on the Bible and Talmud is considered an indispensable tool for Torah study.

R' Yehudah HaLevi (1075 - 1141 CE)

R' Yehuda Halevi was a Spanish poet and philosopher. He is considered to this day to be one of the greatest Hebrew poets of all time, and his liturgical poetry appears in several prayer rites. His philosophical work, the Kuzari, is one of the great masterpieces of Jewish philosophy.

Rambam (1137 - 1204 CE)

Rabbi Moshe ben Maimon (Rambam) was perhaps the greatest intellectual and spiritual figure of post-Talmudic Judaism. He wrote indispensable works of philosophy, law, commentary, and responsa. He was the first to produce a comprehensive commentary on the entire Mishnah. His code of law, Mishneh Torah, is the first and unsurpassed comprehensive code of Jewish law and practice.

Radak (1160 - 1235 CE)

Rabbi David Kimchi (the Radak) was a Provencal rabbi, biblical commentator, grammarian and philosopher, born to a family of grammarians and commentators. His commentaries on the Hebrew bible display his grammatical mastery, and are amongst the most basic and commonly referenced.

R' Moshe Chaim Luzzatto (1707 - 1746 CE)

R' Moshe Chaim Luzzatto (Ramchal) was an Italian rabbi, kabbalist and philosopher who also wrote dramatic works and literary criticism.

R' Nachman of Breslov (1772 - 1810 CE)

R' Nachman of Breslov was one of the most creative chassidic masters, whose thought and teachings continue to resonate within wide circles far beyond his immediate followers. He was a great-grandson of the founder of Chassidut, R. Yisrael Ba'al Shem Tov.

Rav A.Y. Hakohen Kook (1865 - 1935 CE)

R' Avraham Yitzchak Hakohen Kook was one of the major Torah personalities of the early 20th century and influential leader in both Lithuania and the Land of Israel. A master of many facets of Jewish literature, he wrote philosophical and mystical tracts as well as responsa and commentaries.

Rav Daniel Kohn

Rav Daniel was a central teacher and guide to spiritual growth at the Sulam Yaakov yeshiva where Dave and Mike met and learned together. Though little of his Torah is quoted directly here, its spirit permeates the book.

About the Authors

DAVE MASON

MIKE FEUER

Dave and Mike have led bizarrely parallel lives. Born just four days apart, they both grew up in secular, Jewish, suburban communities, then found their way to Colorado College. Despite having friends, interests, and even one class in common, they remained complete strangers. Dave then backpacked through over a dozen countries including Syria, China, and Cuba, while Mike lived in the woods for two years, immersed in wilderness therapy with at-risk youth.

Later, both turned their attention to the environment. Dave went to NYU Law and subsequently became a litigator for the Natural Resources Defense Council (NRDC). Mike studied desert agriculture and water resource management, but ultimately found his calling as a teacher.

Fifteen years after first becoming classmates, the two finally met as part of a core group formed to create a new kind of Torah study institution in Jerusalem, called Sulam Yaakov. There, they became study partners, close friends, and both became ordained as Orthodox Rabbis. Dave was blown away by his studies about the inner workings of prophecy, and was surprised at how little exposure he had to this crucial part of his tradition. He decided to create The Age of Prophecy to bring this world to light for others like himself.

Mike joined the project initially as a research assistant, bringing an expertise in the terrain, history, and stories of the Bible to the book. His deep involvement earned him contributing author status, though Mike prefers the term creative co-conspirator.

Professionally, Dave is a businessman, social entrepreneur, and business strategist. He and his wife Chana live in the eclectic Nachlaot neighborhood of Jerusalem, where they homeschool their son, Aryeh Lev.

Mike lives with his family outside of Jerusalem, at the edge of the Judean wilderness.